Praise

"No one captures a sense of place better than Linda Windsor. Caught beneath the spell of the *Fiesta Moon,* you'll find yourself celebrating the timeless beauty of Mexico, embracing the charming characters, and holding your breath for a happy ending that's as certain as the moonrise."

—Liz Curtis Higgs, best-selling author of *Thorn in My Heart*

"Filled with mystery and Windsor's characteristic humor . . . more riveting and fun than the first."

—Carolyn R. Scheidies, *Author's Choice Reviews*

"Linda Windsor's *Fiesta Moon* is definitely a south of the border recipe for fun, romance, and superbly crafted characters. Corinne and Mark offer a taste of suspense in an unforgettable adventure set in a not-so-sleepy Mexican village."

—Diann Mills, author of *When the Lion Roars*

"Linda Windsor has woven a magical tale set within a small village in Mexico. Her adept use of the area's language and customs take the reader on a journey to another country. The story is captivating. One wishes for the fiesta moon to shine on lovers everywhere."

—Eileen Key, *The Road to Romance*

"Linda Windsor's *Fiesta Moon* is a joy to read, turning romantic locations, exciting characters, flawless descriptions and humorous situations tempered by faith into a feast of words. Hungry readers everywhere will line up for a second helping. Bravo, Linda. You've done it again."

—Molly Bull, author of *The Winter Pearl*

"A pig, a handsome rake, and a spunky young woman all add up to a delicious concoction in *Fiesta Moon* that goes beyond mere hilarity with its theme of how God's grace can touch the most reprobate heart. Linda Windsor has penned another winner!"

—Colleen Coble, author of the *Aloha Reef Series*

"Linda Windsor's *Fiesta Moon* is a treat—a perfect combination of festive setting, intriguing mystery, and heartfelt romance!"

—DeAnna Julie Dodson, author of *In Honor Bound* and *To Grace Surrendered*

"Linda Windsor never fails to tickle my funny bone and touch my heart. In *Fiesta Moon*, her sophisticated hero exiled to a small Mexican village makes me laugh as he struggles like a cat in water. And her loving heroine tugs at my heart as she decides whether to cast her net to the hero or let him drown. A delightful book of wonderful characters."

—Donita K. Paul, author of *Dragonspell* and *DragonQuest*

"Every Linda Windsor romantic comedy is a treat, but, with *Fiesta Moon*, I think Ms. Windsor may have eclipsed her previous work. Only once in a blue moon will you encounter such a loony mix of personalities in such out-of-this-world situations. An enamored pig, three brothers named Juan, and a sombrero-wearing donkey shine bright in a richly woven story, which includes threads of intrigue and deep faith. Enjoy a party you'll never forget, but watch out for the moonlight. You just might fall in love with *Fiesta Moon*."

—Jennifer Lynn Cary, author of *The Hugenot*

"Captivating and comical . . . Linda's refreshing humor and the zany antics of her characters are skillfully interwoven with the adventure and faith journey that all take you on an exhilarating emotional rollercoaster ride."

—Amber Miller, *Romancing the Christian Heart* magazine

"Innovative and daring . . . Windsor is the master of Christian romantic comedy."

—Laura V. Hilton, author and reviewer

"Warm, lovable characters and a heartwarming, intriguing story that takes place in an unusual setting. What more could one ask? Linda Windsor has given us another wonderful read."

—Dorothy Clark, author of *Beauty for Ashes* and *Joy for Mourning*

"Immerse yourself in this enjoyable romp as unredeemable rake Mark Madison and his pet pig get the desires of his heart in Corinne Diaz, a feisty, lovable woman who has spent her life caring for orphans. This story will take you on a joy ride through your emotions and leave you feeling fully satisfied and content. A story you don't want to miss, *Fiesta Moon* is a delight."

—Cheryl Wolverton, author of *Father's Love*

"Linda has given us a winner again. Her writing paints a colorful picture of life in a Mexican village, peopled with equally colorful characters who leap from the page into your heart. There was an air of mystery and the romantic tension sizzled."

—Lena Nelson Dooley, best-selling author of *Gerda's Lawman* and *Scraps of Love*

FIESTA MOON

FIESTA MOON

Linda Windsor

WestBow
PRESS
A Division of Thomas Nelson Publishers
Since 1798

visit us at www.westbowpress.com

Published in Nashville, Tennessee, by WestBow Press, a division of Thomas
Nelson, Inc. Author is represented by the literary agency of Alive Communications,
Inc., 7680 Goddard Street, Suite 200, Colorado Springs, CO 80920.

WestBow Press books may be purchased in bulk for educational, business, fund-
raising, or sales promotional use. For information, please e-mail
SpecialMarkets@ThomasNelson.com.

Publisher's Note: This novel is a work of fiction. Names, characters, places,
and incidents are either products of the author's imagination or used fictitiously.
All characters are fictional, and any similarity to people living or dead is purely
coincidental.

Library of Congress Cataloging in Publication Data

Windsor, Linda.
  Fiesta moon / Linda Windsor.
     p. cm.—(Moonstruck series ; 2)
  ISBN 0-7852-6063-3 (trade paper)
  I. Title.
PS3573.I519F54 2005
813'.54—dc22   2004029429

Printed in the United States of America
05 06 07 08 09 RRD 6 5 4 3 2 1

CHAPTER 1

The sun rising above the Sierra Madres glared in Mark Madison's eyes, despite his costly designer sunglasses, as if to punish him for daring to emerge before it reached the high point of its day. It reminded him of the receptionist at Madison Engineering Corporation, who welcomed him for a rare early morning appointment with cheer-veiled sarcasm. "Good morning, Mr. Madison," she said but meant, *That's what you get for staying out on the town when the rest of us working stiffs have to get up early to make a living.*

Mark's lips pulled into a righteous grimace as he gripped the wheel of his rental car. He did a lot more than those nine-to-fivers thought—especially Blaine—and they'd realize it now that he was temporarily on leave.

"Three strikes and you're out," Blaine said after Mark's most recent DUI hearing. "You've got to pull your life together, Mark. I'm tired of bailing you out of trouble and making excuses for you to Mother." Mouth thinned with disapproval, he handed over Mark's license. "If you are pulled over for anything unrelated to the project, kiss this good-bye, because you won't need it where you'll wind up. As it is, your performance in Mexico will determine whether you have a job when you return."

Blaine's condescension had fanned the fires of Mark's shame into rebellion. "I never asked you to make excuses for me. I never asked for you to bail me out of this DUI either. I'm my own man, whether you believe it or not."

1

At least Mark was as much a man as he could be, with a big brother who filled their ambitious father's shoes to the brim and a baby sister who had earned a doctorate in marine archeology before her twenty-sixth birthday. With ambition and brains taken, all that was left for Mark to claim was charm.

Blaine ran his fingers through the silver salting his dark hair at the temples. "When are you going to get it through that thick head of yours that I'm trying to help you aspire to something beyond liver failure?"

Mark bristled. "I'm a social drinker."

"You're becoming more than that, Mark."

"I can quit anytime."

Blaine drilled him with a challenging look. "Want to bet?"

Mark knew he was being suckered in, but for some reason he bit. "Name the stakes."

"If you keep the hacienda project on target and stay sober while you're doing it, I'll step down from our on-site management and let you take it over. There's nothing I'd rather do than stay in-house and let you do the traveling."

Mark practically salivated. He never minded the work, but hated being confined to the office, filling in the pieces of projects that Blaine had already designed. He envied his brother's travel. What a waste for someone like Blaine to see the world, when he was just as happy to stay in the box with his wife and kids.

Only a fool wouldn't jump at this. "You got yourself a deal, bro."

"I can't watch you, Mark, but God will know if you value honor more than a good time." Blaine had been on a God kick since he'd met Caroline. And while it made Mark a little uncomfortable sometimes, he had to admit his older brother seemed a lot happier now. And when Blaine was happy, Mark's life was easier.

So Mark got a *Get-Out-of-Jail-Free* card. Blaine and his church had used their pull to get Mark's jail time shifted to community service at some remote mission in Mexico—practically elevating Blaine to godly status in their mother's eyes. Blaine had saved Mark from ruin once again.

✦

As though living in a nice neighborhood and having a wife and 2.5 kids was all there was to aspire to in life, Mark thought, gearing down the sweet sports car as the incline became more steep. Not that he didn't like Blaine's wife and kids. What was not to like? Caroline loved everybody. Mark belonged to a mutual admiration society with his teen nieces, Karen and Annie. And he supposed the newest member of the Madison family, little Berto, made the perfect *point-five* of the national family average.

Family was nice, but that wasn't "living" in Mark's estimation. That was squeezing into a box of conformity and pulling down the lid, when there was a world to see and experiences to try before a man got too old to enjoy them. Then, maybe, he'd settle for life in the box.

As a busload of tourists passed him, two young ladies, their long blond hair tossed by the breeze, waved at him. Mark beeped the horn of the Jaguar XK8 convertible that he'd leased in Acapulco and flashed them a dazzling smile. He gunned the engine and soared around the bus, affording the girls, who'd hastily switched sides, a rakish wink. Blaine would have a hissy fit if he knew that Mark had switched his ticket destination from Mexico City to Acapulco, much less that he'd leased a car more suitable to his lifestyle in lieu of taking the bus.

"Well worth the trip," Mark said in a wistful tone, wishing he was still there, sipping a frozen drink—regrettably without the alcohol he'd promised to abstain from—and watching the leggy beach beauties strut their stuff against the sun-splashed blue of Acapulco Bay. Instead he was headed over the season-parched Sierra Madres to do penance in a one-donkey village.

As the distance between his sports car and a truck bulging with produce closed, Mark eased up on the accelerator. The truck groaned and shifted gears as it took the steep incline, its faded plank rails wobbling with the strain of its load. Glancing past the bend to the left, Mark spied Mexican women and children in a ravine cut by time into the worn mountains. It was dry and rocky for the most part, except for remnants of a river running through it. The children played in the water while their mothers washed clothes at its edge in the same manner as their ancestors.

Licking his dry lips, Mark reached for the bottled water in the walnut-and-leather-trimmed console as the truck ahead finally breached the crest and leveled off. To his increasing annoyance, it slowed even more, brake lights glowing. Mark impatiently took a swig of water and nosed around the vehicle. Seeing his way clear, he shot forward, when something in the periphery of his vision caught his eye—something moving out from under the truck. By the time Mark realized it was one of the lumbering vehicle's back tires, it was too late.

The tire shot into the backside of the Jaguar, sending it fish-tailing perilously close to the edge of the road, and dropped down into the ravine. Like a teetering giant, the braking truck skidded on its remaining tires across the road toward the ledge, the bare axle gnashing at the pavement in a trail of sparks. Mark gunned the engine of the Jag, streaking out of the truck's path and swerving back into the right lane. The truck ground to a stop at the cliff's edge, but Mark's overcompensation gave way to a teeth-jarring ride, reducing the Jag's high-performance features to those of the donkey cart sitting by a roadside stand, now dead ahead of him. Braking all the way on loose gravel and dirt, Mark not only upended the vegetable-laden cart, but took out the stand's canopy as well. Staring in disbelief, Mark watched the dust settle over the hood of the now stalled Jag.

Draped over it was a collapsed corner of a blue construction tarp. The other three corners, still supported by poles, provided shelter from the sun for a rustic roadside fruit stand. From the shouts of "*Ay de mí*," barking, and braying emanating from the underside, it was inhabited by Mexicans, dogs, and a disgruntled donkey.

Leery of his sensory report, Mark fingered his throbbing fore-head just as a wet, cool sensation spread between his legs. He quickly uprighted the water bottle emptying in his lap and noticed an assortment of fresh fruits and vegetables scattered on the floor of the car, evidently relocated from the capsized cart.

Just as he registered that things couldn't get worse, the air bag released.

◆

Can things get any worse? Corinne Diaz wondered as she worked her way through the crowd of the village *zócalo*. Not that Mexicalli was that large. Its few cobbled streets snaked their way through a cluster of homes and businesses growing from the lake on which the town had been built. Crisscrossing the streets at whatever angles the landscape would allow, occasional dirt and stone alleys led to orchards or gardens that fringed the settlement landward.

But all of Mexicalli seemed to have turned out for the Cinco de Mayo fiesta, along with their relatives from across the lake or up the mountain. And Corinne was searching the square for a pint-sized French soldier who was only seven—a very proud seven.

"*Ay de mí,* Señorita Corina, that boy 'Tonio makes no good."

Corinne stopped, waiting for her portly housekeeper to catch up. If the steep winding streets of the town were a challenge to Corinne's lungs, poor Soledad was puffing like a tuba player.

"Soledad, why don't you sit here in the square and keep an eye out for Antonio?"

Corinne unclipped the cell phone from the scarlet sash of her embroidered red and green skirt. Everyone sported the colors of the Mexican flag in honor of the day.

"Here," she said, handing the phone to the older woman. "Call the school if you find Antonio, and tell him to wait here until the rest of the cast finds him."

The orphans from Hogar de los Niños were scheduled to put on a play reenacting the 1862 Battle of Puebla, where a few Mexican militia under the leadership of General Ignacio Zaragoza Seguin turned back French troops sent by Napoleon to occupy the country.

Antonio was playing the part of a general of the French army. The young boy was so impressed with his red, white, and blue uniform of crepe paper, with its gold foil epaulets, that Corinne suspected him of coming into the village prematurely to show it off.

"No, no, no." Soledad shoved the phone back at her. "I will catch the culprit by his ear and drag him back to the *escuela*. I don't comprehend this equipment much."

Touch-tone hadn't quite taken over some of the more remote villages. Buttons were for clothes, not *equipment,* which was Soledad's word for anything she didn't understand. She only knew her heavy, black *teléfono*.

"It's like the computer," Corinne explained. "You just push *ocho* and the call button. Then it's just like your *teléfono,* no?"

Soledad arched half of the continuous black hedge of brow that separated her dark gaze from a low, copper-bronze forehead. She marveled at Corinne's wireless laptop, mostly for the photo albums stored in it, but marveling was as close to *equipment* as the Indio woman cared to get.

"My *teléfono* serves me well enough," she replied.

As frustrating as this general attitude was, it was also part of the village's charm.

With a sigh, Corinne reattached the cell phone to her sash. *"Bueno,"* she conceded. "But if you see Antonio, just keep him here."

She didn't want Soledad to have to climb the hill to the orphanage at the outskirts of the village. It was supposed to be her day off, but nothing went down in Mexicalli without Soledad's knowledge. Despite the lack of a phone in every home, news blanketed the town rather than spread through it. Who needed telephone lines when a network of neighboring clotheslines was far more efficient?

"Feed him a *churrito* from the butcher's stand. I'll gather the rest of the troops at the school as soon as they've finished their dinner, and bring them over for the show."

"Do not fret so. 'Tonio will show himself when the fun begins." Soledad reached up to tuck a loose strand of dark hair behind Corinne's ear that had escaped her upsweep. In addition to being cook and housekeeper at the orphanage, Soledad had also assumed the role of Corinne's *dueña*. A proper young lady did not live unchaperoned.

"I wonder that you have one hair left on your head. You are the nurse; you are the teacher; you are the nanny."

"Administrators wear many hats." Corinne wore those hats and many more as assistant to the priest who ran the orphanage. This morning, it had been that of janitor. Would the little ones ever learn to put the paper in the designated receptacle, rather than in the toilet, which was not designed to accomodate paper products? "Besides, I love what I'm doing."

And she loved Mexicalli. Corinne scanned the shaded plaza once more for the errant *commander de jour*. The butcher, the baker, even the candlestick maker had set up makeshift booths on the plaza for the event. Along the adjacent side of the square were a number of Indios selling handmade crafts from *petates,* or woven mats of split palm. The Cantina Roja, Mexicalli's only eat-in restaurant, bar, and gathering place, had moved its tables across the cobbled street so that guests might partake of its food and drink and have a front-row seat for the festivities. Even now, a visiting group of mariachis from the village on the other side of the lake were tuning their instruments near the stage.

"If I were your mama, I would say you should be making your own babies, not chasing after someone else's. It isn't like you need the money, no?"

Corinne turned, a wistful smile settling on her lips. "No, Soledad. I've been very blessed. Although if the ladies at the orphanage where I was left as a *niña* had not chased after me and found me a good home, it might have been very different. I might be begging on the streets of Mexico City or worse. Now, maybe I can make a difference in another orphan's life."

◆

It was a God thing, of that Corinne was certain. The search for her biological mother had begun at Cuernavaca, where Corinne had been adopted at the age of two. From there, Corinne and her parents traced María Sanchez to Mexicalli, which at the time had no orphanage. There the trail ended. As for Corinne's birth father, he'd been recorded as an American artist, John Smith—probably not his real name. Since Corinne had blue eyes and a lighter complexion than the cocoa or copper tones of María's people, the chances were good that he'd been fair.

The search was initiated not out of Corinne's longing to find her roots, but because of a tumor found during an annual physical. It was benign, but it led to a precautionary quest for her biological parents' medical histories. Unfortunately, María Sanchez was a popular name, and "John Smith" could have been any of the numerous Bohemian artists who came and went through the region.

So instead of finding the parents who'd given her up twenty-seven years ago, Corinne had found what her life might have been like had she not been adopted and raised by loving parents. And Mexicalli itself was a charming village, seemingly frozen in time. It felt like home, a part of her she hadn't known existed. The place and the people, especially the orphans, so enchanted her that she felt led to give back some of the blessings she'd received.

◆

"Aha," Soledad exclaimed, drawing Corinne from her reflection. The housekeeper pointed across the *zócalo* to where a crepe-paper-bedecked runaway bowed in front of Mexicalli's wealthy patroness, Doña Violeta. The setting sunlight crept under the jacaranda trees and glanced off the foil epaulets on Antonio's shoulders as he wielded his wooden sword against an invisible opponent.

"Better we hurry before he annoys Doña Violeta, and she ceases to help Hogar de los Niños forever. That one can be eccentric."

Eccentric was an understatement for an eighty-three-year-old woman who rode around town in an upholstered donkey cart. Her *burro* always wore a straw hat with a band to match its mistress's somber dress. The color of the day was navy blue.

Corinne stayed the housekeeper with her hand. "I'll take care of Antonio. You enjoy the rest of your afternoon."

"Pues," Soledad said, easing back down on the park bench without much protest. "Perhaps I should untire myself."

Smiling at the woman's unique grasp of English, Corinne set out through the picnicking clusters of family and friends gathered around the stage under the shade of the jacaranda trees. Her full skirt swished about her calves as she passed by so many familiar faces. Mexicalli was a small town, so even if Corinne did not know all their names, she had seen or dealt with most of the villagers in the two months since her arrival.

She reached the opposite side of the plaza, where Antonio was regaling Doña Violeta with the importance of his role. It had now advanced in rank from general to none other than Archduke Maximillian himself.

"I am second only to the great Napoleon, who could have conquered even the conquistadores," the boy boasted, assuming a proud stance, hand on the hilt of his wooden sword.

At that moment a thunderous clap erupted from the edge of the plaza where the road entered the city at its southern tip. The high-strung Antonio fumbled his sword. Doña Violeta clutched her purse to her chest as though it had been her heart that made the noise.

Corinne looked in the direction of the noise, where a rusty yellow livestock truck belched gray exhaust and hiccuped to a squeaky stop.

With the entire population of the *zócalo* watching, Capitán Nolla—Mexicalli's only policeman—and mayor Rafael Quintana swaggered over to the truck as its passengers streamed out of the cab like clowns from a Volkswagen Beetle. But Corinne's attention was sidetracked by a lone figure that hopped down from the company of grunting swine in the back of the vehicle.

CHAPTER 2

This is definitely not Kansas, Mark mused as he jumped lightly from the back of the livestock truck. And the pink-nosed pig that had snoozed with its head in Mark's lap was not Toto. Feeling as if he'd been pummeled by every stone in the Sierra Madres, he stood on the cobbled street of Mexicalli and stretched his six-foot-plus frame. Instead of inhaling the mountain air, he opted to keep his breath as shallow as he'd done since climbing into the back of the Swine Transport from Hades. After getting up close and personal with pork on the hoof, he wasn't sure he'd ever eat bacon again.

A suit-clad official, who identified himself to the driver as the *alcalde,* or mayor, and a uniformed policeman now approached Mark. With his graying dark hair slicked back from a broad forehead, the mayor resembled a short version of Brando's godfather character.

"Bienvenido a Mexicalli, señor."

Meh-chee-CAH-yee? He'd have to revise his pronunciation.

"The driver tells me that you are looking for our Hogar de los Niños." The stocky gentleman tucked an ample chin to his chest, giving Mark a head-to-toe appraisal. "By chance, would you be the brother of our Señor Blaine Madison of Pennsylvania?"

His sister-in-law, Caroline, had warned Mark that the people of Mexicalli made visitors one of their own. Extending his hand, Mark replied in kind. "Yes, señor, I am. I guess that makes me *your* Mark Madison."

Producing a smile almost as wide as his mustache, the man

shook Mark's hand. "And I am Rafael Quintana, mayor of Mexicalli, at your service. My village has been expecting you."

Mark glanced around, taking in the festive decorations in the plaza. "All this for me? Wow."

"No, no, no, Señor Madison," Quintana protested, Mark's humor zipping over his head. "Not that we would not put out such a welcome, of course, but today is Cinco de Mayo. All of Mexicalli is here to celebrate."

Puffing up like a proud father, the mayor made a wide sweep with his arm, encompassing the town plaza, but Mark didn't miss the unobtrusive way he managed to wipe his hand by shoving it into his trouser pocket.

"I'm kidding, Señor Quintana," Mark said, resisting the urge to sniff his fingers. There was no way a man could ride with hogs for two hours and not smell like them. "I made a joke."

"But of course you do." Quintana's laugh stemmed more of relief than humor. "But tell us, what became of your car?"

A thump, followed by a sharp squeal, distracted them as the pig that had mistaken Mark's lap for a pillow scrambled to its feet. Not quite as large as its companions, it had managed to wriggle under the plank tailgate. Before the driver or any of his compadres could stop it, the pink porker made a break through the crowded plaza.

Mayhem ensued. Small, but swift of foot, the pig eluded its pursuers. Picnic blankets were abandoned; children squealed; their mothers and grandmothers screamed. One of the Cantina Roja tables was upended when the pig sought refuge beneath it, causing the patrons to abandon their seats in all haste. Mark watched in disbelief as the troublemaker circled in front of a stage where a group of mariachis played without pause.

Everyone was so preoccupied with the pig that no one noticed a rather sophisticated cart, with brass rails and polished black sides, heading swiftly downhill, preceded by a bolting burro wearing a hat adorned with a bow. No one, that is, except the pretty señorita and little boy who chased after it. Determination on her face, the young woman hiked her full skirt above her knees, revealing a distracting display of shapely legs. Just then the child, garbed in some sort of paper uniform, lost his footing and sprawled on the cobbled walk in the wake of the cart and the señorita.

With a heroic surge of adrenalin, Mark left the mayor shouting directions to his minions and sprinted across the street to head off the runaway burro. Rushing into its path, he held up his hands.

"Whoa, boy!" he called out, his voice as calm as the staccato clippity-clop of approaching hooves on stone would allow.

Just as it seemed the steed was going to run him down, Mark stepped to the side with all the finesse of a matador and seized its bridle. After a few awkward attempts to dig into the stone street with his feet, he finally succeeded in bringing burro and cart to a halt.

"Easy there, fella," he cajoled, stroking the quivering flesh of the donkey's neck.

Downhill momentum having its way, the señorita gasped as she collided with the cart. "Doña Violeta . . ." She reached into the bottom of the vehicle, drawing Mark's attention to a drawn figure curled on the carpeted floor between twin leather upholstered benches. "Are you all right?" She helped the elderly female into an upright position.

Bizarre as the rich leather upholstered donkey cart and its aristocratic octogenarian were, Mark couldn't take his eyes off the señorita. Her cheeks were flushed and her eyes blue enough to shame a sapphire. Concern surfaced from their luminous depths. Perhaps he'd rescued her grandmother.

Mark handed the burro's reins over to one of the village men, as others gathered around to help the lady out of the cart. She was stooped, no taller than the senorita's shoulders, and clad in a dark blue dress with a high lace collar straight from the Victorian era.

"Doña Violeta, permit Antonio and me to take you home," Señorita Blue Eyes said to the dowager in fluent Spanish. Suddenly, as if she'd just missed the boy, the younger woman cast a frantic look about and found him at the edge of the crowd. "Antonio, are you all right?"

Here was definitely a reason to dust off his college Spanish, Mark thought as the boy answered with a glum nod.

"See to the child. See to the child," Doña Violeta ordered above the cacophony of concern over her welfare. An accustomed authority rang in her voice. "It's not the first time I've taken a tumble in Chiquita's cart."

This old lady was tougher than she looked.

"You are sure?" Blue Eyes asked.

"The boy, Corina," the old woman insisted.

Co-ree-nah. Making note of the name and pronunciation, Mark stepped forward, ready to receive the credit due for the rescue.

But instead of acknowledging him, the young woman rushed to the boy, who stood, chin trembling, with ebony pools for eyes. Was it her brother?

"Antonio," she said, in a tone that would melt butter. "Let me see your hands."

Jutting out his chin in a brave attempt to stall his welling tears, the tattered paper soldier extended them, palms up. They'd been scraped raw by the cobblestones. "My uniform, it is ruined."

"Now you look like a general who has really been in battle," she told him. She stepped back and gave him a once-over. "Yes, this will make you more believable. You must make sure that you show your hands to the audience during your performance, so they will know how brave you are."

Antonio grew a good two inches in height from his former withered stance. *"Es verdad?"*

"Of course it's true." As she drew him into a motherly embrace, she glanced in Mark's direction and smiled.

Mark introduced himself. "Señorita Corina, *me llamo* Mark Madison. I'm glad that I was able to stop your grandmother's cart before anyone was hurt."

Her smile dissipated and her gaze narrowed.

Mark did a quick mental replay of his Spanish to make certain he'd not made an inadvertent insult. *Me llamo* was as basic as Spanish could get.

"Perdoname, Señor Madison," Corina replied, her words stiff as a tuxedo collar. "I did not recognize you with all the calamity your pig caused." She lowered her gaze to Mark's feet.

Following it, Mark was astonished to see the pig standing at his heel, breathing heavily from the chase. "It's not *my* pig," he answered, a confused frown knitting his brow. "Excuse me, but have we met?"

"I shouldn't wonder that you don't remember."

Her pained smile only affirmed Mark's growing sense that they had not only met before, but he hadn't made a good impression. He braced himself. "No, but I have feeling I'm about to be enlightened."

"We danced at your brother's wedding . . . just before you became sick on my shoes." She extended her hand. "I'm Corinne Diaz. And, for better or worse, we'll be working together at the orphanage."

Mark stared. No way could this wholesome Mexican beauty be the pinch-mouthed shrew who had sent him a bill for the cleaning of her dress and shoes, along with a scathing note suggesting a long stay at a good rehabilitation center.

A smirk tugging at his mouth, he took her hand in his and brushed her knuckles with his lips. *"El gusto es mío, Corina."* He rolled the syllables of her name off his tongue in a tigerish purr. "If the mountain air does as well by me as it has by you, the pleasure will definitely be mine."

As he turned away to fetch his luggage, Mark let out the trepidation building in his chest with a long sigh. Every time he thought that it couldn't get any worse, it did.

◆

Mark Madison. Corinne was tempted to look over her shoulder at the retreating, disheveled hitchhiker just to be certain that this was indeed the prodigal of the Madison family. That he had arrived with a truckload of swine, looking like a walking dust bag in designer clothes, was not lost on Corinne's sense of humor. Maybe this, too, was a God thing—as in a rebuke for the man's decadence.

"I have to ask," she began, succumbing to a smile as he returned with his bag. "Who booked your transportation from Mexico City?"

"Cute," he replied. "About as cute as the rest of this godforsaken place. Where is this hacienda anyway . . . on the mountaintop?"

Antonio turned toward the struggling traveler, walking backwards. "Are you the new *jefe*?"

"I guess you could say I'm the boss, hombre. I'm the construction engineer."

"Then you will need a *mozo*." The boy thumped his ragged paper-covered chest. "Perhaps you will consider me."

Corinne chuckled. "I think Mr. Madison can do just fine without a young servant." She rubbed Antonio's thick dark hair. "At least one who is seven years old. Besides . . ." She glanced at Mark. "He has come to *serve*, not to be served."

"But I'll keep you in mind, hombre, if I need someone of your talents." Mark extended his hand to the boy, who shook it enthusiastically.

Corinne turned Antonio face forward again. "Before you fall and skin your backside," she explained.

"How about we stop a minute before I fall on my face?"

Mark shifted his leather suitcase from one hand to the other and stopped to catch his breath as they neared the end of the main street through the village. Corinne and Antonio paused and turned as he wiped his damp brow with the back of his hand, smearing the dirt collected there.

Dust seemed to hang in the air over the parched, faded green landscape. The livestock truck had stirred it even more.

"So, care to explain why you are three days late and arrived in a livestock truck? When you've caught your breath, of course." To herself Corinne acknowledged that the steep streets had nearly done her in at first exposure also.

"Talk about holding a grudge." Mark cocked a sandy brow at her. "You're enjoying this, aren't you?"

Unaware of the strained undercurrent between the adults, Antonio consoled him. "All gringos take their breath climbing the street of our village, jefe. *Ni modo*." He shrugged. "It can't be helped, no?"

"You were to arrive on the Mexico City bus three days ago, according to Blaine's e-mail," she prompted. "I was just curious."

As far as Corinne was concerned, the orphanage could have taken the blueprints and subcontracted the labor itself, rather than subjecting her to Mark Madison with his high opinion of himself and the fruit of the vine. She had little patience with playboys, which, from all that she'd seen and heard, was exactly what the man was.

She allowed that most of her information had come from sorority sisters who'd set their sights on landing one of the area's most eligible bachelors and failed. But when he'd made a fool of himself at his brother's wedding, he'd confirmed his reputation in her eyes.

"If I thought I could get back up, señorita, I would lie down and bare my throat." Instead he sat on his suitcase, his square jaw shifting in irritation to one side. "I decided to take a minivacation in Acapulco instead of flying in through Mexico City. It was probably the last moment of pleasure I will enjoy until this project is complete. This morning I started toward Mexicalli in a fine sports car, but it was arrested after a produce truck threw a wheel just as I passed it."

"The *car* was arrested?" she echoed.

"Until it could be cleared of wrongdoing." He raised his hands, head shaking in equal disbelief. "I honestly think the local *alcalde* thought he might get a hot red, only slightly scratched, Jaguar out of this, but it's rented. Now it's between him and the rental company. I'll have to pay the fine through our contract, I guess. I'm turning it over to the corporate attorneys as soon as I report in."

Corinne had heard of such occurrences, but had never encountered it firsthand. In traffic accidents, the vehicles were impounded until the matter was sorted out and damages paid. But it didn't increase her sympathy for Mark Madison.

"Think of the poor farmer who owned the produce truck. He'll be without his livelihood until it's settled."

Mark shot her an incredulous look. "If he'd tightened his wheel nuts, it wouldn't have happened."

"That doesn't change the fact that his family will suffer—a family most likely living hand-to-mouth."

Of course Madison cared very little about what she was saying. But for God's grace, she might think the same way. They'd both been raised in comfort. The difference was that Corinne had been drawn into helping the needy through her involvement in church missionary programs. Mark Madison, on the other hand, was only here because his irresponsible drinking had gotten him into more trouble than ruining a good dress and shoes. From what she'd heard, his brother had pulled some big strings to get the three-time offender this much lenience.

Mark shrugged, mimicking Antonio. *"Ni modo.* It's not my fault."

Not his fault. That was probably the same argument he'd offered in court. Corinne had no patience for slackers. She'd earned a degree in teaching and, because she carried a heavy academic schedule, a second one in social work at the same time. Why couldn't people simply admit that they made wrong choices and accept the consequences? If one parties the night before an exam instead of studying, one fails the exam. If one gets drunk and gives in to temptation, one may get pregnant. Alcohol addles judgment. People didn't have to drink it.

"Anyway, I hitched a ride from that hole-in-the-wall to this one, and here I am, smelling like a pig rolled in dust." He got up and bowed his head to her. "But at your service, nonetheless."

The western sun frolicked in his rakish gaze as he straightened. Mark Madison's charm was dangerous when he was sober—and down on his luck.

Corinne checked her watch. She had less than an hour to see Antonio fed, treat his scratches, and get her little group of orphaned thespians to the village square stage.

"I'm running late, so I'll have one of the women at the orphanage show you to Father Menasco's guest room. You can shower and change there. I'm not sure if he's home or visiting, but he is expecting you."

Turning in dismissal, Corinne started across an open meadow toward the Quonset hut compound that was Hogar de los Niños in long, hasty strides. The bright yellow blossoms of the surrounding primavera trees cast a sharp contrast to the thirsty mountainous backdrop of milky lilac, grays, and pearls, as though to copy the waning sun's brightness.

"And then you must come to see our performance, jefe," Antonio called over his shoulder as Corinne pulled him along.

"Or the jefe may want to rest in the parsonage," Corinne suggested for both companions' benefit. Her chest knotted in rebellion at her inadvertent use of Antonio's title for Mark. He was no boss, and certainly not hers.

"I wouldn't miss it, Antonio," Mark declared.

"We start early in the morning," Corinne pointed out. She could see it now, being awakened by one of the Cantina Roja's staff to let in a drunken Mark Madison.

"But I don't," the roguish newcomer shot back. "I'm just getting wound up this time of day. A quick shower, and I'll be at your command."

"Just remember, we're here to set a good example for the children."

"Then I'll do my best not to live down to your expectations of me, señorita—and see if the word *forgiveness* means anything to you."

Corinne nearly stumbled at the challenge in Mark's voice. Catching herself, she met a look as brittle as Soledad's caramel nut candy, and not nearly so sweet. Although he said nothing, his expression spoke volumes. He had apologized in person over the phone and by note, as well as returning her things professionally cleaned.

The ball was in her court . . . but she didn't want to play.

"People change, Corinne."

Corinne knew that. Her father had. But had Mark Madison? His untidy arrival three days late was hardly favorable.

"Or don't you believe that's possible?" he asked.

If she was the Christian she liked to think she was, how could she not give him a second chance? Her fingers sought the gold cross at her neck, given to her by the Edenton church and school back home, and she replied with the words engraved on its back.

"All things are possible, Señor Madison." She glanced after Antonio, who had taken off ahead of them, bored with the adult exchange. "My apologies for implying otherwise."

But seeing will be believing in this particular case.

CHAPTER 3

There was little applause at the end of the children's play, not because it wasn't enjoyed, but because, Corinne had observed, it wasn't the custom among the general Indio population. Nonetheless, appreciation brimmed in the audience's demeanor—nodding heads, a raised hand here or there, and eyes bright with enjoyment. It was an unqualified success.

Antonio showed his iodine-smeared hands as he was driven from the stage by General Seguin's minipatriots. Now the actors lined up at the head of the other orphans to lead a noisy parade accented with wooden blocks, painted cans beaten with sticks, and plastic whistles, their eventual destination the *petate* mats that Corinne had spread on the lawn.

"You really enjoy working with the children. It shows over you *completamente*," said Diego Quintana from his seat on the mat beside her. The electric lantern lights of the plaza twinkled in the ebony of his lash-fringed gaze.

The son of the mayor of Mexicalli, Diego had a complexion not quite as dark as the cocoa or rosewood of the Indios, due to a mix of Spanish ancestry, and he bore the aristocratic high cheekbones and strong jawline of his Aztec ancestors. Clad in a loose-fitted poet shirt over Levis in love with his long, lean legs, he looked the Bohemian artist that he was. His exquisite handcrafted jewelry was sold in high-end stores throughout Mexico.

Corinne smiled. "But for God's grace, I might have been one of them."

◆

Her answer had been the same to her parents two months before, when she'd broached the subject in their posh West Chester home after the health scare had precipitated her search for the medical records of her biological parents.

Her father had treated her as though she'd lost her mind.

"I absolutely forbid it. This is insanity." Daniel Diaz slammed his fork down, rattling the turn-of-the century china dessert plate. "What if you get sick? The nearest decent hospital is three hours in either direction, if you're lucky. And I use the word *decent* loosely."

"Daddy, I'm as healthy as the proverbial horse. The lump was fibrous. It's gone," Corinne assured him. "But the coincidences are too much to be anything less than God's calling. He led us to Hogar de los Niños and Father Menasco at a time when my training is exactly what is needed."

"You talk to her," Dr. Diaz implored his wife.

"Talk to him, Mom," Corinne joined in, seeking her mother's alliance as well.

Kathleen Butler Diaz chewed her bottom lip, glancing with apprehension from husband to daughter and back. "I don't want her to go away any more than you do, Daniel, but she is twenty-seven. And with the investments from the money my mother left her, she doesn't have to work."

"She doesn't have to work *period.*" Lips pressed into a hard line, Daniel stared at his untouched flan hard enough to melt it. "First she wants to become a nurse. Two years later, she decides to become a teacher. Now she is to be a social worker. What next?" He shifted his gaze to Corinne. "An astronaut, maybe?"

"Daddy." Corinne covered his clenched hand with hers. "Can't you see that it was no accident that my medical scare led me to Hogar de los Niños?"

"What about the position you accepted at Edenton Christian Academy?" her mother reminded her.

"Exactly," Corinne agreed, but not, she knew, for the reason her mother intended. "How coincidental is it that the academy happens to be sponsoring a mission right in Mexicalli? It's got to be God."

Her parents' silence was the first indication that she was making headway.

"I know that you would rather I remain around Philadelphia, but what if the ones who placed me in your care had ignored their calling?"

Her mother closed her eyes.

One down, one to go.

"It's not forever," Corinne went on. "And you know how hard I've been working with Edenton Christian and Father Menasco to get grants for the renovation." Her social work internship contacts and fluent Spanish had gone a long way to help her with both local and Mexican authorities.

Daniel Diaz cocked his head at her. "How long is 'not forever'?"

"Until the orphanage has expanded to the renovated hacienda. Then I'll come home and . . ." She grinned, mischief lighting in her gaze. "And then we'll talk about this astronaut idea."

◆

"So, might I hope that you will stay until you find your real mother?" Diego asked, breaking into her reminiscence.

"If I find her, I find her," Corinne answered. She meant it. God had given her good parents and good health. It would be nice to meet her birth mother, but Corinne's needs had been more than met. "Either way, my place is here for the time being."

"And for that, I and all of my village are thankful." Diego gave her a slight salute.

Corinne laughed. "You are a shameful flirt, amigo. "

But he possessed such a flair for it that even this twenty-first-century woman didn't mind—she knew better than to take him seriously.

Her housekeeper had warned her from the start that Diego was between señoritas at the moment. Soledad's niece was his last live-in, sealing his fate both in heaven and on earth with her aunt.

Now the lithesome beauty was in Mexico City pursuing a career in dance.

"Will you never take me with seriousness, *mi corazón?*"

"I am not your heart, I am your *amiga, nada mas.*"

Sometimes Corinne wondered if she'd ever take a guy seriously. To date, the distance she kept between herself and the opposite sex had spared her untold grief and disappointment, in her estimation. Forewarned was forearmed—and she'd seen enough to collect an arsenal.

Surely there had to be someone for her, someone responsible and faithful, someone she could admire and respect. But where was he, she thought, glancing through a break in the trees at the moon. Shades of a romantic song played in her mind, the lyrics changed to reflect the void in her heart. *Somewhere out . . .* where?

A cacophony of banging, rattling, and drumming clashed with the melody in her mind. Making enough "music" for twice their number, the children of Hogar de los Niños marched toward her in a single line. Undaunted by the line she'd drawn in the romantic sand, Diego helped her organize the proud fiesta participants in rows on the woven palm-leaf mats until staff teacher María Delgado brought up the rear.

Ordinarily, the children would be preparing for bed by this time, but this was *fiesta,* and the rules had been bent so they might stay long enough to see the fireworks. By the time everyone was situated and *liquados*—frozen fruit drinks—had been passed out, the mariachi band started playing, entertaining the crowd while rickety towers made of scrap wood were set up on each side of the stage.

"And a strawberry sweet for the sweetest." Leaning over the head of one of the seated children, Diego handed her a treat from the box tray he'd used to carry them. As Corinne accepted it, he gave her a peck on the cheek and backed away in roguish satisfaction. All he needed was a mask.

The not-unpleasant shock that filled Corinne's mind dissipated at the sound of a male voice.

"Got any lime?" Mark Madison piped up behind her. Stepping into the periphery of her vision, he added for Diego's benefit, "No kiss on the side, *gracias.*"

One velvet black eyebrow arched over curious appraisal, Diego offered Mark his choice of the last few *liquados* in the box. "Help yourself to them, Señor . . . Madison, I presume? Señorita Corina has told me of you," he continued, extending his free hand. "I am Diego Quintana, a local artisan."

Mark shook his hand. "I assure you, Señor Quintana, that I am not as degenerate as she would have you think. We've shared a regrettable history."

Heat crept to the surface of Corinne's face at the possible interpretation that she might have more of a "history" with Mark Madison than platonic. She put it right at once. "I told Diego nothing regarding what little of your character I've been exposed to, Mr. Madison. He can judge that for himself even as we speak."

With a billowing puff of skirt, she sat down on the mat and patted the place beside her. But before the gaze she raised could invite Diego, Mark dropped down in the place intended for the other man and lifted his frozen drink in a salute.

"Just living up to my reputation, sweetness."

I am not your sweetness, nor will I ever be! Corinne chewed the words and swallowed them, sooner than launch another offensive before she'd assembled sufficient defense for his inevitable retaliation. Instead, she took a handful of the napkins from Diego's tray as he sat down on her other side and, leaning forward, handed them to a boy in the row in front of her to distribute.

"So, Diego, are you related to the mayor?" Mark asked behind her back.

"I am his son, but . . ." Diego lifted surrendering hands. "I have no ambition to politics." He shifted the conversation as Corinne straightened. "So you have come to change the Ortiz hacienda to suit Hogar de los Niños?"

"Yes, that's the plan. Do you know any reliable contractors?"

Clean and scented with aftershave, Mark Madison had made a remarkable transformation. His normally light-colored hair was wet and shades darker. Combed back off his face, curling at odds with the collar of his light blue shirt, he reminded her too much of the hero in one of her favorite movies, *Romancing the Stone*—complete with the dimple in the middle of his chin. She'd forgotten the dimple, perhaps missing it earlier due to a coating of road dust and swine sweat.

"Most of the contractors would have to come in from Cuernavaca," Diego answered.

"What about the Three Juans?" Corinne suggested. "Two of the brothers live here, and the other has a home in the mountains not far from here."

Besides, she didn't come here for dimples. She came to serve God and His orphaned babes. And the suave Mark Madison with his reputation as a lady-killer was definitely not her type.

"They would make your project, how do you say . . . interesting," Diego admitted with a decidedly amused smirk.

Mark frowned. "Why do they call themselves Three *Ones*?"

"*Tres Juanos,* actually." Corinne succumbed to a grin. "Juan Pablo, Juan Pedro, and Juan Miguel." At Mark's head-jerk reaction, she laughed. "I kid you not. Juan Pablo is an excellent plumber—"

"With million-dollar words and creative"—Diego made quotation marks with his fingers—"*projectations.*"

"Juan Pedro is an electrician."

"When he's sober," Diego added.

"And Juan Miguel is a sculptor who does plaster and masonry." Mark jumped in at the pause. "What's Juan Miguel's problem?"

Corinne glanced at Diego. "Nothing . . . nothing really."

Mark gave a short, derisive laugh. "This is a joke, isn't it?"

"*No, señor, es verdad,*" Diego assured him. "But Juan Miguel is an artisan like myself. So when he is involved with his sculpture, he does not like to be distracted."

"And when would that be?" Mark asked. "His sculpting hours, that is."

Diego shrugged. "Whenever he is inspired, *cómo no?*"

A sputtering hiss of fire from the stage area highlighted Mark's bemused expression and ended the conversation as the pyrotechnic show began.

"No Mexicalli holiday is complete without fireworks." Having had to step off the mad, spinning carousel of life back home to the *mañana* schedule of the mountain village herself, Corinne was spurred by a twinge of sympathy. Leaning in close, she shouted in his ear, "Welcome to Mexicalli. It's a world unto itself."

◆

That was an understatement if Mark had ever heard one. If anyone had told him even a month ago that he'd be in a mountain village, surrounded by ragamuffins in paper uniforms, watching a corner market fireworks display as it threatened to burn up the shuddering wooden towers holding it, and sitting on the grass with an attractive, if bristly, señorita, he'd have said the speaker had been into the loco juice. Okay, maybe he'd sit on the grass with the señorita, but the rest was straight out of the *Twilight Zone*. He still hadn't recovered from the runaway donkey sedan with the aristocratic octogenarian at the reins.

Mark laughed to himself. He didn't know life could be so crazy without the help of some intoxicant—or so interesting, for that matter. *And what's the deal with Corinne Diaz and Diego Quintana?* he wondered, watching as Diego shared a few words that put a smile on the lady's face. Not that Mark cared. She was a little too goody-goody and self-righteous for his taste—like big brother Blaine.

"Antonio!" Near the front row, the young woman who'd herded the children from the stage reached over and tugged on the tunic of the French general, who had jumped to his feet in excitement.

"Hey, General," Mark called out. "Come sit back here with me and you won't block the others' view."

With a grin exploding on his face like the Roman candle shooting into the sky, the youngster glanced at the shepherding teacher for permission. At her nod of approval, he scurried to the back row and dropped to his knees on the mat. "Did you ever see such beauty, *jefe?*"

Mark exchanged a smile with the dark-haired teacher, holding her shy, lingering gaze until Antonio jabbed him with an elbow. In

the bright flash of a floral display, she looked to be no more than
eighteen. Maybe she was just a helper or one of the older orphans.
Regardless, she was too young to bat those long seductive lashes at
someone his age.

"It's *muy grande,* no?"

"Very grand," Mark answered.

Someone his age. Suddenly thirty-two seemed ancient as he fixed
his attention on the sky exposed through the trees.

A few more pinwheels spurting colored fire that lasted a minute
or so, some Roman candles, and a finale of shooting streams with
secondary spirals, and the *very grand* show was over. The air was
filled with the scent of the burnt incendiary powder, while clouds
of dissipating smoke hovered in the sky over the plaza.

The children were hustled to their feet and lined up for the
march back to the orphanage.

"Everyone look to the front and follow María," Corinne
instructed.

So that was her name. There'd been too much confusion before
the fireworks for a proper introduction.

As if realizing that she'd been remiss, Corinne turned to him.
"Mark, this is María Delgado, a very capable aide as you can see.
María, this is Mark Madison, the gentleman who has come to
make over the Hacienda Ortiz."

"*Mucho gusto,* María," Mark said across the sea of little heads
between them.

Dipping in a polite curtsy, María nodded. "*El gusto es mio, Señor
Madi*—"

She broke off with an apologetic smile to collar the little boy who
passed out the napkins earlier. Fascinated by a stray dog begging
food from a nearby picnicking family, he'd started to wander off.

"Okay, are we ready?" Corinne said as Paquito was brought back
into the line.

She began to sing the familiar tune of "Jesus Loves Me" in
Spanish. By the second line, the orphans chimed in, accompanying themselves with the clatter and bang of their instruments.

Mark had never thought of the tune as a marching song, but it worked, moving the children through appreciative onlookers who were staying for the music and dance planned afterward.

Cristo me ama,
Cristo me ama,
Cristo me ama,
La Biblia dice así.

The chorus and chaos brought some of the citizens who lived along the steep, winding street to their doorways to wave as the procession moved by. Encouraged, the marchers increased their volume and vigor from block to block until the cobbled street gave way to the paved road leading across open fields to Hogar de los Niños.

While hardly Mark's scene, it was more entertaining than he'd have expected. Not that he hadn't been tempted by Diego's invitation to remain behind for the dancing. A drink would have gone well about now, but oddly enough, he was too tired, not to mention sore. His backside hurt from the jolting ride in the truck, his legs felt the toll of the vertical landscape, and for whatever reason—most likely fatigue—there was an aching void making itself known in his chest. It seemed to grow larger with each line the homeless children sang.

"Cristo me ama," Antonio sang at the top of his lungs.

The earnestness of his youthful spirit flowed from his hand to Mark's.

Jesus loves me. Mark's lips quirked with skepticism. He supposed he might have been Antonio's age the last time he had sung that song and believed it. But the real world wasn't a Jesus world. And real love was hard to find.

Aside from what he felt for his mother, Mark wasn't even certain he knew what real love was. What began as the real thing for him usually wound up being infatuation or desire. He'd seen Victoria's Secret's angels, eager to lift him to heavenly heights, turn into vamps intent on draining the life out of him and his bank account.

"Pues, jefe," Antonio said when they reached the play yard of the orphanage, "remember that I am still available if you need a

27

helper." The tattered general drew himself up to his tallest and gave Mark a salute.

"Will do, amigo," Mark replied. He was beginning to see how easily his adopted nephew, Berto, had wormed his way into Blaine's and Caroline's hearts.

"I am not afraid of the ghost that stole my brother."

Jolted, Mark stared at the boy. "Ghost?" He glanced to where Corinne and María were dismissing the children to their respective huts. "What ghost?"

Antonio looked at Mark as if he had the IQ of an amoeba. "The angry miner who killed the first mayor of Mexicalli—the husband to the good Señora Lucinda."

Come to think of it, Blaine had mentioned something about a ghost. Then the rest of Antonio's words registered. "Wait, what's this about your brother being stolen?"

"We think Enrique ran away." Corinne had stepped over and put an arm around Antonio's shoulders. "But my little brother in Christ would never think of leaving me, would you, *hermanito?*"

Antonio's bravado faded, giving way to a slight tremble of his lower lip. "My brother did not run away. He would never leave me. The ghost took Enrique."

"There is no such thing as a ghost, Antonio," Corinne insisted. "And even if there was, I heard it was la Señora Lucinda, who loved children so much."

"Then maybe she wanted a little boy for her own," the boy suggested. Antonio drew his arm across his running nose.

That was another problem with kids. Something was always leaking or running. Computers couldn't hold a candle to the paper waste produced by child care.

Unaffected, Corinne dug a tissue from her skirt pocket and promptly policed the boy's nose and arm. "Regardless . . ." she said, kissing the top of his head. "We pray every day for his return, yes?"

"*S-sí,*" the boy sniffed. "Jesus will bring him back."

The glaze of dismay in the look Corinne gave Mark over the child's head prodded him into action.

"And until then, we have lots of work to do, right?" What in the devil was he going to get a kid to do? "That is, if it's okay with your teachers at the orphanage."

Before his eyes, Corinne's dismay turned to gratitude with a smile that stalled his impulse to rescind the invitation.

"I'm certain we can spare Antonio after his lunch and recess. I'll talk to Father Menasco tomorrow."

With a loving pat, she sent Antonio toward the doorway where María waited for the last of the strays. Once the door to the large Quonset hut dormitory closed behind them, she faced him, suddenly awkward.

"I know I apologized earlier, but . . ." She looked away as if the words she sought might be hiding in the lilies growing around the entrance. "That was very good of you to take Antonio under your wing. His brother's disappearance has made him so unpredictable. I'm afraid he might be tempted to go look for Enrique . . . . Not even the police have any idea where the boy is."

"No theories at all?"

"There are a number of possibilities. Sometimes older children are lured off by men who make them beg on the streets to support them. You know, like Fagin in *Oliver Twist,*" she explained. "Or he could have wandered into the abandoned mines up in the mountains. If he did—" She broke off with a shudder.

"Yeah, I remember Blaine saying the hills were riddled with silver mines."

"But the ones under Mexicalli's mountain were depleted in the early twentieth century . . . and most are sealed." She heaved a resigned sigh. "There were volunteer search parties of villagers who know this area well, but Enrique wasn't found."

"And the murdering ghost?"

She shrugged. "As far as the records show, Diego Ortiz died of natural causes, leaving Lucinda a widow. But the Indios are very superstitious." She chuckled. "Sometimes it will make you want to tear your hair out. The work ethic is strong, but unpredictable."

"Like the Three Juans?" he asked.

"Like our Three Juans." Her laugh was as melodic as her voice. "But at least with local help, you can easily look them up when they don't show up for work."

Mark grimaced. "I think I'll stick to licensed contractors."

"Suit yourself."

Something about the riveting twitch of her lips both fascinated Mark and made him wary at the same time.

Crossing her arms, Corinne looked over at the parsonage. Dim light shone from one window. "Well, the morning comes early, and it looks like Father Menasco left the light on in the guest room and turned in early. You know where to go?"

Mark nodded. The parsonage was an L-shaped structure with a courtyard wall closing in the other two sides. Fortunately the guest room opened onto the patio, as did all the rooms. And Mark had already made friends with the priest's dog, Monty—short for Montezuma.

"So where do you bunk?" he asked, wondering if Corinne slept in the dormitory.

She nodded downhill to where the lake shone like a moon-silvered mirror, surrounded by trees and dwellings. "I have a room at a bed-and-breakfast on the lake—"

"Not on my account, I hope," he interjected.

The fine, aristocratic lines of her profile against the blue-black backdrop of the night sky reminded him of one of those velvet paintings sold in souvenir shops all over the country—a señorita with dark hair pulled tight from her face into a wild cascade; a faraway look in her luminous eyes; and bronzed shoulders bared just enough by the ruffle of her white embroidered neckline to set the imagination afire.

"No, I just needed the space and . . . maintenance," she added, turning to face him. Her smile distracted Mark before he could latch onto the word *maintenance*. "But I'm hoping that your efforts will soon change that and spare me the expense."

He'd clearly mistaken *faraway* for calculating. "How's that?" He wasn't going to fall for that Spanish angel-with-a-plan look. Besides, at any moment, the pinch-mouthed shrew could emerge.

"I'm hoping that you'll get the downstairs plumbing working right, so that I can move my things into the hacienda. It works, but has some strange quirks."

"You're not afraid of the ghost . . . *ghosts?*" he asked, a half-smile tugging at the corner of his mouth.

"I am cautious, not superstitious."

The upturned curve of her lips set off warning bells Mark didn't even know he had, and all of them said *Run, do not walk, to the nearest exit.* Still, no gentleman would allow a lady to walk alone at night. Besides, with the winding and dipping streets of Mexicalli, it could be five times as far as the crow flew.

"At least let me walk you to your B and B. It's fiesta and probably not safe for an attractive señorita to be out alone." He could almost hear his legs telling him it wasn't safe for him to make promises they had no intention of keeping, but . . .

"Thanks, but no thanks. I enjoy the quiet retreat alone with God. Helps me unwind after a long day," she explained, the first sign of her waning energy emerging in a sigh. "Besides, I have a black belt in kickboxing."

Hello. Nix the angel wings. Add a nunchaku slung over each of those deceptively delicate shoulders. "Well, in that case, I'll just thank you for acknowledging the possibility of my redemption." Without forethought, Mark bent down and gave her a chaste kiss on the cheek.

Both of them backed away, equally startled by the impulse. Chaste wasn't his style, but today had disrupted the status quo big time. Uncertain what to expect, Mark watched disbelief freeze on Corinne's face. Finally they parted. Instead of erupting with an ear-splitting Bruce Lee *heeyah* accompanied by a kick below the belt, she spoke.

"You're welcome." With yet another backward step, she pivoted and started down a beaten path that Mark had missed earlier in his rush to shower and join the fun at the plaza. "Good night, Mr. Madison. Sleep well."

Mark swallowed the urge to insist she call him by his given name. He liked living *on* the edge, not astraddle it.

CHAPTER 4

Morning came, complete with a crowing competition among all the roosters of the village, followed, as if cued in, by a church bell. Mark struggled to keep his eyes shut in the hopes that the noise would subside, but soon someone decided to torture a burro.

The smell of strong coffee brewing cajoled his nose from his pillow. He inhaled deeply, hoping for a vicarious caffeine fix to rouse him from his bed. Instead, it alerted his stomach that the cold plate of black beans and rice he'd been fed by the orphanage cook before he went to the plaza was long gone. She'd called it "Muslims and Christians." Strange, but then this entire place was strange.

Throwing off the covers that had protected him from the cool mountain night air, he finally rose from the bed. He opened the red shutters covering the rear window of his room and peered out. The meager farmstead adjoining the orphanage property gloried in the sunlight as a young boy frolicked with the loud-mouthed burro, while his little sister, perhaps summoned by the head rooster, scattered feed on the ground for the barnyard fowl.

"Thank God I'm not a country boy," Mark muttered under his breath. Leaving the window, he surveyed the scattered clothes on the floor with a sigh of resignation. Things weren't likely to get any quieter. The children sleeping in the dormitory next door would be stirring soon, if they weren't already. From the few times he'd dated women with young children, he'd noticed that the latter's eyelids seemed to open in concert with the sun.

Trudging over to a washstand not unlike the antique piece in his mother's front hallway, he checked the temperature of the water in a painted clay pitcher that was nested in a matching washbowl. The parsonage plumbing was modest at best and concentrated in one section of the house—away from the bedrooms. At least there was running hot and cold water for the kitchen sink and the shower, which was closeted, almost literally, along with a toilet between the kitchen and the dining room. Mark supposed the tiny enclosure had once been a pantry. Washbowls and pitchers served for powder room facilities.

Rubbing a coarse bristle of overnight growth on his chin, he studied the tousled image of the man in the small mirror mounted over the washstand, when he felt something scurry over his foot.

"What in—?"

As he jumped back, a large black beetle dropped off his foot and dashed under the washstand. Along with primitive plumbing, the house also had primitive insect control. Little gauze bags containing some sort of herbs lay in the corners of the room. Obviously the insects he'd heard running around in combat boots on the tile floor during the night simply avoided the corners. Twice he'd pulled the string fastened to his headboard, flipping on the single lightbulb overhead in time to see roaches and beetles scatter. Finally he'd succumbed to sleep and left them to their business— perhaps a soccer game between the two species with some kind of seed for a ball.

Three sharp knocks on the door distracted Mark from his infested reverie. Before he could answer, the housekeeper-cook barged in. Wearing a bright blue blouse and black skirt, she greeted him with a bright, *"Buenos días,* Señor Madison!" Without so much as a glance at him, she made straight for the other window and threw open the shades. The morning sun flooded the room with just as much enthusiasm.

"The good padre is back soon from the morning prayers, so I am ready to fix your breakfast. So how many eggs is it that you want?"

Mark shielded his eyes until they became accustomed to the sunburst. "Two over well would be nice."

"*Bueno, dos huevos* you will have." The same energy that blew her into the room whooshed her back out, drawing the door shut in its wake.

Boy, when this town wakes up, it hits the ground running—and squawking, braying, and cooking.

After a quick shower in the utility room—outfitted with a plastic stall, toilet, and laundry tub—and a shave in his bedroom over the bowl and pitcher, Mark exited onto the patio.

Seated at a table shaded by laurel, the man who'd introduced himself yesterday as Father Menasco read a newspaper. At his elbow was a coffee tray containing a fiesta-red thermal carafe, spare mugs, and, Mark hoped, some of the tempting brew he had smelled earlier. He looked up as Monty left the father's side for an obligatory pat, tail wagging. As Mark rubbed the part-shepherd, part-who-knew-what dog, the priest motioned him to sit down.

Casually clad in jeans and a collarless shirt, Father Menasco still looked like any other man of God that Mark had ever seen—cheerful, exuding a peace that went beyond Mark's understanding. And whatever that peace was, it was better for wrinkles than Botox. The guy had some tanned-in crow's feet and maybe a laugh line or two about his mouth, but that was it.

"*Buenos días*, Señor Madison. I trust you slept well?"

Mark pulled up a chair and joined him, and Monty settled down beneath the table. "The setting took some getting used to, but all in all, I slept just fine."

There was something about being in a priest's company that always put Mark on edge. Perhaps it was due to the number of pinches he'd received from his mother as a boy in church, if he so much as thought about acting up.

Father Menasco's lips twitched on one side as he folded his paper and put it aside. "The cats keep the mice at bay, but the bugs rule around here," he said, as if reading Mark's mind. "Sometimes I think they drum with toothpicks on the tile floor. It takes getting used to."

Mark gave a short laugh. "I thought it was soccer—the beetles versus the roaches."

"Well, it is a big sport down here," the priest concurred, with a playful arch of a woolly-bear brow. Fuzzy and thick like the weather-predicting caterpillars back home, it looked as if any moment it could straighten itself and crawl off his forehead. "Annamaria puts bags with her homemade concoction about, but it only works so well. She hates the smell of the insecticide . . . unlike her sister Soledad. Corinne has named Soledad 'the Terminator,' with her can of bug spray and fly swatter."

"Soledad?" Mark asked.

"Corinne's maid."

"I thought Corinne lived in a bed-and-breakfast."

"Soledad works for the bed-and-breakfast part-time, but intends to leave with Corinne as soon as you can make rooms suitable in the Ortiz place. The two have been over there cleaning . . . and *spraying.*"

"She said she wasn't afraid of the house ghost . . . Corinne, that is."

"I don't think Corinne is afraid of anything—certainly not of hard work," Father Menasco said. "She works in the office or with the children in the morning and then goes to the hacienda with her notebook and tools—"

"Tools?"

"She wanted to get a head start."

Great. All he needed was amateur help. Although—

"We thought it was wonderful when Edenton managed to purchase the hacienda and Madison Engineering donated its services to design and oversee the project—but Corinne managed to get a grant to fund the renovation."

"I can imagine she's a go-getter." *Not to mention a control freak.* "And I'll do my best to remain on target, budgetwise."

"She'll watch every peso, that's certain," the priest reflected with a chuckle. "She used her own money to paint one of the downstairs rooms for herself and is now working on an adjoining one for Soledad." He snapped the newspaper and folded it neatly into quarters, placing it on the table while Mark poured some coffee from the thermal carafe into the spare mug.

"Which brings me to an awkward question."

"What's that?" Mark asked as Father Menasco shifted in his seat.

"I was hoping that you might set up quarters there as well. My sister is coming to spend some time at the end of the month," he explained in apology. "And besides, I'd feel better knowing a man was there with Corinne and Soledad."

"Sure. No problem." That way he could tell Blaine he was literally living at work. Besides, the hacienda had to be more accommodating than the parsonage digs. And a live-in maid wouldn't be hard to take . . .

"*Bueno, sus huevos rancheros están aquí.*"

Edging sideways through the screen door to the kitchen, Annamaria held a large tray pressed against her ample bosom. She crossed the patio and placed the steaming breakfast before them.

"*Gracias,* Annamaria," Father Menasco said.

"Yes, *gracias,*" Mark added, as the two eggs—sunny side up—stared up at him, quivering on a tortilla smothered in bean sauce. Aware that the cook was waiting for him to try them, he picked up his fork, but Father Menasco interrupted with a short grace.

"*Cristo, pan de vida*—Christ, Bread of Life," he translated for Mark's benefit, "*Ven y bendice esta comida*—come and bless this food. Amen."

Mark didn't suppose there was any hope of asking God to turn up the sun enough to harden the eggs.

Brow raised expectantly, Annamaria wrung the fabric of her apron as if her entire livelihood rested on Mark's approval.

He cut up the egg-bean-tortilla mix until the yellow was somewhat disguised and popped a forkful into his mouth. Chewing with a forced enthusiam, he nodded. "Good . . . *muy bueno.*" Thankfully, the other ingredients did a good job of disguising the yolks . . . at least until the cook turned on her worn *huaraches* and darted back to the house with a titter of delight.

Mark grabbed a napkin and rid his mouth of the contents. "I'm sorry, Father," he managed, chasing the taste away with a gulp of coffee. "I have this aversion to runny eggs. I just can't deal with yolks quivering on the plate."

The priest held up his hand, stopping Mark's apology in its tracks. "No need to explain. Unfortunately, that is the only way Annamaria can fix them. She says she cannot bear to blind the eggs or turn them over on their eyes when they stare at her so. And I won't go into her boiled egg hang-up."

Mark could well imagine, with the yolk-eye connection.

"Although I have managed to convince her to cook pancakes," Menasco said, as if that somehow made up for it.

Mexicalli was becoming more like the *Twilight Zone* introduction by introduction. "Well, I hope to move into the hacienda this week . . . I'll hope Soledad is a more versatile cook. That way, I can free up your guest room." *And let the bugs have their own place.*

By the time Annamaria returned to collect their dishes, Mark's plate was licked clean—literally. Monty had been more than happy to help with the egg dilemma. Delighted that she'd pleased her guest, the cook left with the dog at her heels, promising him a special treat in the kitchen.

"You have no idea how much face that dog has saved me with Annamaria. Fortunately, he likes everything she makes. Not that she's a bad cook, by any means," the priest quickly added. "And my tastes are simple."

At that moment, a bell rang at the gated entrance to the courtyard. Father Menasco glanced at his watch. "That would be Doña Violeta."

"The lady with the decked-out donkey cart?"

The priest nodded and smiled. "Every day except Sunday, she buys all the day-old sweets from the bakery and brings them to the orphanage. It's her way of helping."

Mark envisioned a donkey cart filled with Entenmann's. Now, that would be a promo picture.

"Of course, Rosaria and Raul make certain there is enough left over for her to buy." At Mark's quizzical expression, he explained, "They own the bakery. It is their contribution to the *niños* . . . and, I suppose, to Doña Violeta's kindness. She gets a great joy out of being called *Doña de los Dulces.*"

"Lady of the sweets," Mark translated to himself as he followed Father Menasco to the gate.

There was the wizened old lady, dressed in dark purple, which was also the color of the band around the donkey's hat. The entire interior of the cart was filled with white boxes and plastic bags, so that there was barely room for the driver, who held the reins in one hand and an open parasol in the other.

She smiled at Father Menasco, but upon seeing Mark, she brightened even more.

"*Buenos días,* Señor Madison." She extended a delicate gloved hand with all the majesty of a queen in her court.

"*Mucho gusto,* señora," Mark answered.

The glove was made of the same fancy lace that festooned her hat. It reminded him of an old-time stewardess cap, just large enough to cover the very top of her head. Beneath the lace that cascaded from it, he could see the tortoiseshell combs in the back, pulling the rest of her steel-gray hair into some sort of plaited knot.

"Will you come with Father Menasco and me to deliver the children's pastries?"

Her English was heavily accented, but perfect. More surprising to Mark was the pale blue gaze that peered out of the pleasant folds of her eyes. The milky covering of cataracts could not hide the life behind it. Come to think of it, she'd been pretty feisty yesterday, when Corinne pulled her up from the bottom of the cart, but Mark had been so taken by the señorita that he hadn't paid much attention.

"No, but thank you, señora. I need to get to work."

Disappointment grazed the elderly lady's expression only for a moment before her enthusiasm returned. "Then you must know that I have not forgotten my gallant rescuer when Chiquita got ahead of herself on the hill." She puzzled for a moment. "I did introduce you to Chiquita, did I not? I was so shaken, I may have forgotten my manners."

"Chiquita and I have met, haven't we, girl?" Mark rubbed the whisker-bristled nose of the donkey as Doña Violeta nodded in approval.

"Indeed, Mr. Madison, you will hear from me soon."

"You don't have to do anything special—"

She stopped him by raising a gloved finger. "You are in Mexicalli, and here we have our ways. An invitation will be forthcoming."

Her voice of authority left no room for argument. Beside, Mark couldn't argue that Mexicalli had its ways. He'd never been anywhere else where he was on a first-name basis with a donkey.

◆

The rickety ladder beneath Corinne wobbled as she reached overhead with her paintbrush, causing her to catch her breath—and not for the first time. She'd even dubbed the ladder with a name—Squeaky.

"Caray! Qué pasa?" Soledad gasped from the adjoining kitchen. Before Corinne could steady herself, the housekeeper appeared in the doorway, her dark brown eyes wide with alarm.

"The same thing. I stretched a little too far, and Squeaky reminded me *pronto*," Corinne admitted with a sheepish smile. It was hard to decide if the climb down and back up the ten feet of the old wooden ladder was more unsettling than the teeter when she overreached herself. Unfortunately, it was the only ladder the orphanage had.

"It is like I have said before: this is a job for a man. You should have this—" She held up a scrub rag rank with ammonia and pointed to Corinne's paintbrush with disdain. "Not *that*." She considered the room for a moment. "Perhaps you should just paint without the ladder."

"Now, that would look nice, if I left the top four feet dingy white," Corinne drawled as she progressed one rung at a time to the tiled floor of what had been the dining room. With louvered double doors to seal it off, it would serve her well enough as a bedroom and office.

Soledad was impervious to the sarcasm. "You are a lady. Ladies do not do such things," she chastised. "What if your leg breaks itself? Then what will you do? And that can, it shakes like an old woman's legs."

Corinne steadied the lopsided paint rack. Her duct-tape repair had slipped. "I'm almost finished with this wall. What do you think of the color?" Perhaps distracting the mother hen would silence her clucking.

It worked. Soledad's face lit up as bright as the sunshine yellow on the wall. "Who would know? It is just the color that I want."

When Soledad accompanied Corinne to Cuernavaca to purchase paint supplies, she'd been skeptical. The can didn't match the color.

"I'm doing the trim first. Then I'll roll the walls the way we did last week in my room."

Corinne's room was a soft apricot and would have to be painted again when the project was done. But at least she'd have a place of her own before the bed-and-breakfast regulars and Father Menasco's sister arrived at the end of the month.

And since Mark Madison would be displaced too, Corinne already had a room picked out for his office and quarters—the salon just across the grand entrance from her and Soledad. Not that she believed in the rumored ghost, but a man's presence would make her feel better about being alone with Soledad in the big house.

"Then you use the long stick, not that ladder?" the housekeeper challenged.

"Yes. No more ladder . . . after this one section," Corinne added softly, to avoid Soledad's keen hearing.

Just one more section next to the door, and she'd be finished with the trim. The rolling would go much faster. Maybe next week, once the room was cleaned, they could even move in some of the secondhand furniture that Corinne had found here and there.

Scratching her nose with the back of her paint-spattered hand, she walked over to an old radio and found some music that might step up her speed. The lyrics of the songs were in Spanish, but it was the beat Corinne was after. When she couldn't sing all the words, she just bebopped along with the tune.

"Ba, bada, bada . . ."

The ladder wrinkled the drop cloth over the wooden floor as she lined it up with the next section of wall in need of paint. Kicking the wrinkles into submission, she steadied the paint can on the cockeyed rack and began her climb. As a precaution, she braced one hand on the open door to the foyer.

"La, la-la, la, la-la—oops!" She caught the paint can just as it tipped toward the wall. Since there was only a quarter or so of sunshine yellow left, it didn't spill. God was so good.

Braced against the last few of the top rungs, Corinne considered the tipsy rack and dismissed trusting it. But if she held the can in one hand, brush in the other, her steadying hand was gone, unless . . .

Carefully, she balanced the can on the top edge of the door, while leaning it at a right angle against the frame. With Squeaky leaning against it, the arrangement would work fine—as long as she didn't hit the can with her elbow.

Just fine, she assured herself, after testing its stability with a dip of her brush. Taking care not to get any yellow on the white ceiling that she'd rolled the week before, Corinne angled the bristles just so, dragging them along with focused precision. When the paint gave out, she leaned back to examine her handiwork. Perfect. Not a smidgeon of sunshine on the ceiling. Replenishing the brush with a second dip, she eased it up to pick up where she left off.

"Ba, bada, bada bada—"

"Anybody home?"

The male voice hardly registered before the door bumped against the ladder. Squeaky lunged sideways, taking Corinne with it. Dropping her brush, she somehow managed to hang on to the ladder and gain footing on the floor in time to catch the ladder from crashing. Instead it folded, mashing her hand. With a pain-induced dance, she let the ladder fend for itself.

"Ow-wow-wow-wow-wow!"

"What the—?" Mark exclaimed.

Clutching her damaged hand in its partner, Corinne ceased her footwork to stare in astonishment at Mark Madison. Mouth agape and eyelids closed, he stood like a half-human statue. The other half was sunshine yellow.

Her brain froze at the bombardment of reactive thoughts. *What is he doing here? The floor!* Paint was getting on the beautiful hardwood floor where the tarp had been shoved aside. How could so little paint spread so far?

Somehow her body went on automatic pilot. She dropped to her knees and began mopping up the floor with the paint-soaked tarp around Mark's Rockport deck shoes, but all she managed to do was smear shoes, floor, and all.

Exasperation boiled over logic, determined to vent or bust. "Haven't you ever heard of knocking?"

CHAPTER 5

The question gave Mark pause as he slogged through confusion to determine what had just happened. With wet paint seeping into his ears, he wasn't certain he'd heard right. Had he done something wrong?

Wiping the fresh coat of paint from his eyes with his fingers, he saw a young woman wallowing in the paint that puddled at his feet, her dark ponytail swinging from her frenzied mopping. She was a little paint-spattered, with specks of faded blue and egg-yolk yellow to match his shoes. Had breakfast been an omen of the day to come?

Gradually the replay took form in his mind. He'd stuck his head in the door to say hello and was whacked promptly . . . by an open can of paint . . . that was propped overhead . . . like an old Boy Scout camp trick. Anger thawed his disbelief.

"And this is my fault *how?*"

Suddenly, the doorway of the adjacent wall was filled with a plump Mexican woman dressed in black and yellow—the same bright shade as the room.

"*Ay de mí,* look what has happened!" Hands flying to ample hips, she eyed him from head to toe like a mad bumblebee.

"Tell me about it." Mark wiped the paint dribbling off his forehead back into his soaked hair. Instead of attacking, the bumblebee rushed to hand him a dishtowel. It was damp, but damp beat soaked every time. "*Gracias,* señora."

Corinne bobbed up from her paint-smearing delirium. "Soledad, get some more rags. This tarp is soaked, and the floor is going to be ruined."

"What am I, burnt toast?" Enough anger rose to Mark's face and neck to bake on the paint the towel had left behind.

Corinne glanced up as through seeing him for the first time. "What?"

He pointed to the door. "Did you learn that trick at kiddie camp?"

She pushed herself up from her knees and winced. "I'm sorry. It's just that—" She ran a hand through her hair and then jerked it away as she realized that she'd just streaked it yellow. "I couldn't hold on for balance with the paint can—"

Soledad rushed back in with rags and began to toss them on the puddles of paint. Saving one, she promptly began to wipe the paint off Mark until he took the rag with a terse *"Gracias"* and proceeded to get off the worst himself.

"So what was your paint doing on top of the door?" he asked.

The minced question brought the bumblebee out of bending down to help Corinne. "It is that old-woman ladder, señor," she explained. "She makes my Corina to fall."

"Wait!" said Corinne. She lowered her head. "It was my fault. The paint rack wouldn't hold the can, and I only had a few feet to go, so I balanced it on the top of the door." She stopped her confession long enough to turn off the music. "And I didn't hear you coming because of the radio." She lifted her shoulders and dropped them in resignation. "I'm really sorry."

The penitent pout that formed on her lips set Mark's ire back a degree, but as her gaze ran the gamut from his face to his shoe, her penitence turned to humor.

"Here." She leaned over to pick up one of the extra rags that Soledad had tossed on the floor, vainly attempting to hide the full tilt of amusement claiming her face. "Let me wipe some of the paint off."

Still annoyed, Mark folded his arms across his chest as if her ministrations were his due as she raked the excess paint off his back.

"It's just that I've been trying to do this job on a next-to-nothing budget and in a bit of a rush . . ."

Skipping over his buttocks, she continued her downward swipe to his feet.

"You missed a spot," he said, a wicked grin tugging at his mouth. With a grimace, she grabbed one of the extra rags and tossed it to him. "In your dreams, Madison."

Now he remembered Miss By-the-Book from the wedding—a hot number in a bright pink oriental dress that curved in all the right places. Those had been her exact words when he'd suggested they skip the rest of the reception and continue celebrating on his sailboat.

"I was trying to be gracious, considering that your carelessness gave me a fresh coat of egg-yolk yellow," he began in a teasing tone.

"If you'll step out of your shoes . . ." she said.

"Sure." Mark complied, cocking one brow in confusion.

"Good thing this is water-based paint."

"Yeah." He watched the swing of her yellow-streaked ponytail and the sway of her feminine form as she wiped the Rockports inside with a clean rag.

"There's a shower in the utility room." She straightened and pointed to a pass-through between the kitchen and the yellow room, where a wringer washer stood at attention next to a pink-curtained enclosure. "Towels are in the metal cabinet," she said, pointing to the opposite wall. "You can wash the bulk of the paint off and put your jeans back on. Thank goodness it wasn't a full can."

"Are you thankful because you still have another can of paint left, or because I didn't get the whole batch?" Her tactics might not be fair, but they were more fun, especially when she smiled like that.

"Both."

Despite their differences, they had a matched sense of humor— once all stresses were removed.

"Speaking of which, where did you find such a—" No adjective Mark could summon was mentionable, so he picked a lesser one. *"Hideous* color?"

"Soledad picked it out at the premixed counter."

Ah, the bumblebee. That explained a lot.

"What do you have against sunshine yellow?"

"It just reminded me of my breakfast this morning. My unfavorite style of eggs—runny."

She wrinkled her nose. "Eww."

"My thoughts exactly. Imagine my surprise to be wearing the matching color so soon afterward."

"Oh no." She broke into a melodic laugh. "No wonder you looked so . . . so . . . like a cross Big Bird. But," she said, clearing the humor from her voice, "you'll be delighted to know that this is Soledad's room and not yours. I thought you might take the salon across the hall."

"Sounds good. I'll check it out after I get some of this off."

As he peeled off his shirt and tossed it onto the pile of dirty rags, Corinne did an abrupt turn, hastening to straighten the rumpled tarp. Mark grinned from the inside out with mischief as he glanced down at the faded version of the yellow on his chest. "I'll call you when I need my back scrubbed."

Head pivoting in his direction like a tank turret, she aimed and fired. "I don't feel *that* guilty, Madison. But there is a new toilet bowl brush in there."

"You're a hard woman," he said over his shoulder, heading into the utility bath and closing the door behind him.

"Remember that, and we'll get along just fine," Corinne called after him, dismissing the twinge of chemistry that shot through her when he stripped off his shirt. She and Pam, her college roommate, had coined a word for it. *Twickle.*

"Just fine," she repeated, more for herself than for the man in the bath. But she must have been mistaken. How could a barechested Big Bird cause anyone to *twickle?*

Lord, I do not need . . .

"First, you beat on the wall like so, señor," Soledad's voice carried from the kitchen. She demonstrated, knocking three times. The echo reverberated through the empty house. "*Y ahora . . .* turn on the hot water and—"

Mark interrupted. "I can handle a shower, *gracias.*"

"*Así así, así así . . .*" *So-so,* the housekeeper buzzed over and over with undisguised disdain.

46

"Better listen, or you'll be sorry," Corinne called out as she shoved the soaked paint rags into the empty bucket.

But before she could explain why, someone from the front of the house called out her name. *"Hola,* Señorita Diaz? Are you in the house?"

"Coming!"

With a glance at the paint film drying on the floor where the tarp hadn't caught it, Corinne went into the foyer, where a Mexican gentleman stood assessing the damage done to the mural by falling plaster along the rise of the graceful, curving staircase. A tree limb had blown through the window on the upper level, causing water damage during the previous rainy season.

"Juan Pablo, just the man we need to see," she said in welcome. Not that she'd made it a secret that the orphanage was interested in hiring contractors to complete the renovation. "How are your brothers?"

"Bien, gracias." He glanced past her through the dining room door where the paint had spilled.

"Do you think Juan Miguel might be able to repair the mural?" she asked. Granted, the eldest brother was primarily a sculptor, but he had dabbled in some still lifes that sold well in Taxco. A dabbler was all they could afford.

"Pues, as the father projectates, *all things are possible,* no? And perhaps you need him for painting the walls *también,"* he observed, tucking his unlit cigar into one corner of his mouth.

"I had a little accident," she explained. "Thankfully, it will come up if—"

A squeak loud enough to pierce the eardrum came from the utility room, followed by the sound of water—not the gentle fall of a shower, but the pounding of a tropical downpour.

"Mark." Not only had the stubborn man not listened, but it sounded as if he were dancing a polka with the old wringer washing machine, and the tin linen cupboard had cut in.

"Madre de Dios!" Soledad wailed in the background.

Corinne banged on the door. "Mark, just turn it off."

"That is not good sign," Juan Pablo said, pointing to the water oozing out from under the door. "Where is the . . . *como se dice?* . . . poomp?"

Poomp? Corinne pondered the word. "Pump? The pump's in the—" She beat on the door again. "Mark, can you turn off the—"

"I'm try—"

Suddenly the downpour of water ceased. Soledad came shuffling in from the main foyer, face flushed in triumph. "I quit the big switch."

Of course. The electric box was on the kitchen side of the wall. As for Mark . . .

Corinne knocked again. "Mark?"

"What, Corinne?" came the irritated reply from inside the makeshift bathroom.

"I tell him that it will put to lose if he do not do this." Soledad knocked three times with her fist on the wall to demonstrate the proper operating procedure. From within, loose plaster fell.

"Are . . . you . . . all . . . right?" Corinne lost patience with each word. If he felt good enough to be annoyed, he could at least answer her question with a *yes* or *no.*

"Oh, I'm just dandy, Corinne." His voice oozed with sarcasm. "After being blasted with ice water, I decided to wrap myself in bright pink plastic and sprawl against a rusting washtub. I didn't even break my elbow when it jammed in the toilet during my fall." He caught his breath and continued. "And I'll never need Preparation H, thanks to quality bristles of your *new* toilet brush."

"Okay, I get the picture." And it was not a pretty one. Funny, heaven help her, but not pretty. Suppressing a laugh, she pointed to her elbow and mouthed, *"Eso en el lavobo,"* to a bemused Soledad. "Soledad tried to tell you how to get the water—"

"I know she did," he barked back. The tin cupboard clanged like a gong as he evidently slammed its door.

"I tol' you so," Soledad sang in reproach.

"Soledad tol' me so." Mark mimicked her operatic reply. The cupboard door slammed again. The catch was tricky anyway.

There would be no starting over this time, Corinne thought,

exercising every effort not to laugh. But at least it wasn't her fault. Frankly, it served him right for being such a know-it-all.

"And by the way, we need a new faucet. The old one flew somewhere when I tried to turn off the ice water."

Corinne's humor evaporated. She'd forgotten to turn on the hot water heater. An antique itself, they only used it as needed—not for scrubbing or painting.

"So what can you expect—" Soledad started.

Corinne cut her off. "Well, there's good news," she announced, painting her pang of guilt with brightness. "You'll never guess who is here."

"I'm not in the mood for guessing games, *Coreena*." The cabinet clanged again, followed by a muffled word that Corinne didn't care to make out.

Ouch, he is in a foul humor.

"It's Juan the plumber," she said as Soledad retreated down the hall, clucking to herself. "Now, isn't that a God thing?"

"I hope a heavenly hand was not involved in this." The familiar sound of the rust-locked casters on the washtub scraping across the floor underscored Mark's raw demeanor. "Tell him I'll talk to him another day. I'm not in the mood to receive company."

Actually, he sounded more in the mood to burn down the hacienda and take the first plane for the States.

Not that Corinne blamed him. She'd tangled with the shower trying to get water to fill a bucket, and wound up soaked. Soaked and cold, but not sprawled on the floor in the buff.

Wait, she didn't want to go there.

And not with her elbow jammed in the john and a toilet brush scraping her backside. And not after being doused in paint. *The poor guy*, she thought, wrestling with the incompatible mix of sympathy and humor.

"I'm sorry, Juan," she told Juan Pablo, who had heard the whole bizarre thing. Given his sober-as-the-proverbial-judge demeanor, she wondered if the plumber's English allowed him to grasp the entire situation.

"Okay!" she shouted through the door to Mark. "I'll tell him to come back, but I should warn you that Juan has some time open now to work on the plumbing, and his brother is sober."

Yes, it was absurd, she thought, but absurd was often the order of the day in this place. Mark would have to get used to it.

"Señor, are you certain that you do not need help?" Juan offered. He swiveled his cigar from one side of the thick strip of mustache to the other, waiting for an answer.

"No, Juan, I do not need help," came the razor-edged reply. "What I need is a real shower, good soap, and the first ticket out of this place I can lay my hands on. Can you arrange that?"

"*Lo siento,* señor, but no." The Mexican shook his head in regret. "But the plumbing gains on you, and you must put yourself with reason, no? You cannot build on I being able to directate the building for you in the future. There is much work for us in the ordinary."

The door flew open, and Corinne took a step back as Mark came through. His water-heavy jeans hung low on his waist, and a floral-print towel was wrapped in a turban around his head. His face and upper body still had a yellow tint.

Grinning, or at least showing his clenched teeth, he nailed Juan Pablo with his gaze. "How long will it take to replace the utility bath and kitchen plumbing, Juan, and how much?"

The plumber peeked around the jamb. "Hmm." Water stood on the floor, while the shower ring that had once held the curtain in a pink circle at a right angle now drooped parallel to the wall. Across from it, the toilet held on to its seat with one hinge.

"*Pues,*" he said, drawing on the cigar, "I must quit myself to home to projectate the cost . . . but it will be, I think, to your satisfaction."

"*Projectate* it on paper then," Mark insisted, "and get back to me tomorrow . . . *mañana, entiende?*"

"*Sí, entiendo,* but you will be needing a new key for the shower. I will have to go to Cuernavaca for—"

"Key?"

"*Sí, señor,* a key." The plumber moved his fingers as though twisting an imaginary dial. "What it is that turns the water to run."

"The faucet?" Corinne guessed.

Juan Pablo nodded. *"Sí, como no?"*

"How not indeed," Mark drawled with an acerbic smirk.

With the prospect of employment in his grasp, Juan Pablo extended his hand, but had second thoughts on seeing Mark's yellowed hands. *"Biengood,"* he declared as one word. *"Hasta mañana,* jefe."

Waiting until Juan Pablo exited through the front entrance, Mark asked under his breath to Corinne, "Projectate?"

"He's a proprietor and speaks the way he thinks such a man would speak," Corinne explained. "It's just that his use of English is a little skewed. And by the way, while *como no* literally means *how not,* it translates into *why not* or *what else* among the people here."

"Thanks for the language lesson."

Unable to resist, she reached up and straightened his turban. "Flowers become you."

"Back at ya with the paint." Mark pulled a pained grin and walked past her in the footsteps of Juan Pablo.

"You know what Scarlett said," Corinne called after him. "Tomorrow is another day."

Pausing at the door, he looked back, his face stricken. "I certainly hope so. I don't ever want to repeat this one."

"Bad beginnings, good endings?" Or something like that.

To her surprise, instead of reacting with annoyance, he pointed a finger at her and winked. "I'm counting on it, Corina."

Coreena. Even wearing a flowered towel as a top hat, Mark Madison possessed an irrepressible charm. Or maybe it was the six-pack abs and low-slung jeans that brought a heat wave into the room. The moment he was out of sight, she'd open a window.

For now, she'd just admire that deliberate, long-legged retreat. What a waste of gorgeous—like a French pastry—all puff and no substance. And just as bad for a no-nonsense woman like herself.

CHAPTER 6

The water damage was worse than Blaine had counted on in his estimate, Mark thought as he swept fallen plaster into a pile in the corner of the salon the next day. When the former owners moved out, they didn't latch all the shutters and windows. With the onslaught of rainy season and storms, the current damage had been done. Several rooms were littered with chunks of plaster, but for now, Mark was only concerned with the main salon where he was supposed to set up his quarters. Thankfully, the year-round spring-like weather was optimized by the astute design for cross ventilation and surrounding shade trees, making the work to be done bearable without air-conditioning.

It was a crying shame to turn the grand hacienda into an institution. Its history of an elegant lifestyle spoke to him through its graceful arches, murals, and frescoes. Mark could envision settling down in such a place, if it weren't located in the boonies of the *Twilight Zone*.

"*Perdoname,* Señor Madison, but Juan Pablo is here with his pre-supposition," Soledad said from the doorway. "Or so he calls his paper," she added with a disapproving sniff that declared her estimation of Juan Pablo—or at least his use of English—pretentious.

"Great, send him in." Considering the layer of plaster dust and dirt covering him from head to toe, Mark hoped Juan could fix the shower.

"And you must remember to ask him about his wife's brother's furniture store in Taxco."

Mark took a dustpan full of the debris to a thirty-gallon trash can and deposited it. After discovering that all that the orphanage had to offer for furniture was an inflatable air bed and a kiddie desk, he'd asked Soledad if she knew where he could find some things locally. He should have expected he'd be sent to a relative of someone he'd already met.

"Got it." Mark wiped his hands on his jeans and, using his arm, cleared off an old paint-spattered library table that had been left behind. It was wobbly, but he could use it until something better came along.

"Buenos días, Señor Madison," Juan Pablo greeted him, a large, wide-brimmed hat in one hand as he extended the other.

Conscious of the white dust, Mark wiped his hand against his leg once more and shook the man's hand. "Sorry, the place is a mess."

"You have much work to be done, you can build on that," the plumber agreed. Juan Pablo's mustache broadened with an understanding smile. "I work in such conditions most of my days. *No me importa.*"

"Well, it matters to me." Mark encompassed the room with a sweep of his arm. "This is *not* my usual working condition."

His sweat-soaked cotton shirt clung to him, smudged and gray where it had been white. His jeans were dappled with the plaster dust that irritated his eyes. Never would he have thought that he'd miss the modern office of Madison Engineering that he'd grudgingly occupied a few weeks ago. Nor had he realized that he'd taken for granted his designer suits or his massage shower with its consistent water temperature and pressure. The shower at the parsonage was hit-or-miss, and the one he'd taken out at the hacienda was outright vicious.

"Ahora, my presupposition." Juan Pablo put the estimate on the table with a flourish. It was a printed form with *Tres Juanes* across the top, but beneath was the brothers' surname.

"Morales," Mark read. "So you are Juan Pablo Morales. I didn't think to get your last name."

"Por qué? For what is it *importante* among *amigos?"*

The term *amigos* triggered a memory of Blaine's voice lecturing Mark after he'd accepted a bid from a golfing-and-sailing buddy without bothering to shop. "The sooner you learn that one doesn't play with one's associates, the better. It interferes with the ability to keep business *business.*"

Mark's poor judgment that time resulted in the Madison Corporation being underbid by a competitor.

"Besides, in Mexicalli, everyone knows everyone," Juan Pablo went on, oblivious to Mark's fleeting consternation. "When I hear 'Señor Morales,' I know I am in the oven."

"Kind of like when my mom calls me by my full name, eh?"

"So I said," he agreed, chuckling.

"And you can call me Mark."

Juan Pablo's humor vanished. "Oh, no, Señor Madison. That I cannot do. You are the jefe." The plumber hesitated. "And there is only one of you, but three brothers Morales. *Entiende?*"

Mark scowled, not understanding . . . exactly anyway. "But there are three Juans, too." He pointed to the header.

"Como no? But we are Juan Pablo, Juan Pedro, and Juan Miguel . . . not the same."

Time for the *Twilight Zone* theme again. Instead of arguing, Mark nodded. "Got it. You are Juan Pablo, I am Señor Madison."

"Buenogood," Juan Pablo rattled out in satisfaction as the jefe studied the quotation.

It was written in Spanish, although some words jumped the language barrier. At first the bottom line threw Mark, until he converted the 4,000 pesos to dollars. "About $350," he said aloud. A similar job at his Philly condo had cost about that much. "Sounds reasonable."

"Three hundred fifty dollars for what?" Face flushed from her walk from the orphanage, Corinne stepped into the room, a half-eaten orange lollipop in her hand. Surprised to see her this early, Mark checked his watch. It was midday; time flew, whether one was having fun or not.

"For the plumbing fix," he explained, taking note of her skirt and blouse. It was the same outfit she was wearing when he arrived in Mexicalli and just as attractive as he remembered.

Juan Pablo cleared his voice. "There is much damage to the pipe, especially after Señor Madison tore off the key."

Corinne popped the candy stick into her mouth and held out her hand. "May I see, *por favor?*"

Was that color creeping to the plumber's face? Juan Pablo's swarthy complexion made it hard to be sure, but the way he looked away from Corinne's appraisal made Mark suspicious. With a slight sinking feeling, he watched Corinne switch the lollipop stick from side to side as she read through the estimate.

"Have you been talking to your cousin in Los Angeles again, Juan Pablo?" she asked upon reaching the final number.

"*Pues*..." The plumber gave her a sheepish grin.

She finished the candy and flicked the stick into the plaster-filled waste can. "All he's doing is replacing the faucet and the pipe from the wall," Corinne told Mark. "I checked on the Internet, and a simple faucet is only 460 pesos, tops. It shouldn't take you over an hour to cut off the pipe where it comes through the wall, Juan Pablo, and join new PVC fittings. That should cost... what? About ten dollars—or a hundred or so pesos?"

She looked at Mark for confirmation, but he hadn't had nearly the practice in peso conversion. With a chiding press of her lips, she handed the estimate back to Juan Pablo. "Assuming it takes you three hours, and that is really stretching it, you are charging us a little less than a hundred dollars an hour, according to this."

"A little less than one hundred U.S. dollars?" The plumber scowled at the paper as if it were responsible. "Perhaps there is an error in my *mathematics*." He nodded as if that were the answer. "I will hurry myself to return in one hour with the right estimation."

Corinne shook her head. "We'll give you half your estimation, and even then you will be earning wages equal to a Los Angeles plumber and not those of your peers. And that is only because we need it done by the weekend. If you cannot do it then, *pues*..."

She raised her hands as if there was nothing else to be done.

"Then we will have to pay you Mexican wages for the job . . . which is what we expect," she added, "*if* you want the contract to do the entire hacienda. After all, we are in Mexico and not Los Angeles."

"*Como no, señorita?*" Folding the rejected estimate, the embarrassed Juan Pablo tucked it into the brim of his hat. "And I will return *por la mañana,* with the new key and the PVCs, no?"

Smiling as though Juan Pablo had just promised her the moon, rather than tried to swindle her—if he had, that is—Corinne gave him a nod of approval. "That would be wonderful. *Hasta mañana,* Juan Pablo. And give my regards to your wife."

"That you can build on, señorita." With a slight bow to her and Mark, the plumber made his exit, calling over his shoulder, "*Hasta mañana.*"

"Later, amigo," Mark replied as he turned to Corinne. "Boy, I thought you were hard over the toilet brush, but—"

"Some of the contractors practice what I call creative math. It could be a genuine mistake, especially with converting the currencies, or it could be intentional."

"Well, you were right on it." A little flattery always helped, although she deserved every word.

"But that wasn't my job. It was yours."

Mark wasn't certain which was worse, Blaine's criticism ringing in his memory or the unspoken *But I didn't expect any better* in her sigh.

"I wouldn't have signed anything until I'd rechecked the math." Okay, it was a little white lie. The price had sounded reasonable based on his previous experience. Very reasonable. "So I wasn't as quick with the pesos as you. I've only been here two days. And it's like the old 'fool me once' adage. Twice doesn't happen."

Corinne hoped that was the case. If not, her worse fears about Mark Madison's irresponsible approach to life and work would be confirmed. And that was the last thing she needed after the phone call she'd received just before lunch. The body of Antonio's brother, Enrique, had been found above the village by some hikers. Because animals had gotten to it, there was no way to tell how the boy had perished without an autopsy. And his nearest living relative, the boy's uncle, asked to have the body released for burial without one.

When she called to object, Mayor Quintana explained to her that it was the logical way. The body would have to be taken to Cuernavaca, where it would wait in line for who knew how long? There were deceased residents from the smaller villages who had been kept so long that they'd practically been forgotten. There was nothing more to be done, according to the *alcalde*.

"Señor Mark," Soledad called from the kitchen. "Did you forget to ask about the furniture?"

"Aw, man," Mark groaned. "Yes, Soledad, I forgot."

Trying to follow the wisdom of the Serenity Prayer that hung over her desk, accepting what she could not change . . . at least for now . . . Corinne pushed the discussion to the back of her mind and switched to the one at hand. "Furniture? What furniture?"

"Nothing much," he said in dismissal. "I thought I'd buy a desk with a file drawer and a bed and dresser for this place. A television would be nice. Soledad said one of Juan Pablo's relatives owns a furniture store in Taxco."

"A desk, bed, dresser, and a *television*." Annoyance flared in her words. "And I suppose you'll want a satellite dish, since cable hasn't reached Mexicalli."

"Only after I double-check the pricing."

The wisecrack ate at Corinne's already raw disposition. "Juan Pablo's brother-in-law sells *new* furniture. As in, not in the budget."

"So, I don't want a furnished house. Just a few essentials. I don't think that's asking too much." He lifted his hands and turned away. "Sheesh, I feel like I'm married," he said, as if he'd contracted some flesh-eating virus.

"Not hardly." Corinne could feel the serenity she'd struggled for slipping away. "But you do have some responsibility . . . not that you're used to being accountable for anything you do." A part of her cringed the moment the words were out, but it was too late.

Mark whirled about, electric gold flecks snapping in the brown of his gaze. "Okay, let's get this straight. I don't need your permission to do squat, Miss Pinch Penny."

"Pinch Penny?" Anger was not the answer, but at the moment it offered more relief. Her resolve to remain patient melted in its path. "You wouldn't know how to pinch a penny if your life depended on it."

"If you mean that I don't suffer from your missionary mania for self-righteous deprivation, you're right."

"Self-righteous?" Somewhere the word struck a chord of reality, but was choked by her tangled emotions. "I just want to get the most for the money we've managed to raise. So if good stewardship is a crime, *mea culpa*. And all this"—she flung her arms in a wide circle, nearly clipping Mark's nose with the back of her fingers—"is not a mania; it's a passion . . . a passion to help children, who, but for God's grace, might have been me."

Mark braved a step closer, so that she had to look up to turn the full glare of her fury on him, and replied, "And if wanting some semblance of comfort while I'm *stewarding*"—he rested his hands on her shoulders—"is a crime, I'm guilty too. It's the least I should have, considering I'm doing this work for free."

Victory surged in Corinne's veins. "Let's get this clear," she said, shoving his hands away. "You're doing this because you were sentenced to community service for your third DUI. It was this or jail time."

He didn't flinch. "At least they have television in jail . . . and a bed."

"We have an air mattress for a bed. And for entertainment, Father Menasco has a delightful selection of reading materials that he's accumulated during his years."

Mark stepped even closer, as if to stare her down. "*You* have furniture. Or do you get some special dispensation for being such a holy example for all of us?"

"It is used furniture, *which*"—she raised her voice, rising to the tip of her toes until she was almost eye-to-eye with the six-foot-plus ignoramus—"I paid for out of my own penny-pinching little purse."

Time stilled, but not the calculation in her opponent's gaze. He was desperate, on the run. Her breath grew short with triumph so close, so—

"Your what?" the lips just a breath from her face demanded.

Distracted by them, Corinne did a quick mental backtrack and gathered steam. "I said that I paid for it out of my own Penny—with a capital *P*—Pinching Purse."

She was tempted to poke back at him for emphasis, but somehow in the heat of the argument, they'd become too close. Toe-to-toe, chest-to-chest, eye-to-Adam's apple.

Disconcerted, Corinne raised her head, her gaze locking in a dead heat with Mark's. Like two storm clouds on the verge of collision, there was no backing away.

"So," she began, the remainder of whatever it was that she'd intended to say evaporating as Mark pulled her against his sweaty, plaster-dusted body and lowered his mouth to hers.

Corinne heard thunder—or was that indignation pounding in her ears. She felt the lightning shooting through her from the fierce contact, leaving every nerve ending sizzling in its wake. Her mind raced for reason's cover, but her body braved the tempest with shameful eagerness. The hands she placed on his shoulders to push him away curled into useless fists as the fury of the assault gave way to something far more disconcerting—tenderness. And then it was over.

Breathless, she pulled back and looked up into his eyes, where remnants of the storm still snapped and crackled.

"You need a man, lady," Mark said, taking in a shaky breath.

A man? He *had* to be kidding. He was a man—definitely so—and he was the problem. The shredded bits of her fury came together, strengthened.

"But don't look at me."

"You?" Corinne spun away from him, rubbing her arms as if to rub off the aftereffects of whatever it was that had happened. "Believe me, Mark Madison, if I ever wanted a man, much less *needed* one, you can rest assured that it would not now or ever be you or . . . or . . . or anyone like you."

Head lifted high, she spun on her heel and left the room, storming through the foyer to the patio steps. The man couldn't handle a simple plumbing contract, and when it came to a woman's needs, he sure as the dickens didn't know what he was talking about. Hah! A man was the last thing she needed . . . particularly one like Mark Madison.

"Corina!" Soledad's shout stopped Corinne short at the gate.

She turned, impatient. "What?"

"You not going to eat your lunch?" the housekeeper asked.

Lunch. The word doused her anger with a sheepish awareness from tip to toe. From there embarrassment took over. One of Soledad's salads was why she'd come to the hacienda in the first place—lunch and a quiet retreat before she told Antonio that Enrique was not coming back. Suddenly there was Juan Pablo and Mark, and before she knew it, her emotions ran away with her, carrying her into a heated argument that boiled over into, of all things, the arms of Mark Madison.

Ignoring the sensory overload that drove her breath away, Corinne gathered it back. "Can you wrap it for me to take back to the office?" She started toward the hacienda entrance. "I really need to get back."

As far away from Mark Madison as possible until she could determine what and how whatever happened *happened.*

Fool me once . . . Corinne stopped in her tracks, recognizing Mark's words. *Oh, just give it up,* she told herself in frustration, whatever *it* is.

CHAPTER 7

What had he been thinking?

Or maybe that was the problem. No thought had been involved. He'd just kissed her.

Mark paced the floor of the salon, leaving footprints in the dusty coating left from his sweeping. It was Corinne's fault, of course . . . all of it. She'd started in on him, just like Blaine, and driven Mark into saying things he shouldn't have and then doing something he shouldn't have.

"So," Soledad said, startling him to a halt as she entered the room with a tray balanced on one arm and a folding chair under the other. "You and Corina have a disgust about what?"

Mark hurried to help her put the chair at the desk. He'd seen Corinne brush by the salon as if he weren't there and heard her talking to Soledad in the kitchen. Undoubtedly filling the maid with her vile opinion of him. Not that he really cared, but he could have sworn Corinne had been crying. And now her protective bumblebee wanted to know why.

"With all due respect, it's not any of your business, Soledad."

Retrieving a damp cloth from her yellow apron pocket, Soledad motioned for him to sit down and wiped the rickety desk. *"Pobrecita,* she is so upset."

"Yeah, well, I'm a little upset too. I have a right to some creature comforts."

The stocky housekeeper jerked upright, her brow a continuous knit of consternation. *"Qué?* What kind of *creature?"*

"Me," Mark clarified, her misinterpretation bringing a hint of a smile to his lips.

Looking over her shoulder, as if fearing that her Corina had the same radar hearing that she possessed, Soledad lowered her voice. "But of course, the man of the house should be comfortable."

At least one of the females in charge agreed with him.

"Corina is not herself this day. She is very upset. *Ay de mí,*" Soledad sniffed, digging into her big apron pocket for an embroidered handkerchief. After blowing a loud honk into it, she put it away, but her dark eyes were glazed with emotion.

Something told Mark it had nothing to do with his *disgust* with Corinne. He put his arm around the housekeeper. "What is it, Soledad?"

"That Enrique." She shook her head. "He was always running off to the hills. I knew it would finish badly with that adventurous one."

"Enrique?"

"Antonio's brother, who went lost before you coming here," she said, her voice thick with emotion. "And my *pobrecita,* she is gone to tell 'Tonio his brother will not be coming back. But first she must put together herself."

Kicked in the belly by the news, Mark sat down on the chair. "Aw, man," he lamented. "I didn't know." He thought she had just overreacted out of superiority. The fact was, she was just a better businessperson than he; but then, who wasn't?

"So you go say that you are sorry for making her cry."

Mark's head shot up. "Say what? I didn't make her cry. I just—" He stopped speaking as Soledad planted her hands on her hips.

"I just acted like a jerk," he finished. A displaced and very uncomfortable jerk, but a jerk.

But she was such a goody-goody . . .

"So you will say I am sorry and take her a rose."

Mark blinked in disbelief as the housekeeper produced a rose wrapped in tissue from the same apron as the dishcloth. "Have you got a rabbit in there too?"

Soledad burst into a giggle. "Oh, Señor Mark, you are so silly.

I put no rabbit in my apron. In the pot, yes, but in the apron, no, no, no."

Mark took the flower, wondering just how much Soledad knew about his and Corinne's "disgust." Part of him rebelled at the idea of crawling to Corinne with a rose in hand, yet there was another, more subtle side of him that wanted to apologize. He hardly recognized it.

"I'll go in there now. Maybe I can—" Mark blinked in disbelief. Either a small white pig just trotted through the foyer, or he'd been sober way too long. Besides, wasn't the hacienda ghost a Spanish *doña* or a murderous Indio? "Soledad—"

A startled shriek came from the direction of the kitchen, followed by the scraping of furniture. "Mark!"

Flower in hand, Mark raced to the kitchen with Soledad on his heels, only to meet a pink-eared swine making tracks away from Corinne, who brandished a chair.

"*Vete! Vete ya!*" Soledad shouted. "I will not have creatures in my house!"

Instead of exiting out the open patio door, where a young man stood waving his straw hat at the animal, the pig veered into the salon.

"I will get my broom."

As Soledad ran off to fetch her weapon of choice, Mark and Corinne tried to corral the animal in the salon. It scattered Mark's piles of dried plaster debris as it raced around the room. In an attempt to head it off, Mark stepped into its path, waving his hands. Instead of being dissuaded, the pig made straight for him, slowing from a run to a panting trot until it had Mark's back to the wall.

"Corinne, the chair." Why hadn't he grabbed the broom?

But to his astonishment, instead of attacking him, the pig pulled the blossom of the flower that Mark still held. Dumbfounded, he watched as the pig dropped at his feet, exhausted and chewing.

"Wait, I think I know this pig." Even as he spoke, he couldn't believe he heard himself right. But the pig was just about the same size and coloring as his travel mate in the swine truck.

At Corinne's snort of amusement, Mark shot her a dour look.

"You see one white pig, you've seen them all," she teased.

A knock dragged Mark's attention from the snouted visitor to the foyer where the Mexican youth stood, hat in hand. "*Perdonamé,* señor," he began, shifting his nervous gaze to the ceiling as if the rest of his words were written there. "I . . . bring . . . your . . . peeg."

"Pigs of a feather," Corinne said, her mouth contorted with the effort not to laugh outright.

"This is a joke, right?" he asked the man. One brow lifting in suspicion, he cranked his head in Corinne's direction. No, she wouldn't know a joke if it fell on her.

"*Perdonamé,* señor," his visitor repeated. "I . . . bring . . . your . . . peeg." Clearly, that was the only English the man knew.

This was unreal. Mark shook his head. "No. *No es mi . . .* pig." *What was the Spanish word for pig?*

At his feet, the pig grunted.

"Your pig seems to think otherwise."

The man's face brightened. "*Mira,* your peeg."

Soledad buzzed into the room, armed with her broom. "*Salga!* Get out. I allow no creatures in my house."

Startled to its feet, the pig darted behind Mark. "Whoa, wait!" he shouted as Soledad missed the swine and clipped Mark soundly with her broom.

"*Calme, calme,*" he told the riled housekeeper.

"That creature cannot stay."

"I know." Mark looked at Corinne for reinforcement, but her amused demeanor told him no help would come from that quarter. Nonetheless, he tried. "Will you please tell this man to take the pig out into the courtyard until we can resolve this?"

Corinne repeated Mark's request in rapid Spanish, while Soledad stood, broom at the ready, gaze narrowed, until the peasant moved to fetch the animal.

"You go," Mark told the housekeeper. "We will get the *creature* out of your house." Then, "What is it with this pig?" he exclaimed as the animal circled him to avoid the man's reaching hands. "And if you can stop smirking long enough," he told Corinne, "can you find out who this guy is?"

Mark walked out into the courtyard—the only way to get the pig out of the house without further chaos. Only then did the pesky porker oblige. After some questioning by Corinne, Mark discovered that their visitor was the son of the farmer who owned the swine that had accompanied Mark on his trip from the produce stand fiasco to Mexicalli.

Seated at a concrete table and bench set that had been too heavy for the previous owners to move, Mark strained to pick out the story behind this odd delivery, particularly why the animal was deemed *his*.

After a staccato exchange of Spanish, Corinne turned to him, her eyes dancing. "José says that this pig was not supposed to come with your other traveling companions. It seems your livestock entrepreneurs bought this piglet from a *bruja*."

Bruja . . . the translation triggered incredulity in Mark's voice. "A witch?"

José nodded. "*Sí, una bruja que . . .*" The rest was lost on Mark's limited academic knowledge of the language.

Corinne nodded, taking on a sympathetic expression. "*Lo siento, señor*," she said, before turning to Mark. "Your pig is bewitched." Her lips twitched. "But then it would have to be, to be so enamored with you."

"I love you too." He gave her a pained smile. "But what's the witch got to do with me?"

"*Sí, una bruja*," José put in with pride. "Witch."

"The Indios are very superstitious, especially the more rural ones. When José's father discovered the pig had belonged to a witch, he was reluctant to take it, but since it was so cheap, he decided to put it in with the other pigs. But then they started to get ill, so his father said to get rid of the enchanted pig."

"*Y además, el puerco no crece*," José added, shaking his head.

Corinne translated. "And besides, he says, it won't grow."

Now it all made sense. "In other words, no one wants the runt."

Beneath the table, the piglet wormed its way around Mark's leg. "Sheesh," he exclaimed, shoving it aside with his foot. "It's not enchanted. It's just plain crazy."

"You must put off some killer pheromones . . . for swine, that is." Corinne covered her mouth with her hand, but Mark knew a giggle when he heard one.

Annoyed, he glared at her. "You didn't seem to mind them a little while ago."

The sobering sting of Mark's retort brought color to her cheeks. He was not only forward, but he was rude. No wonder the pig liked him. She peeked under the tile-inlaid table at the animal resting its head on Mark's shoe, its little pink-rimmed eyes closed in contentment. It was cute . . . for a pig.

"Bueno, I go *ahora."* José rose from the table bench, addressing Mark. *"Usted debe darme diez pesos para el puerco."*

"Ten *pesos?"* Mark echoed.

"Oh, sí, señor. *Pero eso incluye la carga de la entrega."*

"That's ten *pesos* for the pig, including delivery charge," Corinne explained.

"But I don't *want* the pig." Mark couldn't believe his ears—or anything else about this scenario. "No," he said, pointing a stern finger at José. "Take it elsewhere."

"Now, there's no need to get disgruntled," Corinne said. "No pun intended."

"Just tell him."

"If you insist." With a sobering sigh, she addressed José. "*Lo siento, José, pero tome el puerco a otra parte."*

"It is good buy, jefe," Soledad observed from the door of the hacienda, where she eavesdropped, broom in hand. "If we feed it, it will make good dollars when it is grown."

"How would you know a good buy on a pig, Soledad?" Mark snapped, what little good nature he had going to the hogs.

Corinne suppressed what was rapidly becoming hysteria. As far down as the report of finding Enrique's body had pushed her, this scene was having the opposite effect. If this didn't end soon, she'd go totally crazy.

The cook approached them, a condescending look on her face. *"Pues,* Señor Mark," she began with authority. "I go to the market every day, no? I shop good for *la* Señorita Corina. Why, just this morning—"

Mark held up his hand to cut her off before he received the entire market report and addressed Corinne with measured words. "Tell him I don't want the pig."

José's face fell. "*Ah, bien, dígale que es suyo, gratis.*"

Corinne gave Mark a wicked grin. "Good going. He says it's yours at no cost."

"I will keep the pig in the orchard," Soledad volunteered. "And we will share the moneys when it is grown."

"I don't want a pig."

"No one will take it," Corinne pointed out, "now that it has a reputation. The Indios are very—"

"I know." Mark cut her off. "They're very superstitious."

She almost felt sorry for him as he buried his face in his hands and then ran his fingers through his sun-streaked hair as if to erase the whole affair from his mind. Almost.

"So, does the pig stay or go?" she asked, glancing from Soledad to Mark and back.

With absolute denial in his demeanor, Mark turned to the cook, but the expectation of profit on Soledad's brow practically lifted her off the ground. Corinne watched his certainty wage war with reluctance to disappoint the housekeeper.

"Okay, it stays."

The hard case that Corinne had built against Mark Madison in her mind and around her heart cracked.

Soledad broke into nothing short of worship. "I knew you were a good businessman, jefe, and I am very happy to be in business with you." She wrung her hands with excitement. "There is a— *cómo se dice?—un cajón de abono—*?"

"A compost bin," Corinne translated.

"*Sí, como no?* I can put the leetle creature in that."

Mark rose and shook the bewildered José's hand. "Gracias, José."

"*De nada*, Señor Madison. *Me costó solo mi viaje largo y el precio del puerco,*" the peasant said with a heavy sigh.

"It cost him only the cost of the pig and his long journey," Corinne translated at Mark's bemused expression. "It's only six dollars, Mark. That's a lot of money to someone like him."

With a skyward roll of his eyes, Mark dug into his pocket and pulled out a money clip, flipping a modest wad of bills. "I don't have anything smaller than a ten," he said.

"I'm sure that would delight José. After all, he had a long journey."

With a cutting glance, Mark tugged the bill loose from the clip and handed it to the peasant. "I just bought a pig I don't want when I don't even have a decent bed. This place is getting to me."

Oblivious to Mark's grousing, José took the money and pocketed it before the jefe changed his mind. *"Muchas gracias,* Señor Madison. *Muchas gracias,* señorita. *Adiós."* He repeated himself as he backed through the courtyard gate.

"Come to Soledad," the cook cooed, trying to coax her future fortune pig from under the table.

"Did you buy a boy or a girl?" Corinne teased.

"How should I know? . . . and I don't dare look, or you'll accuse me of some other decadence."

Breathless and red faced, Soledad rose and leaned on the table for support. "Señor Mark, he will not leave from your feet."

"I think I'll leave you to put those pheromones to good use," Corinne said, getting up.

Mark grimaced at her as he followed suit. "Come on, Toto. Kansas isn't anywhere near these parts."

Corinne headed for the gate.

"Wait," he called after her. "Where are you going?"

"To check on a munchkin," she said, taking up the theme.

"Toto." Soledad reflected on the name and, after a second, nodded. "Toto is fitting for such a creature. But Señor Mark, perhaps if you walk to the . . ." She paused to retrieve her version of the new word. "The *composta,* I think the way will be easier. Our pig is strange to this place, and you are all our little Toto knows, no?"

"No . . . *yes,"* he stammered, the thought on his face turning to confusion. He waved Corinne on. "I'll catch you later."

Not if I can help it. Caught off guard once was enough. She still felt the heady effects of his kiss when she thought about it.

Which she wouldn't.

"Sure," she answered as Mark led the contented Toto out of the house with an excited Soledad bringing up the rear. Now, there was a partnership she'd never envisioned.

Stay tuned for the next episode of the continuing prodigal saga. Chuckling, Corinne started out of the hacienda. She couldn't wait to tell her friend Pam about Toto. As for Mark Madison . . . *Pues,* as Soledad would say . . . maybe he wasn't quite as self-absorbed as she'd deemed him after all.

CHAPTER 8

The following morning, Soledad insisted that Mark check on how well she was caring for their new investment. The plank pen was closed everywhere except for a wheelbarrow's width opening, so they'd used a damaged door to close it off. Afterward, the housekeeper mopped and scrubbed the salon, while Mark hauled the trash cans of plaster he'd swept up to a pile of debris next to the pigpen. Each time he went near the pen, Toto went wild, trying to get out.

Pigs. Mark rubbed his temples as if to push the distraction from his mind and then zeroed in on a room labeled *Ballroom-Gym* on the renovation blueprints. Blaine's plan to leave the support walls intact and make the best of the space they had for the dormitory rooms was the cheapest way to go. The ballroom, with its two-story cathedral ceiling, was big enough for a gymnasium, but there would be no room for bleachers. But after all, it wasn't as if the orphans had family lining up to watch them play.

Mark found himself thinking of Antonio and wondered how the little guy was doing. Instead of coming back to the hacienda, Corinne had gone straight to the bed-and-breakfast before Mark could find out anything or make amends as he'd promised Soledad.

When he was Antonio's age, he'd practically worshipped his big brother. If he was honest, he still did, but in a grudging way. Still, the thought of losing Blaine—well, Mark just didn't want to go there.

Laughter wafted in through the open windows from the meadow beyond the open patio gate, drawing Mark's attention to the cute little copper- and mocha-toned kids with shining black hair that cast off the same shades of blue and purple as a raven's wing. They danced and frolicked behind a tall, lithesome young woman. He recognized Corinne as she led them in what appeared to be a game of follow-the-leader.

Like Mother Goose with her goslings trailing after her, Mark observed, kicking back in the folding chair he'd pilfered from the parsonage with Father Menasco's permission. Of course, the prickly young woman bore no resemblance to the nursery rhyme figure, clad as she was in Capri pants and a tank top that hugged her figure. If Mark had to personify her in Mother Goose context, she was Little Miss Muffet, perched on her high little tuffet, purse strings tight in her fists and a smile that, when she was in good humor, was to die for.

Something about that dark hair pulled up into a ponytail with a bright red scarf, bold and perky, and that petulant pursing of her lips—even when he was the source of the peeve—turned Mark into a cross between Jack Horner, caught with his finger in the financial pie, and the girl kissing Georgy Porgy.

"*Caray,* look at you," Soledad chided, bursting into the room with a plate of sandwiches and a bowl of fresh sliced watermelon.

Nursery rhymes. Mark gave himself a mental smack. This place was getting to him. That morning, after the rooster's crow and the starving burro's woeful bray for food, he could have sworn he'd heard the sound of a cow being pushed over the moon. Upon looking out the window, he'd seen a farmer driving his reluctant livestock to pasture. And now he, Mark Madison, had a pig—or at least half of a pig. His money, Soledad's care.

"Whoa, Soledad," he exclaimed as she put the tray of fruit and sandwiches in front of him. "That's enough for two people."

"I will feed the pig on the rind. That is good business, no?" she said, her head moving with a proud sway. "The same shopping for the hacienda and our livestock."

"Excellent thinking." Mark checked out the scored cucumber slices on the chicken sandwiches. The bowl beside it was filled with caterer-perfect melon balls. When had the housekeeper had time to

71

do this? She'd just taken her mop and bucket out a few moments ago. "And this is too fancy for me, Soledad. These are fit for a king—and his court."

"You make such silliness, Señor Mark," the housekeeper tittered. "And for now, you are the king of the hacienda, no?"

She'd better take that up with the queen. Mark kept his acerbic reflection to himself. He knew when to hold them and when to fold them, and he'd best hold on to Soledad's goodwill. Not that it was hard to do. Now that they were business partners, he had the feeling she was completely on his side.

"Who am I to argue?" He forked a melon ball and popped it into his mouth. It helped offset the dryness of the plaster dust he'd swallowed that still made his tongue stick to the side of his mouth. "Delicious."

"Howsoever," she said, looking past him through the open window to where Corinne and children played. "You must make up for your disgust with Corina."

In addition to the ears of a bat, the woman had a memory like an elephant.

"You know I haven't seen her since she left here yesterday."

Soledad kept busy morning to dusk, setting up her kitchen and working in and around the hacienda to make it habitable. Some of her labors were a waste of time, given the construction planned, but she'd not hear of letting workmen come into such a filthy house. Besides, her salary came out of Corinne's budget. He might as well get some benefit from this project.

"*Bueno,* she will come for lunch soon. That will be the time, no?"

"Absolutely. If she's still talking to me."

"Oh, Señor Mark, do not try to fool Soledad. A man so *guapo* as yourself knows his women."

"Corinne isn't taken in—" The cell phone on his belt cut him off, playing an electronic version of Beethoven's Fifth Symphony that would send the master spinning in his grave. Mark took it from the sling and flipped it open.

"Mark Madison here."

Satisfied with the result of her efforts, Soledad gave a broad smile of approval and exited, humming, "Da, da, da-dah . . ." in an operatic effort.

"So how are things south of the border?"

Blaine. Talk about timing.

"I've had saner times." Since Blaine's family was out when Mark had checked in on arrival, he'd yet to tell his brother of the eventful journey and arrival at Mexicalli. Mark wasn't inclined to share recent events either.

"What was it you called it in your message?" his older brother chuckled. "Hades with sombreros?"

"Something like that." Forcing into his voice a brightness he was far from feeling, Mark went on. "But it's improving. The weather is pleasant, the people are loco, but friendly, and I have my work cut out for me. What more could a guy want?"

A pity party with a few drinks at the Cantina Roja came to Mark's mind, but he wanted to prove Blaine wrong even more. His body had yet to adjust to going to bed and getting up with the chickens . . . not to mention the burros and cows and now pigs.

"Have you gone over the specs yet?"

That was Blaine, a line or two of pleasantry and to the point.

"They are on my desk as we speak." And they were—under the melon balls. As Mark leaned back, he spotted a drawer handle on the table front that he'd not noticed before.

"Will they work, or will you have to make some adjustments?"

"Not sure yet. I imagine the usual adjustment or so will have to be made, once we get into the project." Mark could imagine Blaine squirming at the idea that he might possibly have overlooked something. "But for now, the plan is good to go."

"Have you contacted any contractors?"

"Just a local yokel for an immediate plumbing fix." *Who should have been here this morning.* "I think the whole system is going to need replacing." He eased the drawer open and found a thin book inside; some kind of Spanish novella, a romance, he presumed, from the heart on the cover. "The pipe is old and filled with sediment and rust."

The book was just the right thickness to balance the wobbly table—probably the reason it was stored in the drawer to start with.

"I think I included that in the estimate."

"You did," Mark told him, trying it out. "I'm just making a few urgent repairs so that some of the staff can stay in the front rooms of the hacienda—the ones that will eventually become offices. I'm using the salon as office and quarters. Corinne Diaz and her house-keeper occupy the parlor and dining room across the hall—or they will, as soon as Juan Pablo fixes the plumbing."

The book worked like a charm—a first, given his luck to date.

"So how is Corinne, Mark?" his sister-in-law butted in.

Mark winced. *Nothing like being pulled from the pan into the fire.*

"Hi, Caroline. Are you keeping Blaine straight?"

"Not if I can help it." A totally wicked chuckle sounded on the other end.

Caroline was the best thing that ever happened to Blaine. Her freewheeling spirit drew him out of the tight niche in which he thrived but from which he missed life.

"So how is she?" Caroline pressed.

"Fine. She stays on top of things and makes up for the Spanish I've forgotten."

"She's really dedicated to this project."

"Yeah, that's an understatement."

"Did you see the ghost yet?"

A third voice had come on the line. Mark recognized it as that of his little nephew, Berto.

"Not unless you count Soledad coming in from the clothesline with a tarp draped over her."

Berto giggled. "My sisters thought that *I* was a ghost. I was hiding under the tarp."

Blaine cleared his throat before Berto could launch into one of his favorite, often long-winded, reminiscences. "Could I get back to business, people?"

"Uh-oh," Caroline said. "Good-bye, Mark. Give Corinne a hug for me."

He couldn't believe he'd kissed her.

"*Adiós, Tío* Mark," Berto chimed in. "*Adiós, Papá.*"

The tenderness in Blaine's voice betrayed his no-nonsense reply. "*Adiós.* Now, get off the phone, both of you."

"'Bye, all," Mark put in before two hasty clicks sounded in his ear.

"I'm not so sure having an office at home is a good idea," Blaine said, when the static from having three lines open at once quieted.

"Hey, you're off those acid-eater pills, aren't you?"

"Yeah, I guess. And it's great to be here when Caroline and the kids come sailing in every afternoon." Blaine paused.

Mark could almost hear his thoughts being filed methodically into business, home, and miscellaneous.

"So how are you *really* making out?" he asked at last.

"*Really,* I'm fine. I mean, it's not Acapulco." Not by a long shot. "But it's a treat to be out in the field." And it was a far cry from the Hilton and the wining and dining of prospective customers that Mark dreamed about.

"Have you gotten any cantina contracts?"

So that's what Blaine was hemming about. Heat fired under Mark's collar. Blaine would have made a great match for Corinne. Both were control freaks.

"If you mean have I been drinking and partying, the answer is no."

"You really have to be on your toes down there. Mexican time and business time do not often coincide, especially in the country."

"Blaine, I have a *sober* handle on everything," Mark assured his brother. Still, life in Mexicalli made him feel as if he'd had one too many. "I was even a hero to some old lady named Doña Violeta. I caught her burro when it bolted with her in the cart."

If he told Blaine the whole truth, his brother would swear Mark was off the wagon and swimming in booze.

"Just keep me up on the project. Money is tight."

"I know, you feel responsible to the church to stay within budget." With Blaine and Corinne there wasn't any other option. "Nothing like working on a shoestring—a frayed shoestring."

"If you have any questions, call me."

And get another lecture on finance? No thanks. I can get that right here. "Look, just cut me some slack, Blaine, and let me surprise you."

"I'm counting on that."

"Good."

Doubting that Blaine counted on anyone but Blaine, Mark looked up at the sound of someone entering the hacienda foyer.

"Hasta luego, hermano," he said, and closed his phone as Corinne Diaz swept in, her face flushed and glowing. From under her arm, Antonio gave Mark a snaggletoothed grin.

"Buenos días, amigo," Mark said to the boy, returning his grin. "Or should I say *Buenas tardes?*"

◆

With a brightness that had been forced since the news of Enrique's death, Corinne pulled Antonio to her. The funeral tomorrow would be in the village on the other side of the lake, where the boys' family had come from.

"Antonio and I have a grand idea, but we might need your help."

"With what?" Mark answered, guarded. "I don't know much about kids."

"Señorita Corina needs two muscle men," Antonio informed him, posing to show off a scrawny but wiry bicep. "But I am only one."

"To help me move some things," Corinne explained.

Antonio was too overwrought to join the others during siesta, and she hoped that moving her things from storage into her newly painted bedroom might distract the boy from his grief for a while.

"I talked with Juan Pablo this morning. He should be here any time to do the plumbing, so I thought we might get a head start on moving."

Soledad's high-pitched "Moving?" sounded from the kitchen. A moment later she appeared. "We are moving now . . . *today?*"

"Just starting, Soledad," Corinne assured her. "We won't spend the night here until the plumbing is working for certain."

Juan Pablo had voiced his intentions to be here after lunch, but she knew he hadn't specified after *which* lunch—today's or another.

Although given her ultimatum, he'd do his best to earn the extra money offered for completing the task as promised.

"Good, because I will not stay here without a man of the house."

"I could move here," Antonio offered, brightening.

"And then Señor and Señora Altman would have to search all over Mexicalli for you," Corinne reminded him.

"Who?" Mark asked.

"Antonio's new mother and father . . . as soon as all the red tape is worked out," she added.

"Oh!" Soledad clasped her hands together. "God is so good." Before Antonio could dodge her, the housekeeper snagged him and smothered him in joyful kisses.

"Bringing the Altmans and Antonio together was definitely a God thing," Corinne told Mark. She felt her eyes tear up. At least it was with happiness this time. "How like God to place a silver lining around the darkest clouds."

The bad news of yesterday morning had been followed by today's good news. For years Antonio and Enrique's mother had worked for the Altmans, an English couple who vacationed every winter at the lake. She had often brought the boys to work with her, much to the delight of the childless Mrs. Altman. Having heard belatedly of the children's parents' death, the couple had asked to adopt the boys. And as much as Corinne would miss Antonio when the adoption went through, who could complain about a God thing?

Of course, nothing was simple in Mexico when it came to paperwork and procedure. And further complicating things was Antonio's uncle, who clearly didn't want the boy, but kept postponing signing away his right to guardianship. Father Menasco thought the man was holding out in hopes of extracting money from the desperate Altmans in exchange for his signature.

"Hey, congratulations, man," Mark said, offering Antonio his hand.

Pulling away from Soledad, the boy took it in a manly shake. *"Muchas gracias."*

"Let's celebrate," Mark said, shoving the tray of food at Corinne and Antonio.

"We just had a snack."

"But I can always eat more, no?" the boy cut in, helping himself to a handful of the fruit. *"Hay* soda?"

"We have iced tea," Corinne told him.

Soda was too expensive to keep on hand, but thankfully the mountain spring water on the hacienda property was good. Blaine Madison had taken care of all the health department concerns prior to purchasing the place.

"I get it now," Soledad announced, returning to the kitchen.

"So, what kind of *furniture* are we men moving?"

Mark's voice smacked of cynicism, but he'd have to get over it.

"You remember. The furniture I bought with my own money?"

"Ah, yes, with the pennies you pinched from your purse." He popped the *P*'s, mimicking her.

With a short retreat in mind, Corinne lifted Antonio up to seat him on the edge of the desk. "But nonetheless mine," she said. "Be back in a minute." Regrouped and ready to fire. "I'm going to help Soledad with the—"

"Aquí está," the housekeeper announced, heading her off at the door with a pitcher and paper cups. She handed them to Corinne. *"Pues,* I wish to take up some water before Juan Pablo puts it to off."

"I'll take care of this. You go."

Taking a reinforcing breath, Corinne returned to the library table and served the tea. As she leaned over the table to pour it into the cups, a stiff envelope in her pocket reminded her of the invitations she'd found on her desk that morning. She'd been so preoccupied with Enrique and Antonio that she'd forgotten to give Mark his. She fished it out of her pocket and handed it to him.

"What's that?"

"An invitation from Doña Violeta to supper tomorrow evening. It's in your honor for saving her."

At Mark's suspicious lift of the brow, she added. "No, I didn't open your mail and reseal it. I got an invitation too."

Mark slid his finger under the wax seal. "Fancy."

"Doña Violeta is old Mexico," Corinne said, pointing to the elegant calligraphy on the expensive stationery. "She's in her eighties and still has a steady hand. Diego says that he gets his artistic gift from her."

"Not a lot of advance notice though."

"She's also eccentric."

"Doña Violeta Quintana de la Vega," Mark read aloud. "That's a mouthful of old Mexico for sure."

"Can I come?" Antonio asked. "I helped save her too."

Corinne handed him a cup of tea. "It will be late, after your bedtime. And besides, it's for grownups only."

She didn't mention that they would probably be emotionally and physically tired from crossing the lake for the funeral. At least for now, she hoped to keep the boy's mind off Enrique.

"So, are you in or out?" she said, handing Mark a cup.

"Sure I'm in," Mark declared. "I need some entertainment besides the cockroach races under my bed each night."

"No, I mean helping us move."

"*Your* furniture, right?" he asked, hopping back on the pity wagon. "Oh, I'm in, Miss Muffet. There's no sense in all of us roughing it."

"What did you call me?" she asked indignantly.

"You know," he said. "Miss Muffet. Prim and proper and penny-pinching on her tuffet."

"And afraid of the spider," Antonio laughed, unaware of the strong undercurrent between the two adults.

Why she ever thought the man had any redeeming qualities eluded her. He was incorrigible, plain and simple.

"Thankfully, I only need your muscle and not your wit." She grabbed half a sandwich and a cup of tea. "I'm going to see what Soledad has to be moved while you two finish your lunch."

"So we can talk man-to-man," Antonio said, with as much seven-year-old machismo as he could muster.

Muffet, indeed, Corinne thought, leaving before Mark could regroup. Besides, there was nothing wrong with being prim or proper. And yes, she did pinch pennies when it came to using money wisely to help a good cause. What was wrong with that?

Spying a spiderweb in a corner that had obviously formed since Soledad cleaned, Corinne brushed it aside with a sweep of her hand and shook it off along with Mark's cloaked barb. She might be a Miss Muffet, but he'd soon see that she'd not be scared from her tuffet, not for kisses . . . er . . . love, nor money.

CHAPTER 9

"Now, *that* is a fine automobile," Juan Pablo observed through the window of the bedroom, where he was giving Mark a hand with assembling Corinne's wrought-iron bed. *"Pues,* I must quit to my work, if I am to finish this day."

Mark finished with the last bolt and stood, wiping the sweat from his brow. Whoever had crafted this piece would never be accused of undercutting quality. It probably weighed as much as the vehicle he saw easing through the narrow courtyard gate of the hacienda—a new-model four-wheel drive, luxury—with Corinne Diaz sitting pretty behind the wheel.

This was the final straw. Tossing the borrowed wrench back to its owner, Mark headed out to the patio.

"You have a new SUV?" he demanded as the car came to a stop in front of the patio.

He'd wondered, when she left to get her things from the bed-and-breakfast, why she hadn't taken Juan Pablo's pickup, which she'd borrowed earlier to move the furniture out of storage at the orphanage. But he'd been too busy figuring out how to assemble the bed to say anything. Now he understood fully. Why ride in a junker when Miss Muffet could travel in style?

"Don't tell me. *Daddy* insisted," he drawled, still smarting over the new box spring and mattress set waiting to be put on the bed frame.

"That's right." She made no apology as she breezed past him with a box marked *linens.*

"And it has a CD player," Antonio said, explaining his belated exit from the leather passenger seat. "I have never seen such a fine automobile."

Mark had. But his had been "arrested." He grabbed another box identified as curtains and rugs. It was easy to be a saint when *Daddy* saw to one's every need.

"I don't suppose your father would want to adopt a son?" he called after her, following her through the entrance at the juncture of the L-shaped building.

The corporation had funded his ticket to Mexico City and bus fare. The Acapulco switchover and stay had been on Mark's own account, which was supporting his plush condo in Philly while he wasted away in Mexicalli-ville . . . with no margaritas.

No more. He was out of here—the hacienda; unfortunately, not Mexicalli.

Barging into the room to tell Miss Muffet where to stuff it, Mark slowed upon seeing Corinne and Soledad whispering in the kitchen doorway. By their distraught faces, they weren't discussing the arrangement of the furniture.

"Antonio," Corinne called out to the boy who came in behind Mark, carrying a rolled-up scatter rug. "Will you look in the car for me and see if you can find the Ricky Martin CD?"

The boy dropped the rug and, with an eager nod, scampered back outside.

"What's up?" Mark asked, once Antonio was out of earshot.

"We were just discussing the funeral tomorrow and arrange-ments to get there," Corinne told him, the mist in her eyes knock-ing the wind out of his peeve. "I guess we'll have a minicaravan going around the lake to the family's village."

"But they just found the body yesterday," Mark observed.

Corinne rushed into the kitchen and snatched up a tissue from a box on the counter.

"Pobrecita," Soledad said in a hushed tone. "She has so much love it hurts her."

Before Mark realized what the housekeeper was about, she shoved him into the kitchen after the young woman. "Go, go."

Mark gathered his wits as Corinne turned, her face a mirror of wretchedness. "Come on," he said, closing the distance between them. "Let's take a walk." He slipped his arm around her shoulder.

To his surprise, she leaned into him as he led her out the back of the house. The thought slipped inside him and filled him with a sense of awe: for one moment, someone actually needed—and trusted—him. For one moment, it felt as if he was born to fill that need, satisfy that trust.

This place was definitely getting to him.

"I love this time of evening," she said, moving away from him as they meandered up the slope toward the orchard. Above the white-blossoming trees, the setting sunlight cast its last rays on the purple mist tucking in the mountains for the night.

"Yeah."

Although he hadn't noticed it before, it was a spectacular view, almost as grand as that of the pristine village with its red-tiled rooftops nestled next to the lake, which looked like a fire-glazed mirror from their vantage. Beyond the parsonage, Mark spied the farmer with the noisy livestock closing a gate behind his handful of cows. The crack of dark wasn't nearly as annoying and noisy as the crack of dawn.

In the east, the moon, faint but stubborn, pushed its way into its rightful heavenly position in the face of the brighter, bigger sunset. Funny, that was all Blaine and Caroline could talk about, that Mexican moon. And the weird thing was that Mark, like the cows and the chickens, hadn't been up and out long enough to even notice or appreciate it.

Beside him, Corinne drew in a shaky breath and let it out slowly, eyes closed as if drawing on an inner strength. At a loss as to what else to say or do, Mark followed her lead of silence, when snorting and pawing from the direction of the old compost bin gave him the answer.

"Want to go check on my pig before he knocks down the pen?"

A welcome chuckle bubbled up through her distress. "Sure."

Since Toto hadn't been in residence long, the air was still scented with the sweet orange of his surroundings.

Orange blossoms, a beautiful señorita, and a pig. What was wrong with this picture?

"You know, this is embarrassing," Mark admitted as Toto became more excited. He gave Corinne a sheepish look. Corinne smiled, and something inside Mark lit up like a new day.

"I tell you, that pig isn't normal . . . even by pig standards."

Her laugh was worth being the brunt of her humor. Suddenly she sobered. "I know I've been testy of late, but . . ." She exhaled a shaky breath. "They haven't even investigated Enrique's disappearance, short of a brief search. Now there's to be no investigation of his death. Everyone I've spoken to says that he wouldn't have run off. He was happy at the orphanage . . . as much as an orphan could be. He didn't care for his relatives."

She pulled up some weeds and offered them to Toto. Momentarily distracted from Mark, the pig tugged them out of her hand.

"Kids run off to explore," Mark ventured in explanation. "He could have become lost."

"Enrique was not lost."

Corinne spun around, as startled as Mark by Antonio's appearance, the CD that she sent him for in hand. "How do you know, 'Tonio?"

The child looked around as if he expected to be overheard. "The *caracol* got him," he whispered.

Mark looked to Corinne for a translation. "Some kind of native superstition?"

"A snail?" she said, skepticism knitting her brow.

"*Sí*, the *caracol*. It puts to lose all who touch it. I told Capitán Nolla that I feared the *caracol* that kill my *mamá y papá* kill Enrique, too."

No matter how ridiculous it sounded, the boy obviously believed touching a snail led to his relatives' demise. His chin began to quiver.

"The *caracol*, he is bad luck."

Corinne shrugged. "It's a new one on me." She turned to Antonio, who was spinning the CD on his finger. "Where is this *caracol*, Antonio?"

"In the mountain, but I have never seen it. So I said to Capitán Nolla."

"So the police captain knows of this snail?" Corinne was just as confused as Mark.

"He says that I make it up for the bad luck of my parents and brother." Standing on one foot, he dragged the other against the inside of his leg, scratching. "Can I play the CD inside?" he asked, ending the subject as quickly as he'd started it.

Corinne waved him away, watching as he retreated past an overgrown herb garden into the house. "Maybe next week we can head for Cuernavaca and get you some decent furniture . . . as long as it will fit in my vehicle."

Antonio wasn't the only one adept at changing tracks. Mark straightened from leaning against the top ledge of the pen. "That'd be great," he said, pulling a half-cocked grin. "Of course, I'll have to check my calendar."

"Do that." Her knowing look all but pulled his socks up. She knew he was teasing and more. And judging from that sexy curl of her lip, she liked what she saw.

Just as Mark leaned in to see if orange lollipop was the flavor of the day, she turned her face away, staring at the hacienda as if it held the answer to the question that distracted her from the pleasant tension building between them.

"I know it's not a snail," she said, neutralizing the chemistry the same way her despair had shot down his earlier annoyance. "But I'm beginning to wonder if there isn't more to that family's tragedy than we know."

"Why don't we finish up here and head down to the Cantina Roja to unwind a bit? Maybe someone there knows—"

Corinne drew away from him as if he'd grown a second head. "I don't think so. Contrary to popular belief, barhopping solves nothing. If anything, it contributes to one's problems."

"*Barhopping*? It's the only one in this one-bar town."

"I don't drink."

"They don't serve soda?"

"If I wanted a soda, I wouldn't go to a bar for it."

"Do you schmooze?" Mark raised his hand before she could reply. "Wait, no need to answer that. I can see there's no schmoozing up there on that tuffet of yours. What is it with you?" He spun away, facing the downward slope to the village where a few lights were beginning to show. "Are you afraid you'll fall off or something?"

Under other circumstances, this could have been, pig aside, a romantic postcard moment. "I mean, what do you consider a good time?"

"Anything or anywhere without you and your booze." Chin struck in an airy pose, she marched away.

"Well, if I didn't need a drink before, I sure could use one now," he called after her, dizzied by her personality seesaw and determined to get off.

He needed to go somewhere where the girls weren't wrapped up in anything but guys. Somewhere where a come-hither look didn't mean *follow me to the next subject*, which wasn't closely related to what a man and woman should be thinking about on a night like this. He needed . . . Blaine's disapproving face flashed in his mind. Well, the devil with his brother and Corinne. He needed a drink.

A small boat coasted toward the sandy beach of the sleeping village of Mexicalli, its engine puttering to a halt. All along the waterfront, fishing boats had been pulled up beyond the waterline for the night, the sand gutted by their hulls.

After finishing off a bottle of Corona, the older of the two men aboard hopped out of the craft and landed on unsteady feet, going to his knees in the shallow water. Swearing under his breath, he wrung out the fringe of the serape that held the cool night air at bay.

His companion, no more sober, bent over double laughing.

"Hey, amigo, only Jesucristo Himself can walk on water."

"If you talk any louder, I will send you to see Him with my own two hands, *chico*. And don't forget the paint."

Sergio, his wife's dimwitted cousin, made up in agility what he lacked in brains. He could climb the wall to the Hacienda Ortiz like a monkey and gain them entrance. Their boss, who fancied to call himself *El Caracol,* had said that the gringos would be moving in any day now. A handsome reward awaited anyone who might dissuade them.

Lorenzo felt inside his shirt to see if the magic doll that his mother-in-law had made for him had gotten wet. This would put the proverbial fear of Dios in the do-gooders, and much worse among any Indios they might hire to work for them. Lorenzo's mother-in-law was a *bruja,* and he had seen the results of Malinche's spells. She had cursed her sister's only son, Sergio, before he was born, out of spite for the affair her sister had with Malinche's husband. Her sister died in childbirth, and Malinche, who had no sons, took her nephew to raise as her own. But black magic was hard to reverse, and so Sergio remained a boy in a man's body.

Sergio perched on the side of the small craft, waving his arms beneath his serape for balance, like a heron flapping its wings. Lorenzo grabbed his side of the boat before it tipped over, spilling his companion belly first into the water.

"Jump, you idiot! We need to pull the boat up on the beach."

Lorenzo listened with impatience as the drunken Sergio floundered in the water. Perhaps he should just let the fool drown, overcome by a wet serape. After a few grunts and a belch that could have shaken the leaves in the trees along the lakefront, he showed his face over the opposite side of the boat.

Lorenzo glared at him. "Now grab the side of the boat and push it up on the beach like the others."

"My arm hurts, I think." Sergio always had some excuse.

"I should know better than to expect you to be able to do a man's work after a few beers," Lorenzo taunted.

Sergio would do anything to show his manliness. Sure enough, the young man drew himself up for the task.

"On three. *Uno, dos, tres!*"

The vessel's bottom sliding over the damp sand made a shushing sound, as though to remind them that their mission was one of secrecy.

"Do you have the paint?"

Sergio dug inside his water-heavy cloak. After much more poking and flapping, he produced a can of spray paint with a big smile.

Lorenzo exhaled through his nostrils. At least the man's job at the hardware store in Flores gave him access to numerous useful items at no cost . . . and Sergio had no conscience with regard to taking what he wanted.

"Good. Let's get it over with."

Accustomed to the hilly terrain, they reached the Hacienda Ortiz with no trouble. To Lorenzo's surprise, the gate wasn't even locked. Luck was surely with them, he thought, slipping through the wrought-iron entrance into the moonlit courtyard. All he had to do was open a few windows to see his way around inside.

A clang behind him nearly caused Lorenzo to jump out of his skin. He turned to see Sergio wrestling with his soaked serape, which had caught on one of the elaborate curves in the gate. With an oath, he returned to untangle his companion before he awakened the village.

As Sergio came loose, the can of paint he'd brought from the hardware store fell from his disheveled cloak. Lorenzo reached down and picked it up. It was empty. In disbelief, he shook it, the balls inside rattling with little resistance from side to side.

"You idiot," he hissed through his teeth at the clueless young man watching him. "It's empty!"

"No problem, jefe," Sergio replied. After a lengthy search inside his cloak, he smiled and drew out a small plastic box.

Lorenzo had seen one like it before—among his children's toys. "Crayons? You brought *crayons*?"

"So you said, something to write with," Sergio declared in his defense. "These will write as well as the paint, no?"

In a mix of exasperation and desperation, Lorenzo tried the button on the paint can. To his surprise, paint came out. He let up on the valve immediately. He'd need every drop in the can to finish what he came to do. If it was enough, he might not drown his companion on the way home.

CHAPTER 10

Mexican music stirred his blood. Or maybe it was the pretty señorita who'd set the margarita down on the table in front of him with a seductive flutter of dark lashes that could melt the frosted ice on the side of the salt-encrusted glass. Like a rose unfolding, her lush, full lips spread into a smile. She was dressed in a red embroidered skirt and off-the-shoulder blouse, and she smelled exotic, hints of citrus and flowers in her perfume. It made his head as light as the smoke that wafted up from the burning candle in the center of the table. Her long black hair brushed his face as she leaned in and put her arm around his shoulder.

He was in heaven or on his way there, he thought, catching the oval curve of her chin and turning her face to his. With a conjured look of innocence, her blue eyes widened as though she had no clue that he was about to kiss her.

"Ah, Corina," he chided, his voice growing huskier by the heartbeat as he contemplated her lips. Red . . . ripe . . . orange-flavored as the lollipop she'd eaten earlier?

He had to know. Covering her mouth with his, he heard her catch her breath with a snort . . .

Snort?

Jerked from the arms of his seductress, Mark opened one eye to see two small, dark ones staring back at him over a pink snout.

"Whoa!" Shot with shock, he rolled away from his floppy-eared companion and out of the strange bed in which he'd evidently been sleeping. The thud of hitting the floor knocked the last thoughts of sleep out of him. He recognized the soft peach color of Corinne's bedroom walls and groaned. Pulling himself up on the bed he'd assembled the day before, he was backtracking through the pained daze of his memory when a door opened somewhere in the hacienda.

"Señor Mark, Señor Mark, come quick!" It was Soledad at her operatic best. "Our pig, it is missing."

At the same time Toto, who'd trotted around from the opposite side of the bed, gave him a hungry nudge.

Before Mark could assemble enough wit to answer, the housekeeper shrieked, "*¡Caramba!* What are *you* doing *here?*"

A man grunted, at least he thought it was a man, in the salon . . . where Mark should have been.

Mark shoved his fingers through his disheveled hair and concentrated on clearing his mind as he started for the door. What was he doing in Corinne's room? The last thing he remembered was winning a good-sized poker pot from some little German who bought rounds for everyone.

"Where is Señor Mark?" Soledad said, and from the escalating timbre of her demand, she was building steam.

Reluctantly Mark moved toward the commotion at the speed of his sluggish thoughts. He remembered now. He'd met Juan the Electrician. Juan Pedro couldn't go home because of an angry wife, and Mark was afraid of waking up Father Menasco and Annamaria, so together they had come here. Juan took the air bed. *That* was why Mark was in Corinne's bed . . . dreaming of her.

Nah, must have been a look-alike. The señorita in his dream had a sultry, summer blue gaze—as opposed to one icy enough to sink the *Titanic.*

"Here I am, Soledad," Mark called.

The housekeeper emerged just as Toto, who recognized the voice of the hand that fed him, found her. "Where have you been, you little bad pig?"

"I've looked all around the yard, Soledad . . ."

Clad in a somber dark blue dress, Corinne broke off as she

entered the hall from the kitchen and saw Mark, Soledad, and the missing pig. "Well, well, did you two enjoy your night on the town?"

Sinking, sinking . . . there was no wiggle room. He'd messed up big time.

Juan Pedro stumbled to Soledad's side, staring at the pig with confusion. "Oh, *sí,* Señorita Diaz," he assured Corinne, rumpled hat in hand. "We enjoyed us very much, *gracias.*"

Sunk.

Instead of acknowledging the electrician, Corinne swept past the two men as though she could wish them away. But on reaching the door of her bedroom, she froze with a gasp that took in enough breath to fill a hot-air balloon.

"What—"

"I know, I slept on your new bed," Mark said, heading after her before she exploded. "It's not that big a deal. I left the plastic covers on." Of course he couldn't account for what the pig had done.

Straight-arming the doorjamb to steady himself, he paused, a snicker sneaking up on him at the scene he witnessed. Soledad incinerated the penitent electrician with her dark gaze, dodging a hungry, grunting pig that nearly knocked her legs out from under her, while Corinne stood, mouth agape at the possibility of pig doo-doo in her new bedroom.

"Mark?" His name rolled off her lips.

Red, just like the temptress in his dream.

"Mark . . ." It faltered this time, staggered, not by anger, but a trepidation that banished the scant humor he'd dabbled with.

What had they done? he wondered, sparing a glance at Toto, who had also picked up on the alarm in Corinne's voice.

Mark followed her gaze and froze in disbelief. Scrawled across the wall over the bed was a warning. *Leave or be witched.* The *leave* and one letter of the *or* had been spray painted. The rest was some sort of chalk or—

Mark approached the bed and rubbed his fingers over the plastered wall. Wax came off under his fingernail. *Crayon?*

"*Madre de Dios!*" Soledad prayed, crossing herself. "We must get Father Menasco *imediatamente.*"

"*Calme, calme,* Soledad." Mark turned to Corinne. "What does *be witched* mean? Is it like *bewitched?*"

"It means that you have been cursed, señor." Behind Soledad, Juan Pablo made the sign of a cross over his chest.

"Oh, Señor Mark, your hair."

Before Mark knew what she was about, the housekeeper picked at the back of Mark's head. A glance at the mirror revealed that someone had cut a chunk of his hair.

"Aw, man, that ruined a good cut," he complained to his image. Aside from the bad hair, his eyes were red with pockets under them deep enough to carry water. His clothes were rumpled from being slept in, and he didn't even want to imagine what he smelled like after spending most of the evening in a bar without smoke filters.

"The witch collects for her dolls, for to do you harm."

That drew Mark's attention from his condition. "Don't be ridiculous, Soledad. Someone is trying to scare us."

"Your liquor-dulled brain might not have enough sense to be rattled," Corinne said, "but I'm certainly unnerved."

In other circumstances, Mark might have infused more indignation in his voice. Instead, his scorn was tepid, so as not to anger the gods of thunder in his head. "I don't believe in witches or ghosts."

"Neither do I." Corinne crossed her arms, brushing at the gooseflesh pimpling her skin. "But someone sneaked in here while you were in your drunken stupor, wrote on the wall, and cut your hair." She glanced at Toto, who was circling Soledad's feet, rubbing against the woman's legs like a cat. "And they probably let the pig out."

When she looked at Mark again, disappointment, even hurt, grazed her expression. "Somehow I thought . . . I hoped," she corrected, "that you would be different."

The look reached deep beyond Mark's defenses, tugging at the most vulnerable need he had, one he'd never admit to, no matter how it pained him. The need to be needed . . . and trusted.

"Wait . . ." Mark started after her as she turned to leave. "Where are you going?"

"To get ready to leave for Enrique's funeral."

The funeral. Mark had forgotten. He glanced at his watch and groaned. He'd had a full day, and it was only 7:00 a.m. There was no going back to bed after this, he thought, overriding the protest of his remaining mind and body over the decision. Besides, there was something he had to do. It wouldn't get him out of the proverbial doghouse, but it might bring a little joy into what otherwise promised to be a miserable day.

◆

It was hot and dry in Enrique and Antonio's village of Flores when the entourage from Mexicalli arrived, Father Menasco's small sedan followed by Corinne's SUV. Business as usual had stopped for the celebration; at least it would appear a celebration to those unfamiliar with the customs.

Yet, due to Lorenzo Pozas's uneasiness with the church, this observance broke with tradition. Instead of having the wake the night prior to the service at the village chapel and the procession for the interment, a short one was to be held before the ceremony at the man's home.

Like most of the homes clustered in and about Flores, it was a single-story adobe, dingy white, its tiled roof overgrown with vegetation. Corinne had visited similar ones in Mexicalli, sparsely furnished. An old box spring covered with boards might serve as a bed for the parents, with *petate* mats that were rolled up during the day serving as beds for the children on the earthen floor at night. And for all their want, the inhabitants were usually happier and more eager to share what they had than were many of Corinne's acquaintances back home, who lived in expensive homes, drove nice cars, and wanted more.

Enrique's paternal uncle proved the exception. Compact as the concrete barrier barrels along the turnpikes back home and with about as much personality, Lorenzo Pozas was anything but glad to offer hospitality. He welcomed them with a few clipped English words, did an abrupt turn, and motioned for the village musicians to strike up the *jarabe,* a folk dance for the amusement of the *angelito* in the brown box coffin.

Corinne recognized them as the same group who had played at the fiesta of St. John in Mexicalli.

A man in a brightly colored serape proceeded to dance and frolic to the music, making himself appear tall by putting a clay jar on his head as he portrayed a folk character for the benefit of two other guests—a couple on the maternal side of the family whom Soledad said were the godparents of the boys. But it was the attending children who cackled as he pulled one comical face after another, and stumbled about as though one of his legs had suddenly turned to water.

Freshly showered, shaved, and dressed, Mark still looked the worse for wear from his night at the Cantina Roja. He nudged Corinne. "What's the deal here? It's sounds more like the cantina than a funeral." Although he wore concealing sunglasses over the bloodshot eyes she'd seen earlier, his face was still drawn, undoubtedly caught in the jaws of a hangover headache. He deserved every beat of it.

"Since Enrique died so young," Soledad answered at Corinne's hesitation, "we are providing the amusement of the childhood years that he will miss."

As they watched, the man removed the jar from his head, adjusted his serape, and crouched over in another role—a bent crone with a broken walking stick.

Corinne had heard of the custom, but at the moment she wasn't in a talkative mood—particularly when it came to Mark. While he had showered and dressed, she'd called Capitán Nolla to the scene of the crime, informed Father Menasco, who could do no more than she with the funeral pending, and then hurriedly freshened up.

If only Mark had been sober, he might have caught the culprit who had vandalized her room with the threatening message. If he wanted to waste away his life, so be it. It surprised Corinne that he had even managed to pull himself together in time to leave for Enrique's funeral, much less had time for Soledad to even up the sandy hair that had once curled over his collar.

But he had, a voice reminded her, for the sake of the grieving boy at her elbow. Didn't that count for something?

Yes, she argued against herself, lest the fortification around her senses weaken. But his motive was guilt. Plain and simple guilt.

The music ended, signaling the time for the service. Corinne held her breath, uncertain what to expect as Tío Lorenzo opened the lid of the coffin. Usually it was left open so that attendees could view the *angelito,* but in this case, the body barely had been recognizable. When Corinne saw that the child's remains had been covered with a blanket, she gave a sigh of relief.

While Lorenzo watched, puffed with self-importance as the host, the mourners walked in a single line by the bier, dropping in flowers or small toys, continuing an age-old Indio tradition carried over into their Christianized ways—of sending things that the deceased might need on the way to life in heaven. Waiting until the last, Antonio left Corinne's side with a small jar of water. She walked with Antonio to the bier that held the small paint-gilded coffin. Chin trembling, Antonio put the container inside.

"Now you can help the angels water the flowers in heaven, Enrique." The bravado that the boy had tried to maintain gave in to a sob that strangled his voice as he added, "And give *mamá y papá* for me a kiss."

The uncle grabbed the boy's arm with a harsh whisper about men not crying, but Antonio reached for Corinne's hand as though avoiding the devil himself. As she enfolded the crying boy in her arms, Lorenzo glared over Antonio's head, the cold blade of his stare sending a shiver up Corinne's spine. Lips pressed thin and white with contempt, he closed the lid, so hard that Antonio and Corinne started.

"Nine *niños,* he has," Soledad whispered to Corinne as two men fastened it.

The large size of most families was a primary reason for relatives to decline becoming guardians for other children. Most of the time they could hardly support their own. But with Lorenzo, Corinne didn't think it would matter if the man had been childless. Nor, given the personality she'd seen in his eyes—which were said to be the gateway to the soul—would she even want to place a child in his custody.

Not that Antonio's custody was at risk, with the English couple making arrangements to adopt him. *Thank You, Lord, for Your light in these dark times.*

As the men stepped away from the bier, the godmother draped a pink and blue–checked cloth over the little brown box, after which Soledad placed a wreath of fresh flowers and ribbons at its head. In the distance, the church bells tolled the death knell, timed with the opening of the service by Father Menasco as the guest priest.

Corinne dug some tissues from her pocket, taking one and passing the package to Antonio, who blew his nose almost as loud as the bells.

At the end of the *rosarios,* or prayers, four of the village men took the coffin up on their shoulders for the trek to the cemetery. Once again the musicians struck up a tune, one more reverent than the *jarabe* music. Women carrying small jars of burning *copal*—the Mexican version of frankincense—followed, laying a scented trail for the rest of the mourners through the narrow cobbled street. The village priest began to sing a repetitive prayer for the dead child and was soon joined by the others.

A colorful combination of music, mourning, and prayer, the procession marched to the cemetery next to the village church on the outskirts of town. Soledad explained that this church had replaced the original one in the center of town after a fire ten years earlier.

"And just as well," the housekeeper confided behind the cover of her hand. "For the cemetery in the old was full . . . and this is so beautiful for the angels to look upon."

She pointed to Lago Flores, where the morning sun cast light like a shower of confetti from the glittering water's surface. It was almost impossible to see the flowering hyacinth flotillas for which the lake had been named.

"*Recibe, Jesús, recibe. Recibe, Jesús, recibe. Recibe el niño tan pura y lindo. Y mis oraciónes con el. Y mis oraciónes con el,*" the group sang as they approached the freshly dug grave.

"Receive, Jesús, receive," Corinne sang along, soft and low, falling into ranks with her Mexicalli friends on the side of the bier where Father Menasco stood. "Receive this child so pure and beautiful, and our prayers with him. And our prayers with him."

As the group finished the final "Amen," she heard a deep male voice conclude with her, and turned to see Mark Madison standing on the other side of Antonio, holding the boy's hand. Folded under Mark's other arm was a paper bag. Her first thought, that he'd have the nerve to bring liquor along, was quickly negated by the shape of the package. Besides, for all her disgust with him, Mark wasn't *that* bad.

As the village priest began a final prayer for the boy, Corinne studied the iron set of Mark's jaw from behind the screen of her sunglasses. His profile was the kind that sold books: strong, decidedly masculine. Yet, even though she couldn't quite put a finger on it, there was something vulnerable in the way he stared straight ahead through his designer shades, watching Tío Lorenzo lead his family by the grave to toss handfuls of dirt upon the coffin in the bottom.

The musicians, who'd found shelter under a tree nearby, continued with music for the graveside ceremony. The formalities over, men finished covering the grave while others handed out mugs of hot tequila and cigarettes to the guests. While Father Menasco bade his good-bye to the village priest, other guests thanked Corinne and the staff from the orphanage for joining them.

Suddenly Antonio turned and tugged on Mark's sleeve. "It's time now."

Corinne was astonished when Mark pulled a rocket from the paper bag.

"In honor of your brother," he said, handing it over to the lad. "But I forgot matches."

"I can find matches." Proud as a peacock, Antonio planted the rocket at the head of the gravesite. The guests, seeing what was about to happen, stepped back in anticipation. The man who'd played the comic roles for the children earlier moved forward, offering his cigarette lighter for the fuse.

With a loud hiss and a pop, the rocket shot into the air, straight up toward the cloudless blue morning sky. The guests applauded in delight, but the sheer joy on Antonio's tear-streaked face filled Corinne from the toes up.

Since the introduction of gunpowder by the Spanish conquerors, the Mexican people delighted in it. Fireworks were as common at funerals as they were at celebrations.

Wonderstruck, Corinne turned to Mark. "How did you know?"

"Juan Pablo told me last night at the cantina that no funeral was complete without at least one rocket," he told her. "So I bought one, just in case there weren't any." He shifted, uncomfortable under her curious appraisal. "It was Antonio's and my little secret."

What made this guy tick? One minute she wanted to strangle him, and the next, hug him.

"It was perfect," Antonio announced, joining them. "I know that Enrique is smiling from heaven. *Gracias, gracias, gracias.*" The boy hugged Mark, nearly taking him off his feet.

"*Perdoname,* señor *y* señora . . ."

Startled, Corinne turned to see Lorenzo. "My family and I wish to say our *adiós* to my nephew," he explained, easing the child away from Mark. "Will you and your *esposo* not have a mug of tequila for my late nephew?"

My husband? The reference to Mark so stunned Corinne that Mark replied for both of them.

"No thanks. Alcohol puts us to lose."

Corinne wasn't sure whether it was Mark's use of the idiom or his saying that alcohol wasn't good for them that shocked her more.

"I'll be right here waiting, Antonio," she assured the wary child. For Lorenzo's benefit she added, "We have to leave very soon for the orphanage, as we have a supper engagement."

"*Un momento solamente,* Señora," he assured her.

"I thought you'd be all over him like ugly on an ape for that," Mark said, as Pozas led Antonio away.

"For thinking I'd marry someone like you, or for thinking that I'd drink?" she quipped, never taking her eyes off Antonio.

Lorenzo's family surrounded the boy, children hugging, women kissing, and the men shaking his hand or clapping him on the back.

"Take your pick."

Corinne softened her answer with the hint of a smile. "You have some redeeming qualities."

"Oh?" Mark stepped closer, invading her space with the scent of his aftershave, the warmth exuding from his body, his breath brushing past her ear.

Her senses blaring like an emergency broadcast signal, Corinne broke away to meet Antonio as he made his way back from the family cluster with Father Menasco.

"Ready to go?" she asked with a forced brightness.

"*Un momento, por favor.*" He made his way to the small mounded grave site, now covered with bougainvillea and a blanket of flowers made by the women. Reaching into his shirt pocket, he took out a small palm cross that he'd made in crafts at the orphanage, pressed it to his lips, and laid it on the center of the floral covering.

When the boy backed away, it was as if he had left a part of his heart behind.

"*Pues,*" he said shakily, joining her and Mark. "Now I am ready to go to my new family."

CHAPTER 11

The ride back to Mexicalli was blessedly quiet, Mark thought. The tuba player remained in his head, pumping blasts of brass in his brain. For some reason, Antonio gave up his command of the CD player to sit in the back with him, which was fine, since the boy seemed preoccupied with staring at the passing landscape around the flower-dotted lake. In the front seat, Soledad's voice took over where the ejected Ricky Martin left off. From what little Mark could pick out, she ping-ponged between praise and criticism of the affair as a whole.

"Who would think it?" she exclaimed. "First he wants his brother's boys. Then he doesn't. But then with nine children of his own . . ." She paused to tut in disapproval.

"Do you have a brother?" Antonio asked beside him.

Mark unglued his tongue. "What's that, amigo?"

"Do you have a brother?"

"Yes." *Alive, thank goodness.* Somewhere inside Mark, surprise registered. Yes, he'd like to strangle Blaine, or at least shake him into getting a life, but overall, he cared deeply about his elder sibling. So Blaine was overly responsible—someone in the family had to be, Mark supposed.

"Does he like adventure?"

Mark searched the somber boy's dark eyes, wondering where he was going with this. "Not hardly . . . unless you count having cereal once in a while instead of his usual bagel."

"Then you are very lucky." Nodding in agreement with himself,

Antonio turned to look out the window again as they passed a lookout point over the lake.

Some vacationers were waterskiing, skirting around fishing vessels where tiny figures struggled with nets. The square pontoon shuttle that offered a direct, but not always reliable, service from Mexicalli to Flores puttered its way toward the Mexicalli dock, which was just a speck in the distance.

"If I had been the big brother," Antonio spoke up, seemingly transfixed by the passing scenery, "I would not let Enrique explore so much or leave the house without telling where he was going. And if it put him to lose, I would not let him go." The boy turned to Mark with a broken smile. "He would not like it. He would call me *abuelo* for it, but today he would be alive, no?"

"Probably so, amigo." Mark thought of Blaine. He'd not called his worrisome brother "grandfather," but he had referred to him as "the old man" after Blaine lectured him on his less-than-perfect pursuit of life.

"But I would only tell him such things because I love—" The word caught in the child's throat, backing his anguish to his eyes, where it welled over.

Unfastening his seat belt, Mark slid over to put a comforting arm around the boy. "You go right ahead and cry, amigo. Better to get it out than hold it in."

"I should have told someone when Enrique left," Antonio cried into Mark's rib cage. "But he . . . he said that he would come back before bedtime . . . that he had important business with our uncle."

Mark stiffened at the mention of the man with beady eyes. "Did you tell the authorities this?"

Antonio nodded. "*Sí*, and they talk to Tío Lorenzo, *pero*—"

"But what?"

"*Pero* Tío Lorenzo said that Enrique came for the novena the next day and after it, he left to return to the orphanage." Antonio sniffed hard, recovering most of what had come close to soaking into Mark's shirt. Regardless of his aversion to kids' runny noses, Mark held the boy tight against him, willing to take whatever leaked if it would ease the grief.

"If I had remembered that it was the novena," Antonio said shakily, "then I would have gone to pray for my *madre y padre* and eat the turkey too." He straightened with a shot of indignation. *"Pues,* I have only two years less than Enrique."

"And because you were more cautious, you will have many years more," Mark told him. "Age doesn't make a guy smart. That's up here." He tapped his temple and winced.

Bad idea. It not only hurt, but drove home the point that smart had not been in residence when he decided to throw it all out and have a little fun. Soon as that supper party was over, he was hitting his new sack, even if it was an air mattress. Staying at the hacienda would enable him to sleep a little longer. Not only could he keep an eye on the place, but Soledad didn't get as early a start as the chickens, the braying burro, and the protesting cows next to the parsonage.

◆

While Mark napped that afternoon, Corinne and Soledad tackled the paint and crayon marks on the wall. A phone call to Capitán Nolla revealed that he'd taken pictures after they left and was investigating. As they spoke, she envisioned him sitting at his desk, full of himself and cigar smoke, dismissing the case as vandalism by kids.

That man couldn't find his backside with both hands, she thought. She painted over the words that hadn't come off, while Soledad made up the beds at the hacienda. Since Mark announced he was staying over, they'd decided it was time to move in as well. With the three of them in residence, perhaps further mischief would be discouraged. And just in case it wasn't, she had a borrowed baseball bat from the orphanage sports closet.

"You will knock a home run with their heads, no?" Antonio observed, highly amused by her choice of weapon.

"If Soledad doesn't get them with her broom," Corinne quipped.

To keep the boy's thoughts away from the funeral, she'd asked Antonio to help her bring over her clothing, which she placed in a makeshift closet. With the curtains hung and the boxes put away, the rooms called to be occupied. While Mark and Corinne attended Doña Violeta's dinner party, Soledad, with the help of her sister, was to finish moving in her and Mark's belongings.

No doubt that by the time Corinne and Mark returned, every room in the house would be protected by a cross of some nature. Not that the crosses themselves had any power. When Corinne pointed that out to Soledad, the housekeeper nodded in full agreement.

"So I said, Corina," she said, as if Corinne had been loco to suggest anything else. "But it cannot hurt to put the crosses up to scare away the *brujas,* so that He will not have to battle them, no?"

It was pointless to argue. Soledad's faith in Christ was without question. And if the crosses made her feel more safe, fine. Corinne would stick with faith and the baseball bat.

While she and Mark were gone, Father Menasco offered to stay with the women, since the housekeeper refused to stay in the house after dark, with or without crosses, unless a man was present.

As if the man sprawled on the air mattress in the other room could do much to help them out, Corinne thought as she entered her room after dropping Antonio off at the orphanage.

Although Mark *had* been thoughtful in bringing Antonio a rocket for Enrique's funeral. It had brightened an otherwise dreadful experience for the boy. And on the way home in the SUV, Corinne couldn't make out what Mark and Antonio were saying to each other, but when Mark disconnected his seat belt and held the crying child, her peeve at his night on the town melted. The man was a screwup, she thought, but he wasn't quite as self-absorbed as she'd initially thought. Maybe he'd be fine as a friend.

Deciding to take pity on him and give him a few minutes more shut-eye, she hurried through a quick shower, complete with hot water that remained at the selected temperature—as long as Soledad knew ahead of time not to turn on any other faucet. Afterward, she removed her yellow sundress from its sealed dry-cleaner bag and put it on. With Mexicalli's bug-friendly climate, such precautions were wise if one preferred to be the only occupant of a garment.

While she dried her hair, she heard the shower running again and assumed that Sleeping Beauty had awakened and was preparing for the party in his honor. Which reminded her that he had looked beautiful to her for stopping that cart that day . . . until she found out who he was.

Do you think that they were worse sinners? I tell you no; but unless you repent you will all likewise perish.

Corinne stopped, blow dryer in hand, as the words of Father Menasco's sermon at the funeral popped into her mind. He'd been addressing the reason for the tragedy of Enrique and his parents, lest anyone read some divine judgment into it, as people were inclined to do—both in Jesus' time and now. Accidents happened, and only God can tell us why in His time. That had been the message, but Corinne had been so absorbed in her suspicions surrounding the circumstances of Enrique's disappearance that she hadn't paid close attention.

But she wasn't the one Father Menasco was speaking to. She had never thought the tragedy was any sort of divine retribution. *Like hangovers are . . . or maybe community service for DUI.*

She put the dryer down. She was being ridiculous. God wasn't telling her that it was okay for Mark to destroy his brain cells with tequila or waste his talents and jeopardize a bright future. People made mistakes, and sooner or later they paid the consequences. They got what they deserved.

That was in the Word. End of story. She certainly didn't need to repent; the hunk in the shower did. She shook her head to dislodge the thought. The last image she wanted in her mind was that soaped-up, gym-chiseled body.

"Get a grip," she ordered the young woman in the mirror over her dresser. "You don't even like him." Her image, or was it her conscience, mocked her. "Okay, I like him a little . . . but he's bad news. You know it and I know it."

Without thinking, she shook her bottle of perfume, taking her agitation out on it before putting on a few dabs of the expensive scent. Her emotions were tangled enough without adding too much thought to them regarding Mark Madison.

Standing back to get a fuller view of her efforts, Corinne gave herself a nod of approval and grabbed her devotional book. Not having had time that morning, she intended to catch up on the day's reading while Mark finished getting ready.

Unable to access the kitchen through the occupied utility bath, Corinne went through the main hall to grab a glass of tea from the fridge. She sat at the stained and nicked red Formica table in the center of the room and opened the book to her marker. She took a sip of tea as she viewed the topic of the day—Luke 13:1–5.

Do you think they were worse sinners?

Corinne didn't even read the rest, for at that moment, the bathroom door opened and Mark Madison emerged, a towel wrapped tightly about his narrow waist and hips.

Caught in a visual standoff, he found his voice first. "You look gorgeous."

Gorgeous wasn't quite the word that came to Corinne's mind regarding him, but it was close.

"Thanks," she mumbled. Despite herself, her demure gaze followed his retreat as he headed for the salon. Even with his hair wet and shaggy from towel drying, the trapezoid shape of Mark's upper torso and well-formed legs were a feast for the eyes. As she heard the slide of the salon double doors closing, her gaze fell to the bold-faced passage she'd just read.

Corinne closed the book as if stung by it. *All right, Lord, I repent.* She wasn't exactly sure why, but she felt as though it was definitely the thing to do.

CHAPTER 12

The home of Doña Violeta Quintana de la Vega was unobtrusive from the main street. Its stucco wall was as plain as those that joined it, washed white except for the masses of bright bougainvillea that spilled over the wall. A servant swung open the arched Jacobean-dark oaken doors, inviting them to enter a formal garden of ancient boxwood, roses, and azaleas that put the hanging vines to shame as the song of caged exotic birds welcomed them.

"Señorita Diaz, Señor Madison . . . *la* Señora is expecting you," the servant said. His English accented but precise, the short man reminded Mark of a penguin, dressed in a dark, short-jacketed suit with a satin cummerbund. His closely cropped graying hair even came to a point over his brow.

"*Gracias*," Mark said, putting a gentlemanly hand to Corinne's back.

"*Gracias*, Gaspar," Corinne said, shooting through the entrance as if Mark had tried to brand her.

It's going to be a long night, he thought as Gaspar led them to the colonnade that bordered the patio on two sides. Adorned with classical vases brimming with foliage and crowned with colorful geraniums, stars of Bethlehem, and begonias, it sheltered the entrance to the main rooms of the house. Voices drifted through the open door of the salon.

Massive furniture lined the walls to accommodate the room's high ceilings, commanding attention. The rich patina of the wood caught the light from Victorian-style lamps on the tables arranged around the period settees and chairs where Doña Violeta held court with some of her guests. Upon seeing Mark and Corinne, their hostess rose, slowed by the stiffness of age, to greet them.

"*Bienvenida,* my friends."

Corinne rushed forward. "Don't get up, Doña Violeta. We'll come to you."

Mark's eyes followed the sway of Corinne's figure in the form-fitting sundress. She was as hot in yellow as she'd been in bright pink at the wedding.

But I've seen lots of hot babes, Mark told himself, shaking off the unbidden bolt of attraction.

"You talk to me as if I were an old woman," their hostess chided as Corinne gave her a hug.

Though he'd never put a face to his idea of a dream girl, he thought now that it would be something like Corinne's.

"Doña Violeta," Mark said, slapping down the renegade thought as he folded his hostess's arthritis-gnarled hand within his and pressed it to his lips. It was a cavalier gesture, not something Mark normally did, but something about this place—indeed, something about Doña Violeta herself—demanded it. "It is indeed a pleasure."

The elderly woman's eyes twinkled in delight. "Indeed no, Señor Madison—"

"Mark," he insisted.

"Indeed, Señor Mark, the pleasure, not to mention gratitude, is all mine. But for you, I might have wound up in the lake with my Chiquita." Remembering that she had other guests, Doña Violeta introduced them.

"I believe you know my nephew and Mexicalli's mayor, Don Rafael Quintana."

Don Rafael stepped forward, mimicking Mark's gallantry by kissing Corinne's hand.

"No need to kiss mine," Mark kidded as the mayor turned to him. Judging from the quizzical expression and sudden stillness in the room, the joke was lost on present company. Mark thought he saw Corinne's lips twitch—probably at her embarrassment rather than his joke.

Born of a newer generation, Diego Quintana gave Corinne a kiss on the cheek and shook Mark's hand. "How is the project going?"

"Great, if I can find a contractor who will do it."

"Perhaps later," Don Rafael spoke up, implying that he might have someone in mind.

"And Corina," Doña Violeta went on, "you know Dr. Krump from the bed-and-breakfast."

A round man with a touch of white edging the temples of his slick brown hair, Dr. Krump moistened his thin lips beneath a sparse pencil mustache, taking in Corinne from head to toe as if she were the main course. Stepping forward, he clicked his polished black shoes at the heel with Hessian precision.

"Yes, hello, Dr. Krump," Corinne said.

"I take it the funeral progressed as desirous as such things go?" he asked in his clipped German accent.

Corinne nodded. "As well as can be expected."

"I am so sorry, little Corina."

Shades of Colonel Klink. All he needs is a spectacle, Mark reflected as the little German gave Corinne a loud, wet smackeroo on the cheek.

"Dr. Krump is a retired geologist from the University of Heidelberg," their hostess told Mark.

"Herman Krump, at your service."

He had a firm but jerky handshake that made Mark glad that his headache was gone. "So how is retirement treating you, sir?"

"It goes well that I live now where once I only visit."

"Good for you." Taking note of the asthmatic groans the German gentleman made with each breath, Mark wondered if it was wise to take up retirement in a mountain village where the air was so thin.

With the introductions behind her, Doña Violeta clapped her hands. "Now you must tell Gaspar what you will have to drink with us."

"I recommend the port," Diego suggested. "Not too sweet. Just right."

Corinne gave him a gracious smile. "I think I'll stick with lime and soda, if you have it."

"But of course, we do. I knew you were coming, did I not?" their hostess assured her. "And you, Señor Mark?"

Mark started to tell her to ditch the señor, but knew by now that that was out of the question. Formality was ingrained in the lady. "I think I'll try the same, if you don't mind."

Ignoring the wary lift of Corinne's brow, he waited until she had seated herself between Diego and Rafael Quintana, leaving him the place next to Dr. Krump.

"I heard that you have had trouble with vandals at the hacienda," Diego spoke up. "Have you any idea who would do such a thing?"

Corinne shook her head. "No more than Capitán Nolla."

The laconic bent of her voice brought Don Rafael to Nolla's defense. "You must remember, señorita, that Capitán Nolla is only one man in a town of hundreds."

The mayor must be counting the livestock, Mark thought, watching as Diego Quintana leaned back against the settee and stretched, leaving an arm around Corinne. The top three buttons of his shirt were unfastened, exposing more of his chest than Mark cared to see and a silver pendant big enough to anchor a small boat—most likely his own handiwork.

"I know that," Corinne said, unaware of anything but the topic at hand. "But I at least expected him to dust for fingerprints or something."

Don Rafael assumed a patronizing posture. "And whose fingerprints would we compare them to, even if we *could* take such prints from the hacienda? Mexicalli is not like your big cities."

Dr. Krump bristled like a porcupine on Corinne's behalf. "But such allowedness must not be permitted."

"And it won't be," Mark assured everyone. "I'm going to be living there from now on." He caught Corinne's pointed look, reminding him that he had been there the night before to no avail. "As are Corinne and Soledad. With the three of us present, I doubt vandals will show up again with their paint and crayons."

"Crayons?" Doña Violeta echoed. "Like the little children use?"

At that moment, Gaspar returned with the lime and sodas.

"Well, it was surely young vandals," Krump decided aloud.

Once Doña Violeta saw that Mark and Corinne had been served, she raised her glass. "Enough of brigands. I have invited you here to honor my rescuer and hero. You were not present, Dr. Krump, but at the fiesta, a vicious pig spooked my Chiquita and away she ran, throwing me onto the floor of my curricle."

Mark wondered what Doña Violeta's reaction would be if she knew the same "vicious" rascal was now in a pen behind the hacienda.

"I was being carried to my doom," the lady went on, "when this brave young man stopped and calmed Chiquita. It is to him and his bravery that I lift my glass."

Ignoring the roll of Corinne's eyes, Mark accepted the toast modestly. "I did nothing more than any man—or woman—would do, had they been aware of your situation. As I recall, Corinne was also trying to catch up with you."

Horrified that she'd neglected to give credit to Corinne, Doña Violeta apologized. "I am such an old fool." She lifted her glass again, this time to Corinne. "And to my lovely new friend, who did so much to see that I was taken care of." She smiled, first at Corinne and then Mark. "You two are very special. I have no doubt that all of Mexicalli will be rewarded by your presence."

At that moment, Mark could hardly reply. His taste buds were still reeling from the abominable drink that withered his tongue as it went down. It was all he could do to act demure with some semblance of a smile.

◆

Despite her frail appearance, Doña Violeta was a vivacious hostess, whose vitality made Corinne feel the senior of the two. Ordinarily she'd delight in what promised to be a long night filled with stories of old Mexicalli, but the emotional upheaval of the day had begun to take its toll. Determined to remain alert, she asked for a demitasse of strong Mexican coffee when they were seated in the formal dining room, rather than more lime and soda. Once again Mark followed suit, rather than drink the dinner wine, which was as much a staple at the formal table as it was in the old country.

The hot espresso Gaspar served her was as dark as the tall sideboards and cupboards that surrounded them. Overhead, a soft starlit pattern was cast by the teardrop prisms of an elegant Victorian chandelier that had been converted to electric. Candelabras projected their own flickering firelight over the china and silver settings on a tablecloth with floral cutouts filled with Spanish lace.

Cactus figured heavily on the menu. The *Pollo en Pulque* or Drunken Chicken was cooked in fermented cactus juice.

After grace had been said over the table by Don Rafael, Doña Violeta turned a concerned face to Corinne. "I hope that you will be able to eat the chicken, since it is cooked with some spirits," she said. "I do not wish you to become ill."

"I promise, I won't. It looks delicious." Perfumed by cinnamon, chilies, and other spices that Corinne couldn't identify, it smelled and looked delicious. "Alcohol doesn't make me ill," she explained, upon seeing Violeta's confusion.

It was obvious that, to her companions, supper without a modest portion of wine was unthinkable, except in the case of illness. Corinne knew she would have to explain. "It's just because I've seen alcohol ruin so many people's lives that I've chosen to abstain from it completely."

"Haven't we all known those who have been ruined in such a manner," Doña Violeta said, breaking the uncomfortable silence.

"But food cooked in wine or whatever is wonderful," Corinne said, hoping her forced brightness might put her hostess at ease. Why had she bothered to say anything, she lamented, aware that Mark was studying her from his place of honor at the end of the table. Not one to retreat, she met his gaze head-on. But instead of derision, he gave her a supportive wink.

"It all looks delicious," he said, as Gaspar served him a rice dish with peppers, corn, and some kind of creamy cheese blended together.

Toward the end of the meal, Corinne was inclined to blame her earlier fatigue on the fact that she'd not eaten more than a half a peanut butter sandwich all day. Between the food, coffee, and Doña Violeta's fascinating stories, she was feeling much better.

She laughed as Violeta told them how she didn't like the first car that ever rode through Mexicalli, and the new ones were no better. The quickly passing scenery made her dizzy, so she rode in a car only to visit her physician in Cuernavaca, which, blessed be to God, was not often. And when she spoke of her beloved Chiquita, who was from the same stock as Violeta's very first burro, she reminisced the way most people did about their first cars.

When Gaspar removed the supper dishes, Doña Violeta looked at her hardly touched plate with dismay. "But look at what I have done. I've been a poor hostess to monopolize the conversation so."

"Not at all," Mark objected. "The food, the stories . . . I think I've been enchanted."

If anyone was enchanted, it was Doña Violeta with her guest of honor. She looked at Mark as if he could jump small buildings in a single bound. "And I did not believe that gentlemen such as yourself still existed . . . present company excluded," she added in haste. "If only I were younger, Corina would have much competition."

"Señora, I would be proud to sport you on one arm and Corinne on the other anytime."

Charm just oozed from Mark, with no effort on his part, unless one counted the task of donning a suit and tie. The colors he wore complemented his sandy brown hair and the gold-flecked russet of his eyes.

"Before we return to the past," Don Rafael said, "here is a business card of a contractor who has done work for our city before. Perhaps this will help you." He handed Mark the card as he rose from the table. "*Perdoname, Tía* Violeta, but I have important business in the morning."

Diego jumped on the departure wagon as well. "And I have buyers coming from Cancún to see my latest creations."

Undaunted, Doña Violeta raised her hand. "Gaspar, Don Rafael and Diego must leave us without dessert. See that they have cake to take with them."

Diego started to object. "That isn't necessary."

"I insist. You do not eat well without a woman to cook for you."
She reached for her grandnephew's trim waist and tugged at his
belt. "Look at you. A mountain breeze will blow you over."

Diego hugged his aunt. "That is why I always come here when
a mountain breeze is predicted." He rubbed his flat stomach.
"*Ahora,* the worst storm could not blow me away, thanks to you."

"If the señora will be so kind to excuse me as well," Dr. Krump
announced, "I also must hurry to leave. But no dessert for me,
please." He patted his belly and laughed. "I am ample safe from the
breeze, no?"

Doña Violeta put her napkin aside to rise and see her guests out,
but Dr. Krump stayed her with a raised hand. "Please to not leave
your guests. I know well my way to home, but—" He turned to
Corinne, his expression grazed by second thoughts. "But I hurry,
only unless . . . Corina is walking to our lodge?" Before she could
reply, he tapped a finger to his temple. "Silly me. So you said that
you have already moved."

"But thank you for your thought, Dr. Krump," Corinne told
him. "Have a pleasant walk." It was hard to smile, for her initial
pity had turned to discomfort. How could the man think that she'd
be interested in someone twice her age?

At that moment, the efficient Gaspar returned from the kitchen
with the dessert—three plates of caramel-drizzled vanilla ice cream
and Mexican pound cake and two wrapped packages for Don
Rafael and his son.

"Thank you, Gaspar," Don Rafael said, accepting his cake to go.
"We will see ourselves and Dr. Krump out." After giving his elderly
aunt a peck on the cheek, he turned to Mark and Corinne with a
stiff bow. "Señor *y* Señorita, *buenas noches.* May you sleep the sleep
of the angels."

Mark, who'd risen and waited politely while the parting ameni-
ties were exchanged, shook hands with the three men as they took
their leave. "Thank you for the business card, Don Rafael. I'll call
first thing tomorrow. Diego, good to see you again. Dr. Krump, a
pleasure to make your acquaintance."

As soon as the men left the room, Doña Violeta tapped the fine china plate with her fork. "And now we must eat quickly, before our ice cream melts." Her eyes sparkled with the mischief of a child. "And, if I am not mistaken, there is more in the kitchen."

CHAPTER 13

When their hostess insisted on walking Mark and Corinne to the patio gate an hour and a half later, Corinne was certain that a hurricane couldn't have blown them away. Wired from the strong coffee, she hung back, watching Violeta as she showed off her courtyard with pride. Mark was not only as attentive as the most ardent suitor, but he astonished both Corinne and their hostess when he knew the names of most of her flowers and shrubs.

"My mother was always sending me to the nursery for one kind of flower or another," he explained. "And if I couldn't get away in time, I wound up having to help plant them."

"She must be a fine lady to have you for a son, don't you think, Corina?"

"She is," Corinne replied. She'd worked with Neta Madison on a children's hospital project, not to mention knowing her from Blaine and Caroline's wedding.

"And a man who knows his flowers will know how to grow love as well." Letting her point settle, Doña Violeta pointed up at the moon bathing the patio. "It looks like a fiesta moon tonight."

"Isn't a 'fiesta moon' a full moon?" Corinne inquired, staring at the half crescent cut out of light in the star-spangled midnight sky.

The older woman laughed, clutching her hands to her heart. "I call a fiesta moon any that stirs the heart."

"It looks like it's just on the other side of the garden wall," Mark observed, a boyish wonder on his face that was absolutely endearing.

"I know what we must do," Violeta exclaimed, mischief invading her romantic mood. "If you will give me a foot up, I will look over the wall and see."

They were kindred spirits, separated only by age.

"But then," she said, suddenly coy, "you might be naughty and peek at my ankles."

The old woman and young man burst into laughter, and Corinne joined them. It was hard not to become infected by their moonstruck madness. "Doña Violeta, I can't remember when I've had a better time. It was just what I needed after this morning in Flores."

"I second that," Mark said, snaking an arm around his hostess's frail shoulders. "I want to adopt you for my aunt."

"Consider it done." Violeta pinched his cheek with affection. "And do not be surprised if you receive a delivery soon."

Mark shot her a curious look. "What kind of delivery?"

Suddenly the demure lady again, Doña Violeta tut-tutted. "A woman must have some secrets. But you will see. Until then . . ." She turned and linked arms with Corinne. "You two take care of each other. I don't like this business of vandals and such."

She stopped with them at the gate and, unable to look over her shoulder due to arthritis, twisted first one way and then the other before lowering her voice. "Don Rafael told me that he thought the boy Enrique was *murdered*."

The word raised the hair on Corinne's arms. "I knew something wasn't right. I mean," she backtracked, "I suspected as much."

"The animals found his body first, so it was hard to tell . . . but my nephew saw it and insisted that he saw a bullet hole in the torn clothes of the poor boy." Violeta shrugged. "But it could have been a hunting accident."

"Antonio talked on and on about a *caracol* that cursed his brother . . . parents too. Do you know what that's about?" Mark asked.

"A snail?" The older woman shook her head. "The Indios are very superstitious about animals."

"And witches," Mark said with a laconic twist of his mouth. "Speaking of *which*—" He grinned. "No pun intended. We have to get home. I'm afraid we've kept Soledad and Father Menasco up well past their bedtime."

"Oh no," Corinne exclaimed in dismay. "I've been having such a good time listening to Doña Violeta that I forgot all about them."

She really meant it. Their hostess was a very special person, a delicious leftover from a time when vegging out on carryout in front of the television in blue jeans and a T-shirt was never heard of and chivalry prevailed.

"Come back soon, my children." Seizing a hand of each, the elderly woman squeezed them with surprising vitality. "Do not wait for an invitation."

"You can *build* on it," Mark told her.

She raised her finger at him, teasing, "You have been among the Indios too long."

"Good night, Doña Violeta." Corinne gave the woman a hug and backed away.

"I will see you in the morning after I deliver the sweets to the children," Violeta told her. "From this day on, I will check on you myself, rather than rely on the market hearsay."

"Stop by anytime," Mark said, raising her wrinkled hand to his lips. *"Buenas noches, Doña de mi corazón."*

Being called *the lady of his heart* practically lifted Doña Violeta from the tiled patio floor. In a girlish fluster, she motioned to Gaspar to see to the gate.

As they turned away in the light of the coach lanterns mounted on either side of the courtyard entrance, Doña Violeta's euphoric voice rose above the click of the inside door latch.

"Oh, Gaspar, I had the most lovely evening I've had in ages. And that sky . . . did you ever see such a sky?"

◆

Corinne couldn't disagree. The cloudless midnight sky gave the moon full reign. It bathed the town with its light, defining with pencil-point precision the shadows of the buildings along the cobbled street, reminding her of a string of cutouts. Music and laughter from the Cantina Roja at the bottom of the plaza drifted up to them.

"Why didn't you tell me why you were so uptight about drinking?" Mark said as they walked by the dressmaker's shop. A light in the back somewhere silhouetted a headless mannequin in the front window, bedecked in the latest creation.

Jerked from the serene spell of the evening, Corinne was sharper than she intended. "Would it have made a difference?"

"It might have," he admitted. "At least I'd have understood a little better. I wouldn't have thought you such a prude."

Prude. Miss Muffet. Maybe she'd invited his assessment. Maybe she'd been too harsh on him . . . saying words she'd thought, but dared not say to her father.

"I hope I didn't sound 'holier-than-thou' tonight."

"No," he assured her. "I think everyone knew you were speaking for yourself only."

"It's just that so many people use drink as an excuse for their failures. They drink, they fail . . . go figure."

"Like me, for instance?"

Corinne bit her lip. She'd just done it again. With a plank that big in her eye, it was a wonder she could see. "I *am* holier-than-thou," she groaned.

Mark chuckled. "Hey, I don't need you to let me know that too much tequila plus too little sleep makes Mark a dull boy. My aching head beat you to the punch."

"Still, sometimes I act like I was behind the door when tact was passed out."

"No worries. It's not my place to act the judge."

The way she did with him? Okay, he didn't say it, but did he think it? Guilt swept in to stir Corinne's remorse. She heaved a sigh and changed the subject before she dug a deeper hole.

"Some day, huh? I feel as though I'm on an emotional seesaw and can't get off."

"I hear you," Mark agreed. After a few more steps he spoke again. "And since we're putting ourselves under an examining glass, something Antonio said on the way back really rattled my world. I mean, it made me think."

"And what was that?"

"I know this won't come as any surprise to you, but I'll admit I'm a screwup."

It wasn't a surprise, but when Mark the man coupled his admission with that boyish grin, it was enough to turn her knees to rubber.

"And I blamed my older brother for it, pretty much," he went on, unaware of his effect on her.

"How do you figure that?"

"Blaine is so . . . so confounded perfect." Mark ran a hand through his thick hair. "I mean, who can live up to that?" He stepped up on the next rise of the sidewalk, cupping Corinne's elbow to assist her. "And if that's not bad enough, he's a control freak. All I get are the leftovers of a project to tidy up . . . boring, with a capital *B*. Which is why I don't really sweat over them. Instead, I do what I have to do and go play. That's the one thing I *am* good at."

The connection between Mark's irresponsibility in the family business and the morning's events was lost on Corinne. "And Antonio brought this out how?"

"The more I played, the harder Blaine came down on me. Which made me more angry and determined to play more. There were times I thought he got his jollies just watching and waiting for me to mess up." Mark grimaced, lost for a moment in his thoughts. When he spoke again, it was with tortured earnestness. "I even wished he wasn't there."

Corinne put her hand on his arm. "Hey, that's normal sibling rivalry."

Mark shook his head. "No, I really hated Blaine at times for meddling in my life . . . until today." He drew a shaky breath. "That little boy opened my eyes in a way that I wouldn't take from my mom or anyone else."

Corinne felt something inside her open, something that embraced the shaken spirit of her companion. "And we shall be led by children."

"What?"

"A Bible quote . . . or close," she added.

They stopped, and Corinne leaned against the post of the overhang in front of a glassmaker's shop. Mark faced her, hands shoved in his pockets, his jaw squared against an unseen but vicious foe.

"The kid said, in a nutshell, that if *he'd* been the big brother, he would never have let Enrique do anything that could bring harm to him. That if Enrique had listened to his elders, he would still be alive."

"And you realized Blaine's hard line with you was out of love?" Corinne's heart swelled with his nod.

"And I felt so blasted guilty for hating him so much. I *really* hated him at times . . . wished he'd go away." With a poorly disguised sniff, he stared up at the rippled galvanized aluminum overhead.

"I didn't want to kill him or anything," he continued, "but I did not want a brother. And there's this little fella grieving his heart out over his brother. Ain't life sweet?" His inflection implied it was anything but.

"I guess my grandmother was right." A wistful smile settled on Corinne's lips as she pictured her mother's mom—crown of silver-white hair and smooth, pink complexion—a devout soul if ever there was one. "She used to say that we all have our devils, but—"

A terrible crash sounded from the alley running behind the glassblower's, banishing the rest of the sage wisdom from her mind.

Mark pulled Corinne into the cover of his arms and dragged her into the shadows against the storefront. Her breath stopped by the heart lodged in her throat, she searched the empty street with visions of pistol flashes exploding in her mind. But there was nothing more threatening than two dogs that chased each other out of the alley and across to the moonlit side of the street.

Her frozen lungs gave way to relieved laughter, until she met Mark's molten gaze. Her breath caught in her throat once more, and Corinne swayed in his embrace with a sudden need for protection . . . and more. So much more that she couldn't—daren't—define it. She blinked as he released her, disappointed . . . relieved

. . . annoyed that he had been together enough to step back when she had not.

He gave her a sheepish grin that told her she wasn't the only one who'd thought they were about to witness a gunfight.

"Mind if we walk on the moonlit side? All this talk about hunting accidents has made me jumpy."

Corinne didn't mind at all—if she could pry loose the toes that her heart had pounded into the boards under her feet. Whether it was from the commotion made by the dogs or the result of being engulfed in the protection of Mark's arms, she couldn't say. But she could still hear his heartbeat in her ear and feel the heat and power of his body.

Giving her rioting senses a mental shake, Corinne linked her arm in his offered one. "Consider that motion approved, seconded, and carried."

Back the emotions came, stimulated over the most innocent contact, like the playful pups that had just run by. Corinne resisted the urge to nuzzle up against the strong shoulder next to her, or worse yet, lay her head against it.

Lord, I don't need playful pups. I need guard dogs.

Lorenzo Pozas leaned against the clapboard side of the glassmaker's shop, his hand pressed against his thudding heart. He swore an oath at the mangy dogs that had startled him as he made his way from his employer's home to the lake, where his small boat waited. Who could guess anyone, save a drunk trying to find his way home from the cantina, would be out and about at the midnight hour in Mexicalli? And of all people, it would be Doña Violeta's guests from the hacienda?

He fingered the wad of cash in his trouser pants and glared, his contempt renewed, at the retreating couple, now meandering uphill on the opposite side of the street. Instead of being genuinely frightened by his warning, they had laughed at him. Worse, so had *El Caracol.* And he'd cut Lorenzo's pay for the job in half, all because that imbecile cousin of his wife had brought along a nearly empty can of paint. They had just finished scrawling the threat on the wall with the crayons when they heard someone coming.

Although Lorenzo did not believe in ghosts, the thought had gone through his mind when the front door opened and the gringo businessman and Juan Pablo, both well in their cups, had staggered in.

Getting out of the house through the back was no problem. The problem came when Lorenzo realized that he'd forgotten to leave behind the doll inside his shirt. What good was a threat without the magic doll to give the words substance?

He and Sergio waited, wet and cold, while the American and the electrician finished off the bottle of tequila that they'd brought with them and collapsed in the sleep of the dead. Only then did Lorenzo sneak back inside and place the doll on the pillow, next to the snoring gringo's head. Emboldened by the man's drunken state, he'd even snipped a chunk of his hair to show his wife, Atlahua, how brave he was. Besides, if the gringos could not be frightened away, there were other, more sinister ways to get them away from the hacienda—now that he had the gringo's hair.

For that, Lorenzo should have gotten *twice* the pay, not half.

CHAPTER 14

Living up to his name, Salvador Gonzales was the *savior* to Mark's dilemma. The Cuernavaca contractor was not only willing to send a crew to Mexicalli, but his price was right *and* he could start right away. By the end of the week, the demolition of the walls that had to go in order to combine smaller rooms upstairs into one large dormitory had been started. Support walls were stripped and waited for the arrival of steel beams before the thick studs were removed. Those that did not require moving still had gaping trenches where ancient wiring had been pulled or where water damage had taken its toll.

"Now we're making headway," Mark told Corinne six weeks after the workers had started. Having just reported his progress to Blaine, little brother was riding high.

But Mark could tell from the expression on Corinne's face that she wasn't entirely convinced. The view from the balcony off the upstairs hall was that of old plaster and debris covering the wooden floor.

"What did Soledad say?"

Mark winced. The housekeeper had scrubbed the entire hacienda from top to bottom before the work started. War had been declared. Now heavy plastic divided the living space from the battle zone. Armed with a mop and a broom, Soledad let no man pass through unless he measured up to her specifications of clean.

"Sometimes the soul must be broken before it can be salvaged," Corinne mused aloud. "I guess that applies to houses too."

Mark quirked a brow at her. "Funny. That's what Doña Violeta said this morning when she dropped by."

He really enjoyed the old lady's visits. She was interested in everything that was going on and why. That he could project what the future rooms would look like with his computer made her think that he was nothing less than a miracle worker.

"I understand that she's taken it upon herself to organize a grand opening when it's complete." Despite her wry drawl, there was a fondness in Corinne's eye that told Mark she shared the same soft spot for Mexicalli's "Señora Dulce."

"This morning she had Gaspar put a big beverage cooler of espresso in her cart . . . and she saved aside some of the day-old baked goods for the workers. Of course," Mark added on a dour note, "that little break held up progress for an hour while she dispensed her treats and chatted with them."

Corinne laughed. "That kind of 'help' we don't need. Although," she added, "it *is* sweet."

"It is a miracle," Soledad's voice traveled up from below.

"What is a miracle?" Mark asked, moving to the rail to see where she was. The housekeeper's ability to eavesdrop could make wiretaps obsolete.

Clad in her favorite yellow-and-black, Soledad came out of Corinne's room with a can of insect spray in hand, finger at the ready. "The change in Doña Violeta, how not?"

The battle of the *boogses* had become secondary since construction began, but with the erection of the plastic wall, the housekeeper now had time for vigilance on the insect front as well. Mark could only hope that she never discovered the insect bomb. They'd all wind up wearing chemical suits.

"Soledad." Corinne heaved a measured sigh, no doubt in anticipation of inhaling the fumes during her sleep later. "I thought we agreed to spray the bedrooms first thing in the morning, once we'd gone to work."

"So we said," the woman answered, shocked that Corinne should even question the fact. "But all this *work*—" She put her disdain in the word. "It has disgusted the *boogses* at all hours. *Pues,* in your room, this big spider . . ." The span of her fingers said the rest.

With a shudder, Corinne caved in with a nod of absolution. "No problem."

"What did you mean, saying it's a miracle how sweet Doña Violeta is?" Mark reminded Soledad, his interest piqued. He couldn't imagine the lady as anything but.

Resting an arm on the rail of the staircase, Soledad looked up at them. "Doña Violeta was not always so generous of heart and money."

Mark waited, watching Soledad's thoughts weigh upon her face.

"But then . . ." She shrugged. "Then her tragedy made her think about her selfishness and high manners."

"What sort of tragedy?" Corinne asked.

"It is not—" Soledad broke off with a shriek. *"Oh! Mi corazón!* It is your pig again!" She rushed off toward the kitchen, no doubt to arm herself with her pig-herding broom.

Toto was always Mark's pig, he had noticed, when the animal pulled off an escape from its pen.

With Corinne on his heels, Mark ran down the curved staircase and headed in the direction where Soledad had spied the culprit— his room. "How in the world did he get out this time?"

He didn't expect anyone to answer. In fact, he found it hard to believe that Soledad wasn't hallucinating, since he'd gone over the animal's pen to make certain there was no way it could loosen a board or dig its way out. But there it was, making its way around the empty hearth in the salon—where Mark kept the extra copies of the rolled-up blueprints for the quotes that no one was interested in.

"I allow no creatures in my house!" Soledad shouted.

As if Mark needed to be reminded for the umpteenth time. "Toto!"

Instead of going bonkers as it usually did when Mark was around, the pig ignored him. Its attention was fixed on something in the interior of the fire-blackened fireplace. As Mark got closer, he made out some movement. The pig was catching something up in its mouth and chewing for all he was worth.

"Oh-hhh . . ." Corinne exclaimed from the spot where she remained glued in the doorway.

Mark checked himself from doing a back step as he, too, recognized what was in the pig's mouth. It was a snake, big and black and still wriggling.

"You are in the oven now, Toto!" Soledad vowed, bursting into the room with her broom raised. But upon seeing the pig chomping on his victim, she lowered her weapon and backed out of the room, crossing herself. "First they disgust the *boogses*, now the snakes."

"Aren't you going to do something?" Corinne asked Mark.

He looked at the pig, which by now had eaten the snake's head. "You got any suggestions?"

By her silence, she didn't. "Where do you think it came from?"

Moving closer, Mark looked at the blackened walls of brick. "Maybe from some loosened chunks of mortar or down the chimney . . . Or it could have crawled in here from the open walls. This is an old place . . . uninhabited for what?" He glanced at Soledad. "A year or so at least?"

Soledad nodded. "I have heard that the pig can kill snakes, but never have I seen it."

"I'd rather have a cat," Corinne murmured, as if not wanting to insult the swine. "They can be trained."

"The man said, did he not, that this pig belonged to a *bruja?* Perhaps he is trained in such ways." Soledad rested her chin on the handle of her broom. "She must have been a good witch to enchant our Toto so . . . especially after yesterday."

Mark swung toward the housekeeper, incredulous. "He was out yesterday, too?"

"Oh, *sí*, Señor Mark. Almost every day now, he is out. He found the magic doll that I buried in the yard yesterday and ate it."

If he didn't know any better, Mark would swear Houdini had finally made it back to the world of the living in the form of the witch's ex-pet. The longer he lived in this place, the more surreal it became. Not only was the pig an escape artist, but it also could find buried magic dolls.

"You're telling me you buried that doll, and the pig ate it?" Corinne switched her bewildered look to Mark. "Deranged, maybe?"

"Soledad or the pig?" Mark's flippant reply earned him a scowl from the housekeeper. "Hey, this whole witch thing is weird to me, Soledad. I don't believe in this stuff."

"The pig," Corinne insisted. "Do you think it's safe to be around?"

"Pigs eat everything and anything. I checked it out on the Internet," Mark replied. And now he was an expert on swine. He wondered how Blaine would handle inheriting a snake-killing, escape artist, antimagic pig from a witch.

"Soledad," he said to the housekeeper, "why haven't *we* seen Toto if he's been out so much?"

"Toto does not like the noise the workers make. He comes only to the kitchen door to beg for treats like a little dog." The moment the words were out, Soledad realized that she'd given herself away. "And then I put him right back where he belongs."

A knowing smile spread on Mark's lips. "So *you're* the one letting him out."

"Not the night the vandal comes."

Corinne put her hands on her hips in mock indignation. "What happened to *no creatures allowed in my house?*"

"My thoughts exactly," Mark chimed in.

The grateful glance he sent her way for helping him out with the wily but endearing housekeeper was as platonic as the way he'd held her in his arms on the night they'd been startled by dogs on the way home from Doña Violeta's—yet Corinne's reaction was anything but. He'd not only moved her heart that night, but he'd moved the woman in her. And that woman did not want to be moved.

Soledad bought some time with her stretched out *"Pues . . ."* But when the calculation in her ebony gaze could find nothing to free her from her own web of disclaimers, she resorted to the Indio default answer to any question—the shrug.

Corinne couldn't help but smile. There was definitely more to Soledad's bark than her bite.

"It happens like so," Soledad began, obviously thinking on the run. "When Toto eats that doll, I know in here that he is good magic." She tapped her temple, her gaze narrowing in discovery.

"He protects the hacienda . . . like a blessing of God!" she finished triumphantly.

She nodded, satisfied with her reply, and pointed to where Toto had found a comfortable spot at the foot of Mark's air bed. Ears still perked, as if he knew he was the topic of conversation, the pig watched them watching him. Corinne would have sworn the creature's tail wagged, but curled as it was, it was hard to discern a wag from a plain dangle.

"*And* he saves much money when we go to the market."

Corinne swung her attention back to Soledad. "You've been taking Toto to the market?"

"*Cómo no,* but on a leash." Her secret out, Soledad was on a roll of triumph. "Everyone feeds him, and I find the very best prices because he amuses so much." She cast an affectionate look at the swine. "He is a good-luck pig. He belongs in this house."

"He belongs in a pen," Mark said.

Soledad crossed her arms. "Keeping Toto in the pen will put your work to lose," she warned.

Corinne knew she could end the standoff, but did she really want a pig in the house? "That's just superstition, Soledad. And Toto's likely to get hurt if he's underfoot."

"He belongs in a pen, Soledad." With all the authority of the jefe, Mark scooped up the pig. "End of story." He turned to Corinne. "You're not buying all this, are you?"

"The magic no, but—" She shuddered. "He did kill the snake. I hate snakes."

Toto squirmed in Mark's arms. He wasn't a big pig, but he was heavier than he looked. "We can get a cat. Doña Violeta said the other day that one of hers had kittens."

"But what if it doesn't hunt snakes?"

"*You* want to live with a pig?"

Corinne squashed a ready retort about already living with Mark. After all, it wouldn't be true. "If Soledad can keep him bathed and clean . . ." She hesitated, wondering if she was hearing herself correctly. "I mean, people do keep pigs as house pets."

Soledad caught her breath. "And they are not witches?"

"No, they are not," Corinne assured her. "The pigs are a special breed trained to be house pets. People pay good money for them."

"I am *not* hearing this," Mark said, shifting the contented pig in his arms.

"*Cuánto* . . . how much money?" Soledad's thoughtful expression suggested that a future beyond the chopping block might lie ahead for Toto.

At that moment, a horn sounded at the courtyard gate. Through the window, Corinne spied the nose of a truck through the wrought-iron rails, but the setting sun glazed it, making it hard to discern the color.

"Maybe that's the supplies I ordered to be delivered this morning from Cuernavaca." With an exasperated breath, Mark put the pig down. "I leave the fate of the pig for you two to decide."

As he started out the front door, Toto fell in behind him. Corinne had to admit, Toto was cute—at a distance. His pinkish curled tail bobbed with each trot.

Soledad stepped next to Corinne, crossing her arms in satisfaction. "I think Señor Mark has made the right decision, no?"

With a laugh, Corinne gave the housekeeper an impetuous hug. "Yes, I think *he* did." Had the outcome been anything else, both she and Mark would have been in the oven. "But I am serious about keeping Toto bathed."

Soledad crossed herself. "*Cómo no,* I am already bathing him every day. Did you not smell his soap? It is orange citrus."

Corinne screeched to a mental halt. "*My* orange citrus bath gel?"

Undaunted by Corinne's mingle of ire and incredulity, Soledad shrugged. "*Cómo no?* He is accustomed to the orange blossoms around his pen."

Well, heaven forbid that Toto the pig suffer scent shock. Chuckling despite herself, Corinne retreated to the courtyard to see what was going on. Besides, arguing with Soledad was a lot like charging windmills. One might make some headway, but all in all, it was a no-win situation.

CHAPTER 15

To her surprise, Mark and Juan Pablo were busy untying ropes that secured a pickup load of furniture. *Nice furniture,* Corinne thought, taking note of the dark mahogany head and footboard of a bed and matching chest of drawers. There were a mattress and box spring and a large secretary. Perched on top, its back secured to the cab roof of the truck, was a leather chair.

"Buenas noches, Señorita Corina," Juan Pablo said, peering around from the back of the vehicle.

"Buenas noches, Juan Pablo. It is good to see you."

Corinne managed a smile, but it was thinned with disgust. Evidently Juan Pablo's brother-in-law had made a sale. Just when she thought Mark was progressing from self-indulgence to hard work.

"Hey, look at this," Mark called out to her. A kid-at-Christmas excitement infected him. "This must have been the surprise that Doña Violeta kept alluding to."

"Doña Violeta?" she repeated. "You mean Doña Violeta sent this . . . for *free?*"

Mark, who'd climbed up on the pickup bed to untangle one of the lines, gave her an incorrigible grin. "O ye of little faith."

Corinne wrestled between being glad for him and peeved at him. Mark's problem was that everything came so easily for him. Whatever mess he got into, he could either buy or charm his way out. She watched as he shifted the load, his sweat-fitted T-shirt moving with him like a second skin.

Muscles had no right to ripple like that. She crossed her arms against the unbidden provocation to her senses—not unlike that of the predusk breeze catching the bougainvillea spires that spilled over the courtyard walls with its faint breath, making them quiver ever so slightly.

"Although, I was hoping it was the supplies from Cuernavaca," Mark admitted. "They should have been here this morning."

"Then I am sorry that is not the case for your sake, Señor," Juan Pablo spoke up with a doleful look. "It always puts me to satisfaction to order from the local store."

The plumber nodded to where some of the arches supporting the second-floor overhang had been removed and temporary posts of nailed-together two-by-fours put in their place. "They replace the whole arch when only part is rotten? That is much presumption, in my humble opinion."

Glad for the distraction, Corinne pretended to study them, too, focusing on Juan Pablo's disapproval. She'd had concerns about hiring outside the village. At least when no one showed up, Mark could track them down to find out why. But to date, things seemed to be going well.

"I wondered the same thing," Mark answered. "But fact is, Gonzales gave us a contract price, so if he wants to put more into the project than needs be, that's his problem."

"Perhaps." The plumber didn't seem as confident as Mark. "Perhaps not."

Mark was unruffled by the man's doubt. "What, are you a carpenter too? Juan of all trades?" he teased.

The idiom threw the villager. "*Qué?*"

Not that Juan Pablo would laugh. Unlike his brother Juan Pedro, who laughed at everything, business was business.

"It's an English saying that means you can do all kinds of work," Corinne explained.

The plumber's expression brightened. "Ah, *sí*. For plumbing and electricity it is a necessitation to be able to fix what must be pulled apart, no?"

"You're right about that." With a wry chuckle, Mark jumped to the ground, but as he made his way around the truck to join Corinne and Juan Pablo, he stumbled.

His startled oath was followed by a loud squeal. In an instant, Toto barreled around the pickup and bolted straight for the house.

"That blasted pig had better learn to stay out from under my feet or he's going to the butcher, magical or not."

Juan Pablo didn't bother to look after the pig as it rushed into the house. Livestock running loose in Mexicalli was not an unusual sight.

"*Pues,*" he said, pulling down the tailgate. "We must hurry to get your furniture inside. I have much work this coming week to prepare for the fiesta."

"What, another fiesta already?" Mark eased a matching leather ottoman out from between a swivel desk chair and the mattress. "Sheesh, you guys have one a month or what?"

"It's the Festival of Saint James," Corinne informed him. "And yes, there is one almost every month. You'll hear all about it in church Sunday . . . *if* you go." She hadn't seen him attend since his arrival.

"You can fill me in." Mark gave her a wink and offered her the ottoman. "Think you can handle this?"

Another strike against him on her scorepad. The man seemed to avoid church like the plague.

"Wait," he said on second thought. "Maybe you should carry in the chair cushion or—"

"I can handle a stool." With *I am woman* insistence, Corinne took it from him. Her mistake was instantly evident. The stuffing topped a base made of lead, making it much heavier than it looked. Refusing to let on, she waddled under its weight toward the house. She was woman . . . stupid woman, but woman nonetheless.

"Perhaps if we hurry ourselves," Juan Pablo said to Mark in the wake of her retreat. "I can be home before the moon takes over the sky and my Maya is put to romance without her man, no?"

On reaching the front door, Corinne rested the ottoman on the rise into the hacienda from the courtyard, heaving a breath somewhere between a pant and a sigh. She'd seen Juan Pablo with his wife at the market, walking with a protective arm around Maya's plentiful waist, or sitting together in church, sharing a hymnal.

Wiping perspiration from her forehead, she shoved down a rise of envy and despair with resolve and picked the stool back up. In God's time, she'd know such joy. She just had to wait on Him and not take less than she'd asked for—which meant Mark Madison.

Granted, romantic notions regarding him plagued her, but Corinne had no place for a self-indulgent unbeliever in her life. Perhaps there was a place for him in her heart as a friend. After all, they'd shared some secrets—his reason for not taking the easy way out, her repugnance regarding alcohol. But the way he stirred her as a woman meant no more than the breeze moving the bougainvillea blossoms.

I need someone more reliable than the breeze, she thought, putting the stool down in the salon. For good measure, she gave it a little kick. It worked on the stool, which moved, but the thoughts regarding one irresponsible but charming gringo would not. *And now,* she thought as she limped out of the room, *I have a sore toe.*

The following morning Mark was awakened by Soledad's frantic rap on the salon door. "Señor Mark, it is after the rooster's crow, and the supplies are here from Cuernavaca."

Mark rolled over in the comfort of his new bed, with which his thoughtful benefactress had included a box of linens, and squinted at his travel alarm. Nine o'clock? He groaned, tossing back the covers in a sleep daze. He hadn't set the alarm because the workmen usually got him up and moving by now. Swinging his legs over the side of the bed, he struck something warm, round, and bristly. Its startled squeal impaled Mark's sluggish senses. Before he could recover, the sliding door cracked open just enough for the intruder to make its escape.

"Soledad?" Annoyance strangled Mark's voice. "How did this pig get in here?"

"*Pues—*"

Exasperation edged in. It always began with that word. "Never mind," he called out, pulling on jeans over his boxers. As he stood, his right foot would not follow the lead of the left, wedging somewhere around the knee. With a grunt, Mark hopped around on one foot, trying to push out the object blocking his pant leg.

"Mark?" Corinne sounded uncertain from the other side of the door. "You'd better come see this."

She was usually up and gone by now, but then they'd both worked late setting up and arranging the furniture. It was hard to keep the impatience from his voice. He wasn't exactly Clark Kent *à la* Superman in a phone booth. "I'll *be*" —a shoe popped out ahead of his foot—"right there."

"Omigosh, they're coming through the gate."

And what was wrong with that? The courtyard was big enough to stack the supplies to one side and still use the other. "I said I'll—"

A horrible scraping noise, akin to a log of chalk on a giant blackboard, blotted out the rest of Mark's answer. Outside, someone chattered like an excited monkey in high-pitched Spanish over the roar of an engine.

"Ay de mí!" Soledad rushed past Mark as he emerged into the hall with Toto at her heel. She stopped, peering over Corinne's shoulder through the open entrance as if she beheld a monster rather than a delivery truck.

Corinne bit her lip. The slow shake of her head sent a shot of panic through him. Soledad got hysterical over something as inconsequential as her *boogses,* but Corinne wasn't as easily rattled.

"What?" Even as he said the word, Mark bolted to the door and looked outside in the direction of the commotion at the gate.

Or rather, *in* the gate. A giant delivery truck was wedged in the opening of the stone wall, and the intricate, hand-forged gates lay twisted off their inset hinges to either side of the bull-nosed vehicle.

Mark swallowed the oath that came to his lips. Waving his arms at the driver, he vaulted onto the patio. "Stop! Don't!" A sharp stone gouged his unshod arch, stopping him short on the lawn. While he hopped toward the gate, throbbing foot in hand, the driver of the truck gunned the engine.

"No, no, no, no, no!"

Despite his pain-grazed protest, the behemoth on wheels pulled back through the opening. The screech of metal against stone riddled every nerve in his body, making his bruised foot complain even more. In seeming slow motion the truck broke free and rolled backward. It struck a gnarled cypress on the other side of the dirt drive that had guarded the entrance for at least a hundred years, meeting its match with a ground-shaking thump.

The driver's companion bobbed up and down in fast forward, spitting Spanish at the driver of the truck. Aside from a few words, most of the phrases Mark had not learned in academic Spanish, so he had no idea what the guy was saying. All he knew was that now the little man was pointing at him and expounding with the same vigor.

Mark turned toward Corinne and, still holding his wounded foot, nearly fell over. "Will you tell him to wait until I get some shoes on?"

The sound of a thousand pistol cracks split the air, cutting through the rumble of the truck's engine. Awash in another tide of disbelief, Mark swiveled in time to see the truck, trailer tipped as though finished with the entire scene. In its wake lay a pick-up-sticks pile of lumber and miscellaneous supplies, interwoven with the metal bands that once held the various sizes of wood together.

Soledad came up behind him, his Dockers in her hands. *"Dios mio!* look what those fools have done to your gate."

Mark shoved his feet into the shoes. "And they are going to pay," he growled. He marched forward to meet a short, stocky man, with a scowl as dark as his hair, coming through the gate. "What are you do—*Qué hacen ustedes?"*

But when the driver answered in rapid Spanish, Mark realized his mistake and held up his hand. *"En ingles, por favor."*

"I deliver," the driver said, shoving his thumb at the broad, hairy expanse of chest showing through the open neck of his sweat-stained shirt, "you"—a thick-knuckled forefinger addressed Mark—"paint." It then swung toward the side of the truck where the paint and rust that covered the rest of the cab had been scraped off by the gate to reveal gray metal.

"Oh, no." Mark shook his head. The truck clearly needed a paint job long before today. Besides, it wasn't his fault if the idiot had no depth perception. *"Es su error."*

The driver stared at Mark, long and deliberate, as though deciding whether or not to take the disagreement to a physical level. From behind, his companion babbled something about being in the oven. Although the night cool still lingered, Mark felt as though the temperature had been turned up to noonday hot as the man nodded in agreement. When the driver reached down into the top of his mud-stained work boots, the hair prickled at Mark's neck.

"Are you sure you want to do that, amigo?"

Mark emphasized the amigo part. Without appearing as though he wanted to duke it out, he tried to subtly assume a defensive martial-arts position. He'd worked his way to a brown belt, but hadn't kept up the discipline, much less used the training, once he'd broken up with the pretty instructor.

Instead of pulling the anticipated blade from his boot top, the man produced an invoice and unfolded it with a snap. "Sign. I go."

"Usted rompió el camión," the chatterbox injected, jabbing an accusing finger at Mark from behind the bigger guy.

Mark had seen the type—the kind that starts a fight and then backs off to watch.

"He says that you broke the truck," Corinne translated at his shoulder, giving Mark a start. To his further surprise, he noticed she was leaning on a baseball bat as though it were a cane.

"I got that." Much as Mark didn't want any kind of physical confrontation, a part of his pride was pricked that she obviously thought he needed her protection.

"Would you like me to take care of this?" She cut him a sidewise glance, a hint of a smile playing at the corners of her mouth.

If those blue eyes worked on the deliverymen the way they did on Mark, she'd have them paying for the paint job. "Be my guest, señorita. I hate kung fu fighting before breakfast."

The conversation that ensued was too fast for Mark to understand. At least he didn't think he understood. Surely they weren't talking about baseball. Corinne smiled a lot, occasionally swinging the bat pendulum style from her waist and motioning with her head toward the orphanage. No, they were talking about the hospital. Was she asking the driver not to put him in the hospital?

Gradually, the driver's fierce look dissolved into a nod and, at the mention of *rosarios*—prayers—a grin. He dug into his pocket and produced a paper bill.

"*Para el equipo de béisbol para los niños.*"

That much Mark understood—baseball equipment for the kids. Was that why she'd brought out the bat? His wounded ego wavered with uncertainty.

"*Gracias*, señor. You are a generous man," she told him, pocketing the bill in her skirt pocket.

"And Mark and I will pray for your speedy recovery and ask for prayers for the same at the orphanage chapel." Corinne nudged Mark. "Go on and sign the paper."

"We haven't checked to see if everything is on it," he pointed out.

Corinne laughed, a lyrical sound made to distract from the whisper she gave him from behind her hand. "Some things must be taken on faith or fist," she whispered, reaching out to take the invoice.

So she *had* thought he needed her protection. "Hey, I've had martial-arts training. All I needed was help with the translation."

She ignored him. "All *I* need is a pen," she said through a smile, making a pretense of signing the invoice with her hand. "*Una pluma?*"

"*Oh, sí,* señorita." As though he couldn't do enough for the señorita, the driver hastened to the cab for the pen she requested.

"And I don't think it takes much *training* to take on a guy who's just had gallbladder surgery. But if you want to have at him, go for it."

So that's who was in the hospital. Mark regrouped his thoughts, not ready to roll over just yet. "You're the one who's so nuts about the money, Miss Penny Pincher. A paint job just adds to the cost . . . not to mention shorting us on supplies. Vendors do it all the time."

"*Faith*, Mark. I know you put little stock in it, but sometimes we just have to rely on faith." Looking as if she held the monopoly on that particular commodity, she took the pen the driver handed her and passed it and the invoice along to Mark. "Just sign the paper."

"I'll remind you of that when the bills come in and we are over budget." Mark scribbled his initials on the shipping receipt.

All the while his ego shrieked with three aspersions cast at his courage, business acumen, and spiritual foundation. At least two of the three were misses. Yes, he believed in God and Jesus. But he didn't believe that faith trumped a man's own abilities and efforts. If a guy was careless, he missed sometimes. Other times, luck prevailed.

"Maybe you can charm Doña Violeta into paying them off—if his employer's insurance won't cover the paint job."

So that's what her superiority was all about. She was still miffed because his new friend had bailed him out with furnishing the salon. Never mind that the furniture was simply on loan—no way was he going to tell her that. Far be it from him to deprive her of her righteous indignation.

Pleased that he'd completed his business, the driver shook Corinne's hand, avoiding Mark altogether. *"Muchas gracias,* señorita.*"* The rest of his parting words were lost to Mark's distracted ear.

As the truck took off down the road, Mark picked up where he'd left off. "So it's okay for your daddy to help you, but it isn't okay if someone decides to help me? Is that what you're trying to say?"

CHAPTER 16

Corinne could not believe her ears. She'd come out, armed with Soledad's bat because the driver looked as if he were prepared to eat Mark alive and serve the leftovers to his excitable friend. Now Mark had the nerve to attack her for it?

"I said that it's easy to be *spiritual*"—his inflection mocked her—"when Daddy provides everything you need. Anyone can lean on the kind of faith that provides one's every wish."

"Faith is anything but having one's every wish met. Don't confuse needs with wishes." She swung the bat up onto her shoulder. "And don't mix up wounded egos with faith issues."

"And just what does that mean, Miss Penny Pincher?" He propped his hands on his hips, drawing her attention to the fact that he'd not had time to don a shirt.

"It means that I just saved your tush from a good thrashing."

"From a guy just out of surgery?"

Corinne mimicked his stance. "I didn't know that when I grabbed the bat. I thought the two of them were going to make mincemeat out of you."

Evoking shades of a professional boxing match, a bell sounded from the gate, breaking the toe-to-toe, nose-to-nose challenge that held Corinne and Mark a heated breath apart. Wearing a straw hat with a lavender band to match her owner's dark violet attire, Chiquita trotted through the gate pulling Doña Violeta in her upholstered cart.

"Children, children," the matron chided, a smile showing beneath the veil of her hat. "Surely some spilled lumber and a broken gate are nothing to argue over."

As though to object to the trivialization of the trauma, the stones at the entrance seemed to rumble, softly at first. Ears laid back, the burro chafed at Doña Violeta's attempt to rein it to a stop as the rumble escalated into a landslide. Not about to be caught in it, Chiquita lunged forward, but Mark managed to catch her reins, diverting the donkey's panicked bolt into a circular one as the courtyard wall disintegrated to either side of the opening.

As the dust settled, Corinne thawed from her frozen state and hurried to the cart, where the plucky little lady, unlike the last time, held fast to the rail.

"Doña Violeta, are you all right?"

Releasing the rail with one gloved hand to cover her heart, Doña Violeta nodded. "Indeed, I am fine, thanks once again to my Mark."

Running a calming hand along Chiquita's quivering shank, Mark managed a pained grin. "I think this donkey's getting used to calamity."

"And if it didn't, Mark could just use his raw brawn or black belt prowess to save the day." Corinne couldn't help herself. The man's ego was only exceeded by his luck.

Doña Violeta extended an imperious hand to Corinne. "If you would please to help me down, I would love a cup of tea and a prayer to thank God for our blessings."

"Blessings?" Mark and Corinne echoed, incredulity in sync.

The older lady tucked back her veil, her face a mirror of calm in the midst of a storm of chaos. "But of course," she said, taking Corinne's offered help to step down from the cart. "Now the gate is wide enough for *all* your delivery trucks to get through, no?"

Mark snorted. "You could pull the *Titanic* through it."

"And the gate can be widened. The art of iron working still exists," Violeta reminded them.

Her brightness reminded Corinne of how much more optimistic she needed to be. But then, Doña Violeta had not had Mark Madison to deal with.

"I'll keep that in mind," Mark said as he finished tying Chiquita to one of the original hitching posts, a lion's head with a ring through its mouth. "Just as soon as I get this mess under control."

"But you'll join us for tea?"

His simmering gaze softened as Doña Violeta plied his arm with her frail hand, and for a moment, Corinne thought the lady would have her way with the irate Mark.

"I'd love to have tea with you, Doña Violeta, and thank you for your generous loan of the furniture."

His benefactress brushed away the notion that gratitude was due with a sniff. "Nonsense."

Loan? Corinne's breath caught on the word and whooshed out as she quickly looked down . . . up . . . aside . . . anywhere but at Mark. It should have occurred to her that even Doña Violeta would not make such an extravagant and inappropriate gift.

Still, Mark could have told her.

"But," he went on, "I really have to call to find out why the workers from Cuernavaca aren't here. They should have shown by now."

"No worry lines," Violeta chastised, brushing away the furrows on Mark's brow. "I have enough for all three of us. And Mark . . . God is in control, even when it seems like He is not."

Mark smiled in return affection. "I'll try to remember that."

"That's all He asks." With that, the matron turned to Corinne. "Now, about that tea . . ."

Tea was as far from Corinne's mind at the moment as recognizing that God was in control was from Mark's. But her upbringing prevailed.

"Tea is good," she said, cupping Doña Violeta's elbow to steady her as they climbed up on the patio. "And Soledad always has water on the pilot, so it should be ready in a jiff."

"A *jiff?*"

Corinne's peeve dissolved in a smile. *"Muy pronto,"* she explained.

She was glad that she and Soledad had stayed up and put the house back to order after the furniture had been brought in and set up. Doña Violeta approved of the arrangement, even if Mark's bed had been left unmade.

While Soledad prepared the tea, Corinne gave Doña Violeta a tour of the progress to date, watching to see if the older woman's impression was the same as hers. It was futile at first. For all the feedback on Violeta's face, she might as well have kept the veil of her hat down. But as they left the ballroom with its hanging wires and rutted walls, the señora broke her pensive silence.

"And the workers from Cuernavaca did not come as promised this morning?"

"No. Unless they thought the supplies weren't here and there was no need," Corinne suggested.

"Perhaps." Something in the way the older woman said the word suggested that she had her doubts. Did Doña Violeta know something, or was she, like Corinne, merely suspicious of contractors hired outside the village?

Soledad not only had tea waiting for them in the kitchen, but fresh-baked *pan dulces*. "Nothing but the best we have for our Doña *Dulce*," she said, helping their guest into a chair at the kitchen table. "And now I will be outside, if you should need me."

"Nonsense, Soledad. You baked the treats. You must share them with us."

Soledad stiffened. "You are a gracious lady, but—"

"Sit," Violeta commanded with an old-world authority that superseded even Soledad's. But it was the same old-world tradition that prohibited a servant from taking bread with those of the noble class.

Uncertain as to what to do, Soledad sought out Corinne with her gaze. Even though Corinne was a modern woman, it had taken considerable persuasion to convince Soledad that she really was welcome to the same table with her employer.

"Do join us, Soledad."

Toto waddled in, roused by the voices from his spot in the cool-tiled shower adjoining the kitchen. To have a pig found in her kitchen was more than the conscientious housekeeper could bear.

"Ay de mí," Soledad wailed. She scooped up the pig with such haste that she nearly dropped him. "What is this creature doing in my house?" she exclaimed, speeding past the set table and a stunned Doña Violeta as if the devil himself were nipping at her heels.

Her guest started. "Is that the same pig . . ."

Corinne nodded. "I'm so sorry. I can imagine your shock, but it's not really as vicious as we first thought, and it can kill snakes."

This brought Doña Violeta up short. "Snakes?"

"Sugar?" Corinne said, trying to recoup her manners. "Yes, it got in the house, and we found it killing a snake in the salon fireplace."

Doña Violeta helped herself to the sugar and stirred her tea once, taking care not to clink the unbreakable glassware with her spoon. Still caught in thought, she helped herself to one of the sugared bread treats.

"Shall we resume our talk about Mark?" she asked, her hat making the slight cock of her head more noticeable.

"Were we speaking of Mark?"

As though she still couldn't quite believe what she'd seen, Violeta cast a glance at the back door where Soledad had retreated with Toto. "Yes . . . at least that was my intent. Matthew 23:24, I think."

"Matthew . . . what?"

While Corinne did a mental backtrack, her companion said a short grace of thanksgiving. Okay, Mark, pig, and a snake belonged in this picture, but how did Matthew get into it?

"'You blind guides, you strain out a gnat and swallow a camel.' Yes, that's it," Doña Violeta said to no one in particular. Realizing that she'd lost Corinne at their joint "Amen," she leaned over and placed a hand on the younger woman's arm. "I don't want you to make the same mistake I did, Corina. The same mistake the Pharisees did in Jesus' day."

"With regard to the Law, you mean?" Maybe after the wall crumbled behind Violeta, the shock of the pig was just too much.

After another bite of the still-warm *pan dulce,* Violeta let her gaze drift from Corinne to the open casement window over the counter. "Many years ago I was so busy sifting gnats through my idea of God's law that I let a camel through." After a sigh of relief, remorse, or both, the older woman went on. "I was so concerned with what *I* thought a Christian should be that I sifted out my prospect for happiness, judging too harshly instead of looking at my own actions."

"Judging whom, Doña Violeta?" Corinne recalled what Soledad had said—that Doña Violeta was not always so gracious and generous. Had lost love caused her change?

"That is not important. It was in the past, which cannot be changed." She swallowed a dainty gulp of tea, as though the past were with it. "Mark is a good man with a good heart. He needs a chance to prove himself and the heart of a woman who will forgive him and love him, as God charges us to do with our fellow man."

Do you think that they were worse sinners? I tell you no; but unless you repent you will all likewise perish.

The words from Enrique's funeral were totally unrelated to today . . . weren't they?

"I had a loved one who walked on the edge of faith, Corina. And I, in my self-righteousness and judgment, pushed that person off instead of closer to God and to myself. Take the words of an old woman who has lived long regretting it. Treat others with love, as you would wish to be treated if you were on the edge."

Even as her hackles raised in rebellion, there was a part of Corinne that wondered if Doña Violeta was right. Was Mark "on the edge," and was she, as a Christian, ready to push him off rather than pull him aboard?

"Mark doesn't think he needs any help for anything. If he goes off the edge, it's his doing."

"Perhaps."

There it was again, that intonation that agreed, but left the door open to doubt. The Mexicans made using it for all possibilities into a fine art.

"But what Mark does, he will have to live with. How you react to his mistakes or triumphs, you will have to live with . . . as I have these many years, because I extended judgment instead of love."

Corinne did not know Doña Violeta well enough to discuss

such personal matters, yet she felt compelled to defend herself. "So I should love it when he messes up royally?"

"Love the sinner, not the sin." Doña Violeta's hand shook, causing the cup to clatter against its saucer as she put it down. "Easier said than done, I will grant you." She thought a moment. "We waste our time fretting over that which we cannot change. Those things should be left to Him who can change them. It is our calling to focus on what we do have control over—our own reactions."

She picked up the remains of her *pan dulce* and finished it off with a delight that took years off her age. When she'd chased it with her tea, she removed the paper napkin from her lap and placed it on the table beside her plate.

"If I have misread what I see between you and my Mark," she said, shoving away from the table to rise, "then you have my humblest apologies. Please know that I would not have brought up the pain of my past if I did not fear for the same in your future, Corina. Perhaps to talk of it will grant me comfort of mind when I face my Savior, rather than bearing the guilt for having said nothing. I have only spoken because I am moved to, not out of judgment, but out of love."

Corinne hadn't finished her tea yet, but her guest was ready to leave. As she started to rise, Doña Violeta placed a restraining hand on her shoulder.

"Sit, sit. I am not so senile that I can't find my way out of the house."

"I really need to get to work anyway," Corinne objected.

"After you finish your tea . . . and perhaps think about what an old woman has shared with you."

To Corinne's astonishment, Violeta gave her cheek a motherly pinch.

"And who am I to talk about a pig in the kitchen, when I dress my Chiquita and treat her like my own child? Tell Soledad that I am sure he is a dear house pet."

Gathering up her folded gloves, Doña Violeta exited with more spring in her step than she'd had on arriving . . . as if sharing her story had lightened her load.

Recalling how she'd felt the night she'd talked about forgiving her father, Corinne understood at least the lightness of spirit. However, the message—just what she was supposed to do with regard to Mark Madison, treating him with love—needed clarifying.

Faith. Her own advice to Mark came back to haunt her. With no appetite for the rest of her *pan dulce,* Corinne shoved the plate aside and folded her hands.

All right, Father, I'll try to do unto Mark as I'd have him do unto me. But all I can do is try.

Dona Violeta's reply to Mark flashed bold in reply. *That's all He asks.*

CHAPTER 17

Discouraged, Mark stared at the pile of supplies outside the rubble of the courtyard gate. Instead of diminishing with each load he hauled inside, it seemed to grow in the blistering heat of the noonday sun. Self-pity painted a dark mental picture of Mark-against-the-world with brush strokes of Blaine's smug *Knew you couldn't do it,* the silent *I told you so* behind Corinne's tight-lipped retreat into the house, and Mark's own insecurities.

And he was alone, unless one counted the pig that lazed nearby in a cluster of wildflowers. Unlike Soledad, it refused to be driven off by Mark's bad humor. Instead it followed his progress—or lack or it—with pink-rimmed, white-lashed eyes.

Mark wiped the gritty sweat from his brow, squinting in the overpowering sunlight at the sky. If God was in control, He definitely was not on Mark's side. In addition to the delivery debacle, He'd changed the mind of Salvador Gonzalez as to the financial wisdom of sending a crew an hour's drive into the mountains from Cuernavaca. But the contractor's mind could be changed again, if Mark was willing to up the payment 25 percent.

Bottom line: with the hacienda in ruins from the initial work, Gonzalez had Mark over a barrel. He was either going to have to find more funding or—or quit. It was a dumb project, akin to making a silk purse from a sow's ear . . . or rather the reverse. The house was too fine to serve as a dormitory. It wasn't designed for such use.

How not? The Mexican expression reared up with an image of

Antonio and the other children. But for an accident of birth, they could have been born and raised in just such a house.

Try. Doña Violeta's advice surfaced in the whirlpool of Mark's despair.

Try with what? cynicism mocked, as Mark pulled a piece of two-by-four from the pile.

Faith. Corinne flung the word in his memory like a gauntlet.

Sure, cynicism countered. Her faith had come through. All the items on the bill seemed accounted for, but it was all junk grade. How had Blaine ever completed a project in this south-of-the-border *Twilight Zone*? No one and nothing could be counted on.

The whole of Doña Violeta's message streamed through his mind. *Try . . . that's all He asks.*

"I am trying," Mark shouted, slinging the board onto the pile. "I came here, didn't I?"

And now he was talking to himself.

"God, I hate this place, I hate the people, and I hate all this holier-than-thou crap. I could do better, and I don't even go to church."

"Sounds like a challenge to me."

Mark pivoted to see Father Menasco standing behind him. Enough color heated Mark's face to stop traffic in downtown Philly.

"I, er . . . I was just . . . just venting." Fixing his hands on his hips, he pretended to study the pile of supplies. "Been a bad day, Father."

"So I've heard." The priest walked over to a mound of stones from the gate and made himself a seat. "I'd suggest praying, but I see you're well underway on that account."

Mark cut a disconcerted look at the man. Was the priest laughing at him? There was no sign of humor on Menasco's face. Beyond seren-ity, some curiosity filled his gaze as the priest scoped out the damage.

"What do you mean, I was praying?"

The priest returned his attention to Mark. "You were talking to God, weren't you?"

Suddenly ashamed, Mark braced himself from the urge to look away. He was a man now and owed no explanation to anyone.

"I was yelling at Him," he answered in spite of himself. "I'd hardly call that praying."

"Any communication with God is prayer. It doesn't have to be petition or praise or thanksgiving. He hears it all."

Excerpts from previous rants shuddered through Mark's memory. He'd never thought about it that way. Rebelling against an innate certainty that the man spoke the truth, Mark dug in stubbornly. "I'm just saying I wasn't doing the *Now I lay me down to sleep* bit."

But he had been voicing his frustration and anger to a God whom he thought he'd given up on. Was that a remnant of faith?

Father Menasco shook his head, his salted black hair glistening in the sun's halo. "I imagine God gets tired of those canned words from adults, don't you? Not that they won't do in a pinch," he added in afterthought. "I've been so tired that *Now I lay me down to sleep* has served me in good stead at times."

"Look, if Corinne sent you here to save my soul or get me to ask for God's help, forget it. He hasn't been on my side in a long time." The croak of emotion in Mark's confession betrayed more than he intended.

"Oh? When was the last time you asked for help?"

"A long time ago, Father." Bitterness welled in Mark's throat as memories came rushing back. His best friend, ironically the minister's son, had hung between life and death after a skiing accident. Mark prayed with the church for a recovery that never came.

A lightbulb flash of realization filled him with surprise. He hadn't actually stopped *believing* in God, but he *had* stopped trusting Him.

"And that was God's last chance, eh?"

Father Menasco's question stopped the warm beams of wonder—or was it hope?—spreading through him. Mark Madison, screw-up extraordinaire, had given God one chance when his own life had been a series of second chances. Even Blaine had given Mark a second chance.

"That kind of puts it in perspective, doesn't it?" Mark admitted, and he didn't like the way it shook out. "Me giving the God who built the world in seven days an ultimatum, when at the rate I'm going, I won't be able to pull this project together in seven years."

Menasco gave him one of those benevolent smiles that priests always do, but this time Mark saw it—grabbed at it—as encouragement rather than part of the spiritual uniform.

"I imagine so," the priest said, "but that's between you and God." He rose, rubbed his back, and looked toward the hacienda. "Me, I came up for a glass of Soledad's iced tea. She in the house?"

"Yeah, go ahead." Mark motioned at the disorder surrounding him, hoping his stinging eyes did not betray the emotion building inside. "I've got some work to do."

By the time Menasco stepped into the hacienda, he was nothing but a vanishing blur of black to Mark. But in Mark's mind was the vivid image of a picture that hung in his old Sunday school room—of Jesus knocking on a knobless door.

Feeling as if something were ripping the door of his heart off by the hinges, Mark stumbled blindly to the privacy of the stone pile and fell to his knees.

Is that You, Jesus? Do You really want a fiasco like me in Your camp? Look what I've done. I've had everything and wasted it . . . and now, when I'm really trying—You know I am—everything is coming apart at the seams, me included. I don't know what to do except pray for Your help.

I know I've made You my last choice this time, but if You give me one more chance, I am ready. God, I just can't do this alone. Help me.

A barking dog penetrated the numb, empty fog left in the wake of his prayer. His mind and body had been strained from thought and strength, and he lifted his head from the cradle of his folded arms. He blinked, wiped his eyes, and blinked again in disbelief.

A group of a dozen or so men, women, and children were approaching on the dirt road that wound its way up the hill to Hacienda Ortiz. The women, most wearing crowns of braids that made them appear taller than the men, wore the long, colorful skirts of the Indios, while their male compadres sported *calzones*, pajamalike trousers, with loose-fitting shirts, banded at the waist with woven sashes. Patches abounded, but their poverty failed to silence the jovial gestures and expressions as they talked among themselves.

God? Mark was too spent to get wordy, but this sure had the makings of answered prayer. At the end of the entourage there was a man leading a donkey, another an ox, and each was harnessed to some kind of sledlike flatbed. Another pushed a wheelbarrow. Behind them chugged Juan Pablo's beat-up pickup.

By the time the group reached the hacienda, a force more powerful than the sun warmed Mark from the inside out, restoring his broken body and spirit. He resisted the urge to rush the suddenly quiet and somber group in a hugging frenzy, waiting for Juan Pablo, the only one Mark knew, to park.

But it was Juan Pedro, rather than his plumber brother, who climbed out.

"Buenas tardes, amigo," the electrician said, taking Mark into a big bear hug. "The peoples of Mexicalli," he continued, blasting Mark's face with liquored breath, "hear of your misfortune and are here to help *el* Señor *del Cerdito."*

The señor of the pig? Mark's translation barely registered when an elder of the group handed Juan Pedro a stoneware jar, which Juan in turn placed in Mark's hands.

"First," the spokesman said, "we give you the money we have saved for the fireworks of the festival." He removed the lid, revealing wads of small, smudged bills. "There are coins as well in the bottom."

"No es mucho, pero quizás Gonzalez bajará su precio," the Indio spoke up.

Maybe Gonzalez will lower his price? Mark gave himself a mental shake, certain his translation was wrong. No one else knew that Gonzalez had upped the price. Gooseflesh pimpled his sun-hot skin.

"How did they know about Gonzales?" he asked Juan Pedro.

"Pues . . ." Juan Pedro gave a shrug, as if such knowledge were a given. *"Todos . . .* all know it is his way."

"Reputación mala," the senior villager chimed in.

But Mark knew the higher source behind this show of support.

He steeled his jaw, making certain he wouldn't make a blubbering fool of himself.

"*Pues*, do you wish for us to move the materials into the courtyard?" Juan Pedro asked.

Thanks, Lord. It was a pitiful response for an overwhelming blessing, but there was a time for all things, and this was the season to work.

Mark motioned toward the pile. "By all means . . . and *gracias,*" he said, taking in the ragtag group with his gaze. "*Muchas, muchas, muchas gracias.*"

Mind clicking into gear, he studied the situation, trying to assess who needed to do what. "Maybe if the women and children separate the lumber into various sizes . . . "

Juan Pedro waved Mark away with his hand. "Bueno, amigo, this is not the first time we have done such work. You go call Gonzales and make him to lower his price. I am your jefe for this day."

Mark didn't want to look a gift horse in the mouth, but he wasn't sure he could put much stock in the assurances of a drinking, if not inebriated, electrician. But having been tarred with the same brush himself more than once, he considered this a day for second chances.

He gave Juan Pedro a hearty thumbs-up, when a childlike chorus drew Mark's attention toward the orphanage. Coming up the hill he saw a jeans-clad Corinne leading a gaggle of singing goslings carrying baskets and thermos jugs.

Cristo, me ama, Cristo me ama, Cristo me ama, la Biblia dice así.

The words slammed into Mark, twisting and skewering his chest until the pain became unbearable. As if the hounds of hell nipped at his heels, he beat a blurred path to the house, praying that he'd not stumble . . . *anymore.*

◆

Her grandmother always said that many hands made light work. If ever there was a day the old adage proved true, it was today, Corinne thought as she handed out another tray of hot dogs fresh from the stone barbecue pit that had been built into the corner section of the courtyard. It hadn't been used in years, but the bed was sound, and the heavy iron grate had been cleansed by fire and a fervent prayer on her part.

"That's the last of them," she announced.

Father Menasco helped himself to two of the crispy wieners before passing the tray on to the picnicking villagers. Most sat on the tarps that Corinne and Soledad had spread on the softer yard beyond the patio proper and chattered with an enthusiasm that belied their long afternoon's work.

"This is such a treat," he said. "Boiled hot dogs are good, but cooked over a fire . . ." The priest smacked his lips.

"God provides." Still, Corinne shook her head in wonder. "To think that this morning we were wondering what to do with the extra cases of hot dogs that came with our food order . . ."

Corinne had only brought the older children, those who could be trusted to help rather than get in the way. They had a grand time hauling the weeds, brush, and trimmings that the women cleared around the house and yard to the compost heap in the back by Toto's vacant pen.

She and Soledad had done what they could with the yard in their spare time, but the years of neglect had made the task formidable.

As formidable as the project woes that Mark faced. It had been all she could do to hold back guilt upon hearing how the Cuernavaca contractor had jacked up the price now that the job was underway. If she had known, she certainly would have stopped Mark from signing the contracts. But she hadn't known.

At least the villagers had taken some of the sting from the disaster. The materials were sorted and moved inside, and the stones from the gate debacle stacked in readiness for reuse. Even the twisted gate was deemed salvageable.

Next to her, Father Menasco pushed himself up and tossed his plate into the container that Soledad had put out for the trash. "I'd best be getting the little ones back to the orphanage before you and I are both in the oven."

"I could probably get them all in my SUV," Corinne suggested, watching the youngsters frolic in the far yard with Toto. They'd almost taught him to fetch, although once in a while, instead of returning the chunk of wood to the thrower, the pig sought out Mark and dropped it at his feet. "It would be quicker."

She'd never seen Mark so . . . what was the word? It might be *humble,* except that it was more than the fact that he kept thanking people over and over as he worked shoulder to shoulder with them. Reserved? Aside from his gratitude, he hadn't had a lot to say . . . except to the children. Whenever one chased Toto to where the pig dropped the stick at Mark's feet, Mark went into a clownlike tizzy of "Oh, no, not *you* again," to which the children responded with cackles of delight.

She frowned, puzzled. He was always polite, charming, and full of boyish mischief. Maybe it was what she *didn't* see that was different. Had she only been looking for fault before?

God, we already talked about this. I know You're right. I know I've had a plank in my eye.

And I haven't said a word about how I warned him to deal locally, she added, not for God's benefit, but for hers. Just because she'd confessed didn't mean she wasn't clinging to a few fragments of guilt for looking for the worst in Mark and overlooking her own flaws. *Lord, I don't want to become one of St. Matthew's Pharisees with their camels.*

"Why don't you and Mark give some of these older folks a ride home instead?" Menasco said, cutting short her confession. "Between your vehicle and the truck, no one will have to walk back to the village."

An hour later, and after much persuasion, the elder Primitivo, his two brothers, and their wives accepted Corinne's offer to drive them home. Like most of the villagers, the Indio and his brothers made and sold crafts with their women—when he wasn't healing.

In some cases, healing and witchcraft went hand in hand, but Soledad insisted that Primitivo, who had cured her warts, could only be a healer, since witchcraft was illegal. In her estimation, if the old man was a witch, he was a good witch whose power came from the saints he prayed to at his altar.

The lively chatter of the Indios faded the moment the last car door was shut. By the time Corinne put the vehicle in gear, she realized the reason for her passengers' initial reticence and subsequent silence. It was their first car ride.

Behind her, Primitivo squeezed the back of her neck rest with a crushing grip. It did not release until she braked in front of the old man's hut. Upon exiting the vehicle, he regained his composure.

"It is with much thanks that I, Primitivo, invite you to come into my home for coffee."

"I don't know, Primitivo, it's pretty late," Mark started, but Corinne cut him off. To refuse would be to insult the elder villager and his wife.

"You have the heart of an angel, Grandfather," she said, gathering up her purse from the floor.

They ducked under a canopy of vines that shaded the entrance. After Primitivo's coffee, sleep would likely be out of the question.

CHAPTER 18

Mark had only been on the main street of Mexicalli—the one that led from the poorly paved road to Cuernavaca and the one that led to the lakeside development—if one could call the cottages there development. But when Corinne had pulled onto an unpaved, rutted street behind the shops and businesses, it was like entering into yet another world, even further removed from that to which Mark was accustomed.

The white stucco of Primitivo's house turned from yellow to orange with the glaze of the setting sun, except where patches of it had fallen away to reveal the mud-and-stick construction. Near the foundation, rusted corrugated tin scraps from the roof covered some of the holes. Shaded by a vine canopy, atop which some chickens roosted, was the doorway, with a bench on each side. The elder's wife hurried in ahead of them and flipped a switch, flooding the windows with light through the poorly fitted shutters.

Mark gave Corinne a second questioning glance as he motioned for her to precede him into the humble hut.

"It's an offense to refuse hospitality," she whispered as she passed him.

He knew she was one of those *go-native* sorts, but agreeing to enter a house that looked one good wind from collapse, and for coffee—the homegrown kind that had to be taken black because it ate spoons? Exhaustion or not, it would be three days before he got another night's sleep, he lamented, ducking through the low doorway. A single lightbulb, unadorned by a shade or globe, spread its yellow light over the meager furnishings of what appeared to be a kitchen–family room combination.

Covering a hard-packed earthen floor were woven rugs, once as bright and colorful as the ones sold in the markets along the main highway between Mexico City and Acapulco, now faded and dingy from wear. Blankets and linens rolled up in *petate* mats that were suspended on nails between the rafters suggested that the enclosure also served as bedroom at night. Señora Primitivo dragged a chair and a stool from under a dinged wooden table near the kitchen wall.

A strange scent akin to pine smoke assailed his nostrils, growing stronger once Mark was seated in a rocking chair next to an inner curtained doorway that he assumed led to a back room.

"Mientras . . . while my wife makes the coffee, I would speak of your troubles, *el* Señor *del Cerdito."*

It was one thing with the kids, but the Señor of the Pig title was wearing thin with Mark. "Please, Señor Primitivo, call me Mark. *Me llamo . . ."* His Spanish floundered.

"Llámeme," Corinne supplied.

"Call me Mark," he repeated to the man, sparing his companion a grateful look.

Primitivo nodded. "Señor Marco."

"Gracias." There was no point in arguing. With the Indios, he would be lucky to get rid of the pig label.

"You have already helped us greatly regarding our troubles, Grandfather," Corinne put in.

Primitivo fetched a bottle and three chipped stoneware cups from a shelf by the window over an apartment-size gas stove, where his wife put on water to boil. Next to it was a porcelain-covered sink unit fitted with a pitcher pump.

As their host poured a clear liquid from a bottle that had served another use—what that might have been, Mark had no idea, as the label was long gone—Corinne stopped him.

"No *refino* for me, please. I prefer to wait for the coffee and leave the drink of your ancestors' spirits to their descendants."

Refino? Mark took his cup, aware that Corinne watched him, and sniffed it. The astringent bombardment of his nose left no doubt that it was some sort of liquor—strong liquor.

"You must have some happy ancestors, Primitivo," he quipped, lifting the cup to his lips. Whatever it was, it would disinfect any lingering germs in the stoneware. He'd take a small sip to appease his host and dump the rest when no one was looking.

It was just a sampling, but when it reached the back of his throat, having savaged and pickled his tongue in passing, Mark's body temp registered four-alarm status. But it was already searing its way to his stomach, tripping a choking mechanism in the process. Somehow at least a pint of it diverted to his nasal cavities, where another wildfire broke out.

Only by sheer will did he manage to set the cup down on a table before he succumbed to reflex. Tears welled in his eyes and trickled down as he coughed and spasmed, gripping the chair as though his life depended upon his hold.

"I don't think your ancestors like gringos," he rasped, once he realized that he was going to live.

At this Primitivo gave a quiet chuckle. "There is much for you to learn, Señor Marco, but I have seen with my own eyes that you have a good heart." He sobered. "And I have heard with my ears that you have made a dangerous enemy. These are matters that gringos do not understand. That is why I come to you."

Their host's last comment wiped the *I tried to warn you* look off Corinne's face. "What enemy, Primitivo?"

The Indio lowered his voice. "The witch."

"I don't think that a witch who uses crayons is much to worry about," Corinne assured the man.

Primitivo said something to his wife in their native Indio language. In response, she closed the curtains over the windows. After lighting some candles around the room, he motioned for her to turn off the overhead light.

"What I am about to tell you can put me to lose with dangerous peoples," the old man warned, pulling the stool up so that he faced both Corinne and Mark.

Mark leaned against the back of the rocker with a groan. It looked like this had the makings of a long night. His body was being preserved from the inside out and now, lights out, save for some candles, this old codger was winding up for some ghost tales.

◆

An hour later, Corinne climbed into the car, warmed against the cool night air with a brace of strong coffee and armed against the powers of evil with copal and candles—the latter at a cost of twenty pesos. Gooseflesh still pimpled her arms, not from Primitivo's warnings of witchcraft, but from the implications of past deeds. The witchcraft he described was nothing short of murder, disguised as work of an evil *naguale*—the animal form of the Indio soul—in this case, a witch.

According to the healer, whose cousin in Flores helped prepare the body of Antonio's brother, the boy had died of neither exposure nor a gunshot wound—if the boy was even Enrique. Aside from his clothes, little of the body was recognizable. But the neck of the deceased had been broken, snapped—Primitivo clapped his hands, nearly causing Corinne to jump out of her skin.

"*Matones.*" On realizing he'd spoken in Nahuatl, which was the closest dialect to the language of his Aztec forefathers, he added in Spanish, "*Asesinos.*"

Murderers.

Not even the boiled coffee had prevented her shudder, the first of many.

Primitivo went on to explain that the boys' parents had not died of a gas leak, but from the poison of burning viper's vine—another tool of witches. At least that was the word among the Indios.

Now Corinne started the engine of her SUV in front of Primitivo's humble cottage.

"I thank you again, Grandfather," she said to the man standing in the doorway, "for your concerns regarding the hacienda. But our faith must not rest on these candles and incense. They are but a gift between friends. It is Christ who protects us from evil."

Though she might witness all she wanted, she knew better than to refuse. If Soledad found out—and she would—the housekeeper would go behind her and purchase the items to use as instructed anyway.

"*Cómo no,* daughter," her host agreed in disagreement, as only the Indios could. "That is as it should be." He lifted his hand. "May you sleep the sleep of the angels."

◆

As they drove away, Mark turned to Corinne. "Am I just totally out of it due to that vicious swig of the ancestors' brew, or did we just buy protection?"

"A gift for a gift," she repeated. "We gave Primitivo a handout and the promise of our prayers in exchange for his prayers and accessories," she added, nodding toward the sack of goods on the backseat.

"But to *whom* is he praying?"

Corinne tried to think of a way to explain. It was hard when she didn't quite get it herself. "The Indios have accepted Christ and the concept of the Trinity, but in the context of their past. Did you notice all the pictures of the saints over Primitivo's altar in the back room when he pulled the curtain aside to get the candles and incense?"

"Yes, but I had no idea who was who."

"Well, they think God has an army of saints and angels, including some Aztec ones we've never heard of. The Indios think their good spirits were some of God's troops." She pondered her explanation a moment. "At least *some* of the Indios believe that. Others are outright pagan, worshipping the four corners of the spiritual world and their respective rulers. Father Menasco understands them more than I do."

"So the old guy will pray to God *and* the Indian entities?"

Corinne nodded slowly. "They sort of pray up the chain of command. In the meantime, the Church tries to show them that the spirits their ancestors worshipped were just man-conjured figureheads for God's creation, and God is the only God . . . and that they should pray directly to the head honcho. Some get it, some don't. It's really hard to undo thousands of years of belief, especially when some of their practitioners are successful in healing and witching, if you call it that."

"You mean murder disguised in a bunch of ancient voodoo-hoodoo." He shifted in his seat, fastening the seat belt. "And that crap about tying the dead boy's feet together so that his murder or murderers can't leave the area . . . that's outright nonsense."

"Yeah." At least she agreed about the superstition. But the murder part wouldn't give her goose-pimpled skin a rest. "Why would someone want to kill the Pozases, much less a little boy?"

And this was the first implication she'd heard to suggest the corpse wasn't Enrique. But if that was true, where was the boy?

"*If* either was really killed. Gas leaks and kids wandering off and dying in the mountains have been known to happen."

Mark's was the voice of reason. He was most likely right. And the boy's corpse had worn the orphanage T-shirt. Who else could it have been?

Mark shoved his hair away from his face as if trying to wipe out the unsettling rumors that the old Indio had shared. "And I thought I was in the *Twilight Zone* before."

When he first arrived, his hair was styled short with a hint of curl at his collar, but now it was thick with sandy rakish curls begging for a comb—or a woman's fingers. Lest her own be tempted, Corinne tightened her grasp on the wheel as Mark, oblivious of her sidewise study, lurched for it.

"Watch it."

Corinne corrected her steering before she struck a small stone fence marking off the yard of one of the last houses before the road curved into the main one leading to the hacienda.

Keep your eye on the road, stupid.

She faked a yawn. "Sorry. Highway hypnosis."

"You mean dirt-lane daze, don't you?"

Corinne laughed, a little too hard maybe, but it felt good to release all the tension from Primitivo's little spook session. Her composure regained, at least outwardly, she rested against the headrest, which was far more comfortable now that one side wasn't squished by Primitivo's hand.

"So what're we going to do with the witchy stuff?" Mark asked.

"Use the candles as needed for lighting."

"Or for romance?"

"As needed for *lighting*," she reiterated.

Romance, candles, fingers, sandy hair all spun whirligig-style around reason.

"And if I have to cook one night, we can use the copal to cover the smell of burned food."

"But you cook a mean hot dog."

Father Menasco had said the same thing, but his voice didn't have a velvet undertone that skimmed over her senses, rustling them into an unjustified anticipation. She wasn't going to be one of Mark Madison's passing fancies.

No sooner had Corinne's mind settled than this morning's conversation with Doña Violeta tipped it the other way. What happened to her resolution to think the best of Mark, rather than the worst?

Corinne pulled up to the backyard entrance under the jacaranda tree that shaded it. Not one to play games, she cut to the chase. "You're not hitting on me, are you?"

Shoving the car into park, she cut the engine, but her ears still rang with its roar. Or was that her pulse?

Mark threw up his hands. "Wouldn't think of it . . . *much*."

She fumbled with the keys as she pulled them from the ignition, and they dropped to the floor. "Oh, good."

Avoiding the stare she felt zeroing in on her, she got out of the car and felt around the carpet in the dark for the keys, lest he see through her fluster to her inner senses, straining like a pup on a leash toward the prospects of that one little word . . . *much*. Latching onto her purse, she picked it up from the wrong end, only to have it spill its contents.

"It might help if you turn on the switch." Mark was behind her now, leaning through the open door to slide the switch on for the overhead lights. "There they are."

Corinne could have sworn she'd run her hand over that spot a dozen times. "I don't know why I'm such a ditz tonight." Shoving the runaway keys into her purse, along with the papers that had spilled from it, she straightened.

"Maybe you've been witched . . . in a good way," he added hastily.

No, there was nothing good about the breath that caught in her throat as Mark circled her waist to draw her out of the way to shut the door. The lights went out, and gradually the ethereal glow of the moon on the landscape regained its prominence.

Somewhere in the distance a night bird called. Or was that the sigh she could no longer hold as he corralled her against the side of the vehicle?

"Sleepy?"

Corinne shook her head. "N-no, are you nuts?" She should have lied, but that wasn't right either.

Still without so much as a touch, he planted a hand on either side of her, allowing an age-old magic called animal attraction to do its thing. "Did you see that fiesta moon?" He pressed his forehead to hers.

What moon? She'd nearly run off the road looking at him. And if she raised her gaze to seek it out through the tree branches overhead, their lips might touch, and that was the last thing she wanted . . . wasn't it?

"You won't"—more ground rules—"kiss me if I look?"

"Can't answer that on the grounds that I might incriminate myself. But if I did, would it be so bad?"

She really couldn't see the eyes peering just beneath that sun-bleached brow of his, but boy, she could feel them—beating down her defenses and inviting the adventurous woman within to come out and play in the moonlight.

Forgetting she had her purse in her hand, Corinne wiped her palms on her hips. It thudded near her feet, keys jingling.

"O . . . oh—"

Her groan was cut off by Mark's lips planted firmly on her own.

It was magic. It had to be, because she fully intended to grab her purse and run, not put her arms around his neck. The last thing he needed was the encouragement of delirious fingers straining that glorious hair instead of St. Matthew's gnats.

"That wasn't too bad, was it?"

But did she want to let the proverbial camel's head past her defensive tent? Her voice was no more than a squeak. "No, it was good . . . very good. But I'm not sure this is—"

"What is that scent?" he interrupted, his cheek brushing past her face with its past–five o'clock shadow as he sniffed her neck. "It's so familiar."

"It . . . it's orange blossom." She wasn't about to tell him he recognized it from his pet pig. "The orchard in the back was full of them when you first came."

He sniffed again, nuzzling beneath her ear.

"I don't think this is a good idea," she blurted out, shifting her shoulder to drive the nose away to a less distracting distance.

"And what's wrong with a moonlight kiss between two people who happen to be attracted to each other?"

What could she tell him? That he was a camel running over her tent?

She rallied. "But that's all it is." And then shrank. "Isn't it? A kiss that fades in the sun?"

When her heart played, it was for keeps. That's why she had to be selective, not cave in at the first flare-up of butterflies.

"Enjoy the magic." He cupped her chin in his hand. "And just to prove that this is something special, I'll do it again tomorrow, in the sun, Corina."

Co-ree-na. The way he said her name was as irresistible as the mouth that closed over her own. "Cori—"

A sharp scream pierced the still of the night, skewering Corinne's heart in midbeat. While her passion-staggered senses scrambled to regroup, it sounded again, only then breaking the invisible bond that held her in Mark's arms. If she could trust her ears, it had come from the house.

CHAPTER 19

Mark struggled to return to reality as Corinne turned with a gasp toward the house. "Soledad!"

The housekeeper burst from the back door, voluminous nightgown hiked to her knees, and dashed out into the yard, shrieking in surround sound. She nearly bowled Mark over when he attempted to stop her.

"Whoa, Soledad. What is it?"

"No, no, no, no . . ." At close proximity, her continuous hysteria was ear-splitting.

"Un fantasma," she sobbed, struggling to pull away.

"A ghost?" Corinne exclaimed, putting an arm around the trembling woman. "It's okay, Soledad. Mark and I are here."

Still gulping for breath, the housekeeper looked from Mark to Corinne and back again, as if realizing for the first time who they were. Her chin quivered as she tried to speak. "I s-saw her with m-my own eyes. Sh-she is in the ballroom with our T-Toto, even as we speak."

"Wait," Mark said, not ready to believe in ghosts. He hadn't quite digested the idea of witches. "You saw a woman inside the house?"

"Sí! Claro!" Soledad's incredulity suggested he had the IQ of a slug. "I saw . . . S-Señora Lucinda."

"Right," he said, leaving Soledad to the woman he'd just kissed a moment ago.

Now, that was real. The sense of her softness lingered like a whisper around him.

"What are you going to do?" Corinne called after him.

He flung the screen door open, hollering over his shoulder. "I'm going to catch a ghost!"

More than likely it was shadow that played upon the supersized superstition of the local population. Then caution stopped him. If it was someone—perhaps the crayon-carrying witch—forewarned was forearmed. He eased the door back gently.

"What are you looking for?" Corinne called to him from the SUV, where she had seated the shaken Soledad in the passenger seat.

In the car light that flooded the tree-shaded area, Mark spied a piece of the old shower piping that Juan Pedro had replaced with PVC.

"A ghost buster," he replied, picking it up. Reinforced with a length of galvanized metal, he reentered the hacienda.

The moon afforded enough light through the window over the sink for him to see his way through to the kitchen. Hoping that Soledad's wails hadn't left him partially deaf, he stopped at the hallway entrance and peeked around it, listening. Instead of coming from the direction of the ballroom, footsteps sounded in the front of the house, followed by a hiss and a familiar grunt.

A hissing ghost and a pig?

Ridiculous or not, the hair pricked at Mark's neck at the sight of a small figure silhouetted in the moonlight spilling in from the Palladian arch over the front door. At least that's what he *thought* he saw. Soledad had hung clear plastic curtains both coming and going to separate the construction from the living quarters. And the one he looked through rustled as though recently disturbed.

God, I know I'm six-two and in gym-prime shape, but please don't let this be what Soledad said . . .

Mark clenched the pipe and gave the figure one last blink to disappear. It did, in an image of flowing white . . . into the salon.

. . . Or at least don't let whatever it is have a gun. Gun trumps the lead pipe.

A crash of furniture in the front room jumped Mark's pulse to warp speed. Brushing his way through the curtain, he raced down the hall. Knowing where the furniture was, he had the advantage of the culprit now. The only way out was through the windows, which, with no one home, Soledad had locked as surely as she drew breath.

Ghost buster ready, he charged into the room and pitched head-long over something that did not belong in his path. It squealed as Mark slammed against the floor, the metal pipe knocked from his hand by the impact. Advantage lost, he crawled toward the noise of its roll and collided, nose first, into a warm bristly body.

Annoyed beyond the limits of caution, Mark gave the pig a backswing. "Whose side are you on?" But instead of hitting the worrisome Toto, he struck his wrist on the corner of Doña Violeta's hardwood desk.

Pain jolted up his arm and left his hand numb in its wake. The sound of tile moving against tile silenced the flood of expletives that wanted to burst through his sealed lips. Clutching his numb hand to his chest, he groped with the other for the pipe in case the ghost was about to finish him off with a heavy floor tile.

At the cool touch of metal, he seized the pipe and inch-wormed to his knees, trying to listen above the roar of the still outraged pressure point in his wrist. Unlike the hand beyond it, the wrist, unmercifully, had not gone numb.

But above his pain and the stillness of the night, his heartbeat and the click of Toto's feet were the only sounds he detected. Unaware that he had been holding his breath, he released it. Holding on to the desktop, Mark pulled himself to his feet and reached for the chain on the lamp.

The sudden burst of light blinded him, but when his eyes adjusted, he couldn't believe what he saw. Or rather, what he didn't see. There was no one in the room at all. Just Toto, who seemed intent on nosing his way around the overturned library table. The curtains over the windows hung undisturbed, so the culprit couldn't have escaped through them. And Mark would have heard that. The only other way out of the room was over Mark as he scrambled around on the floor. Only a ghost—

No way . . . Right, God?

Ghosts didn't hiss and walk around in boots. So if the intruder didn't get out, he still had to be in there. And since there had been no gunfire . . .

Mark's gaze fell on the bed—the only place where the figure could hide.

"Okay, buddy, I know you're there," he announced in broken Spanish. "Tell me why you're here and you go, *no problema.*"

A long moment passed with no reply. It was probably a kid half-scared out of his wits. The figure hadn't been very tall.

Mark gave the intruder one more chance.

"Tell me, amigo. *No problema.*"

Still no answer.

Mark marched over to the bed. Throwing up the spread, he swept the underneath with the pipe, producing a pair of his sneakers, but no intruder.

But he'd seen it enter the salon.

"Mark? Mark, are you okay?" Corinne shouted from the back of the house.

"Yeah, but stay in the kitchen."

Unsettled and confused, he walked to the entrance and flipped on the hall lights. He and Soledad weren't *both* hallucinating. Someone had been in the hacienda. Remembering the sound of tile, he walked over the floor, kicking at the large decorative tiles inset between the hardwood dividers. After all, a man, or a woman, might be able to drop through one of those to an underground passage of some kind.

But none were loose. Shoulders weighted with disappointment and confusion, Mark turned full circle, looking for any sign of how or where the figure might have disappeared, when he noticed that Toto had climbed up on the raised hearth of the fireplace.

Of course . . . the chimney. He'd seen thugs on TV reality crime shows stuck in chimneys. That was the only place the would-be ghost could be.

"Snake-hunting again, Toto?" Mark tiptoed to the desk to retrieve a flashlight he kept in the top drawer. "Did you see any of those critters?"

Easing onto the stone surface, Mark angled so that he could look up the chimney, but wouldn't be a target, should the perp drop down on him. With the push of a button, the flashlight filled the soot-blackened column with its glow, but again, there was nothing up there but a rusted flue. Mark crawled under the low oak mantel built into the stone wall and maneuvered the shaft of light past the canted flap of iron, but aside from a star-studded patch of sky beyond its reach, there was nothing.

"Mark?"

Bolting upright, Mark cracked his head on the massive beam.

"What?" he snapped, backing out of the enclosure. "I thought I told you to stay in the back until I checked out the house."

"Did you see anything?"

"Yes and no." Hiding the fact that she'd scared him out of three lives, he returned the flashlight to the desk and approached the overturned library table. "I saw someone . . . or something, but I didn't see where he, she, or it went."

"What's that?" Corinne asked as he righted the table. Hanging from the rough unfinished underside was a piece of white gauze.

Mark picked it off. "I'd say our ghost has torn her dress." And it was in here just seconds before he plunged—literally—into the room. "And did I say she wore combat boots?"

Corinne pointed to the floor. "Look, aren't those footprints?"

Sure enough, their "ghost" had tracked some of the plaster dust from the ballroom into the salon.

"Maybe the police can make some kind of cast or imprint or something."

Mark cut his optimistic companion off. "In Mexicalli?"

She winced. "Guess you're right . . . but we should still call them."

He shook his head. "How late do you want to stay up while Capitán Nolla tells you that unless we saw who the intruder was, there is nothing he can do. 'After all, señorita,'" Mark said, mimicking the nasal quality of the officer's voice, "'we are just a small village, and I am only one policía.'"

◆

"After all, señorita, we are just a small village, and I am only one policeman," Capitán Nolla told Corinne the next morning as he retreated into his blue-and-white compact car without trying to lift the prints, or whatever police did with them. "But I will write up a report, in case something else should happen."

Mark had been right. Calling the police was a waste of time, she thought, returning to the house with a weary step. It seemed like hours since a loud snort just before dawn had brought her upright in the bed that she shared with a still-sleeping Soledad.

After coaxing the distraught housekeeper into the house with the promise that all three of them would hunker down in one room, they'd compromised on the use of Primitivo's protection— burning candles as a night-light, but no copal.

And now, they were no better off for Capitán Nolla's visit. He'd looked at them as if they'd made up the entire story, despite the plaster-dust prints and Mark's and Soledad's witness. Determined not to simply roll over and let possible evidence go to waste, Corinne passed the salon, where Juan Pablo, who'd shown up shortly after the policeman's arrival, was studying the blueprints with Mark.

"It is with magnanimous regret, Señor Mark," the plumber expounded, "that I and my brothers cannot assume the projection until after the fiesta next week. But you can build on my promise that we will be arrived on the *mañana* after which."

At least Mark had learned a lesson about dealing locally, she thought, ducking into her room to search through the plastic storage container of craft supplies stored under her bed. After rummaging through assorted colored paper, rolls of tape and crepe paper, and assorted markers and pens, she found what she was looking for. Using scissors from the box, she cut a length of the clear contact paper and returned the supplies to their place beneath the bed.

"Don't pay any attention to me," she told the two men as she entered the room.

"What are you going to do with that?" Mark asked.

"I'm going to lift the print for evidence," she said, picking at the corner of the contact paper's backing with her fingernail.

The clearest of the prints was still surrounded by the kitchen chairs that Soledad placed there to keep anyone from contaminating the evidence. Corinne moved a chair aside and knelt on the floor.

"Right."

Scowling at both Mark's disdain and the resistant backing, Corinne continued to work on it. "I wouldn't expect someone who sleeps with a pig to understand."

"Not literally," Mark informed Juan Pablo. "Soledad keeps the pig in the house as a pet."

"Got it," Corinne said under her breath. With the sticky side down, she knelt and carefully positioned the square over one of the footprints. *It's worth a try,* she thought, easing it to the floor, where she ironed it out with her hands.

"The pig didn't run from the ghost," Juan Pablo pointed out. "The animals see things that we cannot, and then they run."

"A ghost doesn't wear boots and gauze, Juan. I think it was some kid . . ."

"With big feet?" Corinne stood up, wiping her hands on her hips. "All I need is some plastic wrap to seal it on the sticky side."

"I had feet that big when I was ten," Mark told her.

"You're not an Indio," Corinne replied.

"Maybe so," the plumber acknowledged Mark, "but how is it explained that it disappeared like so?" Juan snapped his fingers.

"The kid could have slipped past me when I fell."

"Except that the footprints lead into the room." Corinne looked at the floor as if to confirm the thought that had just occurred to her. "Not out."

Juan Pablo exhaled, staring at the contact paper–covered print, his heavy mustache twitching. *"Pues,"* he said, taking up his hat from the desk, "I and my brothers will work during the day. You can build on that as well."

"Hasta luego, Juan," Corinne told him, pulling up the contact paper from the floor and heading for the kitchen.

A delicious stew of some kind simmered on the back burner of the stove, but Soledad had left to visit her sister at the parsonage. Corinne could imagine that by now everyone in Mexicalli was speculating about Hacienda Ortiz's apparition.

Mark sat at the table, going over a set of figures on *Tres Juanes* stationery.

"So, what's the verdict? Has being second choice brought his *proposition* up?"

Mark shook his head. "Nope. Same as before."

She placed the contact-paper footprint next to his papers, plaster dust side up. "That dear little man," she said, her faith in mankind renewed. "You might have to check behind his math, but I believe he has an honest heart."

"I see what you mean," Mark admitted. "He could have held us over a barrel, too, but he didn't."

"And he really cares about the orphans. Father Menasco said neither of the brothers had ever charged the orphanage for their labor on repairs, only for the cost of the materials."

Corinne pulled the plastic against the serrated edge of the box. But the moment it broke free, it drew up on itself. "Oh, phooey."

Surprising her, Mark got up and walked over to her. "Here, let me help."

"I thought you thought this was silly."

"It won't be the first silly thing I've ever done." He picked at one of the tangled corners. "Besides"—he gave her a roguish grin—"I owe you."

Corinne blinked. "For what?"

"I made a promise last night to prove to you that moonlight kisses don't fade in the sun . . . and unless my eyes are telling a fib . . ." With an impatient breath, he pulled the tangled plastic from her hand, but instead of straightening it, he wadded it into a ball and tossed it over his shoulder. "It's a sunny day."

Even if she wanted to run, she couldn't. Mark slipped his arms about her waist. "I might have shared an air mattress with a peculiar pig last night," he said, lowering his face to hers, "but I saved my kisses for a very special señorita."

Her mouth suddenly dry, Corinne moistened her lips. "Kisses," she repeated. "As in plural?"

Drawing her to him, he covered her mouth with his own. The combination of his fresh-shaven, squeaky-clean scent and the suggested power of his firm but gentle embrace made her knees weak as . . . as the reason that fled her mind. The box of plastic wrap slipped from her hand to the floor, but it would have to wait. At that moment, both her head and her heart were on the line, and sweet temptation was pulling hard for surrender to the tune of the Tchaikovsky's 1812 Overture.

The first measure or two whined in cheap imitation of the passion pounding in her chest, but it gradually gained sway, breaking through with an electronic insistence. Mark let her go, digging at the leather pouch at his waist. Retrieving his cell phone, he flipped it open with an apologetic look.

"Hello?" He motioned for her to stay. "Oh, hi, Blaine."

"Yoo-hoo, I am returned!" Soledad shouted from the back of the house.

Picking up the box of plastic wrap, Corinne tore off a piece and gently placed it over the contact paper, hoping neither would melt from the heat of Mark's kiss. There. She had captured, at least to her inexperienced eye, a perfect footprint.

"Sure, everything's going fine." Catching Corinne's sharp look, Mark added, "For living in the *Twilight Zone.*"

"I'll get Soledad to help me with this," she whispered. "See if Blaine has any ideas about getting help from the authorities for our ghost."

Mark's expression clouded with annoyance as he covered the mouthpiece with his hand. "I can handle this." He turned his back to her. "Yeah, well things have been slowed by plans for a fiesta this week, but everyone will be back on the job come Monday next."

Corinne left him to his delusions of control. His kisses were as good by day as by night, but characterwise, Mark was back to camel status. And she needed to reinforce her tent.

CHAPTER 20

"Well, I have to say that you've surprised me," Blaine said on the other end of the cell phone.

Mark stared at the empty doorway where Corinne had just slammed an invisible door in his face.

"Caroline and I can't wait to visit this winter to see it," his brother went on.

"How are Caroline and the kids?" Mark asked, buying time to sort through Corinne's mixed messages.

Not that they needed much sorting, he thought, making his way down the hall toward the salon. Corinne said it last night. She was for real. He was smoke and mirrors, dancing around responsibility as he was doing now with Blaine.

She'd given him a chance. God seemed to be doing the same. The help of the Indios, even with old Primitivo's contribution, surely fell into the miracle category. Entering the salon-office-bedroom, Mark's thoughts halted. He stared at the corner of the secretary desktop, where he'd placed the village fireworks fund. It was gone.

Blaine's voice shifted from happy family chat back to business. "I told her that I didn't want to put you in this make-or-break opportunity—"

A sick feeling churned in his stomach. Their ghost was a thief.

"—but frankly, I was at my wits' end with what to do with you."

And he wasn't much better. Maybe he was in over his head. Maybe he should just 'fess up before he wound up hurting a lot of good people.

"I wouldn't make any plans to visit just yet," Mark said slowly.

Blaine's voice grew taut. "What do you mean?"

Mark could see his future vanishing like the jar of money, but what was he saving, even if he could pull the wool over his brother's eyes? "Things down here aren't at the break stage, but they are a bit cracked."

Blaine's long sigh across the miles made Mark think his brother could have survived Houdini's underwater feat with air to spare. "Do I need to come down there?"

Okay, God. This is it. The screwup is going to confess.

"I'll let you be the judge." With that Mark began with his night on the town with Juan Pedro and the story of Antonio's family. And how could he leave out Corinne?

"She's one savvy lady . . . good looks and brains." Mark laughed, but he meant what he said. "I think I'm in trouble . . . but in a good way for a change."

"Caroline will be delighted to hear that," Blaine responded. "She said she had a feeling about the two of you." From his wry tone, Blaine obviously hadn't.

Mark told him about the Cuernavaca contractor, and how he either had to hire the *Tres Juanes* or go over budget. The delivery truck incident actually drew a chuckle from his brother, surprising Mark, but the threats of witchcraft and the ghostly visitation quickly sobered Blaine.

"And the authorities are overlooking all of this?" Blaine asked, incredulous.

"They claim there's nothing they can do. I'm telling you, I'm working in the *Twilight Zone.* Antonio's parents died by accident— or not. His brother is dead, if it really was his brother, and he died of exposure or a gunshot wound or witchcraft. I'm threatened by a crayon-wielding vandal, or maybe it was a witch . . . and now I have to file a report that a ghost, who left footprints, stole the jar of fireworks money."

Every word Mark said was the truth, but it was so outrageous that even he had trouble believing it.

But Blaine did. "How much?"

"I didn't have time to count it." Resting an elbow on the desktop,

Mark buried his forehead in his hand. "It's a mess, Blaine. I'm a mess." He hesitated. He wasn't used to admitting defeat. Failure had always been someone else's fault. "Maybe you should get someone else down here. I'll do whatever you think."

When Blaine made no comment, Mark hoped they hadn't been cut off. He'd hate to have to go through this again. He checked the face of his phone. "Blaine?"

"Hold on, I'm making some notes."

Good old meticulous Blaine. *Fire Mark* was probably at the top of his list.

"Look, Mark," he finally replied. "You just keep on with what you're doing."

Mark bolted upright, pressing the cell phone to his ear so hard that it threatened to crack the hinge. Was he hearing right?

"Problems with contractors are normal. There are shysters everywhere there's a chance to turn a buck. And problems on site happen. I was so focused on the hacienda's makeover that I didn't consider anything beyond the patio." Blaine laughed. "Believe me, I could tell you about more than my share of mishaps."

"I never heard about any," Mark objected.

"You never wanted to listen."

It was hard to argue with the truth. "Guess this means we've finally found something we have in common."

"Yeah. If nothing else, Mexicalli's accomplished that." There was a warmth in Blaine's voice that crossed the miles, bolstering Mark's humor more than not being pulled off the job or labeled a failure. "But this witchcraft and threat thing sounds like more than some adolescent prank . . . and frankly, I'm suspicious of the authorities' lack of interest."

"So what should I do?" Mark asked.

"Just what you are doing, but keep your ears open and watch your back. I'm going to give my friend Aquino a call and fill him in on what's going on. Half of his relatives are involved in the government. This has got to be more than someone being miffed over losing out on the real estate."

Mark perked up. "Like what?"

"My first thought is mineral rights. You *are* in mining country."

"I thought the silver was mined out."

"It was, but there are other minerals. As I recall, Mexico owns all the rights, but the government grants concessions to those who own property to mine it . . . for a chunk of the profit, I'm sure. I'm just grasping at straws here," Blaine acknowledged, "but it can't hurt to ask around."

"Ask away. I appreciate all the help I can get." Mark meant it. Just having someone like Blaine to share the ups and downs seemed to lighten the weight on his shoulders tenfold.

"And Mark . . ."

"Yes?"

"You're doing okay."

A blade of emotion caught in Mark's throat. He forced an answer past it. "Thanks, bro. I needed that."

"I give credit where it's due. By the way, have you kissed her yet?" His brother laughed. "Never mind. I just know Caroline is going to ask how things are progressing, and she won't be talking about the house. You know how women are."

Mark did, but he'd never thought Blaine had a clue. "Tell her I'll do my best to make her proud."

And You, he thought as he hung up. *You too, God, if You'll help me.*

The prayer dart stopped Mark in his mental track. It had come so naturally for someone who'd considered himself spiritually estranged. As though God was on the spot, ready to pick up where Mark had left Him years before . . . ready to give Mark another chance. As though God believed in him, even if Mark didn't believe in himself.

Mark stared at the cell phone in wonder. Even more miraculous, Blaine had been doing the same. After all, God was God, but Blaine was . . .

A warmth filled Mark's heart.

Blaine was a godly brother. And more shocking yet, Mark wanted to be like him for the first time in a long, long time.

Fingering the buttons on the cell phone, Mark called up the directory and scanned down the list of numbers. Drinking buddies, golf buddies, yachting buddies, college friends . . . When he reached the *Ps*, he found the name he wanted and pushed a button.

Three rings later, a man answered.

"Pyro, Mark Madison here. I have a favor to ask, old friend."

◆

Despite the three days of intermittent showers that followed the night of the "ghost," when the dawn of the fiesta day arrived, the sun shone over a greener landscape dotted with the golds and oranges of wildflowers. Corinne stood in front of her dresser and stared at the brightly clad woman in her mirror. Mexicalli had made her feel the presence of her biological heritage in her blood. Not that she was no longer the red, white, and blue American that her adopted parents had raised, but she'd developed another dimension to her personality—that of the birth mother she never knew. If Corinne could map out her future, it would comprise summers spent working in Mexico with her mother's people and teaching back home at Edenton during the school year.

How fast the days fly, Lord. It was already August. In a few weeks she'd need to leave these people that she'd taken into her heart.

The image of Mark Madison flashed through her mind. She'd be leaving him as well. And that, she told herself, was probably for the best.

I gave him a chance, Lord, and You heard him putting the spin on his progress for his brother. How can I tell he's not spinning me, too?

She adjusted the sash at her waist, a woven blend of Mexican colors that tied the turquoise of her skirt with the yellow of her blouse.

And why would I want someone whose word I could never quite trust? Even as she prayed, her fickle, smitten heart twisted in protest.

And since I know I can't trust him, what I'm feeling can't be love. It's just infatuation. And it wouldn't be that if I hadn't let St. Matthew knock my guard down.

God surely knew she'd succumbed to Mark's sweet seduction

because she wanted to avoid being a Pharisee, straining out the gnats, Mark's nitpicky flaws, while letting the camel-sized ones slip by. Was that charm of his a camel in disguise?

A brisk knock interrupted her one-sided spiritual debate. Spinning so that her gathered skirt flared around her, Corinne went to answer it, but Mark beat her to the door.

Just outside stood Diego Quintana, dressed in a Spanish suit, a rich cinnamon with black soutache trim on the trousers and the short jacket.

Shades of matador, she thought, noting the flattering fit. Not every man had the height or build to pull that off, much less the bravado to wear the ruffled shirt tucked into his narrow black sash.

"Señor Quintana, what brings you here?" Mark said, surprised.

Diego brandished a smile. "The lovely señorita standing behind you."

Mark gave Corinne a questioning glance before standing aside. "Then by all means come in."

"No need for that," Corinne objected. "I'm ready."

She hadn't told Mark that she was going to the festival with Diego. It was none of his business. Besides, other than passing conversation, she'd not had a lot to say to him, partly because she'd been busy at work and partly because Mark at a distance was safer. So when Diego stopped by the orphanage to ask her to the fiesta, and the ladies there insisted that they could take the children without her, she'd accepted.

"Since Soledad has gone to spend the night with her sister, give me time to get my shoes on, and I'll walk down with you," Mark said cheerfully.

"But Primitivo's nephew isn't here yet," Corinne pointed out through a clenched-teeth smile.

With a smirk of triumph, Mark pointed to the road beyond the courtyard. "Coming as we speak."

The man who had volunteered to guard the hacienda while Corinne and Mark were gone approached with a loaded market bag. Corinne groaned, hoping it contained no more than candles and some incense.

"I will be delighted to await your readiness," Diego announced, gallant to a fault.

Soledad had told Corinne how Primitivo, upon hearing of the apparition's visit, sacrificed a black hen in his cave of dreams, wherever that was, in an attempt to get the spirits to tell him who was behind the mischief at the hacienda. Not wanting to disappoint the old Indio or the poverty-stricken contributors, Mark never mentioned the missing jar of money to anyone except Corinne. And they had agreed it was a waste of time to call Capitán Nolla.

"Besides, that will give me time to present Corina with her birthday gift." Diego's reply stopped Mark in his tracks at the salon door.

"Birthday? It's your birthday?" he asked Corinne. "I never heard anything about it."

"It's not until next week, and I only told Soledad," she called after him as he disappeared into the salon. But then, if the housekeeper knew, the village knew, which explained the lovely rose foil-wrapped package that Diego produced from behind his back.

"Diego, you shouldn't have . . ."

"*Hola,* Señorita Corina. I am here to guard against the evil ones." Primitivo's nephew stood at the entrance, as gray as his uncle, but not quite as drawn and wrinkled.

With an apologetic look at Diego, Corinne beckoned the man inside. "That's wonderful, Tizoc. Soledad has some iced tea and sandwiches for you in the refrigerator, so make yourself at home."

"*Bueno.* I will guard from the kitchen."

By the time Corinne had showed Tizoc to the kitchen and returned to Diego, Mark had donned his shoes and was waiting in the foyer with the artist.

"Aren't you going to open that present?" Mark asked, boyish mischief running wild in his gaze.

Corinne shook her head. "Maybe I should put this aside until my real birthday."

"But I was hoping that you would wear it tonight," Diego chimed in, no less eager to please her than Mark was bent on embarrassing her.

Corinne's shoulders dropped with surrender . . . not that she had much choice. She'd not offend Diego for the world. Mark was becoming another matter. How dare he insert himself into their company without an invitation?

Taking care to save the foil wrapping paper for a possible art project, Corinne opened the small box. She knew it had to be some sort of jewelry, but upon lifting the cotton packing, she was awestruck.

"Diego," she gasped, taking the delicate necklace from its trappings.

Suspended from a twisted band of silver was a breathtaking cross pendant inlaid with some sort of stone. The silverwork alone was beautiful, but the stone's variegated colors of blues, reds, golds, and greens were exquisite.

"I've never seen anything like it. What is it?" she asked, turning and lifting her hair for him to fasten it around her neck.

"Ammonite."

"Ammonite?" Mark echoed, his brow furrowing. "Isn't that some kind of fossil?"

Diego nodded as he turned Corinne to display his handiwork. "But polished to a sheen. The cheap ones are usually red or brown."

If that was true, the one hanging from her neck was not a cheap one. Corinne fingered her gift. "So what am I wearing," she teased, "the jawbone of a woolly mammoth?"

Diego chuckled. "You are wearing a snail."

"Snails, you say." Mark looked at Corinne as if that should mean something, but Diego distracted her, putting a possessive arm at her waist. "But then, even unpolished, you would make the *caracoles* shine."

Caracoles? Now Corinne understood what Mark was getting at. But how Antonio's *caracol* and Diego's *caracol* were related was beyond her.

"Well, it's a lovely snail, and the setting is to die for, but really, Diego, you shouldn't have. I don't even want to think what this is worth."

"Then don't," he said, leaning over and planting a kiss on her cheek. "Are you ready?"

At Corinne's nod, he ushered her out of the house ahead of him, leaving Mark to bring up the rear.

CHAPTER 21

In a matter of footsteps, Mark flanked Corinne's other side. "So where do these *caracoles* come from, Diego?"

Putting Mark in mind of a half-baked flamenco dancer, Diego made a wide flourish with his arm. "From Mother Nature, a gem like the cosmos," he said, an artistic finger coming to point at a patch of pasture with drifts of pink and yellow blossoms quivering above fernlike foliage in the midafternoon breeze.

What on earth could Corinne see in a guy so infatuated with himself? And fit or not, he looked as though he'd been poured into those pants. If that fabric didn't stretch, it was going to be Splitsville, should Diego have to pick up something from the ground.

"What I mean is, where does 'Mother Nature' hide these little gems?" Mark persisted.

"From under the sea or the earth—where else could they have survived all these years?"

Condescension and ruffles on his shirt—the combination almost made Mark laugh. "Or in the mountains." He covered his mouth and coughed. The tickle in his throat that had come upon him during the night was still there, not serious, but annoying.

"I think the mountains count as under the earth, Mark," Corinne answered, her warning glare for Mark alone.

At least a glare was warmer than their relationship had been since he spoke to Blaine. Although remaining civil, Corinne had made it a point to avoid being alone in the same room with him. Although after tonight—

"Unless you are interested in mining them yourself, you can purchase them from wholesalers over the Internet, Señor Madison," Diego said with an edge of exasperation. "Do you have access?"

And now the man was a smart aleck. "I can stumble around on it," Mark said.

"Simply do a search for ammonite—"

"I can stumble that far," Mark cut him off.

"Golly day." Corinne inhaled deeply as they approached the village. "Do you smell the fish frying? It's making my tummy growl."

If she was picking up on what he was, Mark doubted it was the fish. Although somehow, he found it hard to believe that Diego was behind the mischief at the house. First, the guy was wealthy. Second, the figure Mark had seen was small, like an Indio or an adolescent. But he could have hired a poor, short guy.

"Then that is what we will have for our dinner," Diego announced. "I'll tip Rodrigo to save us a table for two near the Cantina Roja, so we can watch the dancers."

Mark got the message. Forced to take his leave or be more of a cad than he'd already been, he extended his hand to Diego. "You two enjoy the evening."

He gave Corinne a peck on the cheek. "Have a good time, birthday girl. You deserve it."

And I'll be watching your back all the way. For now, he needed to find someone who had an aspirin. The dull ache that had lured him into sleeping in that morning had finally grabbed hold of his head and, thanks to Diego-on-the-spot, he'd had to leave the hacienda before he could take anything.

The main plaza reminded Mark of the day he'd arrived at Mexicalli. The same booths had been put together on one side, and vendors sold everything from crafts to food. Diego and Corinne headed to the opposite side, where the Cantina Roja had set out tables for its patrons to enjoy the show. At the moment, the merry mariachis played while some children and a few adults danced in front of the stage by the town center.

Mark headed toward the combination market and pharmacy,

hoping it was still open. Maybe he'd pick up some cough medicine too. All he needed, now that the *Tres Juanes* were ready to start work on Monday, was a head cold.

Making his way through *petate* mats and picnic blankets, he nodded and spoke to more than a few of the villagers, many who had come to the hacienda earlier that week.

"Señor Marco!" Primitivo waved from a group of elderly men gathered around him a short distance away.

Mark picked his way to where the old man sat, a smoking pipe in his mouth. "*Hola,* amigo. I see you are ready to celebrate the saint's day."

Primitivo took the pipe from his mouth. "Each day above the dirt is a day to celebrate."

Mark's chuckle triggered the tickle, forcing him to clear his throat again. "Excuse me," he apologized. "I just want to thank you again for recommending Tizoc." He broke off with a dry cough.

Primitivo's gummy smile faded. "No feeling well?"

"I'm feeling fine," Mark lied, images of some nasty-looking concoction and more candles coming to mind. "Just a little too much plaster dust."

"Tell Soledad she must clean better."

"That might be more risky than the dust," Mark quipped.

Primitivo nodded, missing the humor. "You smoke tobacco?"

Mark shook his head in denial.

"Shame," the elder responded. "Tobacco smoke is good medicine."

Obviously, gazillions of dollars in research to the contrary didn't count down here.

"Well, I'd best be moving. I want to get a Coke before the market closes."

"*Hasta luego.*" Primitivo stuck his pipe between his lips and turned to listen to one of his compadres.

Despite the fiesta, the market was open and would remain so, according to the sign in the front window. A wise decision, Mark thought, easing through the aisles thick with customers.

"*Lo siento,*" he said, bumping into a shopper as he reached for a bottle of what looked like cold medicine. Glancing back when he received no reply, he recognized Antonio's surly-mannered uncle shuffling away behind his wife—the witch, according to Soledad. Or was she the daughter of a witch?

Sheesh, he was starting to think *Twilight Zone*. "Señor Pozas," Mark called.

Reluctantly the man turned. "*Sí?*"

"Do you know the caves in this area?"

Pozas shook his head. "No, señor . . . only that there are caves."

"I was just wondering if there were any *caracoles* around here."

Score. Although whether the surprise that registered in Pozas's gaze was innocent or not was hard to say.

"I am just a farmer, señor," Pozas said. "I know nothing of what is in the caves. *Adiós*." With a slight tip of his head, he ducked around the end of the aisle.

Mark's mind tumbled with possibilities as he emerged from the market, a bottle of Coca-Cola in hand. Pausing long enough to pop one of the cold tablets that claimed to help both his cough and headache, he headed across the plaza toward the Cantina Roja's outside tables. After all, he had to eat, and fish did smell good.

◆

It was a beautiful day, *perfect for a fiesta*, Corinne thought as she viewed the activity in the park from the table she shared with Diego. The young Indio women wore colorful prints and solids, while their elders dressed in their town-best black woolen skirts with multicolored belts. Corinne had little doubt that the fabric had been made on their own looms, just like the white fine-gauge weave of the triangular lace garments some wore on their heads.

"I love this place," she said, taking a sip of the special sangria that Diego had ordered for her. "I feel as though I've discovered a part of me that I didn't know existed."

"You did," he agreed. "Mexico is in your blood, Corina. And all these years you have been misplaced."

"Not completely. I am the product of my North American upbringing, too," she reminded him.

"Then you are the best of both worlds." He lifted his glass. "To the best of both worlds."

After the toast, she contemplated the deep red liquid swirling in her glass. "When nonalcoholic sangria tastes so good, why would you want the other kind?"

With a chuckle, Diego leaned over and whispered in her ear. "It is like separating the heart from the soul, Corina."

"I didn't know it had a heart and soul. I thought it had a bouquet."

The poet in Diego was a little overdone at times, but it was genuine. It was who he was . . . whether Mark Madison appreciated his way with words or not. She still couldn't believe the guy had horned in on their walk to the village. Granted, it wasn't a date, but *he* didn't know that.

Having seen Mark join Doña Violeta, Father Menasco, and the priest's visiting sister at another table near the stage, Corinne couldn't help glancing in their direction. She'd met Dr. Elizabeth Menasco Flynn at the orphanage. She was a vivacious woman who loved hiking and exploring when she wasn't practicing her first love—medicine.

Around the stage, the villagers prepared for their rendition of the Santiago, a medieval dance drama of St. James, their patron saint. Unlike on Independence Day or Cinco de Mayo, today the adults were on stage and the children in the audience. With front-row mats, the entourage from the orphanage squirmed under the supervision of María Delgado and the staff.

"Ah," Diego said as his father climbed to the stage to introduce the entertainment. "So Don Victor's son is Santiago Caballero this year."

"Don Victor the butcher?" Corinne said, watching as someone helped strap a fake horse to a dancer's waist near the stage entrance.

"The same. You see, the role of St. James is elected every year," he explained. "So he inherits the horse from last year's St. James." Diego helped himself to more of the sangria. "Tradition has it that if he does not feed the horse a bowl of corn and water every day, it will run away to another village."

The music of the flute and drum grew louder, signaling the entrance of the characters on the stage from both sides. They were clad in military costume, and all that set apart the dancing and fighting Moors from the Christians were Moorish turbans. Everyone was masked except for St. James, who led the Christian forces into the battle dance on his white horse—the front and back sections of which were secured to his waist by a painted wooden belt.

"Diego, Corina . . ." Mayor Quintana approached from the Cantina Roja behind them. Unlike his son, who'd donned traditional Spanish dress, the *alcalde* wore a pale blue business suit, complete with shirt and tie.

"What a grand fiesta," he said, placing one hand on his son's shoulder and the other on Corinne's. "The vendors are selling faster than they can count."

"Always the *alcalde*—my father," Diego said under his breath.

"And everyone will be especially pleased when they see the surprise your Señor Madison has graciously provided."

"Mark?" Corinne said, taken back. "What do you mean?"

"Since the fireworks collection was given to the hacienda, he said his corporation would provide fireworks for the festival." Don Rafael leaned over between them, extending his arm toward a white van parked near the stage. "Those men have come from Mexico City to put on the show for us."

Corinne didn't want her heart to warm again, but it did. Each time she was ready to toss Mark on the impossible heap, he did something that made her think there was a chance.

"Well, what is this?" Don Rafael said, pointing to Corinne's necklace.

"An early birthday present from your son." She smiled at Diego. "Who really shouldn't have."

"May I?" the mayor asked. At Corinne's nod, he fingered the pendant, turning it to catch the light of the lanterns that gradually overtook over the setting sun's duty. "It is a beautiful piece, but . . ." His lips pressed together, as though censoring his words. "But I thought that you were going to release your new collection this *fall*."

"I am, Father, but I wanted something special for Corina's *cumpleaños*." Diego shrugged, but his dark eyes told Corinne that the matter was far from settled.

"Now your competitors will know of your plans, and perhaps preempt them with their own."

Apparently Don Rafael's dictatorial hold on the village extended to his son's life as well.

"What if I put it away and don't wear it again until after your collection is out?" Corinne suggested. "I really wouldn't mind. I can wait until Christmas and have the fun of getting it all over again."

Diego caressed the side of her face. "She is a princess, no?"

"On that we agree. And if you listen to your father, you will be a prince." With that, Don Rafael pivoted and headed back toward the Cantina Roja.

Diego drew his fists to his side, his dark eyes flashing with anger. "You will wear your gift *every* day," he told Corinne. "My father thinks that he is the only one with a mind for business, that as an artist, I am lost in the clouds somewhere, unable to count past my fingers."

"I think that no matter how old we are, our parents will always look out for us and sometimes second-guess us," Corinne consoled him. "My parents certainly weren't in favor of my coming back here after I couldn't find my birth mother."

A smile returned to Diego's face, banishing the brief storm his father had provoked. After handing her glass to her, he lifted his, clinking the two. "And I, for one, am very glad that you didn't listen to them." He leaned over and lifted her hand to his lips.

Corinne laughed at his cavalier wink. "You are incorrigible."

"Tsk, tsk . . . look at you two." Doña Violeta stood in front of their table, petite but regal in a purple dress and matching gloves. Her lively gaze snapped disapproval. "If I had such actions when I was your age, I would still be locked in the basement of the convent."

"But this is a very different day, *Tía* Violeta," Diego told her. "Besides, I believe it was you who taught me always to make a woman feel like a queen, no?" Rising to his feet, he repeated his gallantry for his aunt, raising her gloved hand to his lips.

"But that is not the reason . . ." Placing a hand to her chest, the elderly woman swayed.

In an instant, Diego eased her into his seat, concerned. "What is it, *Tía?*"

Corinne's voice echoed his alarm. "Should I get a doctor?"

"I am such an old fool," she said, "I must have forgotten to take my heart medicine." She glanced up at her grandnephew. "You know the one."

"I will send someone to get it immediately."

Doña Violeta waved her hand at him. "No, no. Gaspar is here at the festival somewhere . . . and I do not want the world knowing of my silliness," she added, with a slight tilt of her head toward her companions at the other table. Biting her lip, she placed a hand on Diego's arm. "Dear nephew, I am distraught to ruin your courtship . . ."

"We're just friends," Corinne put in, emphasizing the last word for everyone's benefit.

"But if you would take me home," the elder lady continued, "perhaps Corina could find Gaspar and ask him to come at once."

Corinne jumped at the chance. "Of course, we will. You know how much you mean to us."

CHAPTER 22

The pill he'd taken earlier having expired, Mark massaged the growing ache in his temples as the dance on stage wound down with St. James triumphant. It had been a long, boring evening, although he couldn't fault the company. Father Menasco's sister had regaled them with the stories of her latest exploit in the caves over Mexicalli until the entertainment started, but once Mark discerned that she was clueless regarding fossils used as gemstones, he lost interest in both the conversation and the shenanigans on stage.

Some guy dancing around with a fake horse hung from his waist, while other dancers pretended to fight, die, and dance again, just didn't enthrall him as it apparently did his companions. He decided to hang on until the fireworks and then head for home.

Meanwhile, he'd watched Rafael Quintana examine Corinne's necklace and stalk off to the cantina like a thundercloud, after evidently having words with his son. And now Diego was playing Don Juan to the hilt, hand-kissing, no less. But as Mark fisted his hands in frustration, Doña Violeta appeared at their table, causing him to blink in disbelief. A moment ago, she'd been in her lawn chair plying him with questions about Corinne.

"You love her, don't you?" Violeta had whispered.

Mark's senses had reverberated from the word, as though struck by a bell clapper. Unable to avoid her all-seeing gaze, he groped for an answer.

"I know I've never thought about a girl the way I do Corinne."

But was that love? "I mean, I don't really know what sets love apart from attraction."

Violeta gave him a grandmotherly smile. "Attraction consumes the senses, *hijo*. Love consumes the heart and soul." A faraway look gathered in her twinkling gaze. "Love is like God, Mark. It is three things in one. One without the other will not last. She will make you burn for her, and she will burn for you . . . but the fires, like youth, will not last a lifetime."

Mark could believe that. If he'd burned any more the other night, before the ghost interrupted them, he'd have spontaneously combusted.

"She will make you adore her ways, the way she cares for others and for you. Her heart will win yours and keep on until death do you part."

Mark wondered if Doña Violeta spoke from experience, of her husband or of a love denied because of an arranged marriage. He searched his memory of the weeks he'd spent in Mexicalli, recalling the joy he'd felt watching Corinne with the children or hearing her chat with Soledad in the kitchen. And her laughter made his heart rise like a balloon in his chest.

"But her soul, her faith will overshadow it all, when you come to share it with her. That is the cement that will bind you to her through eternity."

Would he ever be as unshakable as Corinne? Bad day or good, she always found a way to make the best of it. His rapport with God was like that of a toddler, sometimes up, as when he'd prayed the ghost didn't pack a gun, and sometimes down, as on the day the padre caught him unwittingly arguing with God. Tonight it rose and dipped like the sangria that swished in Corinne's glass before Diego kissed her.

Alarm shook Mark from his troubled reverie at the sight of Violeta dropping in Diego's chair, patting her chest. What had she done, raced across the park? Not wanting to alarm the others until he was certain there was reason for it—the old woman might just be trying to catch her breath—he excused himself.

"I think I'll mosey over to the cantina for some of those cinnamon crisps . . . *churros,*" he remembered. It wasn't exactly a lie. The tempting smell of hot cinnamon had made up his mind to go for some. "So if I don't see you folks before the end of the festivities, I'll catch you later."

With that, Mark zigzagged across the shaded park in the light of the paper lanterns that had been strung from tree to tree by Juan Pedro. Halfway there, he met Corinne.

"What's going on?"

"I'm looking for Gaspar," she said, looking around him at the crowd.

"Why? Is Violeta ill? There's a doctor right here."

Corinne shook her head. "I think she forgot to take her angina pill. She insisted that Diego take her home and I fetch Gaspar, and she'll be fine."

"She does like to give orders."

Corinne met his gaze, affection shining through her eyes in the lantern light. "She didn't want anyone else to know of her 'silliness.' But just in case . . ." She sobered. "Will you help me find Gaspar?"

Prompted by heaven only knew what, Mark seized her hand, making a bow. "Your wish is my command. You take the cantina side of the plaza, and I'll take the market side."

Mark hardly recognized Gaspar when he found him. Clad in the traditional loose white trousers and shirt, the man was sharing a picnic of homemade delicacies wrapped in tortillas with his family near the right of the stage. The moment he heard of Doña Violeta's distress, Gaspar hugged his wife and said good-bye to the others in his party. Mark assumed they were his children and grandchildren.

"She should be well," the manservant assured Mark. "Usually she takes her pill, rests, and is fine, but, still, I will make haste."

Spying Corinne across the plaza, Mark waved to catch her attention. When she finally saw him, she heaved a visible sigh of relief and indicated through gestures that she was going on ahead to Violeta's home.

"Gaspar," he told his companion, "you go ahead with Corinne, but don't rush too fast or we'll have both of you to care for." Mark wasn't sure of the man's age, but the iron gray of his hair implied he was no spring chicken capable of running uphill. "I'll get the lawn chair and catch up with you both."

"*Bueno. Gracias,* Señor Madison."

By the time Mark fetched the folding lawn chair and explained to Father Menasco and Dr. Flynn what was going on, perspiration cloaked his skin, making his cotton polo and trousers cling to his body. Thankfully, they understood the lady's embarrassment and wishes, but he assured them that he would send for them if there was the slightest chance that Doña Violeta needed the doctor's help.

At the moment, Gaspar was probably in the better shape, Mark thought, as he trotted up the hill. Maybe he was getting a cold. He couldn't seem to draw enough air into his lungs to fuel his energy. His legs burned with each uphill pull, while his heart beat itself against his breastbone. And as deserted as the street was from the celebration, if he collapsed, no one would be the wiser until the fireworks display was over.

The courtyard gate to Doña Violeta's home was open. Once inside, Mark dropped on the bench to catch his breath. After all, the people Violeta needed were there. He was just bringing up the rear with a lawn chair and a head filled with a complete section of timpani. And he'd left his bag of medicine at the square, he moaned inwardly.

Once the burning in his legs abated, and he determined that neither his heart nor head was going to explode, he got up and walked to the open door of the salon. Inside, a bright-eyed, pink-cheeked Doña Violeta held court with Gaspar and Corinne in attendance. *Now, what is wrong with this picture?*

Aha, he thought, stepping inside. *Don Juan Diego is missing.*

The burning rushed back, taking sheer effort to override it. He felt as if he'd inhaled helium, making both his head and his stomach light. What on earth was wrong with him?

Violeta, Gaspar, and Corinne, even the furniture in the room, started to circle around to his right.

"Mark, are you all right?" Corinne's question joined the whirl of sensation inside his head.

"Just . . . a . . ." His voice was distorted, too deep and slow for his malady to be caused by helium. ". . . little . . . winded." It sounded to him as though someone had turned on the haunted hacienda sound effects. *Haunted hacienda!*

Mark fell down with laughter at his private joke. Or at least he thought he fell. The rest faded into blackness.

◆

"Estúpido!" Don Rafael paced back and forth in his aunt's courtyard after Mark Madison had been carried out by Gaspar and Capitán Nolla to the police car for transport to Hacienda Ortiz.

Don Rafael had come with the police captain, who was summoned by Corinne via cell phone to bring Father Menasco and his sister to Violeta's house after the engineer's collapse.

After a warm toddy to calm her nerves, his aunt retired, although it was clear that she was more upset about Mark Madison's malady than her own. *If she had truly suffered any manner of heart problem at all,* Don Rafael thought, recalling the sly wink she'd given him as he and Diego retired to the courtyard.

Perhaps she'd succeeded in separating her nephew from Corinne Diaz when he could not. Regardless, he was at last alone with Diego. "I risk everything for you, and you let your fancy for a woman get the better of you," he fumed at his son.

"No one will be able to present a collection before mine, Father," Diego replied, his tone nothing short of condescending. "The necklace was just a small example."

"You know nothing." And Don Rafael hoped to keep it that way with regard to *Tía* Violeta's confidence and the real source of the ammonite. But if his colleague even suspected that a sampling of the valuable commodity had surfaced before it was secured . . .

Don Rafael stopped short and drew a handkerchief from the inside of his jacket. He was sweating as if he'd been witched instead of Mark Madison.

"And what is wrong with giving a beautiful friend a beautiful gift?"

Rafael snorted. "Then you do not see that her heart is already taken by the gringo?"

Diego pretended to study one of his greataunt's prize roses. "You take life too seriously, Father," he said, changing the topic. "You could not stop to appreciate the beauty of life if you were king of the world, instead of mayor of this pitiful town."

"You are what you are because I took life so seriously."

"There is no reasoning with you," Diego exclaimed, raising his hands in exasperation. "I do not know why I try. I should let you fret yourself into an early grave and inherit what sent you there . . . although I have all the income I need from my jewelry. Someday my name will be known beyond a few Mexican states."

Don Rafael had given Diego the best of everything, including Spain's finest schooling. What had it done? Erased the young man's common sense and replaced it with dreams. Granted, his son's jewelry was showcased in a few fine Mexican stores, but life had made Rafael skeptical. The days of the wealth that his family had garnered from the land had passed. Sheer guts and ambition were what replaced what was lost—not a fancy education or artistic whimsy. Not that Don Rafael was bordering on poverty. But a few poor investments had tightened his purse strings and pressed him to take greater risks.

Gaspar appeared at the salon door. "*La* señora is settled in bed, Don Rafael, Don Diego."

"She is well?" Diego asked.

His son adored Violeta, but then so did Rafael. His aunt was a reminder of better days, even if he sometimes tired of her stories.

"Very tired, I suspect . . . and disappointed to have missed the fireworks." From Gaspar's sigh, *Tía* Violeta was not the only one.

"*Gracias,* Gaspar. You are dependable as always," Don Rafael told the servant. "Lock the door behind us, *por favor.*"

Gaspar inclined his head slightly. *"Como siempre, Don Rafael."*

"Diego, will you join me for a drink at the Cantina Roja?" Rafael asked, taking the lead toward the street entrance.

"*Gracias,* no. I hear the mariachis playing again. I think that I will return for the dancing."

Diego's refusal came as no surprise, but to hear it was a relief. It would make it easier for Rafael to report to his partner. After bidding Gaspar good night, Diego walked as far as the plaza with Rafael in silence.

Rafael followed Diego's progress toward the stage, noting how everyone received the young man with handshakes and waves—genuine ones, not the shallow reception that Rafael had grown accustomed to. Another cost of power, Rafael reflected with a foreign twinge of envy.

"Did I not tell you that my mother-in-law was a powerful witch?" Lorenzo Pozas materialized from the shadows, giving Don Rafael a start.

"Do not sneak up on me like so again," Rafael snapped, "or I will pay her to witch you."

"My apologies, Don Rafael. I thought that you could see me," Pozas answered, precious little apology in his voice. "But Señor Madison, he has the fever, no?"

Rafael cast an astonished look at the man. "How did you know?"

When Capitán Nolla asked the doctor and priest to accompany him, nothing had been said as to the identity of the patient, only that they were needed.

"I saw him purchasing medicine for his cough and headache at the *farmacia.*" Pozas's tobacco-stained grin faded. "And he asked me about *caracoles* in the mountains."

The word shot Rafael's heart with fear, starting a mental landslide of questions. What would an engineer know of the *caracoles?* Had he found something? Did he suspect Diego because of that blasted necklace?

"Have you told *him?*" Rafael jerked his head toward the Cantina Roja, where the man who'd put this entire nightmare into motion wheezed between sips of Corona.

"Oh no, Don Rafael," Pozas exclaimed. "It is best that I not be seen with *El Caracol* in public."

El Caracol. If Rafael weren't afraid of the man, he'd laugh. The conniver took the name for himself, as if it somehow increased his stature to match his girth.

Perhaps his foolish son had mentioned to Madison that the ammonite was the fossil of a prehistoric snail.

"But it is very strange that this Madison should ask me about the *caracoles,"* Lorenzo said, nixing Rafael's hope. *"Pues,* I hardly know him. But he asks me."

Other than Lorenzo, his late brother, and the boy Enrique, no one knew that the fossils had been found. *El Caracol* wanted to keep it that way until the hacienda and its property were his, so that he could file for a concession from the federal government.

"I am only thankful that my Atlahua's mamá is so powerful. She is from Sierra de Pueblo," he added, referring to the northeastern mountains above Mexico City, an area noted for witchcraft in days past and present, despite the laws against it. "The sooner Malinche's magic works, the sooner the orphanage will sell the hacienda."

The Indios and their magic. Despite his disdain, the idea lay like a cold stone in the pit of Rafael's stomach. He'd seen things he could not explain . . . like a healthy young man like Mark Madison coughing and breathing as though someone sat upon his chest.

"Yes," Pozas went on, his beady black eyes glowing as though he himself was possessed—most likely by the *refino* made from corn. "The *caracoles* will be ours soon."

A chill swept over Rafael. It was Lorenzo's brother and his eldest son who'd found the ammonite in the rough. Three suspicious deaths later, Lorenzo had the look of a shark in a feeding frenzy— a shark that had done and would do anything for the *caracoles.*

Rafael wished he'd never heard of it. But with what he knew, he either had to join the frenzy or become another victim of it.

CHAPTER 23

Corinne shifted in the plush leather chair next to Mark's bed, studying the pale man lying against the pillows with sleep-dogged eyes. Despite the even, reassuring rise and fall of his chest, she leaned forward and tested his forehead with the palm of her hand. Thank God the fever had finally broken, after a full day and night of sapping his strength.

When Mark collapsed in the doorway of Violeta's home, Corinne felt as though the life had been knocked out of her. She and Gaspar broke free of the shock at the same time and rushed to his side.

He was burning up with fever. Disoriented, he'd struggled as though drunk, vowing that he was fine. Once he determined that Doña Violeta was in no danger, he had insisted on returning to the plaza to see the fireworks, but his knees would not support him. Since there was no ambulance in Mexicalli, much less a medical facility, Corinne called Capitán Nolla and asked him to bring Father Menasco's sister and his car. A half hour later they arrived, and with them Don Rafael.

Suspecting a bronchial infection, Dr. Flynn sent Father Menasco to find the owner of the *farmacia* to get antibiotics while Mark was transported to Hacienda Ortiz. For the last thirty-six hours or so, Corinne and Soledad spelled each other in nursing him.

With each labored breath Mark took, Corinne struggled as if it was her own. Somewhere in the midst of their verbal sparring, he'd become a part of her, and it scared her. Yet she knew beyond a doubt that her heart belonged to the man lying on the bed before her.

It had to be a God thing, she reasoned. Mark Madison was not the kind of man she wanted to fall in love with. She'd asked God to help her resist, and instead, God changed Mark. Not by leaps and bounds, granted, but Mark was not the same man he'd been when he climbed down from that pig truck.

A banging at the front of the house startled the wistful smile from Corinne's lips.

"Hola, is there anyone in habitation?"

Recognizing Juan Pablo's voice, Corinne shook away the remnants of sleep and hurried to the entrance as Soledad stumbled into the hall, still in her nightdress.

"Ay de mí, I sleep too late and—" She broke off, her dark gaze narrowing as Corinne opened the door. "Oh, and look who is here from the mountains." In a dither, she ducked back through her bedroom door.

"Juan Pablo, you're visiting early today."

Bewildered by Soledad's declaration, Corinne peered around him to see the plumber's brothers taking tools out of his truck. Since she knew Juan Pedro, she assumed that the third man—the source of Soledad's strange behavior—was none other than Juan Miguel.

The mason Juan looked nothing like Juan Pedro and Juan Pablo, who were short, stocky, and sported thick mustaches to match their bushy brows. This Juan was tall, willow thin, and clean-shaven, with salt and pepper hair pulled into a ponytail.

"Los Tres Juanes are ready to work, señorita," the plumber announced, puffed with pride.

It was Monday! Corinne backtracked. She'd missed church yesterday to care for Mark. Weariness had blurred her sense of time.

"And this is my eldest brother, Juan Miguel."

From the truck, Juan Miguel nodded.

"Mucho gusto, Juan Miguel." She waved and then backed inside. "Please, come in . . . all of you."

"And how is Señor Mark?" the plumber asked, taking note of the candles and flowers laid on the patio. "It was a grandiose fireworks display."

By now everyone in Mexicalli knew of *El* Señor *del Cerdito's* malady. The candles and flowers, as well as some curious bags of native healing balms, began appearing yesterday morning. If the villagers appreciated his work for the orphanage, he was even more dear to them now for the unexpected treat of fireworks.

"The antibiotics Dr. Flynn prescribed are finally working. His fever broke last night, but his breathing is still shallow."

Invisible hands squeezed her heart. One moment he was a pain in the neck, and the next, a pain in her heart.

"Has he been in any caves?"

Corinne lifted her brow in surprise. That was the same question Dr. Flynn had asked. An avid cave explorer, she explained how the mines and caves riddling the area were filled with bat dung, the spores of which sometimes infected the lungs. Usually it was only fatal for those who already had lung problems, particularly the elderly and little children.

"Mark hasn't been anywhere, except here in the house . . . unless you count an occasional walk to the village."

"Humph. *Pues,*" Juan Pablo said, dismissing the thought. "He need not to worry. My brothers and I will employ his blueprint according to our projections."

"Great. I'll grab a quick shower first, if that's okay?" Corinne had been so concerned about Mark that she'd only freshened up yesterday. Now she needed one to wake up.

It was okay as far as Juan Pablo was concerned, but no one consulted Juan Pedro, who cut the power to the water pump, fortunately, just as Corinne finished rinsing her hair. While she dressed, the scent of frying bacon on the gas stove in the kitchen tempted her to head straight there, but instead, she returned to check on Mark.

On entering the room, she found him struggling into a pair of shorts.

"What do you think you're doing?" she demanded. Seeing him teeter, she rushed to steady him.

"Haven't you ever heard of knocking?"

"The door was open," she replied, ignoring the dour reminder of their first meeting at the hacienda. She pressed a hand to his forehead to confirm the heat emanating from his bare shoulders. "You still have a little fever."

"The key word there is *little.*"

"How much do you remember of yesterday?"

He scowled, thinking. "I missed the fireworks . . . and Soledad made flan."

"Fireworks were Saturday. Flan was yesterday. Case closed." Corinne pushed him back against the pillows with little effort.

"You always like to take charge, don't you? Although . . ." He flashed a devilish grin. "I could get used to this part."

"I'm glad you didn't try to stand," she answered, making a show of ignoring the *twickle* his comment evoked. She grunted as she swung his legs onto the mattress. "I'd hate to have to lift you from the floor."

"Whoa, you're dripping on me," he said, drawing up his knees to avoid the drip of her wet hair.

"I towel dried, but Juan cut the electricity, so no hair dryer."

"Which Juan?"

The playful arch of his one brow stirred the names in her mind. "Electric Juan." With a chuckle, she slung the sheet over her patient, shorts and all.

"Are we having fun yet?"

Corinne pulled a straight face. "I know someone who is not ever going to have fun if that fever doesn't go away." She retrieved a thermometer from the nightstand and stuck it in Mark's mouth.

He made a questioning grunt.

"Dr. Flynn said if your temp remained elevated, you would be taken to the hospital in Cuernavaca."

The night-light on the desk flashed on suddenly.

"Looks like we have pow—" Before Mark could complete his sentence, a loud pop echoed from the back of the house, followed by an excited barrage of Spanish.

"Desconectelo! Off, off!"

With a groan, Mark closed his eyes.

Corinne rushed to the hall, leaving the thermometer beeping in her patient's mouth. "Juan, *todo está bien?* Is everything okay?"

"*Está bien,* señorita," one of the men shouted back—which Juan, she couldn't tell. "Just a little—how do you say . . . snitch."

Corinne frowned. "You mean snag?"

"*Sí,* a snag. No worries."

"Easy for him to say," Mark grumbled from the bed.

Spinning around, Corinne rushed to take the thermometer he'd removed from his mouth, but he turned it off before she could read it. "What did it say?"

"Just a little elevation."

She propped her hands on her hips. "*How* little?"

"A hundred."

"And what?" She smelled smoke akin to burning wire.

"Just a hundred." Mark reached for the glass of water on the nightstand. "And by the time I drink this, it will be even lower."

"Juan . . . Electric Juan?" she called out, moving back to the hallway. "What is that burning?"

"*Es nada,* señorita," the man shouted back as the lamp came on again, this time without event. "See, no worries."

Lord, please let that be the truth.

"Tell you what," she said to Mark. It wouldn't hurt for her to look, not that she'd really know what she was looking at. "I'll go check on things and be back in two shakes with your breakfast."

At his answering grunt, she made her way to the ballroom. Juan Pedro stood on a ladder next to a hole where one of the wall lamps had hung before the previous contractors had removed and boxed them. A piece of charred wire protruded from the wall. To it, he was tying a coil of new.

"Soon it will all be new, no?" He smiled upon seeing her approach.

"What are you doing?"

"*Pues,* this is old," he said, pointing with a soot-smudged hand to the charred piece. "And it runs to that *enchufe* where the electricity comes." After wiping his nose with the back of the same hand, he nodded to a gutted electrical socket a few feet away. "So, to keep from creating more plaster work for Juan Miguel, I will pull the new wire through as I pull out the old, no?"

She'd used a similar technique to replace worn elastic in some of the children's shorts. "That's brilliant, Juan, but we aren't replacing the wall lamps. This is to be a gymnasium. Aren't you supposed to cover the hole with plaster?"

With knitted eyebrows, the little man came down the ladder and took the set of blueprints from the tube where they'd been stored. After much rustling of paper and scrutiny, he dropped them on the floor. *"Pues,* if that is the way you want."

"Unfortunately, that's what we have to do," she said, leaving the man to his work.

Corinne understood Juan Pedro's reluctance. The ballroom was beautiful, but the orphanage did not need it, with its elegant converted Victorian gas lamps lining both walls. Nor did it need the large chandelier overhead, which had yet to be taken out. What was needed was a gymnasium with fluorescent lighting. And she'd already found a place on the Internet where they could sell the antique fixtures.

"Soledad," she said, marching into the kitchen. "Breakfast smells—"

She broke off. Sitting at the kitchen table, Juan Miguel was finishing off a plate of huevos rancheros and bacon, while Soledad hovered over him with a look of adoration.

"—delicious."

"It is, señorita, and I am very thankful for it." The sculptor-mason munched the words along with his last forkful. After swallowing, he gave Soledad a wink. "But then, Señorita Corina, you must know that you have the best cook in all of Guerrero."

Soledad gave him a playful smack on the shoulder as he rose to leave. "You mean in all of Mexico, *perro viejo.*"

Old dog? Was Soledad flirting?

"Pues," the housekeeper announced, all business after he exited, "I will have your breakfast and that of Señor Mark *en un momento.*"

With that, she returned to the stove where the remainder of the cooked bacon warmed on a plate over the pilot light.

Love must be in the air, Corinne mused, distracted by the pop and sizzle of the coffeemaker on the counter. Craving a cup, she was reaching into the cupboard when she heard someone in the bathroom. *Juan Pablo,* she thought, filling the mug to the brim. Just the scent snapped her taste buds to attention.

"And how is your patient?" Soledad asked, shaking the frying pan to spread the melting butter.

"Mark still has a little temp . . . if I can believe him," she said. "Do you think I should give him some coffee?"

"I'd love a cup." Mark leaned against the jamb of the utility-bathroom door, looking like the cat that swallowed the canary—weak cat, small bird. As if walking on the moving blocks in a fun house, he approached the table and dropped, literally, into a chair.

Lord, help. I'm losing patience with this patient.

CHAPTER 24

"Why are you out of bed?" Corinne demanded.

"There are some things a man can't do from the bed," Mark said, waiting for his meaning to sink in. When it did, he was rewarded with a rose of a blush.

"Oh." She jumped up to get another cup. "Well, you should have called for one of us to help you to the room at least."

Since he felt as thought he'd just climbed the Matterhorn instead of crossing through Corinne's room to the bathroom, Mark almost agreed with her. But he'd had to see just what this cough, or whatever it was, had done to his stamina. Now he knew.

"Did you see what the people have brought you?" Soledad asked.

"What people?"

Corinne put his coffee on the table. "The ones who've been bringing flowers and candles into the courtyard since yesterday morning. I was going to show you, but things have gotten a little busy today."

"Everyone in the village is still talking about your fireworks. They were the best Mexicalli has ever seen. So many beautiful colors . . . And in the market this morning," the housekeeper bragged, "I told them all that I cook for you."

Mark sipped the hot brew, savoring the rich flavor as Toto nosed his way into the kitchen.

"And there is mama's little pig this morning," Soledad exclaimed. She promptly abandoned the eggs in the pan to give Toto some melon rind.

206

"And the Sunday school class made you this get-well card." Corinne presented him with a large card with a childlike drawing of a stick man and a pig. "Father Menasco brought it after church yesterday."

On the inside were fireworks and signatures. Mark thought he remembered seeing the fireworks . . . which made no sense, because he remembered thinking on the way to Doña Violeta's that he would miss them. "How is Doña Violeta?"

"Well enough to visit yesterday after church."

Mark watched the piglet shove the flat aluminum cake tin off its plastic placemat and across the floor in his zeal to finish off his meal. "I don't remember Father Menasco's visit or hers."

"*Pues,* the doctor would allow no one in but us at first." Soledad placed a bacon-and-cheese omelet in front of him. "Here it is . . . your favorite."

The food had as much appeal as what Toto had just wolfed down. "Aw, thank you, Soledad, but I don't think I can eat much. I'm more thirsty."

"Liquids are important," Corinne agreed. "But try to eat a couple of mouthfuls."

"Yes, couple mouthfuls," Soledad echoed.

Two were all Mark could force down. He couldn't even finish the coffee. All he wanted to do was lie down. As Corinne walked him back to the salon, he gave in to a pity party. "This is the worst luck yet. I can't be sick now."

"I don't think the choice is yours to make."

"It was just a little cough and headache," he complained.

"They were just signs of the infection causing the fever. I would count my blessings that an American physician was on hand . . . and that Mexicalli is one of the upland villages that actually has a pharmacy with antibiotics and a blood kit."

"Blood kit?"

"Dr. Flynn took some blood yesterday and sent it to Cuernavaca for testing."

On reaching the salon entrance, Mark wanted more than anything to make a rush for the bed and collapse. But Corinne's gentle reminder of his blessings made him think better of it. Instead of going inside, he nodded toward the open front door.

"I'd like to count a blessing or two before I collapse. To see the flowers," he explained at her bewildered expression. "If the people were good enough to bring them up the hill, I can at least walk a few extra feet to see them."

The burning he recalled from the night of his collapse threatened again, but he forced himself to the front door. Candles, mostly burned down, and flowers, a majority wilting from their overnight exposure, were scattered on the patio. He couldn't recall ever feeling so humbled, so at a loss for words.

As Mark blinked away a welling of emotion from his eyes, he spied movement beyond the patio. Walking toward what used to be the gate was a woman leading a little boy away.

"Thank you," he called after them. *"Gracias."*

The woman never looked back, but the child turned and waved. With a flash of pearl white teeth, he said something, but Mark only caught a few words—*bien, gracias,* and Señor *del Cerdito.*

An uncommon joy filled his being, and with it strength to walk back to the salon, where he fell back on the bed in an exhausted sweat.

"Are you okay?" Alarm filled Corinne's voice.

"You know," he said, breathing with some effort, "I don't think I've ever been better, considering how sick I feel."

She pulled the sheet up over his half-clad torso, and as it settled on his skin, she yanked it back. "You're soaked in perspiration again, *Superman.*"

Instead of replying, Mark watched her fill a plastic basin with water from a pitcher and place it beside the bed.

"Move over," she ordered, nudging him away from the edge so she had room to sit. "I guess your fever broke again."

The cool cloth that she wrung dry over the basin felt soothing as she gently ran it over his face and around his neck.

"Mmm," he moaned softly. "Keep this up and I won't want to get well."

Corinne gave him a stern look, but the pink climbing from the neck of her shirt to the tip of her hairline belied it. "Behave, or I'll get Soledad." Taking up a hand towel next to the pitcher, she flung it on his face. "I'll wash; you dry."

After rinsing the cloth and wringing it again, she began to mop the perspiration from his chest. Mark caught his breath as she made methodical circles from the center, up and over the width of his shoulders.

"Now," she said, "turn on your side and I'll wipe down your back." Forgetting to dry, Mark obeyed. "You know, I changed my mind."

"About what?" she asked.

"About my luck," he mumbled. "I have people who care for me. Very special people." People who had little more than a tin roof over their heads and rags on their back . . . a woman like Corinne, the flighty bumblebee Soledad, and children he hardly knew. "And a brother who, instead of reaming me out as I expected, understood when I confessed everything that had gone wrong on the project."

The cloth stopped. "You told Blaine? About the contractors and . . . *everything?*" she asked, seeming stricken, though by what he couldn't imagine. "God is definitely working here," she murmured, as if in awed prayer.

Mark wiped his eyes on the pillow. Maybe it was the fever, because he was definitely not the sappy type. "I haven't forgotten God," he admitted, suddenly needing to share that with her. Especially with her, because he knew she would understand. He coughed, clearing his throat of the emotion binding it. "Who'd have thought I'd have to come all the way to the *Twilight Zone* to find Him?"

Corinne reached over him, taking the towel he'd dropped. The brush of her body against him reminded Mark of how right it had felt when he'd held her in his arms. He inhaled the sweet scent of her.

"And have you found Him, Mark?" Her voice rang with hope. But then Corinne wouldn't have him any other way, no matter how much charm Mark surrounded her with. He rolled over, holding on to the towel and her hand, and then her gaze.

"I'm not kidding. Don't make any more jokes," her voice warned, but a plea swam in her overbright eyes.

Mark wanted to swim in them forever. "Yes, I found Him. And more."

"More?" She moistened her lips in expectation of his answer.

Not the kiss that was on his mind, he reminded himself. "I think I found the meaning of His love . . . here among the people, who give when they have nothing." He sucked in a ragged breath. "And with a woman who lives it."

Reaching up with his finger, he caught the single tear that ventured over the fall of a dark eyelash to her cheek and put it to his lips, tasting its saltiness. "I want all of you, Corinne Diaz, but I'll make do with this until I can prove myself worthy of your trust . . . of your love."

Stars of emotion glittered in the gaze fixed on him. Kissing the same finger, he planted it on the quiver of her chin. And when he drew it away, her lips descended, touching his, tentative . . . unsure.

Then uncertainty was lost in the sweet burst of desire he held at bay beyond the tender embrace of his arms. He wanted her to know that this intimacy, unlike before, was on her terms, in her time. The last thing he wanted was to scare her away. Her shy, lengthening caress robbed him of breath, yet, if this were his last, he'd count it another blessing.

As he inhaled, the smell of tobacco smoke mingled with the orange blossom of Corinne's scent, setting off an entirely different set of alarms. All of them made him aware that they were being watched. Mark maneuvered so that he might see where the smoke was coming from.

Standing in the door, his expression as wooden as the carvings in the tourist shops, Primitivo waited patiently, a faint trail of smoke drifting up from the pipe in his mouth. As if sensing that Mark was no longer a part of what had become their passionate exchange, Corinne backed away, confusion overtaking her flushed features. Following Mark's look toward the entrance, she gasped and leapt to her feet.

"P-Primitivo," she stammered, reaching for the washcloth that tumbled to the floor. "We . . . I didn't hear you come in."

"We have a custom in the States called knocking," Mark grumbled.

"I'd best dump this water and leave you two be." Corinne grabbed the water basin with such force that the water sloshed over the side, spilling down the front of her jeans.

"You are better?" the Indio asked, as if he was always met by a couple in passion's embrace.

Mark spied the dingy woolen medicine sack slung over his shoulder. *Please, Lord, no chopped chicken liver. I don't even like that at swanky places.*

"My *nagual* entered the land of the spirits," Primitivo said.

"Your *nagual?*"

Primitivo gave him an impatient look. "My animal spirit . . . it is how one travels in the spirit world. Did you burn the candles and cobal as instructed?"

"We burned the candles." *As night-lights.*

Primitivo gave him a dismissive wave. "No matter. You were witched by the ghost before you could protect yourself." He shook his head. "Shame you no smoke tobacco."

"Oh, that would have helped my cough a lot." Mark couldn't help his sarcasm. He felt like the dickens, although Corinne had done wonders to distract him. Talk about a rude awakening. Primitivo gave him the willies.

"How has Soledad cleaned since your visit from the other side?"

"Do spirits wear shoes and swear at pigs?"

Primitivo's gray brow shot up. "The pig drove it away?"

"More likely Toto was mooching attention."

"I heard it belonged to a witch. That is good."

There was no reasoning with this guy. Mark glanced over to where the pig had slept without fail since the night of the ghostly encounter—in front of the hearth. It fetched. It heeled, although of its own accord. Spiritual nonsense aside, could it be part guard dog too?

"Soledad sweeps with a broom, no?"

Mark nodded. Despite his doubts regarding Primitivo's beliefs, he was curious as to what Soledad's cleaning had to do with witchcraft.

"Hmm." Digging into his sack, the Indio produced a candle. After several attempts, he finally lit it with his pipe.

If the old man started dancing and chanting, Mark would lose it. He watched as the healer walked around the room, watching the flame of the candle and kneeling to wipe the floor with his hand.

"No one else is sick?"

"Just me." But if Soledad caught Primitivo insinuating that she did not keep a clean house, he would be needing a healer too.

Toto raised his head as the elder Indio approached him with the candle, but never moved when Primitivo climbed up on the raised hearth and ducked into the fireplace.

"Does she sweep in here?"

Mark had to think. He didn't recall seeing Soledad near the hearth since the snake episode. "I don't know."

With a grunt, Primitivo ran his hand over the brick floor of the fireplace and then looked at it. "It is as I thought," he said. "You have the bat fever."

"Bat fever? Don't I have to hang out in caves to get that? No pun intended."

Even if the pun was intended, Primitivo missed it. "See the flame of the candle? It wavers with the movement of the air. And the air moves this," he said, showing the dark dirt collected on his palm. "It is *mal* witchcraft. Very bad."

"What is it, Primitivo?" Corinne inquired, walking in from the foyer.

"The witch brought the bad air from the cave into this room, making Señor Marco sick in the lung."

Mark smirked. "Are you saying that dirt made me sick?"

Primitivo nodded. "So I said."

"That dirt came from a cave," Corinne said, as though trying to make reason of what the Indio told them.

"I saw it in my dream. The ghost brought the cave sickness into this room, putting Señor Marco to lose."

"So Dr. Flynn wasn't so far out after all," she said.

Mark looked at her in disbelief. Surely she wasn't buying this mumbo jumbo. "Dr. Flynn had a dream too?"

Corinne shook her head. "No, but she said that your symptoms were in keeping with an infection that comes from inhaling spores from bat or bird dung. Cave explorers sometimes come down with it. *Histo-something.* She sent a blood sample to Cuernavaca yesterday just to be on the safe side."

"I've been breathing spores from bat crap?" Maybe he was better off not knowing what had made him sick, since he was improving.

"The cave sickness."

Primitivo probably wouldn't know a spore from a sponge, but somehow the old healer might have found the source of Mark's problem.

"We must remove the dirt and burn copal in its place."

"We'll do more than that." Corinne peered into the fireplace. "With the soot and smoke stains, I never noticed."

"The spirits spoke true to my *nagual.*"

"Your animal spirit?" Corinne echoed.

"In his dream," Mark explained, his mind still reeling over the dung factor. "Don't ask."

CHAPTER 25

"I knew I'd wind up back here one way or another," Mark teased as Corinne turned back the covers of her bed an hour later. It was the only place she could put him until his room was thoroughly cleaned.

"Keep pushing it, amigo, and you'll wind up outside on your air mattress with Toto as a nurse," she warned in like humor. She hoped the heat blooming on her neck and cheeks wouldn't reveal that he'd been there more than he knew—haunting her thoughts and dreams. Somehow this rascal had managed to charm his way through her best defenses. Her mind was on the brink, and her heart had already deserted its post. And if Primitivo hadn't interrupted them earlier . . . Her pulse catapulted, reminding her senses of the heady, yet innocent, seduction.

"Your pillows smell like you. Sweet, fresh, flowery."

She'd never been so flustered, so at a loss to explain what she couldn't.

"Scented shampoo and conditioner," Corinne replied, her effort to remain unaffected and businesslike withering as her body remembered what reason dismissed—or tried to. *God, how does a woman separate passion from love?*

"Orange blossom, isn't it?"

She hoped he wasn't as astute when it came to Toto's *fresh, flowery smell* . . . although Soledad had stopped washing the pig with Corinne's bath-and-body set.

At the moment, the pig was still on duty with the housekeeper in the salon, seemingly fascinated by her efforts to remove dirt. The moment Primitivo left, Soledad began emptying Mark's room for a thorough cleaning—candles and incense burning. It was easier to put Mark in her own bed temporarily than to get into an old debate that went nowhere.

But if there were disease-causing spores in the dirt that had been left in the fireplace, by evening they would be gone—except for the sample Corinne bagged after calling Dr. Flynn earlier. If the police wouldn't do their work, someone had to.

"I have to admit," Mark told her as Corinne opened another window for cross ventilation, "I'm exhausted after that little effort."

Sensing a downturn of spirit, she quirked a single brow at him. "So kissing me was an effort?"

Mark laid an arm across his chest in salute. "It gave me the strength to carry on . . ."

What *was* she doing? She wasn't a flirt and certainly not one of those women who milked men for compliments. She was confident, self-assured.

". . . although I might need another dose."

Okay, that grin was worth it. A major *twickler.* Corinne pulled her scrambled wits together. "That's for your nurse to determine. Right now, I register the blarney factor as full. Now, on a more serious note—"

"I thought heart palps were serious."

He wasn't playing fair. Hearts were serious, and hers was flipping out. "Dr. Flynn said that if it is histoplasmosis, it should run its course in eight to ten days. It tends to linger longer or even become deadly in people who have constant exposure or a chronic breathing problem."

Mark snorted, a good stretch from humor. "At least my witch isn't quite as practiced as he or she could be."

"I don't know," Corinne said, her evasive switch tactic providing time for a little self-CPR. "Putting the stuff in the fireplace was pretty ingenious. No one noticed, and with no fire and the flue open, the draft would disburse the spores into the room." She rubbed her arms as though the ghost in question had walked through her. "We're lucky that Soledad and I aren't sick as well."

"You only slept here one night . . . and Soledad had the place locked up like Attica." Mark's expression firmed with resolve. "If— and I do mean *if*—the test comes back positive, this trying to scare us off is going too far. It takes more than a little bat crap to make me back down."

Is this the same guy who didn't want to be here two months ago? In a mix of admiration and wonder, Corinne studied the stubborn set of his golden, whisker-stubbled jaw. Shaving faces was not in her job description. Too many contours, when it was all she could do to navigate a razor around her knees without drawing blood.

"Maybe you could ask Blaine if he knows anyone who will take us seriously," she suggested.

She and Mark had already agreed that if Capitán Nolla would ignore footprints left behind by a ghost, getting him to come look at some dirt in a fireplace was a waste of time. It was so frustrating, she could just scream.

"Yeah, I can hear me explaining it now," Mark said with a dour twist of his mouth. "Some witch is practicing Aztec germ warfare on me."

It did sound absurd. That was the scary part about the so-called witchcraft. No one of authority took it seriously enough. And if Primitivo was right about this, could the old Indio be right about the Pozases' and Enrique's deaths as well?

"Where's CSI when we need them?" Mark quipped. He heaved a labored sigh.

Corinne placed her hand on his forehead. It was clammy, but not fevered. At least he was recovering according to Dr. Flynn's expectations. The antibiotic was doing its part, and now that they knew the cause—or thought they did—reinfection wasn't likely.

"We'll have to settle for your blood test results for now. Dr. Flynn is expecting them late this evening or tomorrow. Then we'll know for certain." She poured fresh water from a thermal carafe on her nightstand.

"Wake me when the call comes," he yawned with an accompanying stretch of his upper torso.

Corinne watched, mind and body held captive by the rippling interplay of his muscles . . . until the ice water overran the glass in her hand.

"Oh, bother!" She handed the dripping glass to him. "I hate it when the ice breaks from the bottom like that," she excused herself. After all, there *had* to be some ice on the bottom, since she'd just filled it.

As she tore off paper towels to mop up the overflow, a timid knock drew her attention to the open door.

Clad in dark violet, Doña Violeta stood there, looking none the worse for wear from her angina episode that past weekend. She reminded Corinne of a tiny, slightly bent queen, crowned with the shining silver of a thick braid.

"Doña Dulce," Mark called out from the bed. "You're a sight for sore eyes."

The bright smile on the woman's smile-weathered face faltered. "Has the fever damaged your eyes?"

"It's just an expression to say that he is glad to see you." Corinne threw the wet towels in a nearby trash basket. "We both are." She walked over to hug her guest when Antonio jumped from his hiding place behind the woman.

"*Buenos días,* señorita!"

Clutching her hand to her chest, Corinne jumped back with a sharp intake of breath. "Antonio, you rascal," she managed on recovery, giving him, and then his companion, a hug.

"I hope you don't mind," Doña Violeta apologized, "but he was so anxious about his Señor Mark." The sparkle returned to her gaze as the boy bounced on the bed next to Mark. "As was I."

"Well, as you can see, I'm still here," Mark announced. "But Corinne and I were worried about you. Any more spells?"

Doña Violeta waved away his concern. "None . . . and I would not have had that one, had I not forgotten in my excitement to take my medicine."

Was there a pill for what Corinne felt every time Mark flashed that boyish grin, when there was anything but a boy behind it?

"Do you wish to arm wrestle?" Antonio asked him.

Mark chuckled. "Maybe next week, amigo."

"Antonio," Corinne chided, "Mark is too sick to play." She watched as the boy digested her warning.

"When I am sick, I like to be read to." The boy turned to Mark, disappointment vanishing in sunshine. "I brought a bag of things to keep me quiet and in it is my favorite book. It is called *Green Eggs and Ham.*"

"You're kidding," Mark replied. "That was one of my favorites too." He patted the side of the bed. "I haven't heard it in years."

Corinne's heart squeezed for Mark. He would obviously rather be left to his dreams, but he would tough it out rather than hurt the boy's feelings. For someone who hadn't been around children very much, he was a natural.

"And while the men visit, perhaps we might have tea?" Doña Violeta suggested.

"That sounds lovely," Corinne answered, trying to ignore the nick of fear at the nape of her neck.

Corinne was torn between helping Soledad and being a good hostess. But the housekeeper had summoned Tizoc through Primitivo to help with the cleaning.

"He needs the work," the old man told them. "But removing the dirt will not remove the bad spirits. The dirt is but the footprint of evil."

Was this some sort of spiritual warfare beyond the depth of her understanding? Not that Corinne believed in the abilities of man or woman to conjure them and use them at will. But she did believe that good and evil spirits worked through mankind.

Father, in the name of Jesus, protect us, if this is a battle beyond the human realm.

"Is anything wrong?" Doña Violeta asked, sliding into a chair at the kitchen table.

Corinne turned on a burner to bring the water in the teapot to boil.

"Someone doesn't want us in the hacienda, Doña Violeta," she answered, fetching two mismatched cups and saucers from the red-and-white painted cabinets. "And they are using fake ghosts and witchcraft to cover it." She put the cups on the table. "And the worst part is that Capitán Nolla doesn't think it's anything more than some precocious teens behind it."

"Behind what, exactly?" Violeta moved her beaded drawstring purse to her lap.

Corinne told her all about it as she prepared the tea, reminding the old woman of the first warning, filling her in on the ghost's appearance and their suspicions regarding Mark's illness. "I can't imagine what is so special about this place, but it's certainly too much for coincidence, don't you think?"

"Coincidence is as mysterious as truth sometimes," Violeta replied with a Confucius-like wisdom.

But when Corinne gave her a curious glance, prompting explanation, Violeta took up her tea and blew on the steaming surface. Her expression was distressed, while her hands trembled so that the tea lapped nearly to the brim.

"Doña Violeta?" Corinne placed her hand on her companion's arm, soft and frail beneath the thin covering of silk. "I promise, Mark and I will see the orphanage finished. We won't leave until the children have a place in which to live and play."

A tired smile stretched Violeta's lips. "It isn't that, *querida*. I have seen the dedication in your heart and his dedication to you in his eyes. Tell me that you feel the same for him." Withdrawing her hands, she placed them in her lap, her back straight as an arrow. "I saw Diego kiss you at the fiesta . . . so I wondered."

"Diego?" Corinne laughed. "Doña Violeta, we are only friends," she assured the distraught woman. "Which is why I felt a little uneasy accepting his gift. I mean, it could look like there was more to it."

If the eyes were the window to the soul, Doña Violeta's were a pale blue sea of despair. "A gift such as that is appropriate—"

"Still—"

"—between cousins."

Cousins? Corinne practically dropped her teacup on its saucer, grateful that she'd not yet tasted the tea. Otherwise she surely would have sprayed her companion with it.

"Rafael knew my terrible secret, of course, but Diego was but a child. He had no idea."

Corinne's voice finally kicked into gear. "What are you saying, Doña Violeta?"

Doña Violeta clutched her purse as though it contained the last shred of her composure. "Ah, where to begin?" she fretted, venturing to cover Corinne's hand with hers. *"Querida Corina . . ."* She trailed off and braced herself with a breath. "I am your *abuela.*"

Abuela. Corinne translated the word twice and each time she reached the same conclusion—grandmother. She opened her mouth to speak, but the tide of emotion rising from the region of her mind where she'd placed abandoned hopes blocked her throat. It was the last thing she'd expected the woman to say.

Doña Violeta caressed the side of Corinne's cheek. *"Mi niñita linda.* You are wondering why I have said nothing, no?"

Corinne nodded. She'd been in Mexicalli since May, and that didn't count the summer before, when she and her family had traced her mother's roots to the village—when Mexicalli had won her heart.

"Shame is one reason," the old woman confessed.

So the María of record was really María Quintana de la Vega. Corinne could hardly believe her ears, but her heart didn't need confirmation. It was shocking, but it felt right. All this time . . .

"And . . ." Violeta's voice cracked. "I . . . I wanted to get to know you. To see if you had your mother's forgiving heart . . . not my hard one."

The notion that Violeta had a hard heart did not set well with Corinne. "Never can it be said that *Doña Dulce* has a hard heart," she averred. Getting up, she drew the older woman to her. "Not my *abuelita.*"

Her little grandmother. The hundreds of hugs that Corinne had stored away with her hopes of finding her blood family begged to be bestowed.

"But I was not always the woman I am now," Violeta said in a shaky voice.

Corinne gave her grandmother a gentle hug, absorbing her heart-wrenching sob. Nor could Corinne help her own sob of joy. She'd turned her past over to God to fill the void and contented herself with serving the people of her mother's native village. But this—

"God has answered my prayers with more than I asked," she whispered against her grandmother's silver crown. "He not only gave me a grandmother, but He made her extra special because she was you." Soft and scented with lavender, she thought, like the sachets that Violeta had made from her flower garden and presented to Corinne when she first arrived. They were to keep Corinne's unmentionables fresh in the rainy season, the prim little lady confided with a rose pink blush.

"*P-pero,* I threw your mother out," Violeta lamented. "She disgraced our family with that despicable artist."

"You mean my father?" Corinne took no offense. She understood the ways of Violeta's generation and station. "It's okay. No worries," she said, mimicking Juan Pablo. "I think it's ironic that my adopted father was an alcoholic, but you know, he was not me. Nor is my real father. I am my own person and am grateful that I had a good family whom God eventually straightened out. Did you know who he was?"

Doña Violeta shook her head. "I made it a point not to . . . another thing for which I am sorry. If María loved him, there had to be some good, no? And look at the beautiful daughter he made with my María." Violeta's sobs were now reduced to little huffs between words. "And when I first saw you, I nearly fainted. You are her image."

"Do you have pictures?" Corinne hoped so. She wanted to see what her mother looked like.

Violeta nodded. "I have kept them all these years. I threw her out, but I could not throw out her photos. I still miss her."

Corinne's thoughts raced and tumbled forward, then backward. "But what happened to my mother? Do you know?"

Pain renewed its assault on Violeta's face. Corinne wished she could take it upon herself, but she wanted to know. Perhaps telling her about María might provide a long-needed release.

"The authorities told me that it was from drugs," the older woman said, digging into her purse. Upon finding her handkerchief, she blew her nose, taking time to compose herself. "The things that addicts use were on her person when she was found in a church in Mexico City . . . and I shudder to think of the circumstances in which she'd lived."

"She made some bad choices . . . just like my adopted father."

Tears ravaged the old woman's eyes again. "But you did not forbid him to come home. And for that, I will pay before God's throne someday. I, in my pride and righteousness, refused her a second chance."

So that is why Violeta had been so adamant about giving Mark a chance . . . about not making the same mistake that she made with a loved one—Corinne's mother.

"I never had the chance to ask her forgiveness." Folding her arms on the table, Violeta buried her face in them, drained.

Corinne rose to get a fresh cloth from the utility-bath. After wetting it with cold water and wringing the excess out, she returned to wipe her grandmother's face. "Now there, *abuelita,* you mustn't punish yourself any further. Guilt is something that we carry on our own. God is waiting to take it from us, if we'll give it up."

"I have asked His forgiveness seventy-times-seven, but still I cannot forgive myself. She was my daughter, my only child."

"And she died in her Father's arms," Corinne said gently. "Did you think about that? That perhaps her last words were with Him?"

Violeta raised her head. Corinne caught a glimmer of hope swimming in her grandmother's bereaved gaze.

"And if María was right with God, then she had to have forgiven you." Kneeling at Violeta's knee, Corinne lifted the woman's trembling hands to her lips and kissed each one. "And I know that God has forgiven you, because in His way He brought us together." Framing her face with her grandmother's hands, she added in a voice filled with affection. "Perhaps I am your second chance, *abuelita.*"

A twinkle kindled in Violeta's tear-swollen gaze. The lines around her mouth tightened, drawing it into a tentative smile. "So much wisdom from someone so young." She cradled Corinne's face with her hands and leaned over, planting a light kiss on her forehead. "And such a blessing for this undeserving soul."

Corinne rose, the void of her lost heritage suddenly filled to the brim. "Now, as soon as we refresh our faces from all this boo-hooing, I want to share my wonderful news with Soledad and Mark. It isn't every day a girl finds a grandmother as wonderful as you."

Doña Violeta's face brightened. "We could have a party. I love parties."

"My parents would love to attend," Corinne blurted out without thinking. "Unless it would make you feel awkward."

"Querida mia, I would like to thank them personally for raising such a fine granddaughter as yourself."

"I thought the world of you before," Corinne said, giving in to another hug. "And now I do that *and* love you to bits."

"We will have such—"

A child's scream cut her grandmother off in midsentence. As Violeta groped at her chest with a start, Corinne glanced in the direction of the hall.

Antonio!

CHAPTER 26

The scream jerked Mark from a drift of sleep, bringing him upright on the bed. Antonio was no longer perched beside him reading, although the book was still there. Instead, the boy stood at the side of the bed, staring, blanched and wide-eyed, at something on the floor.

"What is it?" Mark shouted, vaulting to his feet. Without waiting for a reply, he grabbed the baseball bat that Corinne had left propped in the corner next to her nightstand.

"The c-caracol," the boy cried, pointing to the floor where the gift box from Diego Quintana lay open, its content spilled and shining in the light from the window.

Corinne burst into the room. "Antonio, what's wrong?"

"The caracol," Mark told her, pointing to the jewelry. "Is that the caracol that killed your family?"

"It does not look like that at first. Papá showed me a picture of this kind," Antonio explained, his voice edged with fear. "Papá said that it is very expensive like this and that people will pay us much money to show them where such caracoles are . . . that we would be rich." He turned his luminous gaze toward Mark. "But instead, all of my family is dead but me."

A mental lightbulb flashed in Mark's mind. Was it possible?

"Do you know where the caracoles are?" he asked the boy.

Instead of answering, Antonio looked away. "To know that is to die. I do not wish to die."

"It's in the caves or mine shafts under Hacienda Ortiz, isn't it?"

Antonio said nothing, but his thinned, bloodless lips spoke volumes.

"But I do not understand," Doña Violeta said from the doorway. "What is this about a snail and Diego's gift?"

"This is made from no ordinary snail, Doña Violeta." Mark noticed the woman's red, swollen eyes. "What's wrong?"

In fact, Corinne didn't look so hot either.

Corinne put her arm around Doña Violeta and smiled widely. "Ask us what is *right*."

Mark was incredulous. Here they were on the verge of finding the reason behind the ghost and its spells, and she wanted to play word games. "What's *right*, then?"

He regretted the bite of his tone the moment the question was out, as it summoned reinforcements to the tears that had already assaulted her face.

"I found my grandmother, Mark. Or rather, she found me." She gave an equally emotional Violeta a squeeze.

"I claimed her," the latter told him, with a regal lift of her gray head. "She is Corina Diaz Quintana de la Vega."

"I'd hate to have to fill out forms with that name." Laying the bat on the bed, he approached the two women and embraced both of them. "But I couldn't be happier for you both. Looks to me like you got a prize in each other."

"And when Corina marries you, I will have two grand prizes, no?"

Mark's thoughts braked at the new twist in the road. But instead of his usual turn and run, he approached with caution. "Aren't you putting the cart before the donkey?" He asked Violeta, but his attention shifted to Corinne's reaction.

He'd grown fond of that shade of rose, but he'd just declared his feelings for Corinne earlier that day. He hadn't gotten far enough to declare his intentions yet . . . mainly because he hadn't thought that far ahead.

"Perhaps yes, perhaps no," Violeta replied, "but they are *both* in my stable. How I love both of you."

"I suggest that we celebrate my family reunion and talk about . . .

about," Corinne stammered, then seized upon one of Violeta's expressions . . . "such *silliness* later." She stooped to pick up the jewelry, replacing it in the box. "Now I'm really worried."

Silliness? Marriage was dead serious . . . which was why Mark avoided it. Women didn't. He wasn't exactly sure what was wrong with this picture, but there was a slap hidden in here somewhere.

"If what you suggest is correct, then I will insist that my nephew call the authorities in on this matter."

If Don Rafael and Diego weren't already "in on it," Mark thought. Maybe he was a cynic, but it was awfully convenient for the jeweler to be using the same stuff that led to so many deaths. But if they were in on it, he might as well pull the snake's tail.

"That would be wonderful, señora." Meanwhile, Mark was going to call Blaine pronto.

"We are going to die."

All eyes returned to Antonio, all but forgotten in the excitement. Mark dragged the despondent boy under his arm. "Nonsense, Antonio. I fought off a ghost the other night and a sickness caused by a witch's spell."

"You really saw the ghost?" If it were possible, the boy's eyes grew wider, not with fear, but wonder.

Mark nodded. "And I chased it out of my room." There was no need to mention the falling-over-the-pig bit. "The evil spirits can't stand up against an enchanted pig and a mad Madison. And this Madison is starting to get very mad."

Not to mention tired. Mark hadn't meant to fall asleep while the boy read to him. Left to his own devices, the kid did what kids did—explored. But maybe this was the answer to the prayer Mark had sent up, asking to get to the bottom of this hocus-pocus.

"May I stay here in the hacienda with you, Señor Mark?"

Corinne knelt before the unsettled child. "Antonio, as long as you do not leave the orphanage like your brother, you are safe. And no one here will let on that you know anything about the *caracoles.*"

Unconvinced, the boy glanced around the room. "But what if

the ghost has heard us?" He grimaced in despair. "I wish my new parents were already here."

"Your mother promised me that you will start school in Devon this fall, so they should be here within the next couple of weeks."

"A couple of weeks?" Mark repeated, surprised at how much the boy had gotten under his skin. Almost as much as one feisty señorita.

"Father Menasco told me Sunday," Corinne said. "But with all that was going on, it slipped my mind."

Doña Violeta coaxed Antonio away from Mark. "Come, little man. I need someone with a firm hand to drive Chiquita to the orphanage."

The boy recovered in instant delight. "I can drive the cart?"

Violeta nodded. "Perhaps by the time Chiquita reaches the orphanage, she will be ready for this old woman to take over."

"I have never driven a cart," he warned her with a second thought of doubt.

The old woman waved away his fear. "With my experience and your strength, I think we will be just fine."

Mark sank onto the edge of the mattress, wet with perspiration. It took nothing to knock his knees out. "If you two don't mind, I'll let Corinne show you out."

"I know my way," Violeta insisted. She cast an affectionate glance Corinne's way. "Although I would not object to any time spent with my granddaughter."

If a heart could smile, Mark's did as he watched the two women leave with Antonio tucked between them. But smiling within did not negate more serious matters. He reached for the cell phone Corinne had placed in the drawer of the nightstand for his benefit and dialed Madison Engineering.

◆

The stench of mold, urine, and cheap cigar smoke permeated the back room of the Cantina Roja. Ordinarily Don Rafael did not notice it, but this afternoon, it nearly choked him. Or perhaps it was the noose of fear tightening about his throat.

"You must kill Madison and anyone else in the hacienda," Dr. Krump said, as though ordering a mug of the special German lager the owner of the cantina imported for him each season. "I am finished with your incompetence."

Lorenzo Pozas scowled at the wheezing little German. "The ways of my peoples take time—"

"Which we do not have." Krump cracked each syllable like a whip.

With wet palms Don Rafael clutched the rosary that *Tía* Violeta had given him. When would it end? At first the German geologist was a jovial little man in love with Mexicalli, but upon the discovery of the valuable fossils, he'd changed. In a delusion of grandeur, he called himself *El Caracol,* though Dr. Death was closer to the truth.

This man and Pozas had to be stopped. But how, without incriminating his own involvement in this dark pursuit?

"Perhaps just burning the hacienda to the ground will suffice." And it would burn to the ground, with the manual pump engine housed in the town hall's garage the only available firefighting equipment.

Krump shifted a weasel-like gaze to Rafael. "If not for your son's foolishness, this would not be necessary . . . at least not at this point."

If only Krump had not been in Rafael's office when *Tía* Violeta came in to insist that he call in police from a larger town to protect the hacienda. In a terrible state of distress, she'd told them of Madison's suspicions—that valuable fossils might be the reason behind the haunting of Hacienda Ortiz, and how upset Antonio had been to see Diego's jewelry.

At least the child was not in danger. Violeta assured Rafael that the boy, unlike his brother, knew only enough to be frightened.

"I will take care of Madison tonight," Pozas answered. "The burning viper's vine may spare him the torture of the flames."

"What is that, some kind of poison?" Rafael asked with unveiled contempt. The German ordered the grisly deeds, but Pozas seemed to enjoy performing them.

"To breathe the smoke of the viper's vine is to die." Pozas's tobacco-stained smile caused a ripple of cold beneath the skin on Rafael's arm.

"To the devil with viper's vine," Krump wheezed. "You will carry enough petrol to accomplish your task this time?"

"Por supuesto," the Indio replied.

"Of course?" Krump sneered. "The last time you were to finish a job, you used a crayon." He turned to Don Rafael. "And you will arrange so that Corina is not to be there?"

Rafael nodded. "My aunt is having her and Diego over for supper."

Krump waved him away. "Then we are finished. Go and be quiet."

Taken back at being dismissed *before* and not *with* Lorenzo Pozas, Rafael cast one last glance at the Indio. In the dim light it was hard to see his face. A chill raked the back of Rafael's spine. What did Krump have to tell Pozas that he could not say in Rafael's presence?

Was he about to be *witched* as well?

CHAPTER 27

Sunset painted a fiery backdrop for the mountains surrounding Mexicalli by the time Mark was settled back in his room. Soledad fussed to make him eat the arroz con pollo that she'd prepared for the two of them.

Freshly showered and changed into a skirt and blouse, Corinne applied a bit of orange blossom after-shower spray and headed for the salon to check on her patient one last time before heading to Doña . . . to her *grandmother's* house for supper.

Mark whistled when she walked into the room. "Wow, I'm starting to feel better already. Besides, I don't like the idea of you walking to the village alone." He started to toss back the coverlet, but Soledad caught it and glared at him, her mouth set like iron.

Mark rolled his gaze toward the ceiling. "I slept all afternoon."

"You no eat my arroz con pollo, "the housekeeper declared, "you not well enough to walk down to the village."

"Much less back *up* to the hacienda," Corinne pointed out. Much as she'd love for Mark to go with her, she knew the high fevers had given way to cold sweats from weakness.

"Then you go," Mark said to Soledad. "Corinne shouldn't go alone . . . especially at night."

Ample chin to chest, Soledad peered at him from under the thick shrub of her brow. "The ghost was *here*."

"It wasn't a real ghost. It was a jerk pretending to be a ghost."

"A jerk who was *here*." The housekeeper tapped the side of the bed for effect.

Corinne couldn't help but grin. "Give it up, Mark. I'll be fine."

Shifting on the bed, Mark met Soledad's stubborn look with one of his own. "Will you go with Corinne if I eat all the delicious food that you worked so hard to cook for me?"

Boy, he knew the right strings to pull. Corinne could see the determination on Soledad's face waver.

"Pues . . ." Calculation whirred behind her dark eyes. Taking a deep breath, she let it out slowly until she had everyone's full attention for her announcement. "No."

"Soledad," Mark moaned.

"I do not belong at Doña Violeta's table. I belong here with you and our precious Toto." She took up the untouched plate and scooped some of the cut-up chicken and rice. "And you will eat; I will not leave this spot until you do."

"Well," Corinne said, stepping up to the side of the bed. "You two take care." She pressed a chaste kiss on Mark's forehead, but memory of a more passionate one sent a frisson of heat through her.

"Like I've got a choice with Nurse Vengeance," he grumbled.

"I wish you could go," Corinne commiserated, "but we're just going to look at family pictures." Excitement surged at the idea of seeing her mother for the first time. "It's not really a guy thing."

"Diego is going to be there."

Mark was pouting . . . and jealous, she realized with a *twickle* of delight. Corinne felt compelled to assuage him with a quick kiss. "He's my cousin," she said.

"Yeah, well, just remember that when he walks you home."

Corinne winked. "I will, I promise."

Soledad's votives on the mantel cast a soft glow on the ceiling as Mark checked the clock there for the umpteenth time. Ten o'clock, and Corinne still hadn't returned. Granted, it had only been three hours, but it was a long three. Tossing the covers off, he got out of bed and made his way to the front door. In the dim light of the electric lantern outside, he padded in his bare feet out onto the cool flat stone surface. Beyond the gape in the courtyard wall where the gate had been, the moon bathed the still landscape with a silence interrupted only by the sound of nocturnal insects.

With no sign of Corinne's approach, Mark let his gaze wander over the stacks of supplies brought in by the Indios. They were dwindling, evidence that the project progressed. Mark rubbed his arms against the chill of the night air.

Lord, I just thank You for taking over, because I've been in way over my head.

Juan Pablo, who'd proved to be a competent site boss, had roughed in plumbing to the two rooms assigned as the new baths and showers. They now awaited Juan Miguel to lay the tile. But Juan Pedro kept Juan Miguel busy repairing the walls as the old wiring was replaced with new. All day long, someone called for another, although how they knew which Juan was to answer was anyone's guess.

"And just what do you think you are doing?" Soledad demanded behind him. She still wore her on-duty black and yellow, instead of the floral housecoat she usually had donned by now.

"Wondering where Corinne is."

The housekeeper glanced at her watch. "Where she was forty-two minutes ago . . . at the hacienda of Doña Violeta." Her stern features softened. "But it makes much longer for a man in love, no?"

"It makes much longer when a man is waiting and worrying." Was that what love was? He couldn't recall feeling like this about any other woman . . . but then he'd not been marooned in the *Twilight Zone* with any other woman.

"Pues, if you ask . . ." Soledad broke off, cocking her head to one side. "Did you hear that?"

Mark came in from the patio. "What?"

"I heard something . . . like someone moving bricks," the wide-eyed housekeeper whispered. She pointed to the salon.

Or sliding tile? Recalling the sound from the night the ghost appeared, Mark took Soledad by the arm and guided her out to the patio. "Go to the orphanage and call the police."

"But what will you do?"

"I'm going to sneak inside, wait, and watch." And if he caught the so-and-so, he was going to give the man a headache like he wouldn't believe.

Soledad hesitated, clearly torn between abandoning Mark to the ghost and remaining with him to confront it.

"I'm just going to watch," Mark insisted, giving her a little prod. "Go get help."

"I can build on that?" she asked.

Mark nodded. "You can build on it. Now, hurry . . . and keep in the cover of the lumber and stone stacks."

Reaching inside the door, Mark turned the outside lantern off. The moon provided all the illumination Soledad would need to reach the gate and beyond while he clung to the shadows.

Heart pounding against his chest at the prospect of catching their ghost in action, he grabbed up a scrap of two-by-four and backed against the front of the house, listening. He hadn't actually heard Soledad's noise, but he trusted her ears above the CIA's best high-tech listening device.

He wiped the cold sweat from his forehead, mind racing. Dare he slip inside and make for Corinne's room? From there he could keep an eye on the house from the front to the back through the utility-bath. But that meant slipping through the glow of candle-light from his room—the only room with brick or tile, not to mention the place where their ghost had vanished into thin air.

Something clattered to the floor. It sounded as though it came from the far end of the house. Peering around the front doorjamb, Mark scanned the empty hallway. Nothing there, but a flash of light from the upstairs ballroom balcony entrance. Someone was in the house—in the ballroom.

The length of lumber firm in his hand, Mark slipped into the hall and hustled toward the dark cover of Corinne's room, when he sensed a presence behind him. Before he could bring his weapon to bear, pain exploded against the side of his face, knocking him to the floor. Through the white blast dazing his vision, he made out someone approaching from the back of the house.

Two ghosts. The thought swam round and round the whirlpool drawing him deeper and deeper into a gray-black funnel where hands pulled and tugged at him, lifting, dropping, hauling, shoving.

He heard Toto squeal. Were they killing the pig? Mark tried to open his eyes, but the room moved, the motion slamming his eyelids shut with such force that his stomach heaved in warning. It was safer to listen.

"Sergio, you fool, tie his feet as well."

Who was Sergio? Mark didn't know any Sergio. But he did know the smell of gasoline. He tried once again to open his eyes, but they were so heavy, only a slit of light came through.

Someone was working around him. Was he in a chair? Mark pulled at the invisible bonds holding him immobile. Wood creaked beneath him.

"He awakens, Lorenzo."

Lorenzo? As in Lorenzo Pozas? The name registered with a chilling clarity, nipping at the daze fogging his brain. Clenching his teeth, Mark forced his eyes open. The room shifted left to right in a semicircle and back before stopping. *Where is Pozas?*

"In the back," a young voice replied, alerting Mark to the fact that he'd voiced his thoughts.

Mark struggled to turn and look behind him in the direction of his captor, but ropes bit into his wrists, chest, and feet. "Who . . . who are you?"

"I am called Sergio." Satisfied that the ropes held, Sergio walked around so that Mark could see him. "Much pleasure."

Much pleasure? What, was the guy simple?

"Why did you tie me up, Sergio?"

"Because Lorenzo said to."

"What's the gasoline for?" As if Mark didn't suspect.

"To burn down the hacienda, *cómo no?*"

Oh, God. Mark's prayer dart faded with the welling of nausea. Would Soledad make it back with the police in time? He worked at the ropes binding his wrists when the press of a cold cloth against his right temple added its sting to his misery. Jerking away,

Mark saw Sergio holding a bloodstained washcloth, his round face a mirror of concern.

"You bleed, señor."

The man had to be mentally deficient to worry about bleeding when he was about to set the house on fire with Mark in it. Had Sergio been the crayon witch?

The sound of footsteps in the hall drew Mark's attention to the door, where his worst nightmare appeared with a fuel can in hand.

"Ahora—" Lorenzo Pozas stopped short upon meeting Mark's gaze. "So, the big engineer is awake. 'I was just wondering if there were any *caracoles* around here,'" he said, mimicking Mark's question in the market.

"So there *are* valuable snail fossils in the ground under Hacienda Ortiz," Mark stated.

"Enough to make me a rich man." Lorenzo walked away, pouring the accelerant around the hall, soaking the area in front of Mark's room. "And you a dead man."

"Soledad knows you are here. She's gone to call the police."

"No one will listen to that foolish busybody," Pozas responded. "Especially Don Rafael and Capitán Nolla."

Mark's bravado faltered. He'd suspected as much, but hearing it didn't make him feel any better. "But the government will listen to my brother. He's already contacted the federal authorities to investigate the ammonite fossils in this area, as well as your colleagues. And he has your name."

Pozas turned, his scowl almost inhuman in its darkness. "So you say."

"So I *know*," Mark replied. "I told him how you killed your brother and his wife—"

"They were witched."

"—by arranging a gas leak. And how you shot Enrique and left him to the animals. He will be dug up, and the authorities will find out the truth about his death."

"You know nothing about the boy." Pozas gave the can a toss toward the curtains, but only a little fuel came out. With an oath of disbelief, he shook the can and glared at Sergio. "Did you fill it like I told you, *estúpido?*"

The young man nodded. "It was all I could carry."

"To the brim?"

Sergio frowned. "If I fill it so, I cannot carry it."

Pozas raised his hand to strike his assistant, but Sergio scampered out of reach and out of the periphery of Mark's vision. "Run, you little idiot. You will get yours, that I promise you."

Run? Run where? Mark shifted his weight, turning the chair a little, but he couldn't see where the retreating noise that Sergio made had come from. The strike of a match drew his attention back to Pozas. In its glow, a yellow-stained smile spread on the assassin's face.

"The secret passage to the mines made my job easy," Pozas said, walking with deliberation toward the gas-soaked hall.

Mark was too distracted by the flickering death in the man's dirt-smudged fingers to dwell on how the ghost came and went.

"It is said that Don Diego Ortiz built this in the days of the banditos, when no one who had money was safe from them." With his free hand, Pozas pulled the sliding pocket doors to the hall almost shut. "But unlike him, you will not escape so."

With a flick of his fingers, Pozas tossed the match and closed the doors. The whoosh of igniting gas on the other side rattled them. Ignoring the retreating man and his taunts, Mark watched the only thing that held the flames spreading through the hacienda from him.

"Die well, amigo," the murderer called from behind. The familiar sound of stone scraping stone followed.

Mark's mind raced. He had one chance. If he could break the chair, he might be able to free himself before the smoke pouring under the door overcame him. Bracing, he prayed, *Heavenly Father, help me now,* and shoved sideways with all his might.

But Violeta's chair was well made, and the ropes would not give. At floor level, Mark watched the black fumes snake their way into the room. The varnish on the doors bubbled and ran from the heat that scorched his cheeks even from the short distance away. Sweat poured from his brow into his eyes, already stinging—or had he reopened his head wound?

He made a valiant attempt to wriggle as far away from the hall as he could between ragged breaths, but the exertion provoked an agonizing cramp in one of his bound legs. Realizing that his efforts were futile, all the squandered times of his life flooded his mind . . . only to be chased away by memories of times when he had been in the right place at the right time . . . in Sunday school, where he'd memorized his mother's favorite psalm for Mother's Day.

Yea, though I walk through the valley of the shadow of death . . .

Above him, Soledad's votives still burned, but given his ability to reach them, they might as well be on the altar in the village church. All the candles in the world burning could not help him now.

I will fear no evil . . .

His only hope was the fourth man in the picture of the three Hebrew men in the fiery furnace.

For thou art with me.

With the faith that he had had when he'd read that Bible picture book, Mark mouthed His name.

Jesus.

CHAPTER 28

Dawn broke, casting first light upon the smoking remains of Hacienda Ortiz. Numb with shock and exhaustion, Corinne stared beyond them at the serrated horizon—dark blue-gray peaks jutting into a summer sky. Mark was gone. No one had seen him since Soledad left the hacienda to report that the ghost had reappeared. By the time the call was routed to Cantina Roja, where Mexicalli's police force of one hung out, the fire alarm sounded at the church. In less than an hour, the roof caved in. Still there was no sign of Mark, which led everyone—with the exception of Corinne—to one conclusion.

Wrapped in a blanket inside Capitán Nolla's police car, she'd cried like the psalmist in the wilderness from night into day for God's help in finding him anywhere but beneath the smoldering rubble.

God would not do that to her or Mark. God would answer the prayers that began the moment she and the others were summoned by the frantic ringing of the church bell to the street in front of her grandmother's house as Mexicalli's old pumper passed them, loaded with volunteers. Corinne's stomach turned to stone upon following its direction up the hill with her gaze. Hacienda Ortiz had looked like a giant torch contained in the cup of its courtyard wall.

Icy fear coursing through her veins, she and Diego had left Doña Violeta to await the hitching of Chiquita to her cart and joined the rallying villagers in an uphill race to what became a nightmare of incompetence, despite everyone's best efforts.

The tanker truck, an antique affair that held just enough water to make the fire laugh, raced back and forth to the lake to refill, while men, women, and children formed a ragtag bucket brigade between the fire and the orphanage, the next nearest source of water. As the tanker left for its third refill, the roof caved in, scattering anyone near the blaze and ending any further efforts.

In the village below, the church bell tolled the morning prayer hour, its gongs single and solemn as Corinne's heartbeat. Villagers, looking like moving miniature dolls in the distance, made their way to the small stone house of worship, which had remained open all night for those wishing to pray for the fate of their Señor *del Cerdito*.

Already the grounds outside the blackened courtyard walls were ablaze with color, although Corinne had hardly noticed the Indios paying their homage. Her attention remained on the smoking hovel where Capitán Nolla and some men picked at the roof, trying to pull it away from the massive central chimney on the theory that if Mark's body was in the rubble . . .

Doubt nipped at her spirit with ugly fangs, but Corinne backed it down with resolve. God didn't open her heart to Mark for this. He had to be alive, because the place that his spirit had filled in Corinne's heart did not feel empty. It was cold with alarm, but not empty. Besides, Soledad had said that Mark had been outside the hacienda when she left to call the police. *Outside,* Corinne thought, scanning with a weary but obstinate gaze the area that she and others had searched with flashlights the night before.

The gun of an engine drew Corinne's attention to where Diego Quintana backed a silver SUV toward them. Her cousin had stayed with her most of the night and, unable to convince Corinne to abandon the scene, left just before dawn for a shower, change of clothes, and some food for the workers.

Diego opened the back of his vehicle, revealing a large thermal container of coffee, a sleeve of Styrofoam cups, and white bags of bakery goods.

"If it isn't *Don Dulce*," Corinne teased, walking over to the tailgate.

"You are in better spirits than when I left earlier. Anything new?"

"No. It's not new that God is good and answers prayer. I'm just waiting to see how."

The scent of fresh baked confections triggered her appetite. She'd been finishing the dessert of their late Mexican supper when the alarm sounded, so she joined the workmen in the refreshments, taking time to thank each one for their efforts.

A little while after the work was resumed, Juan Miguel, having learned about the disaster that morning, arrived to join his brother Juan Pablo. Their brother, Electric Juan, as Mark had dubbed him, had helped fight the fire until the roof fell in. Juan Pablo explained to Corinne that Juan Pedro left for the Cantina Roja, overcome with remorse that he might have made a mistake in the wiring, causing the fire.

"Corina, *Tía* Violeta wishes you to stay with her. You cannot remain here until . . ." Diego broke off at the warning flash of Corinne's eyes. "Until the search is over. It will take at least the remainder of the day just to clear the salon."

She wouldn't allow the worst to be said in her presence. "Then I'll stay here the remainder of the day." She took a sip of the black coffee. "How is Grandmother?"

Having caught up with them in her cart just before the roof caved in, Violeta became so upset that Dr. Flynn insisted she return home with Gaspar, lest the smoke and distress take their toll on her health. Don Rafael had accompanied them with the promise to return. Except he hadn't.

Corinne turned to Diego. "Where is your father?" Usually when Nolla was on duty, the *alcalde* wasn't far from view.

Diego shrugged. "Perhaps resting, since there is nothing he can do here . . . which is what you should be doing." When she declined to answer, he jerked his finger toward the side of the gutted hacienda frame. "You are as stubborn as that pig. The firemen say that it has been circling the debris and nosing in each time they turn over a section of wall or roof."

Emerging from the rear of the house, smeared in soot and dirt, Toto was almost unrecognizable as Soledad's pristine white pride.

"Poor baby, he's going to burn himself."

"Corina," Diego called after her as she hurried up to where Toto nosed the debris.

But she didn't listen. She wanted to hug the little critter that shared her affinity for her precious prodigal. Granted, Toto was just a pig, but right now, he was something warm, breathing, and positive to cling to.

"Toto," she cooed, nudging the animal back from some glowing debris. "Let me see your feet." To her horror, the flesh around the pig's hooves was black and tender. "Diego, go to the *farmacia* and get some aloe vera gel . . . what the tourists use for sunburn."

"For a pig?"

Corinne gave him a sharp look. "For a dear pet."

If Soledad had not been reduced to hysteria and needed sedation, the housekeeper would have taken Toto into her care. As it was, she was with her sister at the parsonage.

"And get some triple-antibiotic cream . . . and some cabbage from the market section."

"You will not come to Grandmother's house?"

Corinne shook her head stubbornly. "Come on, Toto," she cajoled, drawing the pig away with a handful of grass. The pig ignored the grass, but turned from the ruins and walked at her feet toward the pen at the back of the yard.

"I will return with food and supplies for the pig and my stubborn cousin," Diego called after her.

"That would be wonderful, thank you." As he turned away, Corinne raised her voice. "Diego?"

He stopped, his wavy raven hair catching the brilliance of the sun in shades of black and blue as he tilted his head in question.

"Thank you. I'm glad you're my cousin."

A smile tugged at the corner of his lips as he answered in kind. *"El gusto es mío, querida."*

◆

Before Diego returned, a twenty-first-century cavalry of *Federales* arrived, led by a white vehicle with the lettering of the Mineral Resources Council. Recalling that Mark had phoned Blaine about the latest developments regarding the possibility of valuable ammonites being behind the "witching," Corinne watched them with heaviness in her chest.

Too late, she thought, dragging to her feet from the seclusion of the trellis-covered bench near the orange grove.

Capitán Nolla met the men who spilled from the vehicles as she reached the front of the house. Among the smart-suited and uniformed entourage was Don Rafael. Heavy circles from lack of sleep accentuated the darkness of his gaze, which he cast down upon seeing her.

Alarm slowly set in as Corinne realized that he was accompanied by guards. Accompanied or escorted?

"Don Rafael?"

"Corina, I pray that you will forgive this undeserving man." Misery glazed the man's eyes. "I am too late to save your Mark, but—"

"Mark is alive," Corinne interrupted. "I know it."

"Señorita Diaz," said a man clad in a tailored natural linen suit. "I am Carlos Aquino, a friend and colleague of Señor Blaine Madison, and this is my second cousin, Vincente."

"M-Mark was supposed to be in the house, but—" But what? *What, God?*

"Señorita, the authorities will do everything within their power to find him," Carlos Aquino assured her.

"Yes," Nolla chimed in. "As you have seen."

"But if it is of any consolation," Aquino went on, "Don Rafael has told us everything."

"Everything?" Corinne said in concert with Nolla.

"I only wish I had called the authorities earlier," Don Rafael confessed. "Please accept my apologies."

Corinne was incredulous. "You had something to do with this?"

she asked, jabbing her finger at the hacienda ruins. The memory of Rafael's irritation over the necklace Diego had given her flashed through her mind. Bits of the past came together with Mark's suspicions to paint a shocking picture. "And Diego?" she asked.

Don Rafael answered with a vehement shake of his head. "No, my son knows nothing of the *caracoles*."

"And thanks to Don Rafael, those who do know are now in custody," Vincente Aquino told her.

"In custody for what?" Diego Quintana asked as he walked toward the cluster of officials with Dr. Flynn in tow. "Papá?" Diego said, his inquiring gaze landing on Don Rafael. "What is going on?"

He handed the doctor the bag of supplies.

Corinne felt a fleeting warmth. Her cousin grew dearer by the moment.

"Let's take a look at what you've done to yourself," the doctor said, approaching Toto and kneeling at his side.

Corinne soothed the wary pig, listening to Don Rafael's story of how the Pozas brothers showed Dr. Herman Krump the *caracol* fossils, initiating a series of sinister events that included murder committed by Lorenzo Pozas. It never occurred to her that the congenial little German could be behind such a travesty of murder and intrigue, yet it made sense. If anyone would know what the fossils were worth, it would be a geologist.

"He was furious when he learned that the orphanage had purchased the land out from under him."

"Indeed he was," Carlos Aquino recollected. "Señor Madison and Father Menasco had just signed the contract on behalf of the church when he called to make an offer."

And that was when the revival of the legend of Doña Lucinda Ortiz's ghost came into play . . . except that Mark and Corinne hadn't been scared off. So Lorenzo resorted to his mother-in-law's witchcraft, scattering spore-rich dirt from a local cave in Mark's room so that he'd get sick.

"And you allowed this?" Diego asked of his father.

"I did it for you, Diego, so that you would be the first artisan to use the local gemstones," Don Rafael answered. "But I did not know, when Krump invited me to help him cover the knowledge of the discovery, that it involved murder."

A mix of pain and disbelief tore at Diego's handsome features. "But why, Papá? Have you so little faith in my work?"

"It was only to help you, son."

"Because you did not think that I could help myself." Resentment vied with disappointment in Diego's voice. "And if you suspected Lorenzo of murder, why did you not call the police then? Why wait until a child's death followed?"

"I did not know if his brother and sister-in-law's deaths were murder or an accident," Rafael replied. "God forgive me, I would have spoken, had I known for certain."

"Even so, it would be hard to prove," Vincente Aquino told them. "Gas leaks are common in such villages where the Indios sometimes change their own tanks. And Pozas is denying everything."

Pozas. The image of the man's hostile glare across the small coffin at his nephew's grave site sent a shiver up Corinne's back. She easily could believe him capable of murder. She glanced up from wiping Toto down with some of the wet wipes from the market bag. "And what about Enrique?"

Don Rafael frowned. "That is what I cannot understand. Dr. Krump wanted Pozas to offer the boy money to show them some of the other sites that he and his father had found in their hunting and exploring together. Killing Enrique made no sense."

"Maybe Enrique wouldn't tell them what they wanted to know," Corinne thought aloud. The whole world was going mad and taking her with it. "And what about last night?" Much as she dreaded the answer, she needed to know.

"That is when I knew that Krump would stop at nothing. He ordered Lorenzo Pozas to burn down Hacienda Ortiz and everyone in it. I knew I had to stop him."

Corinne's chin quivered. "So why did you wait so long? Why didn't you send Capitán Nolla after Lorenzo right then?"

Rafael dropped his head. "Because a coward does not run *to* the fight. I waited until I saw for myself how far Pozas and Krump would go."

"You waited until the fire?" Diego exclaimed in contempt.

"May God forgive me."

Diego cupped Corinne's arm as she struggled to her feet. She couldn't believe her ears. The man admitted to letting the hacienda burn, possibly with Mark inside, and yet he did nothing until he saw the fire.

"God might forgive you, sir, but that is too formidable a task for me." At least for now. *Maybe someday, Lord, but not today.*

She wanted to run away, but there was nowhere to run to escape the pain. A sob tore at her chest, welling to her throat as she stumbled toward the orchard.

"Corina!"

She heard Diego's footsteps behind her, felt his hand catch her arm as she ran toward the jacaranda tree where Mark had kissed her the night Lorenzo Pozas left the disease-carrying dirt behind. Diego easily caught up and blocked her way.

The dam of her emotions burst with the impact. Mark was gone, and Don Rafael could have prevented it.

"I am so sorry for my father, Corina," Diego whispered brokenly against the top of her head.

"It . . . it's not y-your fault," she cried against his chest.

"Would that it had been me in the fire, rather than see you in such despair."

"Toto, wait!"

Dr. Flynn's exasperated shout drew Corinne from the shelter of her cousin's arms in time to see the soot-splotched pig race by them toward the orange orchard, a long string of gauze trailing from its hind foot. Approaching the edge of the hacienda yard, a filthy man hobbled toward them, leaning heavily on his shorter, equally filthy companion. Although his clothes looked like something from another century, there was something vaguely familiar about him as he pulled himself upright and planted his hands on his hips.

"That does *not* look like a cousinly embrace to me, Miss Muffet."

CHAPTER 29

"Mark!"

Corinne bounded away from Diego Quintana, arms out-stretched, skirts flying around her legs. She was more beautiful than ever. And if Mark had any doubts about her feelings toward him, they dissipated as she threw herself into his open arms.

"Oh," she gasped, clutching him as her momentum carried them backward a few steps.

Mark regained his footing and laughed. "I'm glad to see you, too."

Rising on tiptoe, Corinne linked her arms behind his neck and kissed him long and hard on the mouth.

Hello, Miss Muffet!

The fatigue that made Mark's legs ache on the downward climb from the mountain faded in a surge of pleasure and relief. Could a man die of joy overload? He held her tight against him and returned the affection, just as he'd promised himself, once he real-ized that he wasn't dead and in some cold, black hell. Except the devil didn't look like the shaggy kid from the late nineteenth cen-tury holding an oil lamp over his face.

"I love you, Muffet," he moaned as she backed a breath away. If a woman could fill a man's mind, making him want to linger in a smoke-filled inferno rather than go on to that bright spot people talked about, then she had to be the one.

Her kiss-dazed expression exploded with renewed vigor. "Ohhh."

Once again her lips sought his, her fingers raking at his temples, giving new meaning to the adage *love hurts*. The invasion of raw pain forced Mark away.

"Ow, ow, ow . . ."

"What? Oh, Mark," she fretted, seizing a section of her full skirt and dabbing at the fresh blood from the barely sealed wound at his pounding temple. "I'm so sorry." Flustered, she turned away, shouting for Dr. Flynn.

Mark caught her at the waist before she got too far. "It's just a little sore," he lied, not wanting to let her go. She and her stubborn faith had given him a lifeline in his darkest hour.

"Still, it would be wise for the doctor to examine you," Diego Quintana suggested. "And by the look of him, your companion also."

Mark shot him an accusatory look. "No thanks to you and your father's cohorts."

At that moment, recognition registered on Don Rafael's face.

"Enrique!" The man staggered backward, looking at the youth as if he'd seen a ghost. "But it is not possible. Pozas said that the boy was dead."

"Perhaps my uncle lied to you because he feared what Dr. Krump would do if he learned that I escaped," the disheveled boy suggested. "Papá and I were the only ones who knew exactly where the *caracoles* were. Not even *Tío* Lorenzo had been into the mines." Scuffing his bare feet in the dirt, he added, "I should not have left the orphanage."

"You see what your Don Juan and his friends are capable of?" Mark told Corinne in triumph. "Terrorizing kids for profit, not to mention murder."

Ignoring him, she stared, incredulous, at Enrique's long hair, filthy outdated clothing, and face smeared with black coal dust and soot. "Enrique!" She rushed to the boy and enveloped him in her arms. "We thought you were dead."

Mark cut her off. "You had quite a little game going here, you and your father, didn't you, Quintana?"

"But Diego knew nothing of the *caracoles*," Don Rafael spoke up, directing the disclaimer not only to Mark but to a number of official-looking men that Mark hadn't paid much attention to until now. "If you must cast blame," Rafael said to one of them, "then cast it on me."

Were the suits and *Federales* Blaine's cavalry? Mark wondered.

"Don Rafael called the authorities and told them everything," Corinne told Mark, stepping into the circle of his arm with Enrique in tow. "Dr. Krump and Lorenzo Pozas are in jail already."

That explained all the cars and uniforms, but whose side were they on? Rafael wasn't in cuffs, which suggested that more pieces of this puzzle were missing.

A tall, broad-chested man in a linen suit stepped forward, offering Mark his hand. "I am Carlos Aquino, your brother's associate."

One for the good guys. Keeping Corinne close—if he had his way, he'd never let her go—Mark accepted it, much relieved. "Glad to see you arrived with the troops."

"I called my cousin Vincente." Aquino nodded toward another man of much the same build, but in blue tailored linen. "Vincente works for the Mineral Resources Council, so naturally he was interested in your suspicions regarding the possibility of fossils in the area. However, Don Rafael had already notified the state authorities by the time we arrived with the *Federales* to check out your strange story."

"Strange isn't the half of it," Mark quipped.

"When we saw the smoking ruins," Vincente Aquino spoke up, "we thought that we were too late to help you."

"Everyone thought you were inside," Capitán Nolla told Mark.

Frankly, Mark suspected Nolla, too, but decided to keep quiet until he heard more of what had happened on this side of the *Twilight Zone.* It couldn't be any more outlandish than what he'd seen in the last twelve hours.

A network of mines riddled the mountain under Hacienda Ortiz, connected to the house by a tunnel from its underground chamber. That was where Mark had found a treasure trove of Ortiz memorabilia, including the turn-of-the-previous-century duds.

"Well, thanks to Enrique"—Mark motioned the timid boy forward—"I'm fine."

"But how—?" Corinne started.

Mark put a finger to her lips. "We'll tell you everything, but right now, we both are exhausted and starved."

"We'll go to my grandmother's." Corinne framed Mark's jaw in gentle hands. "She is going to be almost as happy as I am." She unleashed the love that sparkled in her eyes in a soulful kiss that ended in a sigh. "Almost."

◆

The patio of Doña Violeta Quintana de la Vega was populated with well-wishers coming and going, as the news of Señor *del Cerdito's* homecoming spread through the small town. Soledad was as tearful with joy as she'd been with grief the night before.

After Mark retired to the guest room to shower and change, the housekeeper bustled about with full intentions of helping Gaspar and her sister put together a buffet of deli meats from the market and food that came in from all parts of the village for the impromptu celebration. But at the slightest snag, she broke down in a fresh torrent of emotion.

"Soledad," Corinne said, giving her a gentle hug. "You must try to celebrate God's goodness, not focus on the bad that could have happened."

With a loud sniff that sent her digging into the pocket of her bright yellow apron for a tissue, the emotional housekeeper agreed. *"Pues . . ."* She withdrew an embroidered handkerchief and blew her nose loud enough to put the church bells to shame. "I will make the struggle."

"Go check on Toto, wash your face and hands, and then see what you can do," Corinne ordered gently.

Front legs bandaged and nose smeared with aloe from the damage that his foraging for Mark in the ruins had done, Toto had been relegated to Doña Violeta's pantry. That was as much leeway as Corinne's grandmother would allow the animal in her elegant villa, despite his exemplary dedication to the search.

Later Dr. Flynn checked out Enrique, amazed that the boy had survived so well in the maze of mine shafts. After a bath and a joy-ful reunion with Antonio, he proudly regaled them all with tales of hunting, trapping, and roasting his kill over an open flame kindled with matches he'd found in the storage rooms hidden behind the hacienda fireplace.

"*Tío* Lorenzo, he looked for me, but I know how to walk like a ghost and hide in the darkness."

Antonio took in his brother's every word with nothing less than sheer adoration. "How I wish I could have been there too."

At this, Enrique's bright gaze sobered. "I am glad that you were not, 'Tonio. It is fun to hunt, but not so fun to be hunted."

Corinne's heart felt squeezed as she imagined what the boy must have gone through emotionally. Granted, Enrique had survived like a man, but he was still a child, with all a child's fears and insecurities. She hoped the authorities put Lorenzo Pozas behind bars forever.

Since Enrique was so wired with excitement, Vincente Aquino opted to take Mark's statement while the boys ate their fill in Doña Violeta's kitchen under Soledad's doting eye. Freshly showered, shaved, and dressed in clothes borrowed from Diego, Mark sat very much alive and warm next to Corinne on the sofa in the salon and shared what he knew regarding the burning of Hacienda Ortiz.

"Lorenzo Pozas and some guy named Sergio, whose elevator doesn't go all the way to the top, knocked me up the side of the head, hogtied me in a chair, soaked the hacienda in gasoline, lit a match, and left through a hidden opening in the fireplace. The last thing I remember before blacking out was falling over in an attempt to break the chair."

"And that is when the boy found you?" Vincente Aquino inquired.

Prayer availeth much, Corinne paraphrased, overwhelmed that she'd received more than she'd asked for. Not only had God deliv-ered Mark, but Enrique as well.

Enrique told Mark how his uncle had imprisoned him in the mine shaft without food and forced him to show Lorenzo where other fossils had been discovered. But Enrique escaped, relying on the hunting and survival skills that his father had taught him and on the items that he found in a chamber beneath Hacienda Ortiz. It sounded like an underground museum filled with mementos from the past.

"Just in time," Mark told him. "I'd run out of the Twenty-third Psalm."

He squeezed Corinne's hand, and her heart swelled with even more thanksgiving for the spiritual connection they now shared.

"It is incredible that a child of nine could survive in the mines," Vincente marveled. "But the Indios know the ways of the land."

"As Enrique said, he and his father spent a lot of time hunting and trapping," Corinne reminded him. "But whose body is buried in the boy's place? We went to the funeral."

"The government will exhume the body," Vincente informed her, "although I feel certain that Pozas will tell us, once we are through interrogating him. Don Rafael really thought Enrique was dead."

"I was lucky that Enrique followed his uncle and Sergio into the tunnel last night and saw what they were up to, or I'd have been a goner." Mark turned to Corinne. "I want to do something for him . . . get him a mountain bike, something."

"That would be up to his new parents," she pointed out.

Father Menasco had promised to call the London couple as soon as he heard the news about Enrique and Mark, and they were overjoyed to be able to bring Enrique home too.

"And now that Pozas is going to jail, the adoption should go through without a hitch."

"Can you tell me more about what is in this underground chamber you and the boy talk about?" Carlos Aquinos asked. He glanced at his cousin. "That is, if your official interview is over."

Vincente eased against the high back of one of the matching chairs across from the sofa. "With Señor Madison's testimony and that of the boy, we have enough to send them all to prison."

"Even Don Rafael?" Corinne asked. "He didn't try to kill anyone . . . and he called the authorities on his own."

"But he covered for the ones who did try to kill me," Mark reminded her.

"But—"

"As I assured your grandmother, great consideration will be given in the matter," Vincente said, helping himself to a bowl of chili-spiced crackers and nuts.

"Don Diego Ortiz's secret chamber—you say it was connected to the Hacienda Ortiz by a secret passage," Carlos Aquino intervened to bring the conversation back to his original question. "But neither I nor the previous owners ever found it. How was it built into the fireplace?"

"Shades of Zorro," Mark said with a chuckle. "I never looked closely inside the hearth, and when Enrique pulled me through, I was unconscious . . . but I'd like to have another gander at it after the roof is pulled away."

Behind them, a telephone rang, almost as loud as the church bell. As Corinne recovered from the start it gave her, Gaspar appeared, heading straight for a massive writing desk under her mother's portrait, and answered it.

"I always thought that the measurements of the fireplace and hearth were overdone," Mark went on. "Too much space for—"

"Pardon me, Señor Mark, but your brother wishes to speak to you," Gaspar announced. "There is another phone in Doña Violeta's room, if you wish to speak in quiet."

"I'll show you." Corinne jumped to her feet, glad for the interruption. Mark was tired, despite his can-do show for everyone. "I really think, since the interview is over, that you gentlemen should let Mark rest awhile . . . although you're welcome to stay and partake of my grandmother's hospitality," she added, every inch the hostess she had observed her grandmother to be.

"As you can see from the activity on the patio . . ." Corinne glanced to where Diego and Violeta sat at a table, conversing with the guests. "She is holding court."

Although Carlos Aquino looked disappointed not to hear more of Hacienda Ortiz's secrets, he was gracious. "But of course, you are tired," he told Mark.

"I will return tomorrow to take the boy's official statement after he has calmed down a bit," Vincente chimed in, rising to take his leave. "If I think of anything else, perhaps I can ask you then." He shook Mark's hand. "*Adiós*, señor, señorita."

"We'll take the call in the other room," Corinne told Gaspar, who passed the message along to Blaine on the other end of the line and put down the handset to show the Aquino brothers out.

The moment Corinne and Mark entered the privacy of her grandmother's bedroom, Mark pulled Corinne into his arms with a rejuvenated vigor, backing her against the closed door. "Alone at last."

"Mark."

He kissed his name from her lips, letter by letter, and when he drew away, his breath was shallow and fast as her own. "Did I tell you that I loved you?"

"Yes, but I want to hear it again and again . . . after you speak to Blaine." Although duty first was the last thing she really cared about.

He gave her a wicked wink. "Come on." Grabbing her hand, he led her, *twickled* to the tips of her toes, to the antique black phone by Violeta's high poster bed. With his free hand, he picked up the receiver, tucking her into the curve of his arm with the other.

She nuzzled the curve of his neck with her head.

"Hello, Blaine." Moving the mouthpiece aside, he whispered behind her ear. "Think Grandmother would object to our honeymooning in this?"

Honeymooning? Was she hearing right? Corinne looked up at him.

"It's been quite a night," he admitted, all business for Blaine. "I'm afraid the hacienda is lost."

"I don't recall being proposed to," Corinne said, sidling closer.

"Yeah, I know there's insurance." He stole a quick kiss from her earlobe and whispered, "If I did, would you?"

His words tickled, stirring Corinne's confusion. "What? The wedding or the bed?" She tried to wriggle around to face him, but his arm locked her waist against him.

"Frankly, I haven't had time to think about it."

"What?" she hissed in impatience. Was he talking to her or Blaine? Somehow the idea of sharing a proposal with her future brother-in-law didn't ring her romantic bell.

Mark covered the mouthpiece. "Did you know the insurance money plus what we already have will build exactly what the orphanage needs?"

It was great news. But at the moment, her reactions were skewed with an urge to snatch the phone from Mark and beat him with it.

"Blaine wants me to draw up the plans and see the project through."

"That . . . that's good," she managed, still hung up on *honeymoon*. Honeymoon meant marriage. Corinne made a face. She didn't want to honeymoon in her grandmother's bed.

"Caroline wants to know about the honeymoon."

"Caroline is on there too?" Corinne gasped. Her proposal, such as it was, was being broadcast all the way to Pennsylvania.

"She's running on about colors."

Colors? She hadn't said yes yet. Heat shot up Corinne's neck, fueled by anger and embarrassment. "Have you lost your mind?"

"And about how lucky you are to have a guy like me." Mark grinned.

Glaring at him, Corinne tried to grab the phone, but he held it out of her reach, laughing.

"Easy, Muffet . . ." Switching it to the other hand, he spoke. "Blaine, Caroline, I have to go. I think this woman is trying to say yes to my marriage proposal, and she means business."

Corinne gaped. "Oh!" If he was for real . . . if they were in on this . . . she . . . she'd . . .

"They want to say congratulations," he told her, handing her the phone.

Corinne jerked it to her ear. "I haven't said yes, and after this stunt, I may have to think about it." When Blaine made no reply, a cloud of suspicion gathered in her mind. "Blaine, are you there?"

Mark hopped up on the raised mattress without the aid of the antique steps kept by the bedside. "Will you marry me, Miss Muffet?"

Corinne slammed the handle into the cradle. "Before or after I strangle you?"

"I love a woman with fire."

She winced. "Don't say that word."

"Right." Mark sobered. "But I am serious." He motioned her closer with his finger. "I promised myself that if I ever got out of that inferno, I'd make you my wife and soul mate."

"Soul mate?" It made her heart ring.

"I know I'm not perfect," he said, "but knowing you has changed me for the better." Mark slid off the bed, folding her hands to his chest. "Corinne Diaz Quintana Vega, et cetera, et cetera . . . will you marry me and be one with my heart . . ." He brushed the knuckles of one hand with his lips and placed it behind his neck. "My body . . ." he said, doing the same with the other. "And my soul?"

His gaze reached into hers, kindling the light of a million stars within. "With this kiss," he whispered, cupping her chin and raising it so that their breath mingled between them, "I vow to make the struggle too."

He covered the twitch of Corinne's smile with his mouth, dissolving her amusement over the Indio turn of phrase with an infectious fervor that lifted her off her feet—or was that the strong arms around her, molding her to him so that their hearts beat in counterpoint?

Her heart and body shouted yes a thousand times over, but it was Corinne's spirit that penetrated the dizzying storm with its calm affirmation. God asks no more of anyone but to make the struggle. To do so with the man she loved was a no-brainer.

EPILOGUE

Red peonies of fireworks burst in gay profusion against the background of a fiesta moon over Mexicalli's new orphanage. From the windows of the structure, the little round faces of the younger orphans watched with wide-eyed delight. On the grounds, the villagers murmured in approval while Corinne applauded with the local dignitaries and other gringos from Pennsylvania, who'd gathered for the official opening day ceremonies. Blaine and his family sat on the other side of the stage with Father Menasco, while Neta Madison and her daugher, Jeanne, sat behind Corinne and Mark.

Now that the brief formalities were over, the celebration looked more like a carnival than anything official. Half of the town's new prefabricated stage had been moved up from the village proper for the daylong affair, along with many of the portable vendors' booths. Some of the orphanage's older children ran game booths to raise money for basic sports equipment, handing out prizes to the winners from a treasure chest of promotional toys donated by Madison Enterprises.

By the time the fireworks started, almost every child in the village and orphanage sported glow-in-the-dark somethings somewhere on their bodies. Corinne could see them running in and out of the onlookers, who watched the show seated on *petate* mats, swathed in woolen serapes. The January days were warm enough, but winter waited with frosty breath for night to fall on the mountainside.

"Your friend Pyro did it again," Corinne shouted in her husband's ear as pinwheels came to life a safe distance away from the new structure. She rubbed the arms of her woolen-silk–blend jacket and tried to move closer. What was she thinking, choosing something with a short, fringed skirt?

"He knows the best in the business for the buck." Mark slipped his arm around her. "Although I'd like to make a few of our own a little later."

His devilment sent a tidal wave of *twickles* warm enough to make her forget the nip in the air. But then her husband of one year had not lost his knack for starting romantic fires and satisfying them beyond a woman's wildest dreams.

Sixteen months ago, the smoke drifting on the mountain air had come from Hacienda Ortiz instead of a fireworks display. Lorenzo Pozas and Dr. Krump had been sent to prison for multiple sentences of attempted murder and kidnapping, since the death of the boys' parents was officially ruled an accident. Don Rafael got the consideration that Vincente Aquinos mentioned for reporting their crimes. The former mayor served two years in a minimum security institution, while Diego reluctantly served Mexicalli in his stead until the elections. Talk was that Juan Pablo—Plumber Juan—might run for the office.

Two months after the fire, Soledad married Juan Miguel. Corinne couldn't help but think that the breakfast the housekeeper made him on his first day at work must have been something else. Soledad moved to his small abode above the village with Toto, although she did accept a job as a commuting housekeeper for Doña Violeta.

As Mexicalli's only enchanted pig, Toto, now a full-grown hog, continued to live a dog's life, which included going to market with Soledad and enjoying food given him by the villagers. Corinne wasn't certain what scent he used these days.

Because flying was out of the question for Corinne's newfound *abuela*, who considered her upholstered donkey cart a modern convenience, Corinne and Mark had chosen to get married in Mexicalli by Father Menasco during the holidays, so that all their families might attend. As if she were the mother and grandmother of the bride combined, Soledad fussed through tears of joy to make the grand reception held in Violeta's villa courtyard as elegant as any Mexicalli had ever seen.

After a honeymoon in Hawaii, Corinne returned with Mark for the construction of his first solo project. Due to the remote location and working on Mexicalli time, the project of building the new orphanage on the Ortiz location took nearly a year to complete, even without the hindrance of "witchcraft." Of course, old Primitivo and his cronies smoked over each stage of the project, making the struggle up the hill on a weekly basis to see that all was going well.

Corinne scanned the crowd, looking for the hard hat that Mark had given the old Indio for his service as an unofficial supervisor, but with the flashing fireworks it was almost impossible. Primitivo had confided in Corinne upon completion of the final phase that he'd thought a lot about praying to angels and assorted Aztec spirits, and had come to the conclusion that it was a waste of time when he could petition the Creator directly. But the incense he sold was like that the wise men brought to Jesus, and the candles were a light of faith in a dark world, so the canny village sage continued to sell them along with his advice on healing and protection.

"Señora Corina!"

Seated at the edge of the stage, Corinne blinked, half-blinded by the explosions of light, in the direction of the voice. Antonio Pozas Altman ran toward the podium from the area of the game booths, a cluster of glowing bracelets in his hand. He and Enrique had moved to England with their new parents, although the Altmans still spent winter breaks on Lake Flores at the lakeside B and B, where Corinne and Mark had breakfasted with them and Father Menasco earlier that day.

"Look what I won for you!" the boy said, his breath frosting the night air.

"Don't you think you should save some for your mother?" she asked, hoping she didn't snag her hose on the plywood as she knelt to receive her gift.

"No, Enrique already won more than she can fit on her wrist."

Mark snorted. "Humph, I don't know if I like some dude giving my woman jewelry."

Antonio produced a grin missing two front teeth. "You are so silly, Señor Mark. I already have a girlfriend at home. Her name is Gloria."

"Did you save a bracelet for Gloria?" Corinne inquired.

"That is what I am going to do next. *Adiós.*"

"Thank you, Antonio," Corinne called after the boy as he darted back through the crowd of sky gazers. Taking Mark's offered arm, she eased back into her seat and shook the glowing bangles on her wrist. "Wasn't that sweet?"

"I think I'm jealous," Mark growled in her ear.

"But you still have Toto," she reminded him.

"Nah, whatever attraction I had for Toto is over," Mark told her. "You saw him. He didn't even know me anymore. Besides, as I recall, he snores and has bad breath." He gave her a playful nudge. "And you're much nicer to sleep with."

Corinne coughed, partly from her husband's mischief and partly from the tickle of a wayward drift of sulfur smoke. "Talk about a left-handed compliment."

Mark pulled her under his arm, as if to squeeze the tickle out.

"Mark, have you forgotten that your mother is sitting behind you?" Jeanne Madison piped up from behind them.

Mark's "little sister" was almost as tall as he was and had earned a doctorate at age twenty-six, but was as unassuming as they came. Her golden brown hair and tawny eyes drew men's attention like a magnet, but Jeanne was oblivious in that area as well.

"Mind your own business, kid, or you won't see those letters I promised you."

"That's low, and you know it."

"He's incorrigible," Corinne told her sister-in-law. It was part of his charm.

Mark knew Jeanne was chafing at the bit to read the letters and ship's log from the *Luna Azul,* which had been found in a chest in the chamber beneath the hacienda. Diego Ortiz's family had owned the Spanish merchantman, which took on water during a storm in 1702 and was abandoned, sinking with a fortune in gold and silver coins.

If Jeanne could interest backers, this could be her golden break . . . as well as another break for the orphanage, since the contents of the hacienda belonged to it. An investment company was already at work to mine the *caracoles*. The orphanage would receive a share as owners of the property, with the Mexican government and the new corporation as partners. But the treasure of the *Luna Azul*, if it could be found, promised to be far more lucrative than the fossils, which to date were not as valuable as first thought.

Above them the grand finale erupted like machine-gun fire versus cannon. As the last white streams of light spiraled to the ground, Diego announced the conclusion of the celebration. Blaine's family immediately dispersed, Karen and Annie running off with their little brother, Berto, to try their luck at the games before they closed. With Mark on Doña Violeta's other arm, Diego helped his grandaunt into the cart hitched to the rear of the stage.

Enchanted by the lady and her mode of transportation, Jeanne and Neta joined her for the ride to her villa, where a Mexican supper catered by the orphanage cooks awaited Mexicalli's guests. At the front of the cart, Chiquita, wearing a chic straw hat bedecked with ribbons to match Violeta's dark blue dress, bobbed her head, ready to go.

"If you will excuse me," Diego said, handing Violeta the reins with a short bow. "I will join you momentarily with María."

Corinne wasn't sure when Diego had begun courting María Delgado at the orphanage, but it delighted Doña Dulce.

"Just look at that moon," her grandmother sighed, shifting her sparkling gaze from the retreating *alcalde* to Mark and Corinne. "Do you remember what I call it?"

"A fiesta moon," Corinne responded. How well she remembered the night. It was the first time that she and Mark connected, not just with a kiss, but with troubled souls reaching out for one another.

"When Blaine and I met, I thought it looked too perfect to be real," Caroline said, snuggling up to her husband. "Like one of those paper-perfect ones that hang on our October bulletin boards."

"Such a moon says that it is a night for love," Violeta told her guests. With a romantic sigh, she snapped the reins gently, and Chiquita pulled the cart away to her mistress's recount of that evening. "Mark and Corinne had only just met, but I knew . . ."

Mark slipped his arm around Corinne from behind and pointed to the sky. "I think I knew too," he confided, nuzzling her neck.

"I think it had more to do with finding the right woman than the moon," Blaine observed, stepping forward and offering Mark his hand. "Well done, little brother." He glanced from the new orphanage looming behind them to Corinne. "On more than one account. I knew you had it in you."

"With the right woman." He squeezed Corinne even tighter.

Basking in the subtle spice of his cologne and his affection, Corinne followed his watery gaze toward the horizon, where the moon spilled silver light over the jagged mountaintops. It seemed no more than a finger's breadth from them. So close and yet so far—as she and Mark had been.

"I think God put that moon there that night for us," she murmured softly, after Blaine and Caroline left to reclaim their brood. "He knew we belonged together."

"It's a night for lovers. Grandmother said so."

"So what do you think . . . later, after we escape the in-laws and outlaws. You and me, the guest room, the moonlight . . ."